The Messenger

Dedication

*This book is dedicated to Haven,
my beloved sister and biggest fan.*

Table of Contents

ISBN - 978-1-7388456-2-0

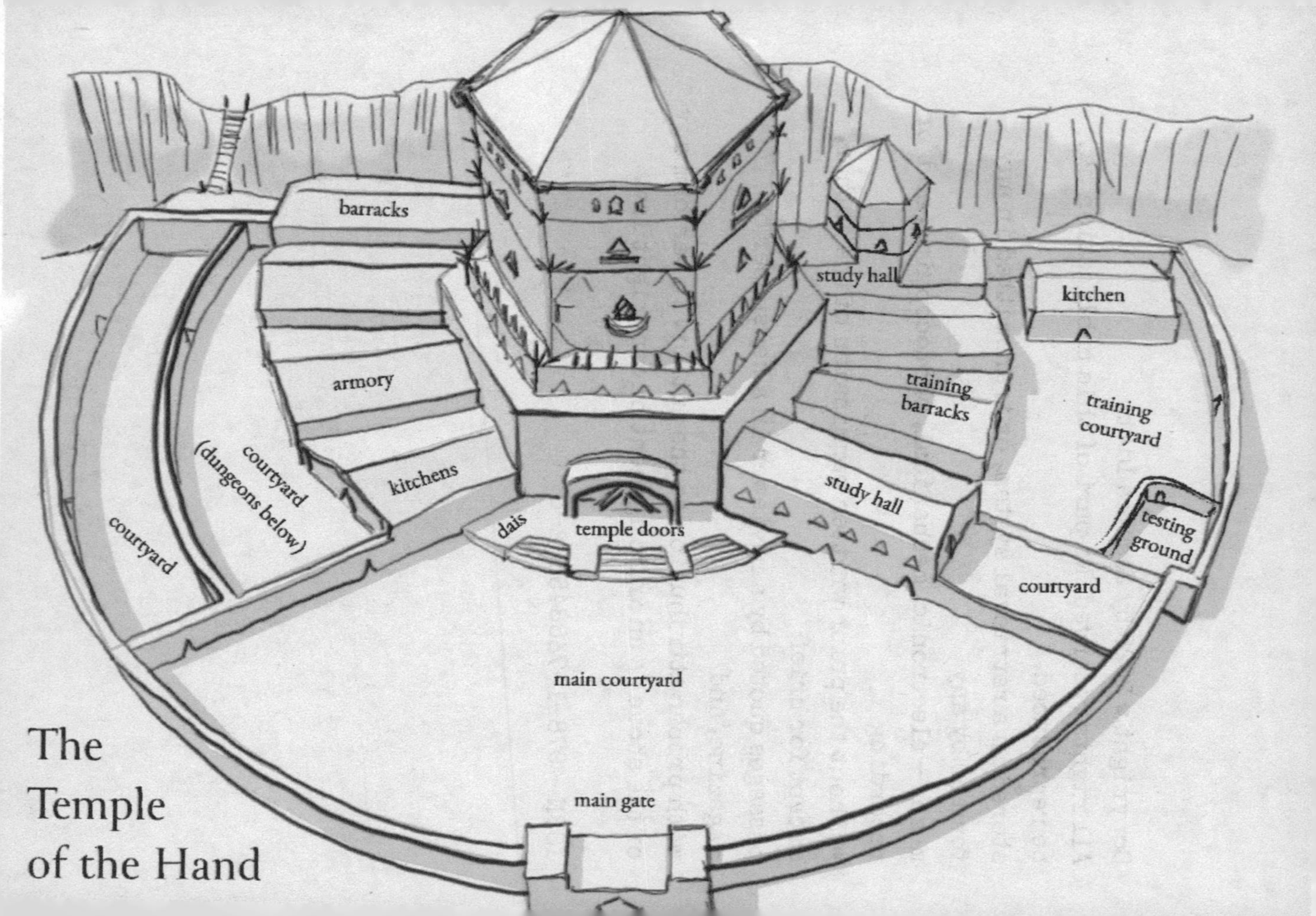

barracks
study hall
kitchen
armory
training barracks
training courtyard
kitchens
study hall
courtyard (dungeons below)
dais
temple doors
testing ground
courtyard
courtyard
main courtyard
main gate
The Temple of the Hand

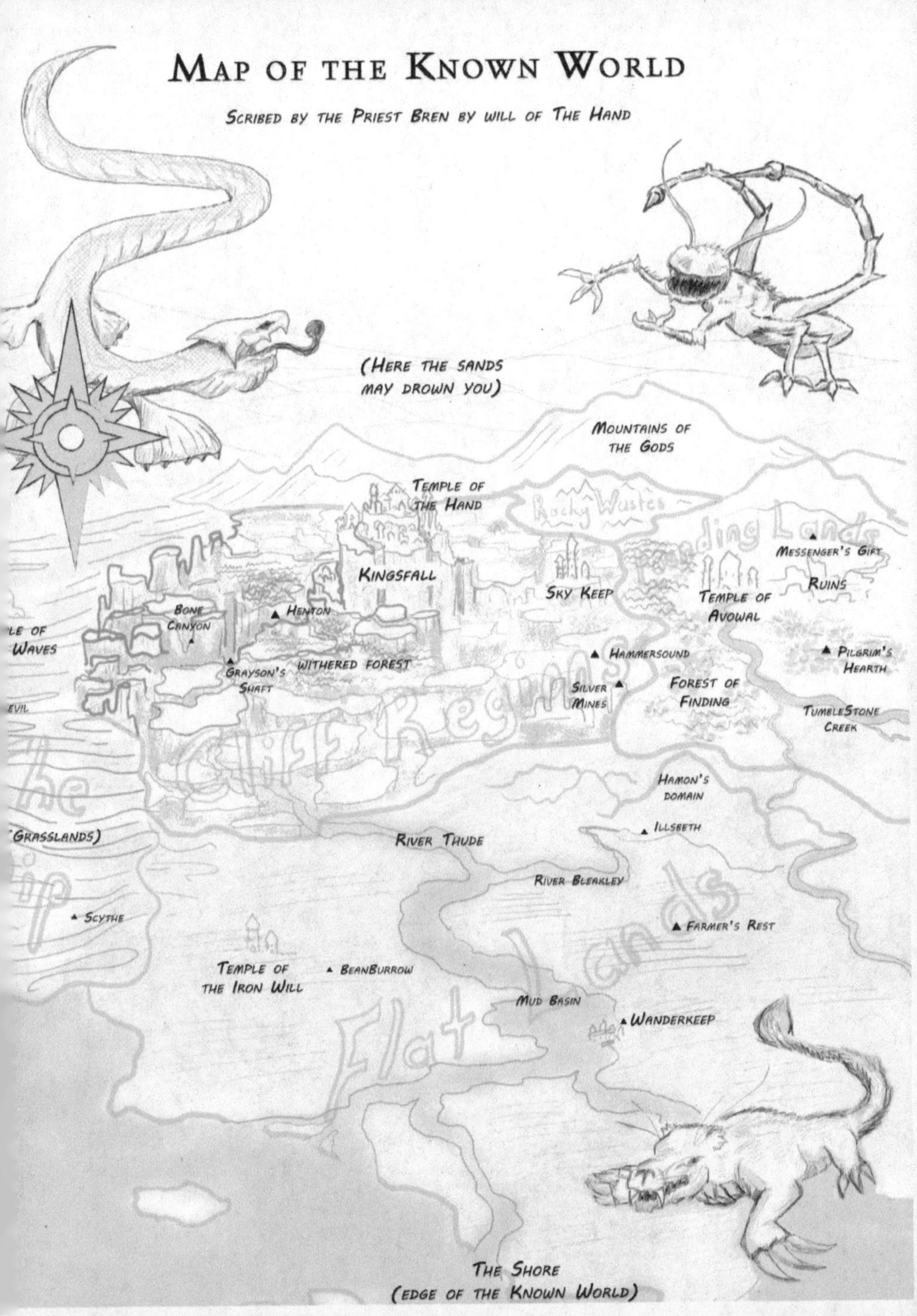

MAP OF THE KNOWN WORLD
SCRIBED BY THE PRIEST BREN BY WILL OF THE HAND
(HERE THE SANDS MAY DROWN YOU)
MOUNTAINS OF THE GODS
Rocky Wastes
ding Lands
TEMPLE OF THE HAND
KINGSFALL
SKY KEEP
MESSENGER'S GIFT
RUINS
TEMPLE OF AVOWAL
LE OF WAVES
BONE CANYON
HENTON
HAMMERSOUND
PILGRIM'S HEARTH
EVIL
GRAYSON'S SHAFT
WITHERED FOREST
SILVER MINES
FOREST OF FINDING
TUMBLESTONE CREEK
the Cliff Regions
HAMON'S DOMAIN
(GRASSLANDS)
RIVER THUDE
ILLSBETH
RIVER BLEAKLEY
ands
SCYTHE
FARMER'S REST
TEMPLE OF THE IRON WILL
BEANBURROW
Flat Lands
MUD BASIN
WANDERKEEP
THE SHORE
(EDGE OF THE KNOWN WORLD)

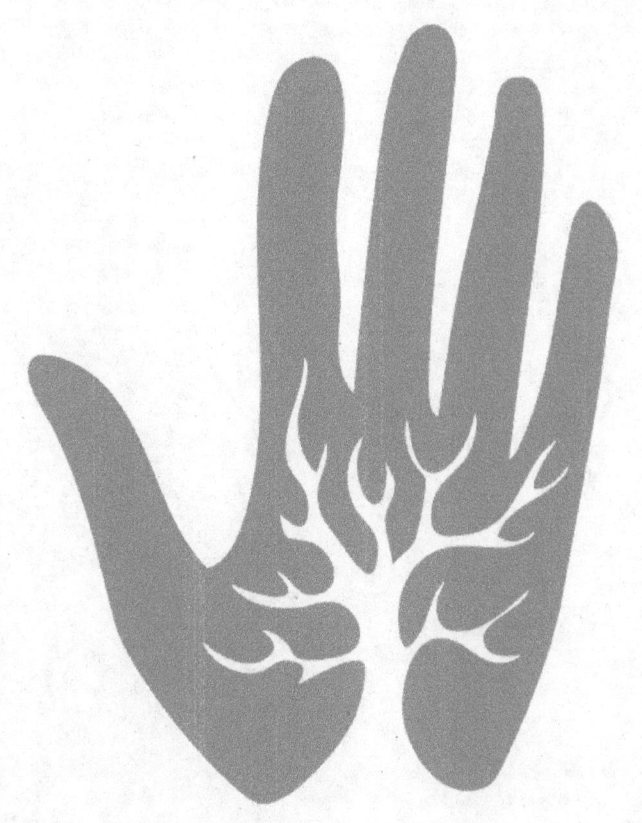

Part One
The death of an acolyte

The sun was so hot the very air seemed to be boiling. It made the wrestling figures seem hazy and unreal. Everything in the courtyard was the baked brown colour of midsummer – the hard clay ground, the spiked wooden barricade around the courtyard, even the wrestling figures themselves. Leaning in the shadow of a triangular doorway watching them was an equally sun-baked and brown boy in a rough robe. However, the sweat running down his face as he watched the wrestlers was not from the sun.

There were many other boys and some girls in the courtyard, all wearing the same brown robes. Some were wrestling and training for the coming ordeal, but most just sat and conserved their energy. The only sound that penetrated the hazy air was the groans and thumps of combat and the soft murmur of voices. Another boy joined the first in the doorway. He sauntered up and stood for a moment, scrutinizing the boy.

"You sure you want to go through with this, Col?" he asked at length. "We all know you're not a fighter."

Col let out a short laugh.

"I've got to do this, Rig. It's not for me. *They* need me to do this. You know how it is."

The taller boy sighed, scratching at the bridge of his crooked nose.

"Yeah, I was afraid you were going to say that. I'm sorry, then, in advance. I can't go easy on you."

Col looked at the bulging, toned muscles of the taller boy's arms and gulped.

"Why not?"

Rig glanced around to make sure they were alone, dropping his voice.

"I've got to do my best, Col. I need this. If anything, I need it more than you do."

He dropped his voice still lower.

"If the rebellion is ever going to succeed, we need people on the inside."

Col snorted. "As if they don't already have people everywhere."

Rig flushed. "Well, not in *this* cohort, at any rate. If I get in, it will be a big strike for our side. I can't fail. I'm sorry."

Col bit his lip in thought.

"Yeah, alright. I understand."

There was an awkward silence, as both thought of the task ahead. The silence was broken as a short, brawny youth came stumping up and stopped in front of the pair.

"Hey, Col," he shifted his feet uncomfortably.

"I'm really sorry about how I'm gonna beat you up in a minute. I like you, but... you know how it is. We all got to do our best."

He met Col's eyes hesitantly.

Col gulped, but managed a small smile.

"I forgive you. Really, it's fine."

The other boy straightened with relief. "Great, now that's over with. The other guys, they're sorry too." He gestured with a short, thick arm at the group of youths who had gathered behind him.

There was a mutter of agreement.

"We all know you're not cut out for this. Why you're doing it at all is anyone's guess. All of us want to win, but we don't really want to hurt you. It's just the way it is. So... no hard feelings?"

Col had turned a sickly shade of green. Despite his dread, he somehow still managed to make his grin seem real and lighthearted.

"Sure. No hard feelings. Besides, I'll beat you all when we get to the Knowledge Trial."

His comment was met with a few rueful smiles, so he pushed on.

"Who says I'm going to lose, anyway? Maybe I should be

apologizing to *you.*"

The other boys started laughing outright at that. Their lifted spirits served to cheer Col up as well. He relaxed a bit and joined in.

Suddenly, a shout rang through the courtyard.

"They're coming!"

Instantly, all training in the courtyard ceased. Every boy and girl stopped what they were doing and turned toward the sound. Others spilled from the many triangular doorways in the walls, where they, like Col, had been seeking shelter from the sun. A man walked into the courtyard, flanked by two women. Each of them was armed with two swords and a long, metal-tipped staff. The boys all stood silent, taking in the sight with awe. All Priests and Priestesses of the Hand were incredibly fit and dangerous.

However, the man who stood before the youths now was something else entirely. He stood at least two feet taller than his female bodyguards, and seemed to fill the doorway. His beard was so thick and long that it almost covered the symbol blazoned across his barrel-like chest. It was the outline of a hand, faint but edged in gold so that it glittered in the sunlight. His face was rough, sun-scorched leather. As he stood there in the doorway, surveying the youths through one clear eye, they saw that the other eye was clouded, an old scar running through its corners.

"Well," he said at last, his voice deep and grunting like that of a forest hog.

"We seem to have a likely bunch this year. Never have I seen a bunch of stronger-looking lads, or tougher girls."

His words caused all the boys to stand taller and puff out their chests. Standing near the back, Col felt his heart sink as he noted yet again that he was by far the slightest and shortest boy in the group. His lean, wiry muscles were pitiful compared to those of the youths on either side of him.

Maybe I can beat some of the girls. He thought ruefully, but doubted it. He'd never been good at fighting. The huge Priest was still talking. His voice had changed, taking on the ceremonial tone of a recitation.

"Acolytes. Today will be your third Trial. Many of you will be sent home today, back into the dreary, meaningless lives you once led. But not all. No. Some of you, those chosen by The Hand, will go on. You will prove yourselves worthy and enter into the higher calling we offer. A calling of measureless glory and honour... as well as many earthly benefits."

Here he pulled aside his beard to reveal the golden Hand of Office he wore around his neck, giving the crowd a wink. Col felt his gut suddenly turn with disgust at the irreverence of the priest. Like most others in his family, he had never really believed that the Hand was real. This only reinforced the feeling that it was merely a ploy to gain power. The gigantic priest wagged his finger at the crowd, grinning.

"But not all of you will be chosen for this calling. Oh no. You must first prove yourself to the Hand, by feats of strength, wit, endurance, knowledge, and worthiness! In order to bear the double swords of the Order, you must first prove yourself worthy to use them. Follow me."

He turned and walked across the courtyard to a door set in the wooden wall. Unlike the rest, this one had a square frame, and a tiny symbol of another hand burnt into the wood. He opened the door and they filed through one by one. On the other side was yet another courtyard, but this one was surrounded by tier upon tier of seats. Every single seat was filled with a watching priest. Stepping through the door, Col felt as though he was entering a whispering sea of black cloth. The place stank of sweat, and the hard packed ground was stained red with old blood. Gold symbols of the Hand glittered on many of the priest's robes, so that Col felt as though they were waving cheekily at him. In a high box in the corner of the courtyard, Col thought he could see the Hearer of

The Hand himself, wearing the golden headdress and ceremonial sword. He couldn't see the Hearer's face through the golden veil, but he felt as though the great priest was staring straight at him – and smirking. He took a deep breath. *It's all right. Just last as long as you can.* The large, bearded priest pushed his way to the front and faced the small crowd of nervous acolytes.

"Today, you will fight without weapons," he bellowed, "no, not even a stick. You fight until you're knocked out, or you give up. Every man fights for himself, to the best of his ability. No biting or eye-gouging, but anything else goes. The last one standing will be accepted immediately, the rest will be judged based on their performance. ARE YOU READY?"

The answering cheers were somewhat halfhearted. The rusty stains on the ground had caused all the youths to become more sober.

The bearded priest shrugged.

"All right. When the gong strikes, begin." He stepped back, and the two women with him vaulted up into the stands. At that same time, the crash of a gong reverberated through the small courtyard, echoing off the high walls.

The next few moments were complete chaos. Several boys went down right away, while the rest of the group quickly separated itself into struggling knots of fighters. A few joined into groups and teamed up against some of the more formidable youths, but the alliances quickly dissolved as they turned on each other.

For Col, most of the fight was a blur. He had barely taken a step before he was clocked on the head and knocked to the ground.

"Stay down," he heard Rig mutter, "I don't want to have to hurt you."

Col shook his head to clear it, then jumped to his feet.

"Too bad for you then," he started to say, but was whacked in the teeth by someone else before he could finish. Spitting blood, he whirled, only to catch another blow to the jaw. He tried to dodge and duck, but people were everywhere and he couldn't watch them all at once. Most of his blows landed on empty air. Those that connected hurt his fists almost more than they hurt the other person. His head spun.

The world was whirling after the first minute. Col didn't remember hitting the ground, but it just seemed to keep jumping up at him every time he got up off of it. He could see splashes of his own scarlet blood mixing with the old stains. Then he couldn't see anything, because the blood was dripping into his eyes. His ribs were screaming. His head felt as though it was splitting open. The taste of blood and dust clogged his senses.

He got up, swiping blood out of his eyes. Those who had originally knocked him down had moved on, and so he had a moment's peace before someone noticed that he was still standing. Then the pain began again as several people sprinted at him.

Blood. The taste of dirt. Swollen eyes, broken teeth. On his knees now, he fought blindly. One by one, the other acolytes were picking each other off, until he realized that he was only fighting one person. A girl with furious eyes who used her feet as much as she did her hands. If she hadn't been hitting him so hard, he would have recognized her as Naia, his cousin from two villages away. She didn't hate him, but she hated losing. Her blows were swift and brutal. Already on his knees, he gradually slipped closer and closer to the ground until he was curled up in a ball on it, just trying to protect himself. Although he was technically on the ground already, and therefore out, Naia didn't stop. The blows kept falling, as if she wanted to make sure he would stay down. With his ear pressed to the ground, Col heard the running footsteps before she did. There was a swift *crack* of bone on bone. Naia let out a groan and collapsed beside him. Through slits in his swollen eyes, Col could see a large, muscled youth standing over her. He vaguely recognized him as Garan, a blacksmith's son. The skin on his knuckles was split, his lip was swollen, and a bit of bloody drool leaked out of the side of his mouth, but he seemed otherwise unharmed.

Garan looked around the courtyard, then raised his arms in the air in victory. Many watching priests broke into cheers.
This is it. Col thought painfully. Muscles screaming and legs shaking, he pushed himself to his feet. The cheers swiftly died off in confusion. Garan turned, saw him, and hit him. His fists hit as hard as the hammers they were accustomed to swinging.
Col went down again.
The cheers resumed.

Although the blood was pounding in his ears and he couldn't put a single thought together straight, Col pushed himself through to consciousness. Every bone in his body seemed to be connected wrong, and his muscles weren't working. Nevertheless, he somehow managed to stand up again. Garan looked confused.

"You again?" he demanded. Many of the priests broke into laughter. As Garan's fist swung toward him, Col blinked blood out of his eyes just in time to see it coming. He dodged. However, the effort of dodging caused his already shaking legs to give out. He lost his balance and crashed back to the ground. Now the laughter was roaring through the stands. No one was cheering anymore, so Garan didn't raise his arms again. He kicked Col once in the ribs, then took a few hesitant steps toward the door. Seeing him, the large, bearded priest swung down from the stands and advanced across the blood-splattered ground.

Col got up. Although he was swaying like a sailor on a storm-tossed ship, he took a few steps after Garan, bloodied fists raised in a drunken challenge. All sound in the courtyard stopped as everyone stared in shock. The world was spinning so hard in Col's eyes that he could hardly see the look of utter astonishment on Garan's face. As the bigger boy stumped back toward him, Col seemed to see several boys advancing from different directions. As Garan swung his fist, seven boys seemed to swing their fists at the same time. Col didn't even try to dodge, or figure out which of the duplicate boys was the real one. His legs were already giving way to the sheer weight of gravity, and it was all he could do to stay standing long enough for the blow to fall. The thud sounded through the silent courtyard. Col's head snapped back as he spun from the blow and crumpled to the ground like a broken puppet, landing flat on his face in the dirt. However, no one saw him fall. They were all too busy staring at the Hearer of The Hand, seated in his special box. For the first time in five years, the Hearer of The Hand was laughing.

2

The Hearer sat, relaxed, in his special box as they brought him his lunch. This year's batch of acolytes were proving to be particularly entertaining. He reflected on the morning's Trial as the servants approached, bearing cold wine and an iced dragon fruit salad, then dried curls of meat and roasted squash on skewers, so spicy you could see the red sauce dripping onto the plate. The last servant brought a tray with a single sheet of paper, the names of acolytes for his consideration. Normally, he only paid attention to the name of the boy or girl who had won the challenge. The rest of the page he usually just split in half, sending the top half on to the next challenge, and the last half home. The lesser priests had already done the work of balancing every acolyte's time with the amount of damage they had inflicted on other acolytes, and the amount of attacks they had survived, then ranked them. However, this year, he reached out and stopped the servant. The young girl trembled. Even to be addressed by the Hearer of the Hand was a great and terrifying privilege, let alone to be touched by him.

"Y-y-y-yes, your Divine Eminence?" she stuttered, eyes big.

"What's the name of that boy they're dragging off the field right now? The one who kept getting up?"

The girl looked to the field, going a little pale at the sight of the bloodstained ground and injured youths.

"Nikolo Wolf, Sacred One," she said immediately, without having to check her papers. Her eyes lingered on the distant figure with both pity and admiration, her cheeks flushing a bit.

He snorted, then started laughing outright.

"Wolf? *Wolf?* Ha! More like a baby goat."

He sat there, smiling and chuckling to himself behind his veil, for a long time before pulling the cord that dropped a curtain around his box, allowing him to remove his veil and eat in privacy.

A horrible, warbling shriek pulled Col out of the dark. It ripped through his head like a dagger through paper. He groaned, throwing a hand across his face. Both his face and his arm screamed in protest. He bit back a yell of frustration and forced his eyes open. He lay in a small, sunlit room. The warbling shriek was still coming from outside the window, and he realized that it was a bird. He lay there for a good twenty minutes longing to kill it, until it finally shut up and flew away. The door creaked open. The sound of the hinges was almost worse than the bird. Col slowly turned his head far enough to shoot a look at the person standing in the doorway. A small, bare-footed acolyte stood frozen by Col's bloodshot glare.

"Nikolo Wolf?" he asked hesitantly. Col grimaced.

"Go away." His voice sounded rusty as it grated through his throat. The acolyte looked confused.

"You are Nikolo, then?"

"Yes."

"Great! I have a message for you. The Hearer said to tell you that you've passed the test... If you ever woke up, that is. The Hand has chosen you to continue onward in your training."

Col sat up so fast he nearly blacked out. His muscles screamed, but he ignored them.

"*What?*"

The acolyte took an involuntary step back.

"Yes... That's what he said. You passed the test of Endurance. Your next test will be Knowledge, and it will occur in a week, giving you some time to recover."

Col slowly wilted back into the bed, a tide of relief springing up inside of him. The acolyte turned to go, but paused in the doorway and looked back.

"You're so lucky," he sighed, his face a mixture of envy and admiration.

"They say that the Hand's will had nothing to do with it, but that the Hearer couldn't bear to let you go after you'd made him laugh like that. Some of the other priests say they've never seen a more hopeless fighter. No one can deny you've got endurance, though."

Col laughed hoarsely. "I *knew* he was smirking under that veil. Now I've got to live with the reputation of the greatest joke that ever made it through the test."

"At least you made it, though," the acolyte muttered with a touch of bitterness. "I'll never make it through mine."

He continued out the door, throwing a casual "Washrooms on your right, food down the hall," over his shoulder. Col stared reflectively after him. After a moment, he attempted to get up. That didn't work very well. With a groan, he flopped back on the bed.

"Wake me up tomorrow," he muttered to the empty air.

It was two days before he was finally well enough to leave the barracks of the Hand. He bounced away down the hill on the back of an old, fat horse, feeling every bump slice through his nerves. The barracks and the temple of the Hand were situated at the top of a high rise of cliffs, with everything else stretching out below them. The Temple was a massive hexagonal tower, with a few smaller towers and several long halls radiating outwards from its base. Several courtyards curved around the structure, with a few outer buildings dotting the grounds. It was a mighty fortress as well as a temple, with a deep canyon protecting its back, and a massive wall curving around in the front to separate it from the rest of the city. Col continued down past the King's fortress, crouched on the edge of a precipice like an old, tired watchdog. The rest of the city was scattered around it, the houses clinging to the flat tops of cliffs, anywhere there was level ground. Partially hidden behind other houses, the beautiful, sandstone spires of the Silent Speaker's temple glittered in the sunlight. The sandstone was a rare material, the only indication that, while small, elitist, and fundamentally peaceful, this was a powerful religion almost to rival that of the Hand. The stone was a shimmering, dark orange crystal which reflected the sun, making the towers look like glowing fingers reaching up from the city towards the sky. A few hooded priestesses shuffled through the crowd, the tattoos below their lips and eyes making them look both tragic and terrifying. They weren't dangerous, but he still avoided them instinctively. Col passed through the outskirts of the city and didn't stop. Instead, he headed over bridges, across clifftops, and eventually down a winding path, deeper and deeper into a remote canyon.

The village huddled in the shadow of two cliffs, dry and brown because sunlight rarely reached it. Even pushing his horse as fast as it could go, it was still late in the evening when he caught sight of it. As Col rode down toward it, a joyful chorus of barks rose to meet him. Ten or twelve dogs catapulted out of the houses toward him, closely followed by a crowd of cheering children. For the first time in weeks, a genuine smile lit up his tired, bruised face.

"It's Col! Col's back!"

"Sing us a song Col!"

"No, tell us a story!"

The children danced around his tired horse, clamouring with excitement. Col smiled, but his eyes peered restlessly over their heads, looking for a specific face. He pushed his horse forward, riding deeper into the village with the pack of children and dogs in tow. Finally, he saw her, leaning tiredly on the doorpost of her house with a dishcloth in hand. When she saw him, her brow creased and she pushed forward through the crowd.

"Yes, tell us a story, Col." Her voice was rough. "Tell us the story of how my little boy went away for three months, and the Hand only now sends him back to me, half-alive with his beautiful face a smashed mess."

Col hung his head.

"I had to go, Ma. You know that. It's the only way for me to save this place. Otherwise we'll never get anywhere."

Her eyes were dark with sorrow. She pushed her way to his side and placed a hand on his ankle.

"I know, Nikki. And I'm proud of you, but I'll never forgive them for what they're doing to you. This..." She gestured helplessly at all of him, sitting slumped in the saddle.

"This is a crime. It hurts me, here." She pressed her hands to her chest. "Come home, Nikki, please. Don't go back there."

He shook his head wearily. The disappointment showed in her eyes, but she nodded in resignation.

"Then at least stay the night."

Without waiting for an answer, she grabbed the bridle of his horse and led it through the crowd, back toward the house. At the door she held out her arms and he half fell out of the saddle. Strong arms steadied him, and he looked up into the grinning face of his older brother Tonis.

"What'd you do this time, Col? Fall off a roof?" he asked cheerfully. Their mother shot him a look, but Tonis continued, oblivious.

"You look like an old meat-pie. I didn't even look this bad the time I fought all three Cooper boys and their dog."

He supported Col as they stumbled into the house, where two other boys were waiting. Their mother held off the crowd of children at the door.

"Col doesn't have time for a story today. Today he stays with his family. Tomorrow you can come back and harass him," she scolded, shooing them away.

Inside the house, Col's brothers were greeting him with various levels of empathy. Terren, the youngest, looked stricken. He rushed from the room before the others could see his tears. They saw them anyway. There was a moment of silence, then Tonis grimaced at Col.

"He'll be okay. It's just a shock, the way you look, but it will fade with time. You'll look normal in a few weeks, then he'll come out and start idolizing you again like before."

From the corner, Col's third brother spoke for the first time.

"I don't know about that. You're messed up pretty good, Col. Nothing for the girls to look at anymore."

He examined Col's face for a long time, and a teasing smile tugged at the corner of his mouth.

"Maybe Elis Cooper will finally pay attention to me now."

"Hankin!" Their mother's sharp voice cut through the conversation as she strode into the room.

"Don't say such things. Can't you see your brother's hurt? What a selfish boy!" She twirled the dishcloth and gave Hankin a hard thwack with it as she passed. Before he could yelp in protest, she cut him off.

"Come help me with dinner, all of you. Col, sit down before you fall down."

A variety of cousins and relatives, most of them boys, tumbled into the house from the surrounding shacks and barns. They filled the kitchen with light and noise, cheerfully working together to prepare the meal. Tucked away on a stool in the corner, Col rested his head against the wall and basked in it, finally relaxing for the first time in three months. He'd done it. He'd passed the hardest test. The rest should be easy. His bruises hurt, but they were worth it for this hope, this chance at a better life for his family and his people. The cheerful ruckus gently lulled him into sleep as no silence could have. He woke with a crick in his neck, to a light tap against his boot. The room smelled strongly of his mother's classic garlic soup, the aggressive flavor doing wonders to disguise the fact that the broth was thin and the meat scarce.

"Col, wake up. Stop drooling on my wall and come have dinner."

His mother's voice was gentle and amused. As Col eased himself into a chair by the small table, a hush settled over the room. A few concerned voices asked how he felt, but most of them just stared, eyes glowing with pride.

"That's our boy. He might look beaten, but he always gets up."

"You'll save us all, Col."

Col flushed a bit at their admiration. At the same time, a small hard knot of determination tightened inside him. He wouldn't let these people down. Not ever. He *would* win a better future for them, even if he had to spend his whole life working his way up in the Order of the Hand, and worshipping a god he didn't believe in. The room was still hushed. People milled about, some taking their dinner elsewhere and others coming in from elsewhere to eat. Col looked around at their expectant faces.

"Alright, out with it. I know what you're all wondering, why don't you just ask?" His voice scratched a bit in the silence, but it wasn't painful to speak anymore.

"Did you pass the test?" a tall, gangly man in the corner finally voiced the question.

"I did." Col smiled. "Only two to go, and the hardest one is over. Knowledge will be easy, and Worthiness is more just a ceremony, from what I've heard."

A collective breath dissolved the tension in the room, and the easy chatter resumed.

"Tell us the story?" his youngest brother asked hopefully. Col laughed, a pure, clear sound.

"Of course."

The night sped away in a blur of golden firelight and eager faces. Col's gentle, gravely voice seemed to weave a spell around his audience; the joy and hope in the room was almost tangible. When the visitors finally left for their respective homes and Col collapsed into bed, the joy still hung like a haze in the air, spreading throughout the village in peaceful waves. Staring at the patched, leaky ceiling, Col knew that he would carry this night in his heart in the months to come, a warm memory of firelight and hope.

3

The day of the Knowledge trial finally dawned, as bright and dry as all the others. Col found himself alone in a tiny study, with nothing to focus his attention on, save his own nervousness. The study was of wood, with no windows, no table, no carpet. The only things in the entire room were himself and the closed door. He breathed deep, trying to fill himself with confidence. Remembering was one thing he was really good at. Dates, names, facts, and especially faces stuck in his mind, so that he rarely forgot them.

Just when he thought he would die of boredom, the small door opened to admit an angular man of middling age and middling height, with a flat nose and a sharp chin. He didn't seem to have any particular office, since he wore no swords, no chain, and his black robes had only a small hand-shape stitched in white thread. With a creaky sigh, he settled himself cross-legged against one wall and motioned for Col to do the same. They sat studying each other for some time before the man spoke.

"Who is the Hearer?" His first question came out sharp and antagonistic. Col found himself relaxing. The question was easy.

"No acolytes are permitted to know, but he is chosen by the Hand itself, from among the priests of the highest rank. The priest who proves himself greatest in combat, power, skill, and knowledge is chosen, and he leads the country in the will of the Hand for as long as he remains strong. The Hand speaks only to him, and even the high king cannot dispute the Hand's will. The present Hearer is well over one hundred years of age, but those who have seen him affirm that he looks no more than fifty. They say that the more time he spends in the presence of the Hand, the less time's passing seems to affect him. The Hearer is the official head of all religions in the world, or at least the world that we know of. Although the high king is officially the ruler-" Col paused, seeing a frown twitch the face of the man across from him. His mind flew back to a conversation he had overheard a few days back. News travelled very slowly in the seclusion of the barracks, but the city had definitely been in somewhat of an uproar over the past few days.

"The late high king, who passed away recently." Col hazarded a guess, and was rewarded by the barest hint of a nod. Col's mind scrambled.

"And so Prince Drystan is officially the ruler, but the Hearer of the Hand is the spiritual ruler, and so, some might argue, holds the most power." *All the power,* Col thought, but he didn't voice the thought. It was best to keep up pretenses and only parrot what he had officially been taught. The man nodded.

"Good. And what is the Hand?"

Col took a deep breath and settled into his storytelling mode. His voice took on the old, familiar tone that consistently mesmerized both his fellow acolytes and the people of his village. His eyes became soft with thought.

"Long ago, a band of travelling monks were beaten by a king's soldiers and thrown out of a town for begging. They meant to find another town, but, along the way they became lost in the dark confines of an ancient forest. Paths that seemed to travel straight twisted in mind-boggling ways. Under the trees, ancient stone buildings and cobbled paths fell apart like grim ghosts of stone. The day grew late, and the monks became afraid of wild animals, or worse, in the shadows. Desperately, they sought the light, and light they found. As the day was fading, they stumbled forth into a clearing filled with the ancient ruins of some bygone civilization."

Col's voice dropped with suspense. Although he didn't believe the story, he could clearly picture the scene.

"The sky was darker than before, not with the coming of night, but with a great storm, sweeping down from the mountains." He closed his eyes, and he could almost hear thunder. "The rain began to fall in torrents. The ruins held no shelter, for little more than the foundations remained. The monks were soaked and chilled to the bone. Desperately, they sought shelter as the thunder rumbled and the lightning raked the sky. Never had they seen such a storm, as if the heavens were at war with themselves. As indeed they were, for suddenly there was a bright light and the leader of the band suddenly received... Divine guidance. He headed toward the mountains through the ruins, as if called by a voice from within him. Hours later, the band had barely the strength to take another step, but their leader pressed on. Finally, when they felt near to death with exhaustion, they came to a cave. As they descended into it, eager to escape the storm, they were met by a soft light, which quickly grew to blinding brightness. At the very back of the cave, they found a large crystal. This crystal shone so brightly they could hardly look at it, but they could just barely make out the shape of a kneeling person trapped inside." Col's voice dropped in hushed wonder. He was thoroughly immersed in the story now. "Pressed against the inner side of the crystal was a human hand. The leader of the monks insisted to the others that he could hear a voice calling from within. He pressed his hand against the shape of the hand in the crystal, and that was when the Hand spoke to him, and he became the first Hearer."

"What did the Hand say?" The other man's voice was soft, and he had a faraway look in his eyes. Col came out of the story with a start, suddenly remembering that he was being tested.

"The person in the crystal claimed to be a messenger of the gods-" he began, but the man shook his head slightly.

"The exact words, Acolyte."

"Ah, yes. Of course." Col racked his brain to remember the entirety of the Declaration Chant that they had all been forced to memorize months ago. After the first few words, it flowed easily to his tongue and he settled into the rhythm.

"What is your name?

I have none that you could speak.

Why are you trapped?

I am not trapped, but hidden.
The light of my immortal form
is too great for your eyes to see.

Where did you come from?

From the storm above the peak.

The peak of what?

Of the mountain of gods,
the home of those who live forever.

How did you get here?

I was sent to warn you.
warn you of the wrath of the gods.
The gods are angry, small human.
They tire of the ways of man.
They will tear apart the world,
unless you heed their commands.

But we know of no such commands.
How can we heed them?

From the heavens I come,
to tell you of them.
I am the mouth of the gods
set here in stone as their laws are,
that I might remain among mortals and teach them.
You alone will I teach, small human,
and you shall teach others.
You will rule them with a will of iron,
and they will obey you or suffer wrath
the wrath of the Messenger,
the wrath of the gods,
on the mountain of the gods.

And the people gave their gold,
and the king gave his land,
and the Hearer built there a temple,
a temple for the Hand."

       Col took a deep breath. "And so they took the crystal from the cave and built a temple for it on the highest cliffs of the kingdom, and the Hearer of the Hand taught his followers the will of the gods. He also taught his followers the ways of war that they might administer the wrath of the gods on those who disobeyed."

       He looked up warily at the man across from him. The man's flat nose was squashed upwards in a large smile.

       "It's, 'You will rule them with a will of stone,' not, 'a will of iron.' But other than that, no mistakes at all."

       Col let out a long breath.

       "Then I pass?"

       "So far, yes. There are a few more questions, but I have no doubt you will find them easy in comparison."

A half hour later, Col left the tiny room feeling dazed, the hearty praise of the priest still ringing in his ears. He had passed. More than that, his mesmerizing storytelling seemed to have won him an admirer in the ranks of the priests, and that was a weighty accomplishment indeed. As he rounded the corner into a hallway, he was met by a riot of cheers. A large group of boys and girls waited in a huddle in the hall. All those who had failed the test had been immediately hustled out of the barracks, and these were the ones who had passed. Their faces were glowing with triumph, but Col's heart still sank at how few remained. At the start of the year, there had been over a hundred acolytes training with him. Now there were less than thirty. However, he cheered up at the sight of several of his close friends still smiling among the group. There was Rig, the fanatical supporter of the Rebellion and even more fanatical friend, Col's cousin Naia, and two other close friends, Beckett and Haynes. Col gave them all a glowing, encouraging smile.

"Good job everyone!" he beamed. "This calls for a celebration." The hall erupted in an excited clamour. Even Garan the blacksmith's son was there, grinning from ear to ear, although Col couldn't imagine how he had passed the test. He couldn't even read.

The night that followed was riotous and joyful. For once, the priests turned a blind eye to the acolytes as they broke the oppressive stillness of the barracks with their merrymaking. All those who had passed would be subject to one, final test at the end of the month but there was nothing they could do to prepare for the Worthiness test, so they had collectively decided to put it out of their minds. Someone had smuggled a large date cake into the sleeping chambers, and everyone gathered there after the meal, each of them savouring their portion. The room was silent for a good while, save for the sound of licking honey and date sugar off sticky fingers. There weren't many girls left since the endurance trial, but those that were left had crept from their rooms into the boy's quarters to share in this treat. After a moment, one of them broached the subject they had all been thinking of.

"What do you think they use to determine who's worthy?"

There was a dark, brooding silence.

"I heard you have to accomplish a dangerous feat to pass," one of the boys volunteered. "My brother told me it's something to do with snakes."

Everyone shuddered, their minds filled with images of deadly poison and writhing pits.

"One of the priests said something about bowls of blood," one of the girls, a dark, dangerous-looking one, said from the corner. Her eyes glittered with something that looked disturbingly like anticipation. There was a stricken silence as everyone stared at her.

"Hey, come on. It can't be that bad," Beckett forced a smile, "I bet it just has something to do with if the Hearer likes you, or if your family has influence, that sort of thing."

"That might be worse," Rig grumbled. "Some of us are poorer than dirt."

There was a mumble of assent. Beckett looked uncomfortable. His family was well-known in the city, as they owned several wells in the region, and taxed heavily on water drawn from them. They were rich, but not well-loved by the poor folk. Eventually, all eyes turned to Col. He thought they might.

"What do you think?" they asked, eyes begging for something. He knew what they wanted, but how was he supposed to cheer them up when he didn't have any more idea than they as to what was coming? Nevertheless, he gave them a bright, confident smile.

"It's more of a ceremonial thing, I don't think it's really hard, just a big ceremony where you get the double swords," he said calmly. "I heard it's not a real trial at all."

His words had an immediate effect, and the tension resolved. Of course, he didn't really know, but since there was no way to prepare there was no use letting his friends worry.

The following weeks sped by in an agony of training. Although they weren't being tested, the acolytes still had much to learn in the arts of war before they could join the ranks of the Hand. Some were innately skilled at weaponry, while all those less fortunate limped to bed each day covered in cuts and bruises. Col was one of those less fortunate ones. Every step of progress he made was paid for in bruises, blood, and sleepless nights. All thoughts of his family and his reasons for doing it faded, until nothing was left but the driving desire to just live through each following moment. Time dragged slower than one of the Hearer's speeches, and yet Col still found himself surprised when he was finally looking at the golden double doors of the temple of the Hand.

4

The Hearer stood perfectly still. He found that it intimidated people when he didn't move at all. In his golden robes with his tall, dominant stature it made him look more like a statue than a man. It was important to remind the people, and even his own priests, of his divine status. There was only one Hearer, greater than the king, greater than all the people in the world. His citizens were blessed to live in this city where they had a chance to see him once a week as he stood on the highest balcony of the temple. Soon, he would have to go. He had many things to oversee. However for now he simply stood, letting the light of the sun light up his golden robes. They had mirrors sewn into them, making him shine like the sun itself as he stood there. The people needed a reminder every now and again of who they served. A reminder that, while he demanded much from them, he also had the right to do so. Without such reminders the lowly masses had a tendency to get... unruly.

It was a murky day, with a smell of electricity in the air that promised a thunderstorm. The gigantic temple doors glittered dully in the subdued light, their entire surface covered with a giant image of the golden hand symbol. Col decided he was quite sick of it. He stood in the courtyard with his fellow acolytes, each of them dressed in solid black warrior's garb, with full capes and hoods pulled low over their faces. Each of them had empty sword scabbards buckled across their backs. A line of four priest-guards guarded the doors, only instead of hiding their armour under robes like most, they wore it openly. Out of the corner of his eye, Col caught a glimpse of black leather and glittering weapons that told him there were other guards behind the pillars on either side. The doors opened a crack, and the guards reluctantly stepped aside to let the acolytes pass through one by one. The interior was entirely dark, and wisps of bitter incense smoke drifted out. As he stepped through, all the rumours he'd heard about this trial came crashing back into his mind. His heart beat hard with dread.

The doors opened onto a large, decorative hall, but today it was shrouded with sheets and a row of flickering candles led to the side, directing the acolytes into a dark, narrow hallway to the right. Usually, the door to this dark passage was locked. It sloped sharply downwards into the stone foundation beneath the tower, and seemed to lead even deeper into the earth than the level on which the Order kept the dungeons. They walked silently, afraid to breathe. Finally, the faint light of fire beckoned them out of the dark, and the hall spilled them into a lighted chamber. The walls were stone, with ledges covered with candles, years of melted wax running in rivulets down to pool on the floor. The entire room was funnel-shaped, with long, wide steps stretching to the very back of the room, where there was a large dais. The edges of the steps were lined with robed priests and small pillars topped with bowls of incense. But Col saw none of this. His gaze was transfixed by the thing on the dais. The Hearer of the Hand stood there, with a large goblet in his hands, but Col barely noticed him. Even the fact that the Hearer was wearing a veil so thin it almost revealed his whole face didn't shock him. Because there was something else on the dais. Something his eyes could barely comprehend.

"By all the gods that be," he whispered in utter awe, "it's real."

At first glance, it might be taken for a large, uncut diamond or piece of quartz. But its edges weren't sharp, they were blurred and seemed to blend with the air as if the entire thing didn't quite exist. It was a mind-boggling thing, a thing that fractured reality. A thing that shouldn't exist. The inside would have been clear, but it was clouded with sharp, tangled lines, glowing faintly as they meshed together and swarmed around... Something dark in the centre. It vaguely resembled the shape of a kneeling human, with head thrown back and one hand outstretched. The lines of light swirled in a hurricane around this hand, as it stretched out from the centre almost to the edge of the crystal. The hand was so close to the surface it seemed about to break through. Around him, Col heard the other acolytes catch their breath in awe.

One by one, the acolytes were called up to the dais. One by one, the Hearer commanded them to kneel, and place their left hand against the crystal, almost touching the Hand itself. Over and over, the Hearer repeated the same question.

"Do you feel anything?"

The first few acolytes nodded. They described vague sensations, a bit of warmth, a surge of emotion. One by one, they were led back down the steps and presented with two gleaming swords, then led away to the Armoury to be fully outfitted as a priest. The remaining acolytes were beginning to relax. That was the entire test? It seemed so easy. Col was barely paying attention, his mind still reeling with the realization that all his assumptions about the Hand had been wrong. It was real. How could it be real? Did that mean that the myths about it were also true? Then Col felt someone seize his elbow. He looked sharply around, and found himself staring into the urgent eyes of his friend, the priest from the Knowledge test.

"You have to feel something." The priest was almost snarling, his voice barely audible but fraught with urgency.

"Even if you don't feel anything, claim you do. Understand? Most people don't, they're just smart enough to pretend. You have to pretend!"

Col frowned and agreed uncertainly. The priest vanished back into the watching crowd, and Col watched him go, a cold sense of unease seeping into his heart. Why had he seemed so distressed? Still frowning, he turned back to watch the proceedings. The fourth acolyte to go up still hadn't answered the question. He knelt there, brow furrowed with concentration.

"I... don't think I do," he said at last. "Give me a little more time." The Hearer's expression went hard behind his thin veil.

"There is no time to spare for those who cannot feel the influence of the Hand. You have not been chosen. Step forward."

His voice was soft and deadly, sending chills down Col's spine. The acolyte on the dais began to tremble.

"No, wait! I maybe can feel something! A sort of warm feeling," he began, but it was too late. Several priests strode forward and dragged him away from the crystal, turning him to face the Hearer. He crouched there, shaking violently as the Hearer bent down and offered him the goblet.

"Drink." It sounded like a gentle invitation, but the restless energy of the watching priests said otherwise. The kneeling boy shook his head.

"Please, no. I don't want to."

As one, the priests holding him drew their swords and pressed them to his neck. The Hearer's voice grew colder.

"Drink."

Hiccuping sobs escaped the boy as he pulled the brim of the cup closer with trembling hands. The entire room seemed to hold its breath.

The boy took only one sip, then cried out in horror. He gasped and fell to the ground, writhing in pain, bloody foam forming on his lips. The Hearer looked on coldly until the boy grew still.

"We must cleanse ourselves of the unworthy snakes among us," he said calmly. The other acolytes stood transfixed by horror. Several started crying. Col felt cold dread seep into his bones, along with dawning comprehension as he stared at the priests dragging the body out, and then at the goblet in the Hearer's hands. It's snake venom, he realized with a shudder. The goblet is filled with snake venom. That was when the Hearer called his name.

"Nikolo Wolf."

The name fell clear and cold in the dead silence of the room. Col stepped forward, feeling numb. Several of the priests recognized him from the arena, and a few whispers and chuckles flew about the room. He barely heard them. Each of the low steps took several paces to cross, and with each one Col felt his dread mounting. He pushed it down. It doesn't matter if you can't feel anything, just pretend. As he approached the stone, a cold hush settled over him. It felt as if time were slowing down as he drew closer. On the last step, he almost tripped before noticing that there were shallow bowls placed at intervals around the stone, with incense and candles burning between them. His toe accidentally bumped a bowl, and blood sloshed over the rim. He shuddered. Then he was at the stone, and all other thoughts flew out of his head. The hand pressed to the inside of the crystal was both delicate and strong, with long, muscled fingers. Looking closely, it suddenly occurred to Col that it was rather strange for a messenger of the gods to have calluses, specifically those calluses formed from drawing a bow. He placed his hand over the Hand, heart pounding. His hand was just a little bit larger, covering it completely. He stared into the glittering mess of threads shrouding the figure inside. At first he felt nothing.

"Do you feel anything?" The voice seemed to come from far away.

"Yes..." Col whispered, and he didn't need to lie, because now he could. Gradually, a warmth was spreading through the thin layer of crystal, growing warmer, stronger. Then he felt something else.

"I feel... warmth, and..." he gasped, "a pulse."

Murmurs of shock spread throughout the room.

"No need to overdo it," one of the priests standing nearby muttered. But Col was staring into the crystal, mesmerized. The threads of light were moving. They swirled slowly away from the figure in the centre, and the stone began to grow clearer, even as the lines of light glowed brighter. Then, a last layer of light peeled away, and Col found himself seeing the figure clearly. Only, it wasn't the messenger of the gods at all. It was a girl. Beautiful, but very obviously human. She wore a dress of rough cloth, and there were dark runes of blood painted all across her bare arms. They swirled up her neck and across her cheeks, nose, and forehead. Her features were delicate, but they bore an expression of such cold pride as to make her look strong, bordering on terrifying. However, it was her eyes that captivated Col. They were dark brown, focused in a frozen stare at some point slightly over his head, and they held so much tragic pain in them that he couldn't look away. Around him, he could hear the conversations growing louder, more surprised, finally escalating to cries of alarm. The light was growing unbearably bright. Then several things happened at once. His hand sank through the thin layer of stone as if it were water. His hand met that of the girl's. He felt the flutter of her heartbeat against his skin, strong and very real. Her eyes suddenly snapped to focus directly on him. Their eyes met, and then the stone exploded.

5

My cousin stole everything from me. Or perhaps it was the other way around, and I was the one who was trying to steal from her. All I know is, we were born rivals. When we were very young, the rivalry was lighthearted. You could almost say we were friends. She was the daughter of the king, I was the daughter of a respected general. She was charming, I was headstrong. Everyone said I would make a valuable supporter for her when she took the throne. We did everything together, along with the rest of the high-born children, from eating to taking lessons with the elders. However, as we grew older our friendship grew strained. She was the only child of the king, destined to rule. Her bloodline was ancient and filled with the power of the world around us. But the issue was, she wasn't powerful. She was weak. The earth never spoke to her, and even the simple act of making the flowers bloom gave her headaches. This wouldn't have bothered our friendship, except that we both saw it bothering the adults so much. Rulers were not meant to be weak. The power of the earth ran only in royal veins, and that was how we held our kingdom against the many nations surrounding us. Strong blood, strong wills. It worried them, to see my cousin struggling, and it worried us to see them worried. Gradually, as time passed I started to see something else in their eyes. Fear. At first, I did not know what they were afraid of. Then there was a day where everything became clear.

I was only twelve, my cousin was fourteen. We were in the courtyard, receiving a lesson on trade from an aged man with barely any teeth. I was bored, grinding a slow hole into the dirt with my toe, when a flicker of movement under the archway caught my eye. It was a group of druids, their rough brown robes contrasting starkly with the fine clothes of the king, with whom they were talking. They watched us, the noble children, for the better part of an hour as we rotated through lessons. An old soldier with only one leg taught us the arts of war. He looked with approval at me as I conquered my sparring partners one by one. I knew he admired my ruthlessness, the way I used everything I could to my advantage. The earth spoke to me as my bare feet twirled on its surface, and I spoke back. One adversary stumbled as the dirt shifted beneath him, while another was tripped up by the grass clinging to his feet. I could feel a gleeful grin growing on my face as I touched the dull end of my spear to his neck.

"I win."

The one-legged soldier chuckled appreciatively.

"Good. Now with Morning."

I turned to face my cousin. Her superior height and age did nothing to quell my confidence. I could see the slightest twitch of uncertainty in her stance, and that was enough for me to know I was going to win. We circled each other, and the group of druids by the wall began to shift uneasily. I ignored them, busy coaxing the earth to do my bidding. Morning frowned in concentration as we moved in towards each other. She seemed distracted, and her parries barely managed to block my strikes. I began to push her harder. The earth moved with me, dancing to my song, my bare feet tapping rhythm. Many people in the gathering crowd lost their footing and fell. It was all Morning could do to hold the earth steady as she backed away from me. I could see the effort taking a toll on her. I danced in a circle around her, blocked her half-hearted strike, and twirled. Her eyes widened, realizing I was only playing with her. She lunged, but the grass whipped around her ankle, sending her staggering. Her spear flew from her hand. I laughed, and stomped on the ground. It split, and suddenly Morning was buried up to her waist in the hard earth of the training yard, my spear point resting on her collar.

The yard was silent. I looked up at my uncle, expecting approval; but the only emotion on the king's face was naked fear. That's when I realized that it was me they all feared.

It was a while before I understood why, but now, looking back, it seems clear. The only thing keeping the royal line on the throne was the power in their veins. But what might happen if another had more power than the royal line?

From that day forth, I saw fear everywhere. The druids, the king, and his advisors all watched me with wary eyes. But the soldiers admired me. The peasants looked at me with awe. I focused on their admiration, and told myself it didn't matter what my uncle thought, what my own family thought. But it hurt, to lose their trust. So I nursed my pride, and told myself that if they saw me as a threat, I would become one. No longer did I hold back when I sparred with my cousin. Again and again I defeated her and the other children, until no one was left who dared face me. When they shouted insults, I lashed back ruthlessly until they were crushed into submission. I no longer had friends, but I had subjects. I told myself it was right that they should respect me. After all, was it not fate that gave me greater powers than my cousin? She was weak, while I was strong. I was strong enough to rule where she could not. Why should she get the throne, when she would doubtless be unable to keep it? Why should she get everything she desired when she didn't deserve it? While I, who deserved respect, received only cold shoulders from the people who mattered most. I despised her for her weakness, for her good fortune, and for the fear that showed in her eyes when she looked at me. And so, by their own actions my family shaped me into the very thing they feared most.

When no one would spar with me any longer, I took to visiting the soldiers. There I met Storm. He was a brave young warrior with a bright smile and laughing eyes. He talked with me when no one else would, and trained with me when I didn't feel like talking, although he rarely won. There were times when even just a glimpse of him would bring a smile to my face.

On my sixteenth birthday, he gave me a necklace and a kiss. I treasured both, knowing that here was something my cousin could never have, even once she became queen and gained everything else. That year was a beautiful one. Every minute that I was not having lessons I spent with Storm. I basked in this new love, and my only other friend, the earth, rejoiced with me. The forests glowed with health, and the crop was more bountiful than ever before. Then I turned seventeen. My uncle died, my cousin took the throne, and everything changed.

It was a late night when they came for me. My cousin, some elders, and a whole pack of druids. My father let them in. He claimed to love me, but I suspect that deep down in his soldier's heart, his first loyalty had always been to his brother and the throne. I didn't let them come get me. When I heard the door open, I went to meet them.

"What is this about?"
There was a very heavy silence. It was my father who first greeted me.

"River, the druids have foreseen your destiny."

My breath caught in my throat.

"My destiny is my own to choose." I said it with certainty, thinking of Storm, but my heart was unsure. My father smiled, a pitying smile. I hated it instantly.

"No, Darling, you were born for great things beyond your choosing. Your blood is strong. Stronger than any we have ever seen."

My mind froze. Could they have finally realized that I deserved the throne, more than my cousin? But no. My cousin was watching me with scornful eyes. Whatever this was, it wasn't good for me. My father went on, that same unhappy smile still fixed on his face.

"It is clear you are destined to be a great queen. Greater than any before you."

I couldn't breathe. My heart leaped with joy. But he wasn't done.

"But this kingdom is not great. We are small, at war with many around us. This kingdom is not worthy of one such as you."

The smile fell from my face as I stared at him, confused. Never had I heard him speak such words before. What on earth could he mean?

Then a druid spoke.

"We have foreseen a future where all these lesser kingdoms will become one. If our kingdom is strong now, how much greater will it become in a thousand years?"

He paused, allowing me to comprehend what he spoke of. Despite myself, I could not help contemplating the possibilities of such a vast kingdom. What could one do, with such power?

"We have foreseen another thing." The druid's face was drained, weary. "This blood that runs in our veins will only grow weaker, more diluted with time. Soon even the kings of that great country will cease to feel the earth; the rulers will walk blind to its power. This is the future we saw. And with it, we saw your destiny."

He stepped forward, gesturing for me to kneel. I have always had a great dislike of kneeling to anyone, but with a druid this was not a pose of submission but of receiving a gift. So I knelt, and his warm, moist palm pressed against my forehead.

"You, River of the house of kings, are not meant for this time. Your power is meant to be wielded in a different time, when all kingdoms are one and a great high king rules over all. You are to be sent as a gift to this distant time, to wed the high king and bring your strong blood to that great house. You will rule at his side over the greatest kingdom known to man, and your children will wield the power of the earth, never to be conquered until their blood again grows as weak as the common man's. This is your destiny."

He pronounced this with great passion, but I saw through his words at once when I caught the glint in my cousin's eye. This is her way of getting rid of me. I almost laughed. It was too ridiculous, all this talk of great kingdoms and high kings. The truth was that they were afraid of my power but also too afraid of the earth's wrath to kill me. So she was banishing me. She'd convinced the druids to foresee a future for her without me in it. A wave of rage and grief swept over me. I looked at my cousin with all the bitter hatred of a thousand vipers. She flinched. I couldn't speak, couldn't face anyone with these raging emotions. I swept past her and out into the night, to hide my tears in the darkness of the forest where my cousin couldn't see them and gloat over me. The others tried to follow me, but the forest would not let them pass.

For the next week, I mourned. This was a fate far worse than losing the throne, for I would lose all that I knew, cast out of the very world I lived in. The druids said the spell would take time. I doubted they could even accomplish such a spell, but I had no doubt that they would try tirelessly. To my cousin, this may have been merely a way to get rid of me, but I could see that they truly believed in what they told me. Your destiny, your destiny, your destiny. The words became a mantra throughout the following weeks, until they finally began to sink in, and I began to believe them. Although I did not want to be cast out, the idea of a great kingdom began to hold more and more appeal. Was I really to become so great? To rule the whole world? The thought took fire in me. My pride grew greater, but my heart grew small and cold, for I would be leaving Storm forever.

On the day the druids finally finished, they sent for me. I made the long journey to their temple at the roots of the mountains, dressed in a rough robe, my feet bare, as though I were destined for sacrifice. A crowd followed me at a distance, noblemen and peasants alike trailing along, drawn by their curiosity. I could barely think for my fear. Never had I been so afraid, for in a way I was indeed to be sacrificed today. I was sacrificing all I knew for an unknown future, one that perhaps would never come to pass. The druids claimed that I would sleep outside of time, only to be woken by the touch of a high king over all the world. But in my heart was a nagging suspicion that I would never wake at all. Nevertheless, I pressed onward. Never did it occur to me to rebel against the will of my father, of the elders, of the druids-- who knew more than any others about the will of the earth. So I walked on, fearful but refusing to show it. I would not let my cousin have the satisfaction of thinking she had beaten me.

The druid's most holy place was not on the mountain, but under it. I walked down through dimly lit caves until it seemed I had reached the very heart of the world, and the joyful song of the earth seemed deafening to my ears. It calmed me, somewhat, to know that the earth would always be there, no matter the civilization that walked on its surface. Storm followed me. The druids tried to stop him, but the earth rumbled my anger and they backed away.

They had me kneel in the darkest recess of the cave. There they worked their spell. Lines of time spun free of the air and wrapped themselves around me. My heart slowed and a great pressure settled on my chest as if the small lines of light were heavy chains. I panicked.

"No, I don't want to do this. I can't."

I stretched out my hand, and Storm caught it, his fingers gently twining with mine.

"You have to, love." His voice was low and broken. "This is your destiny. There's nothing we can do to escape it."

He held my eyes as tears streamed from his, as our fingers came apart until only our palms were touching, as the crushing weight of eternity wrapped its cold fingers around my heart and squeezed. Or perhaps that was only my heart breaking at the look in his eyes. I took one last deep breath and my spirit calmed as I faced my destiny. The last thing I saw before eternity claimed me were his eyes, those beautiful, joyful eyes now so empty of the laughter that once flooded them.

There was a breath, only a breath. I breathed out once, as an unimaginable, crushing pressure pushed down on my lungs. My vision went black. Then the pressure lifted and I breathed in again. My vision came back, strangely warped as if I looked through frozen water. A pair of eyes were looking back at me, and my breath caught because they were so, so familiar. Joy and laughter flickered playfully within their green depths, and I felt my heart start to leap in response. But the face. The face was not Storm's. It was a foreign face, a stranger's face, on the body of a man slightly shorter, and younger than the man I loved. He was wiry and slim, with brown skin, freckles, and bizarre, pale hair such as I had never seen before, nothing like Storm. I stared at him, and then the world exploded around me, full of noise, light, and chaos.

6

The Hearer stood, in his golden robes, and felt as if the floor had been torn out from under him. At the touch of a single boy, an insignificant boy, the crystal around the Messenger shattered. Such a catastrophe had not been thought possible, not in the thousand years of the Order's reign. He felt his strength sap, as if a string had been snipped somewhere inside of him, cutting him off from the source of his energy. Worse than that, his mind reeled at the implications of what was happening. Incoherent rage and panic roared within him, and he almost fell over. However, he sucked the feelings back inside, forcing himself to think clearly. If he didn't act now, everything he had built could come crashing down around him. There had to be a solution, and he *would* think of it. Whatever was happening, it was absolutely critical that he put a stop to it.

The girl stood and stepped forward, swaying slightly. Her eyes were fastened on Col with a startling intensity, taking in every inch of him. Then she spoke, and the room grew suddenly quiet. Everyone strained to hear her words.

"But who are you?" she asked softly, confused. "They said only a high king could wake me, and I was to be his queen. But you are only a boy. Where is your crown? Your throne?"

She looked around, taking in everything – the candles, priests, incense, and bowls of blood. A slow understanding dawned in her eyes, then a growing horror.

"You fools." Her eyes flashed with sudden fury. She turned on the Hearer.

"You have meddled with the spell! You are foolish children, mucking up what you do not understand, and you have brought doom upon the world!"

The Hearer's eyes, at first wide with shock, narrowed at this. His calculating gaze swept the room, and he nodded sharply at several priests.

"Seize them."

Col struggled fruitlessly as hands landed on him. The girl's eyes widened in shock and fury. Her voice rose.

"I am River, daughter of General Ironwood the Victorious, of the ancient blood of kings, and destined to wed a high king over all the world! You will not touch your queen." Her voice was so regal and furious that one of the priests grabbing for her let her go for a moment, and she delivered a sharp uppercut to his chin. Then more priests descended, and she was lost to sight behind a flurry of robes. The Hearer's voice rang out over the confused crowd, improvising wildly.

"The Holy Messenger is clearly crazed from being trapped in such a humiliating, mortal form. Clearly this is some evil spell cast by the wicked acolyte. Never fear, we will free Her Divine Being from this cursed shape-shifting spell. However, the Messenger must not be seen by mortal eyes once she is released. Clear the room."

Col watched as his fellow acolytes were escorted swiftly out. Rig caught his eye, his expression confused and furious. He tried to fight his way toward Col, but was shoved bodily from the room. Col's cousin Naia was also making a ruckus, even going so far as to bite a priest in her attempt to rescue Col. The priest hit her hard, and Col caught a glimpse of Beckett screaming her name, his mournful, love-struck puppy eyes fixed on her. Then a wave of priests blocked his vision and he lost sight of his friends. Meanwhile, the Hearer turned and exited through another door, and the priests holding Col dragged him after. He caught another glimpse of the girl, River, as they were hustled through the passageway. She was walking swiftly, head high, with a cold fury on her face. Her arms were linked through those of the priests on either side of her, almost as though they were her escorts rather than her captors. She didn't even look at Col as she swept past.

He was dumped unceremoniously into a cell. The barred door was slammed shut, and he dared breathe again. At least they weren't going to kill him quite yet. He had no doubts that they would, eventually. He had disrupted their ceremony, perhaps their entire religion. There would be a price. But for now he was out of danger. He heard more bars slam close by, and the girl's voice, cold and quiet.

"Is this how you treat royalty here? How pleasant."

The Hearer ignored her, pacing back and forth in front of the cells.

"This can't be happening," he muttered, furious. "The Messenger is not a mortal. We have claimed for centuries that she is too brilliant and holy to look at, so what are we to say now?"

The other priests stood silent. The Hearer grabbed the bars of the girl's cell.

"Who are you, really? How did you come to possess the spirit of the Messenger?"

His only answer was an icy silence. He let out a breath in frustration.

"No matter. We'll figure out a way to solve this, and 'free' the Messenger from within you, or at least loosen your tongue. There are other matters that must be attended to first, before this city falls into chaos."

He turned and left. The other priests left with him, and there was silence. Col stared numbly through the bars of his door at the wall across from him. His mind gradually turned from gloomy thoughts to curiosity about the girl beside him, just as she spoke.

"Tell me your name." Her voice was close, suggesting that she was also standing at the bars of her door, looking out.

"Nikolo."

"And who is your family, Nikolo? You are not a king, that much is clear. A prince, perhaps? Or merely a nobleman's son."

"No. I'm the second son of a peasant woman; nobody, really." Col felt a strange sense of shame. For some reason, he didn't want to disappoint this strange girl. She said nothing for a long moment. Then,

"They truly did tamper with the spell, then. I should not have woken."

Her voice was soft and full of pain.

"So much for glorious destiny."

"Why was it so important for you to be woken by a high king?" he asked, curious.

There was a long silence.

"They said I was to be queen of a great country that spanned the whole world. They said my own country was too small, too insignificant for one such as I. That I was to sleep until a kingdom worthy of my rule came to be." She paused, and her voice turned bitter.

"They were right. I am worthy to rule. I deserve a great kingdom of adoring subjects, not this... cell." She sounded disgusted, and Col found himself growing slightly annoyed.

"Well, I hate to be the bearer of bad news, but you're not going to get that. Nine chances to one, we're going to be killed or left to die here in these very cells. We've seen too much, and caused too much trouble."

"You know nothing, peasant boy. Be silent," she snapped. Col stared at the wall thoughtfully.

"Well, they'll for sure kill me, but maybe they won't kill you. After all, they think you're a messenger of the gods."

"What do you mean?" She sounded reluctantly curious. And so Col told her the legend of the Hand, starting from the very beginning. She didn't interrupt him, but stayed silent as his voice painted pictures in the cold, dry air.

When he was finally finished, she let out a little snort of astonishment.

"Common folk are so foolish. That is truly the most outrageous pack of lies I have ever heard. If these gods were so powerful, why would they need a messenger to speak for them? And a human to speak for her? Could they not speak for themselves?" Her voice turned thoughtful. "However, I admire the weaver of these lies. Surely you see that with a few words he won himself so much power."

There was a short silence as she contemplated this. Then her voice rang out again, commanding this time.

"Tell me more about your world. It helps to pass the time. Does this kingdom you live in truly stretch across the whole world? Does it have one king, or many?"

Col found himself amused at her ignorance, and stubborn pride.

"The world is incredibly vast," he explained patiently. "No one knows how wide it is, but all the kingdoms that we know of have come under the rule of one king. Only he's dead. His son, the crown prince, is due to take his place soon. His coronation may have already happened, for all I know."

She had many questions. Gradually, as the day passed and his voice sped the hours onward, she stopped asking them in such a commanding tone. However, she consistently avoided questions about her past. When he pressed her, she said only, "It matters not," and then asked a question of her own, or ordered him to be silent.

It was drawing near evening when a sound from outside disturbed their conversation. Far away, a door creaked and boots tramped somewhere above their heads. They fell silent as someone descended the stairs. The hooded head of a priest came into view. Col was surprised to recognize the friendly priest who had warned him during the worthiness ceremony. Bren was his name, but Col didn't dare call out to him. He was followed by several others. To Col's even greater surprise, some of them were not priests at all, but soldiers bearing the crest of the high king. They walked past Col's cell and stopped in front of the girl's.

"You are fortunate," Bren remarked dryly. "Somehow word reached the prince of your words in the Stone Chamber, and he has publicly claimed you as his betrothed." His lips twitched in a bit of a smirk. "The Hearer will be furious, of course. Not often does he get prisoners stolen from directly under his nose."

He unlocked the door and River stepped into view. She accepted the soldier's arm regally, and nodded once to the priests.

"Thank you for your hospitality." Her voice was coldly sarcastic. As she passed Col's cell, she turned to look at him.

"See how much you know, peasant boy."

Col shrugged and gave her a cheerful smile.

"I'm not always right." His smile disappeared. "Watch yourself, though. You've made a powerful enemy."

She snorted and walked on, out of his sight. Bren gave Col a momentary glance of disappointment and regret as they passed, confirming Col's fears. This man would not help him. He let out a long breath and slumped down against the door. Without anyone to distract him from it, the heaviness of certain death weighed down on him. He put his head in his hands. How would his mother react when they gave her the news? Or would she never find out, and live her life wondering what had become of him, just like she had with his father?

"If there's a god out there who doesn't need a messenger, who's actually powerful," he muttered into the empty silence, "I could use some help."

7

The prince had snatched the Messenger right out of his hands. The Hearer hadn't thought the young, distracted soon-to-be king capable of such sneaky treachery, and it made him furious that the girl was temporarily beyond his reach. Unable to do anything about that loose end for now, he redirected all his irritation at the boy. Nikolo Wolf needed to die.

The dungeon door clanged. The boy raised weary, resigned eyes to meet those of the Hearer. It soothed the Hearer, somewhat, to see that the boy had been thoroughly beaten prior, although he would have rather done the beating himself. Unfortunately, the prestige of his status also came with certain drawbacks. He couldn't lower himself to such menial work. The amusement he had once felt toward this boy was gone, replaced by pure hate. He would have liked to strike the lad, but instead he lashed him with bitter words.

"It's a pity, boy. I liked you. You made me laugh once. But you've been a thorn in my sandal ever since. You have betrayed the Order, and destroyed our most sacred artifact. This offense is unparalleled, and the worst punishment imaginable is too good for you. Even for tripping in front of me, people die." He let the ominous silence linger, then finally spoke in a soft, deadly voice.
"Nikolo Wolf, are you ready to die?"

The boy looked pale. He spat blood. The Hearer could see him gulp in fear. Then, to his complete astonishment, the boy grinned. It was fake, it had to be fake! But it was extremely convincing, as if he had just offered the boy a present, instead of grueling death.

"Boy oh boy!" he said, wryly. "Too bad the girl got away!"

The Hearer sprang to his feet, ready to kill the boy then and there. Then he stopped himself, took a deep breath, and held himself back, realizing that this was the boy's intention. He was trying to get a swift death. Not to mention, if he let the boy get under his skin, he might do something undignified. The boy would deal another blow to the security of his station without even trying. Instead, he hissed at the guards holding the boy.

"Take him to the chasm."

As River walked up the stairs, her mind couldn't help but turn back to the boy she had left behind, the one with familiar eyes and a beautiful voice. As well as a singularly unobjectionable face. Despite his scars and some fading bruises, she couldn't help but admit that that boy she had left in the prison had possessed one of the most winsome faces she had ever laid eyes on. Her steps slowed.

"What's to become of the other prisoner?" she asked, trying to fake an unconcerned tone. The guard holding her arm snorted.

"With the Hearer as angry as he is? Nothing good. He'll be lucky when death finally takes him."

"Oh." Despite herself, her heart sank a bit. He was only a peasant. Why should she care? But she did.

"What manner of death would that be?" She tried to sound merely curious.

The guard hesitated.

"It's not a fitting conversation for a lady..."

"Tell me," she snapped. He sighed.

"Very well. The priests like to keep their worst prisoners not in the dungeons, but hanging from chains off the edge of a cliff. They'll probably hang him until he's half-dead, then cut out his tongue, put out his eyes, and generally mutilate him before hanging him back out for the crows."

The others in the group looked uncomfortable.

River suppressed a shudder. That was far worse than anything that had been done in her time. The thought of those familiar, lovely eyes being put out was extremely disturbing.

"That's... less than pleasant." She couldn't keep the nausea out of her voice. "Torture methods have clearly degenerated since my time."

The soldier shrugged.

"You asked."

"So I did."

They emerged from the dungeons into the main court of the temple, and all thoughts of the boy were banished from her mind. Never had she imagined such architecture. Wood, stone, and some manner of mortar blended seamlessly into intricately patterned structures. The doorways were mostly triangular. The walls of the temple were mainly made with stone, but there were long beams of wood that angled and crossed each other, framing the doorways and windows and giving the wooden towers a strangely unfinished, spiky look.

Everywhere, she saw gold. The shape of a hand was patterned repeatedly on almost every surface, its edges glittering. River caught her breath at such opulence. Even the curtains of the doors and windows were made of finer cloth than any she had ever seen. Everywhere, priests hurried on business, but these, also, were like no priests she had ever seen. They wore beautifully crafted black leather armour, and long black cloaks, adorned with a single golden hand, clasped at the shoulder. They were armoured to the teeth, every one of them, and their weapons were sleek, perfect. River couldn't help herself. She gaped.

There was little time for gaping, however. The soldiers escorting her hustled in a distinctly nervous way as soon as the priests left them, and she was swept from the temple and through the city in a close huddle of guards, barely able to admire anything.

After the glory of the temple, the palace was a bit of a letdown.

Yes, it was big. But that was all it was. There was no gold, no beautiful towers, only endless halls of thick stone, with bored soldiers lounging about. The prince met her in a private audience hall. He was tall and handsome, in a distracted sort of way. He wore the finest of clothes, and golden jewellery, but they hung crookedly on him as though he had thrown them on in a hurry. He turned light grey, curious eyes on River, and motioned the soldiers from the room. She swept a deep curtsy.

"You are the high king?"

"Soon to be, yes." A hint of interest flickered across his face.

"They said you came out of the stone itself? Then are you the Messenger?"

River shook her head.

"There was never any Messenger. You have been lied to, my lord. There was only ever me, imprisoned in the stone until I should wake."

The prince looked stricken.

"No Messenger... But that's impossible. That means the Hearer's power is built on lies... And I betrothed myself to what I thought was their source of power... I thought I was stealing it from right under their noses, but if you're not the Messenger... No wonder they let me have you so easily." He stared at her, disbelieving and disappointed.

"But if you're not The Messenger, then who are you?"

River, nettled, drew herself to her full, rather insignificant height.

"I am River, of the blood of kings. I was enchanted to sleep outside of time until such a moment as a high king over all the lands should wake me, that I could rule at his side."

The prince's eyes, taking in her bare feet and rough clothes, were not impressed.

"You may have been some sort of princess where you came from, but what makes you think you have any right to rule in this time? What could you possibly offer me?"

River had been expecting this. She gave him a cool look.

"My right to rule comes not from other's wills, but from the very blood that runs in my veins. What could I offer you?" She drew closer, holding his eyes as she dropped her voice.

"I could offer you the guarantee that you and your descendants would remain powerful rulers for generations, never to be toppled because their blood would hold such power as to strike fear into the hearts of all who came against them."

His eyes widened.

"What sort of power?"

She smiled, a little condescendingly.

"Do you not know of the power your ancestors once wielded? How the earth itself would do the bidding of the one who sat on the throne? Or has your generation forgotten even this?"

The prince frowned.

"Those are just myths."

River's smile grew wider, as grass began to push its way up between the tiles on the floor. The act was strangely difficult, as though something blocked her access to the power. However, her face remained confident.

"Are they?"

His face cycled through expressions of boredom, then surprise, then awe, finally settling on greedy desire. Striding forward, he took both her hands in his, kissing them.

"I would be delighted to marry you," he said, his eyes so sincere that she almost believed it was herself, and not her power, that he wanted. She didn't really care. Her own heart beat cold and broken in her chest, and her fake smile mirrored the prince's. Deep down, she felt that she could never love anyone again. Love was a thing of her past. The future held something far more desirable: power.

The prince gave her a lavish set of rooms previously belonging to his sister, who had moved away to marry a country nobleman. Of course he did.

After her display in the audience hall, he could not do enough for her, so anxious was he to have her for his queen. He assigned three servants to do her bidding, and River felt a quiet tickle of pride as she ordered them about. The rooms were rich, but not suitable at all. They were far too lavish, and while she appreciated the luxury, she didn't appreciate the tasteless glitter of the princess's bedroom. Her day was consumed with restyling the area to her liking, in a far more elegant and sombre style. She fell immediately into the hectic rhythm of creating a new wardrobe, starting with some of the princess's things. As the hours flashed by in fine silks and finer weapons, she relaxed, entirely forgetting the boy in the dungeon. This was what she was meant for, this life of privilege and luxury. This was what she deserved. She leaned out over the balcony railing and gloried in the sight of the vast, majestic city that she was about to rule.

River woke, sweating, from a dream. Even awake, Storm's face haunted her memory, tears of blood streaming from his beautiful eyes as he called her name, hanging from chains off a cliff. She shuddered, wrapping the blankets more securely around herself. This country was far too hot and dry for blankets, she decided, kicking them off again. All the materials were light and airy, but still the heat seemed to creep into one's bones. She stared out the window, trying to rid herself of the memory of Storm. Gradually, her mind drifted to another set of beautiful eyes, and she frowned, thinking.

The morning light streamed in through the small, high windows of the throne room. It was still too early for visitors, and the prince slumped alone in the gigantic stone chair, looking bored as River entered on silent feet. Her black hair hung in a shining river past her waist, jewels glimmered in the delicately braided crown that framed her face. All the runes and dirt were gone, leaving her skin pale and soft compared to the sun-darkened skin of the people around her. She was dressed in a flowing dress of blue silk that hugged her body and trailed out around her feet, accentuating what feminine curves she possessed, and granting her the illusion of height. Silver threads glimmered in the fabric, matching the silver jewellery she wore. Makeup accentuated her exotically beautiful features. Never before had she had access to such finery as they possessed in this land, but she had quickly adapted to it.

Some maids bustled in with a table and breakfast. She watched them for a while as they worked, completely unaware of her presence. Then she stepped out of the shadows.

"Your Majesty."

He started violently, then he recognized her and relaxed a bit. His eyes took in her apparel and widened gratifyingly. She felt a thrill of success. After all, she had intentionally dressed to please him. She wanted something. He noted the serious look on her face, and waved the servants out of the room.

"What can I do for you?" he asked, exactly as she had hoped he would, gesturing for her to come closer. She lowered her eyelashes demurely.

"Drystan, darling, there was another prisoner in the dungeon with me when I was rescued."

She carefully toned her voice to seem only mildly concerned.

"He seemed harmless, and I see no reason why he should be imprisoned or killed for helping me. Would you have him released? It would be most gracious of you."

"What?" The prince looked as if he might choke on his toast. "You want me to just release one of the Hearer's prisoners? Are you mad?"

River was both confused and offended.

"It is only a small request. You are soon to be the high king. You need only give the order."

He scoffed.

"I'm not that sort of king. Do you have any idea of the Hearer's power?"

River just stared at him, uncomprehending. He sighed in frustration.

"It was all I could do to get you released, and he only allowed that because I publicly betrothed you to myself, and he's got to keep up appearances. I appreciate your empathy, but I can't just go saving every poor fool the Hearer decides to torture."

Then River understood. The weight of realization came crashing down on her with crushing force.

"You're a puppet," she accused, "you're no real king at all; only a figurehead for the kingdom, while the Hearer has all the real power!"

Drystan's face flushed bright red. He shot her a look of severe irritation.

"No need to be rude. Welcome to the real world, princess. No one has the power to do whatever they want, like the primitive rulers of your time. Politics aren't so simple."

She looked at him, her face grave.

"But they could be."

Then she turned and left the room.

Once she had returned to her rooms, River fumed. How could she not have seen this? How could the spell have gone so wrong? This empire was great, but the king was the weakest ruler she had ever seen. He had no power. And she was betrothed to him, which meant neither did she. It was all she could do not to cry. Was this to be her fate? Chained to a weak man and subject to the whims of a pompous priest who wore a veil like a widow woman? She threw a vase at the wall of her room in rage. The servants tried to come in to clean it, but she drove them out with threats of beheading and continued to throw things.

It took a long time before her rage gave way to the feeling behind it. She stood with her back pressed to the wall and stared at nothing, unable to understand the loss carving a hole in her chest. She was afraid. Afraid to see him die, afraid to lose the only familiar thing in this broken, sun-scorched land. He wasn't Storm. She knew that. Still, he was Storm's descendant. He had to be. Those eyes were unmistakable, and she couldn't help but feel a pull towards him. The thought of his eyes being put out was unbearable.

"Why should I care?" she asked the wall. But she did.

8

The moon was slow in rising over the high clifftops where the city lay sprawled. Its feeble light drifted down, filtering through slatted bridges and casting strange shadows on the city streets. The huge tower of the temple of the Hand cast strange shadows indeed, with its odd architecture. The shadows made the cliff-face right behind the temple even darker. The chasm seemed to stretch downwards eternally, the bottom far too distant for the weak moonbeams to touch. However, the beams did touch something. They glinted off of chains hanging down the rock face, glittered across a stream of blood sliding down a knotted arm, the veins standing out from strain, and illuminated the beads of sweat on a young man's upturned face. His face was contorted in a silent grimace, his breath coming in weak gasps and his whole body shivering. He hung there by his arms from long chains, his feet swinging gently over the unfathomable expanse below. Above him, four soldiers shifted restlessly, leaning on their staffs.

The wind howled, disguising the sound of soft, sprinting footsteps.

The moonlight glinted off of something else. The sharp flash of a blade, then another across two throats. The pair of soldiers on one side of the prisoner fell before they had time to act. They might have jumped back in time, but their feet seemed somehow rooted to the ground.

Col glanced up at the sounds of yells on the ground above him. They slowly grew weaker, then died out entirely. A dark head peered over the edge.

"Peasant boy?" He didn't answer, merely stared uncomprehendingly. After a silence, the voice tried again.

"Nikolo? Are you awake?"

"I'm not sure," he confessed. "At any rate I'm hallucinating."

She let out a soft, relieved laugh which confused him still more.

"Hold on, I'll get you."

The whole cliff-side seemed to shake slightly, or perhaps it was only the wind. At any rate, it set Col swinging wildly, and he smashed hard into the rock. He yelled, panic flaring as the chains jerked, threatening to snap. Something wrapped around him, its hard scratchy surface pressing against his ribs. Something fluttered against his arms and face, feeling like nothing so much as large leaves. He felt himself rising, and struggled to see what sort of disturbing creature had ensnared him.

It was a tree. Even as he stared, thin twigs entwined with his chains and grew, bursting the links so that his arms were freed.

He was released unceremoniously onto the ground at the feet of his rescuer. She knelt at his side, her hands lightly running over him.

"Are you hurt?"

At first, he couldn't meet her eyes because his attention was entirely captured by his erstwhile guards. Two lay in pools of blood, while the other two were frozen in place, dull eyes staring, their bodies completely wrapped in something dark and thorny that looked like nothing so much as... Roses? It couldn't be. It didn't make sense.

He finally pulled his attention back to his rescuer and made out her face under the hood. He gaped in astonishment. River met his eyes, and her own were conflicted. The silence dragged out. He knew he should answer, but he couldn't find the words. Then nearby yells distracted them both. River pulled him roughly to his feet.

"Because if you're not you need to run with me."

He stumbled, but regained his feet. She slipped under one of his arms to support him, and he almost screamed at the pain in his shoulders. Nevertheless, he gritted his teeth and forced himself forward.

Three guards burst from a back door of the temple and charged at them. River stopped running for a moment, stepped away from him, and planted bare feet on the ground. Col suddenly found himself knocked to his knees. It felt as if the entire world had convulsed suddenly. The echoes of a deep rumbling sound still shivered in the air. He looked behind them, but the soldiers had disappeared entirely, as if they had never existed. He blinked.

"I'm definitely hallucinating."

River took his hand.

"Come on."

9

When they were certain they had lost all pursuers, they stopped. She looked around at the empty city street, and it was a good thing he couldn't see the look on her face because it would have broken even the coldest heart. For the first time, she realized just how lost she was. All he could hear was her catching her breath, then her breaths started coming faster and faster until she was gasping. She fell to her knees, eyes squeezed shut and jaw clenched. He staggered a little without her support, and looked down at her in confusion. Pain was written in every line of her hunched body, and his heart instantly went out to her. He knelt, gently placed a hand on her shoulder. She stiffened. When she looked up, her face was wearing a prideful mask again. He was about to say something sympathetic, but she cut him off.

"You know someone who will take you in? Hide you from the priests?"

He looked around, recognizing the street.

"Yeah. Rig lives a few streets down."

She nodded and stood up, taking his arm again.

"Lead us."

Rig's house was a small building, huddled between two larger buildings. There were no windows, and only a flickering light under the door hinted that someone was home. It wasn't Rig who answered the door. A stranger opened it and stood in the gap, the light behind him making it impossible to see his face. His voice was harsh.

"What do you want?"

Col let go of River and stepped forward into the slanting light beam.

"I'm Col. Rig might have mentioned me. We're on the run from priests of the Hand and I figured he could help us out?"

The man's posture relaxed slightly, but he didn't open the door further.

"Us?"

"Yeah." Col turned back towards River. "This is-" He stopped. She wasn't there.

The street was empty, and there were hundreds of alleyways she could have disappeared into. Or... Maybe she didn't need an alleyway to disappear. The memory of the scene on the cliff top rushed back to Col's mind, and he couldn't keep himself from shivering. There was no way for him to deny that the girl was far from normal. There was something mystical and unnerving about her, and he began to wonder if he had hallucinated the whole past hour.

"... She's gone." He stated the obvious, mind reeling. The man snorted. "I can see that. Probably off to tell the authorities where you are."

He stepped back, opening the door wider. The light illuminated a harsh face, but Col caught a bit of grim cheer in his eyes.

"Come in quickly, and we'll make sure they don't find you."

River strode blindly through the city. The echo of priest's steps reached her through the earth and she changed direction to avoid them. Inside her chest, her heart beat a cold, broken rhythm. Even the earth felt strange in this city, like a dying, half-wild animal. Half her mind was berating her for running away from a life of luxury, while the other half screamed defiantly that she would never, never marry a puppet, and become nothing but a figurehead queen. Nor would she associate with peasants. The boy was safe now, so she would put him out of her mind. If there was a destiny out there for her, she would have to find it on her own. Her heart spoke a different opinion, but she ignored it.

It was nearing dawn when she finally found herself wandering up to a small side door of a large temple. A forest of towers of varying heights surrounded a many tiered, central building with wider levels. Bridges, balconies, and shorter wings connected it all, lending a certain elegance and unity to the complex structure. Its sandstone spires rose as if filled with ambition to pierce the clouds and rise higher than all the other buildings. Her heart warmed with a sort of empathy. As she approached the doors, her eyes widened in astonishment to find that the words engraved above them were in a writing she understood.

With Silence comes Wisdom

Before she even realized what she was doing, she was pushing open the doors and walking inside. The room was small, with intricate paintings of some manner of gods on all the walls. Narrow doorways led away in several different directions. A hooded woman stepped out of an alcove and hurried towards her. She had tattoos beneath her lips and eyes, strange symbols written in another language River didn't know. She looked into River's eyes with an expression that was a little too intense – almost hungry.

"What do you seek?"

River took a bit of a step back before considering the question. What did she seek? Power, that much was certain. But also other, more subtle things, like a sense of belonging. The hooded woman shuffled closer.

"You seek Knowledge?" she prodded. River nodded. She did seek knowledge, for with knowledge came both power, and an understanding of the new world she found herself in. The woman's eyes lit up with delight.

"You have come to the right place. Here, we welcome all seekers. Welcome to the temple of the Silent Speaker. For in She alone is true wisdom found."

She began to lead River towards one of the doorways, but River hesitated.

"Who is the Silent Speaker?"

The woman's eyes widened in shock, and she clicked her tongue softly.

"Such shameful ignorance. No matter. All can learn, and all knowledge will be given to those who seek it. Come with me."

River followed her through a door and up a gently sloping spiral walkway with doors along one wall. On the other wall were murals made with bits of colourful glass which she observed with interest. The first picture depicted an alarmingly buxom woman with golden skin and bright yellow eyes whispering into the ear of a desert traveller. In the following scene, she was surrounded by many other people with the same skin and eyes, pointing accusing fingers.

"The Silent Speaker is a nameless goddess of Knowledge," the woman told River in reverent tones.

"She once told the deep secrets of the world to all mortals, and it is from her that we have everything we know. But the other gods were unhappy with her. They thought that mortals did not deserve such knowledge. They forbid the Speaker to speak or ever again visit mortals. But she did not heed their warnings, for she felt the need to share her knowledge."

The murals continued up the entire passage with various eventful and somewhat disturbing scenes all involving the buxom woman, before finally ending with a picture of the woman seated in a dark room with a hood over her eyes, her mouth a thin line. They stopped, having reached the end of the passage. They stood before a door. The woman traced the last mural gently with her fingers.

"And so the gods cut out her tongue," she said softly. "But still she speaks. Not with words, but silently into the minds of those who are worthy, of those who have learned how to truly listen."

She looked long and hard at River, whose mouth was open with questions burning on her lips.

"The only way to truly listen is to be silent." Her tone caused River's mouth to snap closed, as she turned and opened the door.

The room beyond was wide and well-lit, its many windows opening up onto a stunning view of the city spread far below. There was a woman in the room, seated in the middle of the floor, her many colourful robes spread out around her, turning her into a shapeless mass of long, bright strips of fabric. Her head was bowed, and she looked to be asleep. The woman who had accompanied River strode forward and knelt in front of her.

"Mistress, we have welcomed a new seeker."

There was a long pause, and then the strange woman lifted her head. River sucked in a soft breath, for the woman was horrifying to look at. Every inch of her skin had been tattooed so that her eyes shone out white in a sea of crowded blue runes. Even her eyebrows had been shaved and the skin tattooed. Her cheeks were strangely sunken. She opened her mouth slightly, and River realized with a barely suppressed shudder that it was because she had no tongue.

"This is our mother of knowledge," the other priestess said softly. "She is the wisest one in the world, one who has made herself so eternally silent that she hears the Speaker's voice even when she sleeps. If you wish to find wisdom here, step forward and kiss the rune on her palm."

The woman looked at River and raised her right hand, palm out. River just looked at her, thinking that if this was what it took to gain knowledge, she would rather remain a beautiful fool. She smiled as guilelessly as she knew how.

"This is a weighty decision. May I have time to consider?"

Both women bought the smile, and gave her possessive, hungry smiles in return. The tattooed one made a waving motion with her hand and the other priestess interpreted.

"Of course, have as long as you need. We'll provide you with a quiet space to think."

Col barely had a chance to see the room he had entered before he was blindfolded. He had time to glimpse several people in the room, more than he would have expected, as Rig's family, like Col's, lived in the countryside, and he'd never mentioned living with others. Hands spun him several times and led him off, keeping a firm grip on his shoulders. Doors opened and closed softly, revealing that the house was much bigger on the inside than the tiny front would suggest. No one spoke, but he heard the tread of several different feet keeping pace as he was hustled along. There was a creak of hinges from below him, and the hands suddenly shoved him forward. He let out a yelp as his feet found nothing where the floor had been. His shoulder and head clipped against the trapdoor's edge as he fell. Someone caught him at the bottom, but the help didn't do much besides slow his fall and ensure that his teeth made hard contact with someone's shoulder. They swore in the unmistakable voice of his friend Rig. Despite the pain blindsiding him from the fall, Col let out a breath and relaxed.

"Rig." He couldn't keep the smile out of his voice. Rig sucked in a breath.

"Col! What are you doing here?" Col would have expected him to be delighted, but he sounded worried.

Behind Col came the sound of several sets of boots descending a ladder.

"You know our visitor, Rig?"

"Yeah..." Rig sounded reluctant, "he's my friend."

"I see. Can we trust him?"

There was a very long pause. Col's heart sank.

"No..." Rig dragged out the word, his voice uncertain. "His loyalty is to his family and not to the Hand, but if the priests threatened his family at all he could be working for them."

"I see," the other voice said again. A hand roughly seized Col's chin and jerked his head back. A cold, sharp edge pressed up under the hollow of his throat.

"Say goodbye then."

Rig gasped.

"No! Wait! He might not be loyal to us, but he's very useful all the same. He's the one who caused whatever it was that happened in the temple, with The Hand."

The knife disappeared.

"Ah. So it's his fault the priests are swarming everywhere in a panic," the other voice laughed softly. "You've stomped in a dangerous nest of ants, boy."

Col didn't reply. He was spun around again, then shoved into a chair and tied down. Not that he needed it. His head lolled from exhaustion and he slumped against the ropes. When the stranger's hands pulled his arms free of his sleeves to tie them, they stopped, feeling the heavy *clink* of the metal manacles still clamped around his wrists, trailing a few links of broken chain. The man let out a grunt of surprise at the raw, bloody stripes trailing down from where his own weight had dragged against the manacles. They had used spikes on the inside to keep him from slipping through, but he had slipped a bit anyway and the spikes had left deep score marks in his wrists. Blood soaked his sleeves, despite the thick fabric.

"You been cliff-hanged, boy?" his voice was incredulous. "How in all the hells did you get free? I've only ever seen these marks on dead bodies they cart back from the temple. Nobody comes back alive after they've gone over the edge. How'd you do it?"

"I was rescued," Col muttered. His chin sank to rest on his chest and he barely heard the next words.

"By who?"

There was no answer. It took the others in the room a moment to realize that it was because Col was fast asleep. One man reached to roughly shake him awake, but Rig caught his hand.

"Let the questions wait."

10

When the priests ran panting into the room, the Hearer already knew something was wrong by the looks on their faces. They stopped at the base of the stairs leading up to the high dais where his massive golden chair sat, backed by a halo of ceremonial golden weaponry of all kinds, a reminder of his deadly prowess. The priests looked at each other. They were never so hesitant to speak when it was good news.

"Your greatness," one of them finally said, almost too softly for him to hear from above them, "the young acolyte is no longer hanging from the cliff. And four priests are dead, four more are missing."

"WHAT?" the Hearer roared, disbelieving. "You had better explain yourself, before there are five guards dead!"

The man trembled.

"That's just it, it's unexplainable. They died in ways we can't understand, and we don't know who did it."

He died. The Hearer rarely stooped to violence these days, but his body moved before he had time to think through his anger. He waved to a servant to retrieve the golden throwing axe, turning to the other priest who stood next to the bleeding body of his companion, eyes wide.

"Explain better," the Hearer ordered.

When Col woke to the soft rasp of Rig's voice in his ear, it was still dark. They hadn't let him sleep long, but the few hours were better than nothing. He blinked grit from his eyes and realized that he could see. They had removed the blindfold, although he was still tied to the chair. His manacles were gone, and his arms were bandaged to the elbows. Rig's crooked nose and even more crooked smile filled his vision, lit by the smoky light of a torch.

"Hey Col, we got some questions for you okay?"

At Col's wary look, he hastened to explain.

"They're not gonna torture you or anything. You're among friends, sort of. When they saw your wrists everyone knew you couldn't be working for the Hand, so they're not going to kill you. Besides, we aren't like the priests. We don't engage in needless violence. Just tell the truth okay? And everything will go fine."

Col grinned with a confidence he didn't feel.

"Of course."

Rig left, and Col looked around the empty room. There were no windows, so he assumed he was in some kind of cellar. The trapdoor leading through the ceiling was closed. Rig hadn't left that way. Instead, he had disappeared through the bricks of what had seemed to be a solid wall a moment before. The bricks had come apart to reveal a hidden doorway. Rig had left the door open, but there wasn't much to see behind it but a dark tunnel. Voices echoed through the darkness. The glow of torches grew bright on the brick walls as a large group of people approached. He closed his eyes. In the back of his mind, he imagined his mother's voice.

"What are you doing, Nikki? These people will only give us trouble, you know that. Do you want to get us all killed?" He sighed.

"I'm precious short on choices right now. This is the only way to survive." His mother's voice fell silent in his head. He imagined her saying, *"I know, I love you."* But it didn't ring true. She wouldn't understand. Not without a long and painful argument. And she would be right to be worried. These people were dangerous. He opened his eyes again as the room filled with people. Col was surprised to see that not all of them were tough, dangerous ruffians like the man who had answered the door. Many of the men would not have looked out of place running a shop or merchant's stand, and there were quite a few women. However, looking

closer he saw they all bore the same subtle look about them, a slight tightness of the lips and eyes that suggested they were never fully relaxed. He knew he bore it too – the mark of a hunted man.

One of the men stepped forward and bent down to look Col in the eyes.

"So, talk. Rig told us what happened during the Worthiness ceremony, but you were the only one right there. What really came out of the stone?"

Col told them. They weren't surprised that the Messenger wasn't real, but as hard as he tried he couldn't get them to comprehend the nature of the girl who had really been imprisoned in the stone. The best they could understand was that the priests had somehow imprisoned some poor girl inside a crystal and that Col had freed her. They were delighted, every one of them, with the revelation, and determined to expose the Hearer's secret. Their voices rose, and Col found himself shouting to be heard.

"You don't understand!"

A few heads turned in his direction and he forged ahead, his voice urgent.

"She's not normal. More than that, I would almost say she's not human."

The room fell silent.

"You mean the Messenger really was trapped in the rock?" a beak-nosed woman demanded. Col shook his head.

"No. She's not the Messenger. There is no Messenger. But the girl that came out of that crystal is not an ordinary human."

"Then what?"

Col hesitated.

"I don't know. But she's dangerous, and I don't think she'll do as she's told. She doesn't want to overthrow the priests, she wants to rule them, and everyone and everything else, including us."

They didn't believe him. He could see it in their eyes. In their minds, if the Messenger was made up by the priests, then it automatically followed that all things remotely resembling the supernatural were also lies. They looked at him in awkward silence for a moment, and then a dark, rough-looking man stepped forward. He had a thick white scar on his chin that split his beard in half and twisted his lip into a grimace. The others dropped their eyes in respect as his stern gaze swept the crowd.

"So, the priests have lied to us," he said with no surprise. "Think, men. This is our chance to topple them. The girl is proof, and we need to find her."

There was a mutter of excited agreement. Col opened his mouth again, but the scarred man held up a hand to silence him.

"This lad says she's not as harmless as she looks, so we'll send out search parties in groups of six, fully armed. She can't have gone far."

Col's heart sank. Six rebels, fully armed with their makeshift weapons, were still no match for three of the priest-guards, trained as they were from a young age with hundreds of ways to kill. And yet Col had seen River take down all four of his guards in seconds. This would not end well.

"Please don't threaten her," he pleaded. Several men laughed.

"We'll do what's necessary," the beak-nosed woman snapped, and the others nodded.

Desperately, Col sought the dark, scarred man's eyes.

"Take me with you please?"

The man hesitated, then nodded.

"You'll go with Rig and Myrtle's group. But only because the priests are hunting you, so you can't betray us without betraying yourself. And we don't have the men to spare to guard you here."

He looked Col in the eye, his expression suddenly hard.

"But beware. Myrtle may be a little girl, but she'll stab you dead without a thought if you sabotage the mission. Understand?"

Col nodded.

Although the intention was to leave as soon as possible, it took several hours for the rebels to devise a plan in which they could search for River without drawing the attention of the priest-guards, who were swarming the city. What made it complicated was that those devising the plan could not be the ones searching. The chance of them getting caught was too high. As a result, each of the rebels were drilled with their own assignment and told nothing about the role of anyone else. Col was told nothing at all. After he was untied from the chair, and fed by an apologetic and compassionate Rig, he crawled into a small storage closet and fell asleep on a pile of clothes. The next thing he knew, his collar was seized by hands and he was dragged out into the aggressive light of a torch. He was dropped abruptly, and there was the sound of someone being shoved and Rig's voice.

"Hey, be gentle!"

Rig's house, or, the Rebel hideout that Col now knew it to be, was deserted, except for Rig himself and four others. Their quizzical faces looked down on him from where he lay on the floor.

"Can he fight?" the girl, Myrtle, asked Rig. She looked doubtful. Rig shook his head.

"Not well. Probably not at all right now. Look at his arms."

He was right, but Col flushed to hear it stated so bluntly. The others began to grumble.

"Why do we have to bring him?"

"He'll only slow us down. We're already the last group to leave."

Rig shook his head emphatically.

"Remember, he's the only one besides me who actually knows what the girl looks like. And I never got a very good look."

Myrtle shot them all a withering glare.

"It doesn't matter if he's useful or not. Grimald says we're taking him, so we're taking him. If anyone has an objection, feel free to bring it up with the Grim."

The others fell silent at that. Col got to his feet and Rig led the group through a kitchen and out the back door. The only instruction Col got was a hushed, "Follow me," from Rig.

The moment they stepped into the street, Col noticed a difference. There was an unmistakable tension in the air. Every few minutes, a group of warrior-priests shoved through the crowd. They were everywhere, overturning market stands, breaking down doors, or pulling young girls and boys away from their families to get a closer look at their faces. The panicked milling of the crowd reminded Col of the movement of a herd of Canyon Cows just before they stampeded. These people were terrified, he realized. He stared until a sharp tug on his elbow reminded him that he was one of the ones the guards were searching for. He ducked his head.

The group progressed slowly through the crowd, dodging and ducking in a seemingly aimless manner but somehow always staying within sight of each other. Watching them from behind Rig's bobbing shoulders, Col was struck with the thought that these people would be formidable opponents indeed. They didn't move with the same deadly grace as the priest-guards, but the very fact that they didn't made them all the more dangerous. They were completely invisible, indistinguishable from the general masses. The warrior priests could have been entirely surrounded by rebels and they would have been unaware. However, preoccupied with his thoughts, Col forgot that he was not nearly so skilled. He was shuffling along absentmindedly past the doorway of a bar, closed this early in the morning, when a hand fell on his shoulder from behind.

"Name and business?" The priest-guard's voice was a combination of bored and irritated, so they clearly didn't realize who he was yet, but Col's mind still froze up in terror. The priest behind him reached out a hand and yanked Col's hood off, his fingers digging into

Col's shoulder with a firm pressure to turn him around. Col resisted, but he could only resist so long without the man getting suspicious. Seconds ticked by, and still he could think of no escape. Rig was nowhere to be seen. Slowly, heart sinking, he began to turn. A blur of motion caught his eye as Rig suddenly returned. He took a few quick paces out of the crowd and fixed the priest with a furious look. The glob of spittle sailed through the air in a surprisingly violent motion and landed with a small splat on the bare toes sticking from the priest's open sandal. There was a shocked bubble of stillness in the shuffle of the crowd. The priest stared in speechless outrage. Rig sneered with hatred. Col saw that he had smeared dust in his face, making him almost unrecognizable. In a shrill voice several octaves higher than his usual one, he shouted

"Get outta our streets, you fat temple rat!" The priest let out an inarticulate howl of rage, shoving Col away as his swords flashed out. But Rig was already gone, his hurried passage masked by the frantic rush of the crowd at the sight of the priest's drawn swords. Shaken from his paralysis, Col took the opportunity to make good his own escape, silently marvelling over Rig's genius. The street was in an uproar. Everywhere, Priest-guards were seizing people, but the people were not being compliant. In a panicked rush, they fought back with blind ferocity to escape, trampling priests and other peasants alike. Col hurried into the smaller streets in an attempt to avoid capture, but it was like avoiding ants while stepping ankle-deep in an ant's nest. Priests were everywhere. Glass was breaking and wood splintering as they forced entry into homes. Nowhere was safe, and the group of rebels had vanished. Col felt panic cloud his mind as he darted into the shadow of a refuse-filled alleyway. Someone had bricked off one end, and the stench of the trash was intense, so it was no wonder people avoided it. Breathing slowly, Col considered his options. How could he get out of the city? But a thought was poking at him with a needling intensity. He wasn't out here because he wanted to escape. He was here because he needed to get to that mysterious girl before anyone else found her. His breathing calmed as this new goal clicked into place. But how could he do such a thing, when he was only one person? Well, the first thing was to lose any pursuers. He set about climbing the jagged wall that blocked the alley. As soon as his head poked over the top, a wind ruffled his hair. At the same moment, a chill slid down the back of his neck. The day wasn't cold, exactly, but there was suddenly an unsettling feel to the air. Instead of smelling of refuse, as he would have expected, the wind smelled... Ancient. It took him a moment to see why. On the other side, the alley led toward the high sandstone spires of the Silent Speaker's guild. That place had always scared him, with the tattooed priestesses wandering about in their rough, fluttering cloaks like misplaced souls. That whole area of the city was devoid of noise and the familiar smells of life, smelling only of dust and old stone. However, there was something else in the wind. Something that made the hairs on his neck rise. Something that didn't belong. It was the smell of green, growing things. In a city atop dry cliffs, under the baking heat of the summer sun, such a smell was unthinkable. Just as unthinkable as the pale, delicate flower that crushed under his boot as he dropped from the wall. He stared, unbelieving. Then broke into a run towards the forbidding spires.

Further on down the alley, pale shoots of grass were poking out between cobblestones. Moss clung tentatively to the dry walls. Col's footsteps quickened. He couldn't be the only one noticing this. Some strange power was affecting this area of the city with new growth, and he couldn't help thinking that it was connected to the strange, mystical girl from the stone. What else could it be?

11

The doors of the temple were open. Col looked carefully for priest-guards before entering, but it seemed the two religions avoided one another. Really, it was a brilliant place for the girl to have hidden, and he almost wondered if he should turn and leave her undiscovered in this unnerving place. But, there was the strange, spring atmosphere to consider. Surely someone else was going to notice the change. She wasn't safe here any longer. He steeled himself and entered.

Almost immediately, he was accosted by a tattooed priestess.

"What do you seek?"

He tried not to take a step back, unnerved by her eager stare.

"I seek a girl, a bit shorter than me, sort of foreign-looking, with skin that's too pale, dark hair and brown, angry eyes?"

The priestess's expression immediately froze into something much more hostile.

"You will find no girls here. The only women here are in training, and have cast off the attractions of men, to live a life of silence and wisdom."

She glanced with intense disapproval at the symbol of the Hand that showed through a gap in his cloak. He was still wearing his initiation clothes from the ceremony, although the rebels had given him a new cloak.

"And we of the Silent Speaker have no use for warmongering men such as yourself. Begone."

She advanced threateningly, shooing him towards the door. He resisted.

"Wait, it's not like that. I'm not a suitor, I just want to help her. She's in trouble."

The woman's lips tightened in scorn.

"She has no need of your help, and no trouble will reach her here."

Col seized upon her words, a grin spreading across his face.

"So she is here!"

"What? No. Don't you dare- come back here!" The woman's words cut off as Col darted past her and through one of the many narrow doorways, deeper into the temple. The place was a maze of narrow stairways. He quickly realized that he had acted rashly, as he was running aimlessly through the unfamiliar passages of a place that was swiftly becoming a wasp's nest of angry women. Every room he opened was the wrong one, disturbing yet another priestess from her contemplation. He soon had to stop his search and run for his life, as every corner he turned was filled with angry individuals. The corridors rang with the distant shrieks of the first priestess, who was yelling about an intruder rampaging in a holy space and desecrating the sacred silence. He dashed past a door, then stopped and dashed back. The door had been green with moss. Heart pumping, he ducked inside and slid the door closed, just as the hurried footsteps of a dozen priestesses rushed past.

Only once they were gone did he turn to look at the occupant of the barren little room.

River sat on a narrow cot. Dressed in the fine pants and loose, hooded shirt that she had worn to rescue him, with her long black hair swept over one shoulder, she looked as regal and out of place as an eagle perched on a heap of trash. She stared at him in surprise.

"Peasant boy? How did you find me?"

"You're not very good at hiding," Col smiled. Despite the danger they were both in, he couldn't help an immense sense of relief at having found her. She bristled.

"How dare you! Uncultured peasant! You have no right to be in here, or to speak to me at all!"

"I may not have the right, but I'm going to tell you anyway. You're in danger," he cut her off.

"Other people will follow the same trail I did and find you. We need to leave."

"There is no 'we'," she replied coldly, but stood up from the bed. "I haven't yet decided if I want to be found. I'm to be queen if I marry that puppet. Perhaps I could yet make a strong kingdom through him."

Col stared at her.

"You really think that would work? That you could stay queen for long without meeting a bad end?"

She gave him an irritated scowl.

"You know nothing of such things."

"I know that the city is full of Priest-guards, outnumbering every King's soldier on the street," Col remarked dryly. "If they find you, alone and unprotected, do you think the prince would ever find out what became of you?"

He watched, with some satisfaction, as she considered the validity of his point.

"Because you ran from the palace," he added, "the Hearer will have a perfect excuse to make you disappear forever into his dungeons."

She bit her lip in consternation, then raised her chin defiantly.

"No matter. I chose to turn my back on the palace, and I will walk this path to the end, wherever this path leads."

She started for the door, then stopped.

"What was your plan of escape, boy?"

Col felt a sudden surge of dismay. He'd never made a plan past finding her.

"I don't have one," he admitted. She stared at him for a long moment, then shook her head in disgust.

"Peasants."

A faint commotion drifted through the door from the halls outside. She gave the door a calculating glance, then threw it open.

"Follow me." Her command was thrown imperiously over her

shoulder, and Col didn't feel much inclined to obey. However, he reluctantly stepped forward to follow her. Just as he stepped up near her shoulder, she suddenly jerked backwards, crashing into him in an attempt to slam the door closed again. He tripped and they both fell backwards onto the floor, while the door, which had bumped her foot, bounced gently open again. A woman stood on the other side.

She was quite tall, but she was stooped with her head jutted forward out of her robes like a turtle's. Her robes were long and confusing, pooling around her feet and trailing down the hall in a multicoloured mess. But her face was what captured Col's eyes. It was completely bald, and every inch of shaved skin was covered in tattoos.

She stood there, looking at them long and hard. Her eyes fixed on Col with a blazing intensity, and then on River with a sharp look of greed. By the time they both scrambled to their feet, she was already stepping forward to fill the doorway, leaving no room to edge past her. Although she didn't advance or make any sound, a sharp pang of fear stabbed into Col's gut.

"Ah, excuse us ma'am," he was glad the fear he felt didn't reach his voice, "we were just about to head out on a quick stroll, if you wouldn't mind stepping out of the way?" His voice was everything he wasn't, calm, self-assured, confident. But despite its persuasive tones the woman didn't move. She just stared at the two youths, her eyes unblinking. River had lost her customary arrogance, and seemed to shrink into herself, looking uncertain.

"Most honoured mother, I have come to a decision," she said cautiously, "I have decided that this way of life is not a good fit for me."

The woman gave no answer, didn't even turn her accusing glare from Col's face. He took a deep breath and attempted to brush past the woman. Her skinny arm shot out and barred the way, gripping the door-frame so that he couldn't pass. He fell back in confusion. With her other hand, she swiftly drew something from her robes and brought it to her mouth. Before he could stop her, she blew into the object and an ear-piercing whistle shredded the air. Now the small knife of dread that had been twisting its way into Col's stomach drove home. They were in trouble.

Throwing caution to the winds, Col charged into the silent lady. She was stronger than she looked, and grappled ferociously with him as she was bowled backward through the door. Col knew that what he had just done was probably deserving of some manner of death penalty, but with the Hearer already out for his blood, he hardly cared. No other threat could possibly compare with the danger that the warriors of the Hand posed. They grappled, the lady clinging leech-like to Col's cloak even after he had pushed her backward out of the way. The clasp broke as he pulled away, his cloak coming off in her hands. River, having regained her composure, stepped smoothly out behind them. The lady scrambled to her feet and drew back, staring at them with hate and blowing furiously on her whistle. Over the deafening shrilling, the sound of shouting and drumming feet reached them. The temple of the Silent Speaker was no longer silent. The sounds came from both directions of the corridor. Col and River glanced at each other in panic. She turned and darted away down the corridor. Heart pounding, Col followed, wondering what she could possibly be intending. The sound of feet and whistles behind them grew fainter, but shouting sounded close up ahead. It was no longer just the shouts of infuriated women, either. Col could hear gruff men's voices, and the panic closed around his throat when he considered what that might mean. They seemed to be rushing headlong towards disaster and capture. Then, at the last instant as voices sounded close around the next corner, River suddenly turned and disappeared through an open door. They had only just closed the door when sounds of pursuit rushed past.

Col was panting softly, and River shot him an irritated glance, motioning for silence as she hastened across the room. Nevertheless, she looked slightly shaken. They had entered a large room, with tall, narrow windows and a pool of some sort at the far end. Three other doors stood against the far wall. River turned to him with a raised eyebrow.

"Surely one leads out, no? Which shall we try first?"

For a second he thought that the impossible had happened – was she really asking his opinion? He opened his mouth to answer, but then realized that she had been merely thinking out loud, as she turned and reached for the middle door without waiting for him to speak. He felt a sharp spike of annoyance. The middle door opened onto a room where several women sat in a circle, apparently lost in meditation. River softly closed the door again before any of them had looked up, but nevertheless she looked spooked and hurriedly walked through the door on the left. The sounds coming through the door behind them were growing louder, as if more and more people were entering the temple in search of the two fugitives. Despite how much he disliked her imperious attitude, Col followed River through the door, finding himself on a narrow staircase. To his dismay, it didn't lead downwards. Instead, they found themselves climbing higher into the spires of the temple. Now all the rooms they passed began to have balconies or out-facing windows, and the stairs spiralled around in a slow circle so that Col could tell they were heading up a tower. His heart sank. There could be no way out in this manner. Feeling as one might when about to touch a hot stove, he reached out and caught the edge of River's wide sleeve. She whirled on him, as he'd expected, with an outraged expression, but at least now he had her undivided attention.

"We can't go this way, lady," he said firmly, suddenly unsure as to how he ought to have addressed her. Maybe Highness or Majesty? A small part of him refused. She was just a girl, an outlaw, the same as him. He didn't have to cave to her preference for putting on airs. He put his chin up, despite the glare she was giving him.

"It only leads higher into the tower, and we need to get out. We can't fly."

After he said that, he suddenly realized that he had no idea what she could or couldn't do. She'd been acting normally for so long that he'd almost forgotten the events at the cliff's edge. Her glare gave way to an expression of worry.

"I thought only to escape those tracking us, and to avoid being trapped in a room," she confessed. The two of them were silent for a moment, contemplating their situation. No sounds of pursuit sounded from below. Instead, only the gentle songs of birds echoed through an open door, accompanied by the faint mutter of the city below. Glancing sideways at River, Col saw her mask slip for a moment, revealing a completely lost expression beneath. He felt a surge of compassion.

"Let's follow the sound of birds," he suggested. "Maybe there's a tree we can climb down."

River nodded in relief, resuming her confident stride up the stairs.

It didn't take long. The open door led them into a vacant room with three connecting rooms. One of these opened onto a balcony. They stepped through into a tiny forest.

The platform was crowded, from the walls to the railing, with potted plants. The source of the birdsong was quickly identified in the occupants of the cages hanging from several small lemon trees. Col looked over the edge of the railing with dismay. They had gotten into the tower through an adjoining wing from the main building, but the roof of that wing was too far down to jump without getting injured. Additionally, the balcony on which Col stood faced the wrong way. He would have had to leap at least ten feet sideways to even have a hope of landing on that roof, instead of crashing to the ground below. The ground was much further than he had thought, they were several stories up. Not only that, but it was swarming with Priest-guards. Their ranks were disrupted by agitated priestesses, their dark robes flocking in defence of their home. Col was struck by how much they looked like crows from above. As he watched, a troop of King's guards marched up, aggressively confronting the priest-guards. The sound of angry voices carried even over the squawking of birds. This was remarkable, as the birds were getting louder. Col pulled back from the railing just as a bird fluttered past his face. From behind him, River's voice sounded.

"What's happening down there?"

"Nothing good." Col looked down again, scanning for some means of escape. The tower wall dropped too far to jump before it reached another balcony below. The distance seemed impossible.

"Even if we could get down, there are more guards outside than there are inside the temple," he added, his heart sinking.

River gave no reply, but another bird suddenly fluttered past Col's face on its way to freedom. Col suddenly felt a flash of irritation. While he was looking for a way out, while they were running for their lives, this haughty girl was just passing the time releasing trapped songbirds? He turned around to snap at her, but instead stared.

The cages weren't open, they were completely destroyed. The metal bars were bent and twisted, as what had once been small lemon twigs supporting them had swelled to the size of pillars. River knelt next to a shattered pot with roots snaking across the stone around her. She had both her hands on the trunk of... What? Col gaped at the monster she had created.

The delicate lemon tree at one end of the balcony had grown to twenty times the size, and was writhing like a snake as it stretched still further. The leaves were gone, and the spines along its branches had grown to the size of swords. The tree was stretched out from the balcony, curving to the side, and straining to reach a corner of the main building nearest the tower, its bark a dark, unhealthy colour as its roots lashed out and sank into the tower, crumbling sandstone, breaking into other pots and stealing the dirt from them. River's teeth were gritted, her eyes closed and brow furrowed in pain. Col watched with a mixture of awe and horror as the grotesque plant lashed itself around the railing of another balcony and finally stopped moving. The dust of crumbled stone filled the air. Col sneezed, trying to regain his composure.

"Not exactly subtle, are you?"

The corner of River's mouth twitched in a smile.

"First you are saying that there is no way out, now you are complaining when I made a way."

She stepped out onto a branch and began making precarious progress across the living bridge.

"Make up your mind, peasant boy."

Col quickly realized that, although he had no fear of heights, he did have a fear of disproportionately large lemon thorns. Hesitantly following River, he became preoccupied with the vision of losing his footing and impaling himself. Although the thorns were sparsely scattered, they jutted at just such an angle as to make it very easy to imagine the consequences of falling. He was so concentrated that all other thoughts faded away.

An arrow swished past his head, nicking his ear and bringing him painfully back to reality. Shouts sounded from the balcony behind, and the tree beneath him shook. Suddenly, the lemon spines seemed small and friendly. He quickened his pace, heart hammering as the branch shook with footsteps. Hot blood splashed against his cheek, blurring his vision as he looked down, trying to see his footing. The air filled with yells, then a scream as someone fell. He didn't dare look back. Instead, he looked forward. River had reached the opposite balcony, and crouched on a railing, her hand against the tree trunk. It was no longer wrapped securely around the rail, but only connected by a single branch. He stared in horror as that last branch began to uncurl. River looked up, and for a moment their eyes met as he ran desperately towards her. She looked stricken with guilt, and quickly looked away. The branch stopped uncurling. Then she looked up again, but not at him. At something just over his shoulder. Col whirled, just in time to see a Priest-guard lung at where he would have been. Col stumbled in under the sword swing, the top of his head connecting hard with the priest's chin. They came together with a crash, both overbalanced on the narrow bridge. The sword flew over Col's head and impaled itself in the trunk behind him. The priest seized Col's hair and jerked his head back, struggling to draw his second sword. Col clung to his arms, throwing all his weight sideways and swinging the man into a long thorn. He screamed, and jerked backwards. Col let go of his arms, and there was a snap as the thorn broke off in the priest's side. Maybe not so small and friendly, Col thought with hysterical humour as he began backing carefully away, not taking his eyes off the struggling line of priest-guards picking their way toward him. He felt a strong hand land on his shoulder.

"Crouch down." River's voice spoke softly in his ear. He obeyed, and she stepped on his back, jumping to land in front of him on the bridge. She held the priest-guard's sword in her hand.

"Back up." She bit the words out, just as the wounded priest lunged at her and she sprang into action. Col didn't wait to be told again. As he hurried toward the railing he heard the sharp ring of steel, the cries and grunts of the combat behind him. River made very few sounds, but he heard sounds of pain from the men. When he reached the railing and turned, she wasn't far behind him, desperately fending off blows as the bridge itself writhed beneath her feet, trying to shake off her attackers. Cries filled the air as men plummeted to the ground below. When she reached the railing, the whole lemon tree simply let go of the tower and fell away. They watched with a mix of awe and horror. Portions of the far tower crumbled with the tree, as the whole mess fell down, down, down. Several dozen priest-guards clung to the bark. Although it took only an eye-blink, it seemed like forever before the crash sounded. It split the air, and shook the courtyard, now swarming with men. Col looked down once, then couldn't bear to look again. The distance was not so great to hide the destruction the fallen tree had wreaked below. His last meal became yet another thing to fall from the tower. Cries of fury began to drown out the ringing in Col's ears. The priest-guards were no longer merely trying to recapture a prisoner. They were on the warpath. Col backed away from the railing. He turned to River, to notice with surprise that she, too, was leaning over the rail, looking a little green. The second thing he noticed was the red, red blood seeping steadily down her leg, from a dark gash across her thigh. She let out a small noise. It might have been a gasp, it might have been forced laughter.

"What manner of creatures are those priests? I have never faced anything like them."

He stared at her, feeling a sudden surge of panic. How could he possibly escape without her support? She slid to the ground and pressed both hands over the gash. Something in her grim expression suddenly brought a small flame of determination to life inside him. He stripped off his shirt and shredded it into sections with his teeth. It was old and still blood-stained around the wrists from his own bandages, but he found a clean section near the waist that he tied around her leg. When he was a boy in the village, he had often helped his mother to care for mild injuries. However, this was different, with arrows swishing and bouncing off the tower around them. His hands shook. She watched his efforts with an unreadable expression, then snatched the cloth from him and yanked it tighter. He helped her to her feet, and they began a stumbling run into the tower.

The balcony was connected to a large meeting place of some kind, cluttered with chairs. An altar stood in the centre with a round opening in the roof above it. They ran through the room and into the one beyond. It was a wide entryway, with four staircases leading different directions. The Temple of the Silent Speaker was no longer silent. Instead, sounds echoed up from every opening in the room, footsteps and shouts from the levels below. For the first time, River looked truly afraid.

"This wasn't meant to be, for me to die like this." She sounded so very lost, and almost petulant, like a child denied dinner. Col could see her start to give up, and he knew that if she did they'd never stand a chance. He looked around, desperation making his mind work at twice the speed.

"No one knows what's meant to be. And we're not dying today," he snapped. She looked sharply at him, her fear giving way to irritation. He grinned.

"Go back into the room." His tone was commanding, and her eyes flew wide with fury, just as he'd hoped they would.

"You are insufferable," she hissed. "Why must I die in your company?"

"Because you're insufferable too," he baited her, stepping backwards into the room they had just exited. "We make a good pair."

"Peasant!" she hissed, striding after him. "How dare you speak to me this way? I should have dropped you off the bridge when I had the chance!"

They were both inside the room now, and Col had a plan forming in his mind. The hole above the altar for smoke was almost the right width for a person to fit through. And the altar was tall, it had several stone steps ascending to its peak. He turned back to River.

"If you want to kill me, I'll let you do that later, ok? Just first help me live through this." He let his voice sound as desperate as he felt, but with a note of determination and command that made even his own heart a little stronger to hear it. River hesitated, her eyes narrowed.

"How are we going to do that?" she demanded.

Col pointed upward.

"Stand on my shoulders."

12

River panted and struggled as she hauled Col up onto the rooftop after her. The slate roof tiles were almost burning to the touch, having absorbed an inordinate amount of the days' sunshine. The momentum of pulling him up after her unbalanced River as he finally fought his way through the small hole, and both of them fell onto the roof. Her breath whooshed out of her lungs, hot against his cheek. As soon as she regained her breath it was quickly followed with curses, her voice rising a dangerous amount as she demanded he get off her. He rolled over and lay beside her, as she continued to protest. However, a sound from below caused him to sit up and press both hands over her mouth. Her eyes widened with so much outrage he thought she might shoot daggers from her eyes and impale him. However, she stiffened as she heard the sound, as well. Someone had pushed open the door to the room below.

They both froze, tense. The roof was not overly sturdy. The tiles seemed fragile and made a hollow sound when Col had fallen onto them. He didn't dare move for fear of the noise. Footsteps sounded below, along with the slight creak of leather armor. A voice rang out, far too close for comfort.

"This is the right tower. There's blood on the balcony. Push those chairs out of the way."

There was an explosion of noise, sounds of destruction as the room was searched. A loud crash sounded, that Col assumed was one of the chairs. Then more barked orders.

"Search under those benches. Someone go look for a way down from the balcony."

More crashes, and the shrill voice of several women rose in protest. The priestesses of the Silent Speaker were clearly not as silent as their mistress.

Col's sweat was dripping down his face from the sun. A glance to his left revealed that River was in much worse shape. Her eyes were glazed over from the heat and the blood loss. The bandage around her leg had soaked through, and blood seeped out of the bandage, dripping slowly to the roof.

Drip...

Drip...

Drip...

At first it hissed and dried on the roof, but slowly it began to pool and slide across the tiles, headed... oh no.

Col stared in panic as the trail of blood slid slowly towards the hole in the roof. He didn't dare move, lest the sound be heard. Down below, the men sounded frustrated.

"They're not here." The gruff voice that had been barking orders previously sounded furious. "Check the rooms on the lower levels of this tower, and make sure we have all the stairways blocked! They are NOT getting past us."

Footsteps began to shuffle out of the room. The blood had reached the hole and gathered on the lip, drying in the sun almost as fast as it dripped from River's leg. She hadn't even noticed, her gaze blank as she listened to the sounds below. Footsteps faded, and the drop of blood finally stopped clinging to the roof and fell, splashing down toward the altar. Col held his breath, but there was no sound of anyone returning to the chamber. All sound grew more distant. It was not until he was certain all of their pursuers had descended to a lower level, that he dared let his breath out in relief.

They lay on the roof until night fell. By then, the sounds of the search were inaudible. Col slowly rose to his feet, stiff from sore muscles. He tried to help River to her feet, but she slapped his hand away with disdain, and struggled to balance awkwardly upright on her good leg. She was pale and shaky. Careful of where he stepped, he took her arm and supported her as they limped across the roof. The roof of the altar room proved not to fully connect to the main building. There was a gap between themselves and the center of the sandstone temple, which was a little lower than the roof they stood on. Col eyed it, hope flaring in his heart. The other roof was an easy jump away. However, there was no way River could jump it with only one leg. He looked at her.

"I don't suppose you can fly?"

She shot him a glance that instantly made him feel like an idiot.

"Do I look like a bird?"

"Well, no," he muttered, his cheeks flushing, "but you can do other things I never thought possible. Like on the cliff, and with that lemon tree..."

She snorted in derision. "I can speak to the earth. Does the earth fly? You see me coaxing plants from the ground so you assume I can sprout wings and leap into the air? Stupid peasant. Do you even know the difference between plants and animals? Earth and sky?"

He felt himself flush still harder, gritting his teeth. Why did this girl have to be so stuck-up? He almost wanted to throw her off the roof. Then, suddenly, a brilliant thought struck him.

Still supporting her, with his one arm under her shoulder and across her back, he reached down with his other arm and scooped up her legs, picking her up like a baby goat. She went as stiff as a board, eyes bugging with indignation.

"What are you -- " she sputtered, her voice a whisper, barely able to get the words out.

Col disregarded her, sizing up the distance to the other roof.

"I may not be a good fighter," he muttered, "but you don't spend years as a peasant without becoming strong enough to throw an unruly baby cow into its pen."

Her eyes got even wider and she flailed, trying to push away from him.

"You're comparing me to—what?"

He didn't reply, but with a tremendous heave, threw her off the edge of the tower. She flew through the air and landed with a yelp square in the middle of the opposite ledge. There was a distinct cracking sound, which he prayed no one had heard. Her eyes were wide with pain and surprise, and he hoped the sound had been the roof under her, and not her tailbone. Sure enough, a section of broken tile slid down the slope a ways, almost falling off the edge to the ground below. She spread her arms for purchase and didn't slide after it. As he leaped across after her, several other tiles cracked. However, he barely spared a thought for them. River was giving him a look of such withering hate and outrage that he felt the skin on his face might crack and burn off from the heat of it.

"You revolting little toad!" she hissed, practically spitting. He couldn't help but grin. From the tone of her voice, he assumed she meant some deeply offensive insult. However, he didn't even know what a toad was. Doubtless the meaning had been lost somewhere far in the past.

"Trust me, it was the only way to escape," he said soothingly. "You couldn't jump with that leg."

She wasn't placated, and protested with what he assumed must be a string of biting insults as he helped her to her feet again. He only understood half of them.

"You really need to learn some modern swears if you want to get your point across," he told her as they continued their slow trek across the roof. "Your language is several hundred years out of date."

His good mood increased, both at her impotent rage and at his rising hope as he saw more roofs open up below them in every direction. Most were interlocked, and many sloped downward. However, the journey quickly became tiresome. For the next hour, River maintained a steady stream of criticisms and complaints about the pain in her tailbone. She seemed to have no comments about her leg, but only resented the injury which he had caused. He gritted his teeth and pressed on.

On the ground below, men carrying torches still passed often. However, the two fugitives moved as quietly as possible, staying in the shadows of towers. It was well into the middle of the night by the time they found their way down progressively lower rooftops and across empty balconies until they reached a wall that seemed a possible escape. It was the top of some manner of low storage shed, and the edge extended beyond the temple grounds, into the city beyond. Like the alley Col had reached the temple through, it was mostly blocked and deserted. No temple doors opened nearby, and so no guards had been stationed there.

Col dropped the short distance, landing in a roll. He meant to catch River, but by the time he had turned around she had already reached the ground, chin up in stubborn defiance. He noted that a vine on the stone wall was now growing in a different pattern, resembling a ladder.

"They'll notice that," he pointed out. She said nothing, merely shifted a bare foot slightly on the ground, and the vine shrank back into the cracks in the wall. Her brow creased.

"This is a dead land you have woken me to, peasant boy. The earth barely remembers my people."

He didn't know how to respond, so they exited the alley in silence.

–13–

There was rioting in some portions of the city. The Hearer was set upon by a constant stream of messengers, reporting outrage from the Silent Speaker priestesses, suspected Rebel activity, the young prince sending his own troops out to interfere, and, now, rioting. He felt an overwhelming sense of irritation. The little brat, Nikolo, had started an avalanche of problems that were proving extremely hard to deal with. Not to mention the disturbing rumors of unexplainable events. Two of his priests were strangled by a rose-bush, then many others had died falling from a tower, accompanied by a giant *lemon tree*, of all things! He rubbed his temples, then adjusted his veil and straightened, waving for a priest to bring in the next group.

A group of priest-guards were ushered in, looking young and awkward in their brand new robes. The Hearer looked at them.

"Congratulations, your service to the Hand has begun!" he smiled. They shuffled, looking uncomfortable.

"But what happened to Col? Why didn't the ceremony complete?" one of the girls asked. The Hearer ground his teeth, trying to remain calm. He couldn't afford to kill everyone who had been in the room, so this conversation was necessary.

"Nikolo failed initiation and betrayed the Order. But you, you succeeded! Your first order as Priest-guards is this: The happenings in the chamber of the Hand are sacred and secret. You will not ask for an explanation, you will not speak of it at all. Anyone who breathes a word of the doings in that chamber will be considered a traitor for spilling Order secrets, and will be sentenced to Cliff-hanging. Is this clear?"

No one spoke. The Hearer looked carefully at the blank faces, trying to spy signs of rebellion. He saw none.

"Good. Now go."

There was a tension in the streets where Col and River found themselves, like the moment when a lit match has been dropped into dry grass but hasn't yet ignited it. Most citizens were sleeping, more than was usual. However, the great city of the Hand, capital and center of all the world, never really slept. Because it sat atop high, dry cliffs, it was never truly dark, even when the sun was down. Under the light of the bright, close stars and moon, the streets would usually be full of those eating a midnight meal, shopping for the next day, or visiting with friends. The Order of the Hand was oppressive, but it meant the streets were safe from crime at all hours. Often people would stay up all night, and catch up on sleep during the blazing afternoons. However, tonight was different. The street vendors had banked their fires and closed their shops. The dust in the streets swirled with the swish of robes, instead of the stamp of bare urchin feet. About a third of the people on the street were Priest-guards, and the rest were going about their business in a tense silence. Conversations were carried out in hushed voices. River and Col slunk through alleyways, terrified. Luckily most of the priest-guards would not know their faces. However, they would probably have descriptions out by now, and it was hard to hide the way River limped. With her bloodied, makeshift bandage, and Col's bare chest, they were nothing if not conspicuous. Even the darkest alleys were not safe, as patrols of guards were everywhere, poking into corners and demanding entrance to buildings. Col didn't even know where he intended to take River, only that he wanted to put distance between himself and the two temples of the city. They waited until a troop of guards had marched past, then moved quickly to cross the small street from the shadow of one alley to an alley on the opposite side. Col was so busy watching the backs of the departing soldiers, ensuring they didn't turn around, that he didn't hear the footsteps behind him until a hand landed on his shoulder.

"In a hurry, are we?" a soft, lazy voice drawled. "Why would two young people be dashing through shadows with such urgency, I wonder?"

Col's heart stopped. He turned slowly, seeing River's eyes widen. The man who had his shoulder was a priest-guard. Behind him stood two more. Time seemed to slow as the priest opened his mouth to shout to the other group of guards, now almost out of sight down the street. He saw River's stance shift, as she started to draw two knives from her clothes. At the same time, he caught a glimpse of something on the chin of the priest-guard behind the one holding him captive. He yelped.

"River, don't!" She hesitated, just a moment, as the second priest-guard, the one with a scar on his chin, drew his own knife.

In the next moment, several things happened in quick succession. The man holding Col grunted, eyes bugging out, as Grimald stabbed him in the back. He brought the knife curving in through the side, where the straps were, to bypass the man's leather armor. At the same time, a random street vendor jumped forward and swung a thick wooden stool into the back of the last priest-guard's head. Two men went down before they could make a sound, leaving The Grim, the leader of the rebels, standing alone in front of them in the garb of a Priest-guard, with a golden Hand of Office glimmering around his neck. He stood naturally in the clothing. Col saw that he had underestimated the rebels. He hadn't considered that some of them might be such high-ranking priest-guards themselves. And, no matter the training, no one could defend against a knife in the back. The street vendor, who was doubtless another rebel, began dragging the bodies into the alley. Several other people in the street moved to help him, while the rest silently grouped themselves in a threatening crowd around River and Col. He could hardly believe his eyes. What had seemed to be chance bystanders idling in the street was now clearly transforming into an organized group. River looked taken aback, but still held her knives in a threatening way. Knowing he was risking losing a hand, Col grabbed her wrist. He received a steely glare, but nothing worse.

"Don't kill them," he hissed, "they're friends, here to help us."

She raised an eyebrow, but relaxed slightly, still looking at the threatening crowd with deep suspicion. The rebels mirrored her expression. She looked at the leader, the man called Grimald. It was like seeing two predators eyeing each other, both considering the other to be prey. Col didn't want to find out which was more dangerous. He let go of River and spread his hands, trying to ignore how pathetic he must look, a bruised, dirty, half-naked boy with old bandages on both his arms.

"I'm so glad you found us!" he panted. "I found the girl hiding in the temple. We escaped, and we were looking for you!"

He gestured at River, trying to make the rebels see her as non-threatening. She glared, not helping.

"She needs medical attention. We're both so exhausted, we almost weren't able to make it this far." He looked around with a tired but grateful gaze, the look of a bedraggled dog that had finally returned to its master. He tried to drain intelligence out of his eyes, dulling his gaze in exhaustion.

River opened her mouth, about to object. Then a new expression crossed her face, different from the pride he had grown so used to. She looked serious, and a flash of understanding entered her eyes. She slumped, her hands falling to her sides, where her knives disappeared into the folds of her loosely draped shirt. Col wrapped her arm back across his shoulder. Supporting her, he turned to look at Grimald.

"Do you have somewhere safe nearby?"

In truth, they were both exhausted. River's sudden change in mood wasn't very believable, but the sight of their bedraggled state must have lent to their unthreatening image, because the Grim nodded to several of his men. A few broke away from the group and continued to mill randomly through the street, while the rest hurried Col and River away. As Col had hoped, they weren't bound, or blindfolded. The Grim continued to march down the street with the quick step of a priest-guard, while the others followed in a random movement that seemed almost the natural flow of a crowd. As they walked, Col felt River's hot breath on his ear.

"I sense a plan here," she muttered softly. "I'll go along with it for now, peasant boy, because I don't like killing people if I don't have to. But you are going to tell me what we're doing as soon as possible. And --" and here her voice turned threatening, "I had better like this plan." Col responded with a barely perceptible nod, his mind racing as he tried to come up with a plan.

To his delight, Col wasn't blindfolded this time as they entered a house. However, River was. She endured it with extreme reluctance. When they first brought the blindfold out, she pulled away from Col, backing towards the door of the house. He stared at her desperately. She looked back at him, and the sight of his pleading eyes seemed to have an effect on her. Her own eyes were conflicted, and she seemed to be in pain. A rebel put the blindfold over her eyes, and she stiffened, but let him do it. Col frowned, wishing he could understand this girl. One moment she was proud and cold, a strange, dangerous predator of a woman who seemed to want to rule the world. The next moment she was staring into his eyes with a strange vulnerability. And yet, she clearly despised him. He couldn't understand it, but still felt an odd sense of protectiveness for this crazy person from another time. She was the reason his entire life had fallen apart, and despite her apparent willingness to leave him at a moment's notice, he felt he had to stay with her. She may not realize it, but she needed him. And the mystery surrounding her drew him in.

They travelled for some time through cellars, underground tunnels, and occasionally places that seemed to be behind the walls of houses. When River was finally un-blindfolded, they were entering a vast space that seemed to be an abandoned indoor marketplace. All windows and doorways that faced the outside were either boarded up or collapsed. Holes in the roof shone shafts of dim, early-morning light onto the cobbled floor, and the walls and rafters had clearly become home to many birds and rats.

Several other groups of rebels were already waiting. Col looked them over, as River's indignant voice sounded from behind him where two rebels were supporting her limping progress.

"Was that really necessary?" she demanded.

All eyes in the room turned and focused on her as her face was revealed. She didn't look quite so dignified, blinking in the light with her hair sticking out at odd angles from the blindfold. Col couldn't help but smile. The man called Grimald looked her over.

"Welcome to my palace!" he said sarcastically, gesturing around. "You'll be staying here for a long time, so you'd better get used to the mess." At his confident tone, River's eyes flashed. However, she seemed to remember the situation at the last moment, so instead of giving him a haughty retort, she carefully hung her head in exhaustion. Col sighed. She was truly terrible at pretending.

"She's injured," a woman noted, bustling forward. The Grim nodded to her.

"Take them both to the hospital, Hennah. I'll have guards on rotation, but I doubt they need to be chained in their state." He turned and began giving quiet orders to the gathered crowd, and groups began breaking off to follow his instructions. Col and River were hustled into what seemed to be a repurposed stable. The stalls had stone walls, and they had been fitted with new doors and filled with cots. Many were filled with the injured. For the first time Col let himself consider how much the recent hunt for River might have cost the Rebellion. As he was led to a cot next to Rivers', his mind worked furiously. She expected a plan from him. He needed a plan to get them both out of this mess, before she killed someone, or they both became tools for the Rebellion. As he tried to plan, he made the mistake of lying back onto the bed. The room blurred instantly, as did his thoughts. Sleep grabbed at his mind like a greedy child, and he couldn't resist it.

14

River leaned her head back against the wall as she sat on her cot. She watched Col sleep. With his eyes closed, he really looked nothing like Storm. It was a stranger's face. He'd saved her life, but she didn't trust him. How could she, when she didn't know his motives? She didn't really know anything; not only about him, but about this world she'd found herself in. She felt powerless, and not just because the earth seemed unfamiliar. She had no home. No friends, no family. She didn't even have money, which she would never have considered important with her noble upbringing. She watched the peasant boy sleep, and felt an overpowering wave of jealousy. Her, feeling jealous of a mere peasant! She shook her head in frustration, trying to push the homesick feelings down. Several people entered the room, their baskets of bandages and bloodstained sleeves pegging them as some sort of medical people. She welcomed the distraction, pushing all thoughts away as she steeled herself, watching a woman pull a thread and needle from the basket.

The pain was excruciating. Not as bad as the initial sword stroke, but the incessant, tiny stabs soon had River so agitated she could barely resist the scream building up in her throat. Despite having extensive battle training her entire life, River had not in fact ever been in a real, life-or-death conflict. She had never been wounded before, except for a few sprained ankles and such similar accidents. As royalty, and a potential heir should her cousin die, she had been closely guarded from harm her whole life. This was a new level of pain she had never encountered before. Only her pride held her back from weeping like a child at the sensation. After what seemed far too long, the healers finished their work and left her to rest. She could not help but notice that four guards replaced them, standing in the shadows just outside the room's open door. She was a guest, for now, but they would not give her any opportunity to escape. She wondered what they could want from her. It seemed everyone in this god-forsaken land wanted something from her. And none cared what she wanted. Sleep was slow in coming.

When she woke, the room was dark. The torches had been removed, and she seemed to have slept through the long hot day. A moment after waking, her skin began to prickle. Someone was watching her. She glanced swiftly to Col's cot, but he was still sleeping; splayed with several of his limbs hanging over the edge of the bed, one elbow flopped backwards onto his face, and long hair stuck all over his face with sweat. He made a strange snorkelling sound through his nose, squashed flat under the weight of his own arm. She couldn't help but smile. However, the prickling sensation remained. She glanced around warily.

There was a deeper shadow in the corner beside the doorway. A solid shadow. She sat up quickly, reaching for her knives. They were gone. At the sight of her motion, the shadow stepped forward. It materialized into a young man, dressed in black flowing garments that blended with the dark. His skin was also dark, darker than most of the tanned cliff-dwellers she had seen thus far. His black eyes had a sharp, dangerous look to them, and his black hair curled loosely around his chin from under a hood. His eyes darted to her hands, reaching furtively into her cloak.

"You think we'd leave you armed?" he asked, mildly incredulous. "Beg your pardon my lady, but no one here is that stupid. The stupid ones all die within a week or so." He loomed over her, a good head and a half taller. Weaponless, her instinct was to back away from those sharp eyes, sizing her up. However, her bed was already in a corner.

"What do you want?" she demanded, trying to sound imperious. It was hard, in the dark, unarmed. The floor was carpeted, with wood beneath, and she knew the earth could not feel her through it. The stranger gestured curtly at the door.

"We're having a meeting. I'm supposed to escort you to it."

Warily, she stood up and edged toward Col's cot, reaching out to wake him. But the man shook his head.

"Not him. Your friend is of no particular importance just now."

Feeling even more uncomfortable at the prospect of being separated from Col, River reluctantly did as told and preceded the stranger through the door. He offered her an arm in support, and she took it gratefully, taking weight off of her injured leg.

There were no guards outside the door. Clearly, this man alone was considered more than enough to keep her captive. River became even more uneasy at her proximity to him. She was leaning on him, so he was real, not some sort of shadow. Nevertheless, his silence and dark hooded robes were disconcerting. In her head, she had already named him Wraith. He supported her without any apparent effort, and without once speaking to her as they walked.

They made their way back into the covered market area, and from there entered a vacant storefront and climbed some stairs to the attic. There was already a small crowd gathered. In the dim light of guttering lanterns, their faces seemed more gaunt and hungry. All eyes turned to River.

"Welcome," the large man with a short beard and a scar on his chin greeted her. She nodded politely. The man turned and beckoned a youth forward, a boy with a crooked nose who seemed vaguely familiar.

"Rig, is this the same girl?" the man asked. The boy, Rig, nodded uncertainty.

"I think so..." He came uncomfortably close to her and examined her face.

River's temper flared.

"How dare you treat me like some prisoner or captured animal! I came of my own free will, and I should be treated as an honoured guest, as one of my station deserves! Do you have any idea who I am?"

Rig nodded decisively. "Definitely the same girl."

The Wraith whose arm she was leaning on gave a small huff of amusement, the first noise she'd heard him make since they left the hospital.

The gathered crowd erupted with voices. With just a single wave of his hand, the large man commanded immediate silence. After seeing him take down a priest-guard earlier, and now seeing how he inspired obedience, River felt a healthy respect for him growing in her heart. He bowed, somewhat mockingly, to her.

"Please, have a seat. I apologize for not introducing myself earlier. I am Grimald, and these people you find yourself amongst are the last defense this city has against that tyrant, that leech, the Hearer of the Hand, who seeks to drain this country dry."

There was a mutter of bitter agreement at his words. River sat stiffly, and Wraith left her to go stand by the doorway. Her chair was surrounded by curious and skeptical faces. Grimald walked leisurely around her chair.

"As everyone here knows, there has been a bit of a hue and cry in the city of late," he remarked. "Both the King's garrison and the Priest-guards are out hunting for you. Care to tell us all exactly why?"

River shook her head. "I have very little knowledge, I'm afraid. I was trapped in time, and it seems over the years a religion has sprung up, and these priests worshipped my prison. Now that the prison is gone, they are after me."

"Most likely to kill you and pretend nothing has changed!" a shortish, balding man piped up with enthusiasm. "Those dirty thugs want to keep everyone believing that they have a divine right to oppress us!"

There was a murmur of agreement. Another shortish, roundish, balding man sat next to the one who had spoken. The two looked very similar, like a matched pair of innkeepers who fought over each other's customers. This man was giving her a hard look.

"Hold up." He raised a hand and eyes turned to him. "What do you mean, trapped in time? That's not even possible! How would that have happened?" His voice dripped with skepticism. River gave him a withering glance.

"You people in this age are weak. You have no idea what is possible when all the magic of the world is at your fingertips, and your blood runs thick with it." Her remark met with a stunned silence. Then scattered laughter.

"Magic?" several people chimed at once, their eyes alight with amusement. "That's ridiculous."

River stiffened, and said nothing. What did she care if these people believed her? But despite herself she couldn't help the shame and anger. She hated the feeling of being laughed at. This had never happened to her before. Her cheeks flushed. Grimald raised his hand, and the crowd silenced, slower this time, and quiet snickers lingered.

"Twenty-seven priest-guards are dead," Grimald stated. His words were soft, but they inspired instant stillness.

"I saw the bodies. You all know how they fight, and yet, in the pursuit of two runaway youths, twenty-seven died. The idea of magic seems ridiculous, but I find myself at a loss for any other explanation."

The room seemed to hold its breath. The eyes looking at River now were shocked. No one was laughing anymore. Wraith was now looking at her cautiously from the doorway, his posture no longer relaxed. She stared back defiantly.

An older woman with a lean build and elaborate hat clapped her hands for attention.

"Surely you can all see what a golden opportunity this gives us! We have but one course of action. We must expose this girl to the entire city, as proof that the Hand is a fake, and that the priests have been lying to us! The sooner the better!" She turned to Grimald, who nodded.

"All who agree with Mauve, raise your right hand. All who disagree, raise your left fist," he commanded. There was a flurry of movement, and most of the people in the room raised their right hands.

There followed a long debate over how to best get the word to the public, and how to prove that River was who she said she was. The girl in question began to feel more and more uncomfortable with the idea. She did not like the thought of becoming a pawn in this revolution of ragged peasants. She shifted in her chair, and from the doorway the Wraith snapped his head sharply to look at her. He stepped quickly up to Grimald and muttered something in his ear. The bigger man also glanced at River, then addressed the room.

"We will adjourn this conference for now. The final planning and preparations shall be made elsewhere." People began to stand up and leave, still talking animatedly. River felt herself growing extremely indignant.

"I am Prince Drystan's Betrothed, and a princess in my own right! I shall not be excluded from any counsel, most especially a counsel that is deciding my future! How dare you treat me like this!"

At her exclamation, Grimald looked at her with amusement.

"We don't respect the High Prince, any more than we respect the Hearer here. That man is a worm with no backbone, and he has betrayed his country by refusing to fight for us."

He came closer, leaning down in her face. "You are merely a guest here, not a Rebel, so you have no part in a rebel counsel. If you refuse to be a polite guest, then you shall be a prisoner."

At these words, she realized that everyone had left the room except eight or so armed guards. She stood up, but Grimald pushed her back down into her chair.

"Stay here."

River shot him a glare. She felt so helpless here, and if they imprisoned her here she might never escape. She needed to get out. She tried diplomacy.

"Please, sir," she tried to sound reasonable, "I am still feeling exhausted. I will not follow you to your meeting if I am simply allowed to return to the infirmary. I left a friend there."

He narrowed his eyes. Her heart sank. She had never been good at pretending.

"No," he said at last, "you will stay here until we have decided what to do with you."

She heard what he wasn't saying. At some point during the conference she had forgotten to feign weakness and innocence, and he had decided she was dangerous. You don't put a dangerous prisoner in the infirmary, where there are more possible exits, and more possible casualties. This room was much more defensible, with thick walls and only one doorway. Her heart pounded with urgency. She needed to get out of here, to get her feet on firm ground again. These rebels were not a refuge. They were taking her hostage.

15

Grimald was still leaning over River, so she could not stand up. She let her muscles relax, so that he began to rise, satisfied that she would obey him. Then, she threw herself backwards. As her chair fell, she brought a knee up into the big man's face. His head snapped back with the force. River arched her back and landed on her hands as the chair crashed to the floor. Her momentum continued, and she dealt a kick with both feet into the face of a guard standing behind her. They fell to the ground together, but he was unconscious and River was already rolling to her feet. The cut on her thigh screamed in protest, but the adrenaline was pumping in her veins now and she did not slow down. She charged toward the door, dodging the guards who leapt at her. Grimald began yelling orders, his voice sounding garbled through the blood pouring from his nose. Two guards were moving to block the door. River charged, then let herself fall into a slide, aiming to shoot between their legs. A spear stabbed down frighteningly close to her head as she slipped between them. One of their boots clipped her shoulder, but she was already past them and scrambling out through the door frame.

The staircase before her seemed free of obstacles. She leapt the first five steps. While she was still in the air, she caught a motion in the corner of her eye, a swish of black cloak. Suddenly, a weight crashed into her, knocking her sideways against the wall. They both fell down several steps, and by the time they stopped rolling River found herself pinned to the floor by Wraith. His eyes were impassive as he grabbed her by her hair and slammed her head into the boards. Everything went dark.

River woke back in the same room, in the same chair. Her wounded leg throbbed, and this time her head did too. She tried to jump to her feet, but found that she was tied fast to the chair. The wound in her leg had been stitched up again, and some manner of shiny ointment covered skin that was already starting to heal. It itched horribly, however.

No one was in the room, but in the stillness she could hear the soft shifting and creaking floorboards that meant someone stood outside. She banged her head against the back of the chair in frustration. This proved extremely unwise, as a flash of pain threatened to knock her out again. She sat perfectly still, then, and tried to think her way out of her predicament. The ropes were tight, and she spent what must have been hours trying to loosen them. Finally, she managed to wriggle herself down on the chair until one of her toes could touch the ground. The floor was wood. Sometimes, a spark of life still lingered in felled trees. However, the instant she touched the floor, all hope fled. The boards were ancient, bone dry, and very dead. Not even the faintest memory remained of what they had once been. They were dead, like this scorched land, like the magic in these people's veins. An overwhelming sense of loss engulfed her. She leaned her head back, and let the tears run down her cheeks. She was utterly powerless, in a land where she didn't belong. There seemed no hope at all.

Some time later, she snapped awake. A familiar voice had woken her, just outside. It was the peasant boy, Col, and he sounded annoyed.

"This is madness!" he pleaded softly. "It's far too dangerous to expose River to the city right now. The priest-guards will be down on us and she'll be killed long before the word can spread. We have to get her out of the city to keep her safe."

"You'll have to speak with Grimald about this." The voice outside the door was faintly raspy, the voice of the man in the dark cloak. "He's at council currently."

"Oh, I would never want to disturb the Rebels while they are busy!" Col sounded genuinely pained. "But this is incredibly urgent, I need to tell them what I know, or I fear they may make a decision that will cause much bloodshed." He sounded so earnest, so worried. There was a long silence. Then a new voice spoke up.

"I'll take him to the Grim! What can it hurt?"

"Very well," the soft rasp of the man in black finally conceded.

Footsteps receded.

River sat alone in the room, wondering what was happening. She did not trust Col's motives, as he had led her to these dangerous people in the first place. However, she felt a grudging respect for him. Since seeing him fight, she had considered him a helpless, awkward fool. Handsome, but a fool. However, now she felt herself re-evaluating him. How had he slid himself so smoothly into the guard's good graces, that they took him to a secret meeting even she was forbidden from? The boy certainly had a way with words. She had never met anyone so winsome and likeable. She strained against her bonds, wondering what Col was planning. Then she wondered when she had started thinking of him as Col, instead of Peasant Boy. Somewhere along the way, he had changed from an irritating, impudent stranger with Storm's eyes, to Col. Still irritating, but now she missed his presence.

She waited two days. The light didn't filter into the room except from lanterns, so she measured the days by the morning and evening meals that they brought her. The food upset her stomach, too full of dry, long-stored grain and salty meats. She sorely missed the rich fruits and vegetables of her homeland. She thought she would explode from misery at being stuck in the room, tied fast to a chair except when they changed the bandage on her leg or she was released to relieve herself, in an utterly humiliating fashion into a mere pot in the corner. She had to sleep in the chair as well. They were taking no chances after her escape attempt previously. By the second day, her back, neck, and rear were so sore that she didn't think she would ever be able to stand again. Her legs fell asleep so often that she even considered pretending to relieve herself just for a chance to stand. But the humiliation of that option was unbearable, so she suffered in the chair. Her mood fluctuated between miserable homesickness and furious pride.

Steps sounded up the stairs. She wasn't surprised. Guards often changed shifts outside the door. However, it was after her evening meal, so no one would be coming in. Then, the door creaked open.

Instinctively, she straightened her slumped posture and lifted her chin, trying to look as if the chair were a throne. She threw a scathing glare toward the door. Col peeked in. When his startled expression met her furious look, he looked as if he wished he hadn't entered. But he was already inside now, propelled by the man behind him. The Wraith entered as well, looking her over with a blank expression. Several other people entered behind him, but her eyes were pinned on Col.

"What are you doing, peasant boy?" she demanded. "What is happening?"

He opened his mouth, but the man called Grimald interrupted him, placing a fond hand on his shoulder.

"This peasant boy is one of the smartest lads I've ever met, so I would treat him with more respect," he told her reprovingly. "He has already saved your life by warning us that exposing you to the public in this city was foolish with this current turmoil. It would doubtless have gotten you killed, and many rebels with you. You owe him your thanks."

River stared at him. She hated the chiding tone he was using. Hated even more the idea of thanking a peasant boy. But, most of all she hated the knowledge that Col had, yet again, saved her life. She was starting to owe this boy far more than she was comfortable with. Although, she still clung to the memory of dragging his half-dead body up out of the chasm where they had hung him. Surely that counted for something. She glared at Col.

"Thank you." She then turned away from him. "Will someone please explain what is happening?"

Grimald snorted. His eyes on her held a strong dose of dislike and some wariness. His jaw and nose were still bandaged from where she had kicked him.

"We don't owe you any explanation. You decided to be our prisoner, not our guest."

Two guards unstrapped River from the chair, but bound her arms to her sides. She didn't even bother to struggle. When they lifted her, every muscle and cramped limb screamed pain through her mind. She could barely stand, never mind fight back. Besides, she suspected it was no use. Not with so many guards, and that dangerous, black-cloaked stranger in the room.

They brought her down into the main square of the abandoned market. There was a small gathering there. Dusk made the whole place look even more deserted. River relished the sensation of packed earth under her feet again. However, she did not immediately attack. She didn't know what these people were planning. It might still work out in her favor. She shifted her foot tentatively on the ground, sending her mind searching. The earth seemed almost as dead as the boards of her prison. Then, she felt it become aware of her. Not entirely, but like a wild thing sniffing the hand of a forgotten master. It lurched in response, but the reaction was out of her control. Moss suddenly spread all over the ground like spilled water. Grass and weeds whipped wildly, climbing walls. Even a few tree saplings began to poke up, cracking the dry ground. Col whirled around to stare at her in surprise. As did every rebel in the group. She shrugged in apology, still focused on the sensation. The earth had always been her steadiest friend, something that never changed and never turned away from her, even when her own family betrayed her. Now, even that link to her past was broken. Still, the awe in her captors' faces was gratifying. Until someone burst into the marketplace. It was a girl who looked to be even younger than River. A child, really. Had River seen her anywhere else, she would have assumed the girl to be a harmless street urchin, not a member of a dangerous rebel group. Her eyes were wide and terrified.

"They know where we are!" she yelped, voice rising into a squeak. "A patrol two streets over saw something growing out of the ground and they ran off to the temple!"

The air in the entire market seemed suddenly charged with tension. People poured out of shadows and doorways with practiced efficiency. Each scattered group was doing something different, but all of them went about their tasks with a certainty and speed that bespoke training. River herself was not so calm. She felt her heart beating fast as she stood there, held fast by two guards on either side. What was her fate to be? Should she try to escape right now, or would that only lead to her death? Grimald watched for a moment to ensure the evacuation was going well, then turned to her.

"Get her out of here," he snarled, "out of this city. And kill her if she tries to give us away again."

He fixed his glare on her. "Idiot girl. Do you think the priest-guards will treat you better than we do? Is that why you betrayed our location?"

She shook her head emphatically.

"I didn't try to!" Her protest didn't dissuade his accusation. His eyes held both blame and fear.

"If any of my rebels die today, it will be on your head."

At that, River was shocked into silence. Ever since she had arrived in this country, her thoughts had always been on her own plight, her own goals. Looking around at the desperate people rushing around her, she suddenly felt a hot flush of shame creeping up her throat. Most of these people were young, average-looking townspeople. None of them looked like fighters, and she had endangered them all by her carelessness.

Her guards began hustling her off. As the feeling began to come back to her legs, she found herself able to keep up. Grimald waved to the Wraith.

"Dominik, we need her. Keep her safe."

Ah, so he had a name! Somehow, knowing his name didn't make him any less frightening in River's eyes. Col, however, caught Grimald's arm.

"Let me go with her? Please? I feel... responsible. For her, and for all this chaos, because I brought her here."

Grimald nodded slowly.

"You may go, but you do whatever Dominik says."

Col nodded and turned to follow, but Grimald held him back.

"Remember, lad. You've said your oaths, so you're allowed on your first mission. But you're one of us now. You aren't acting in your own interests, but with the interests of the Cause always in mind. Don't fail us."

As he jogged up to walk beside Dominik, he shot River a sideways glance of relief. Her mind scrambled to put together the pieces of what she had heard. This boy, who owed her nothing, had been initiated into the group and sworn his loyalty to the Rebellion, simply so that he could be allowed to stay with her, and help her escape. This was his plan? But, how could it possibly benefit him? She felt herself becoming more and more indebted to this insignificant boy, and she did not like it at all. She had no idea what his aim was. He had done so much for her, there was no doubt in her mind that eventually he would want something back.

As they left the main courtyard of the marketplace, there was a shattering noise from the far end. Someone was trying to smash through the stack of rubble and old wood that covered what once had been the main entrance. The group rushed faster, around a corner. Dominik took the lead, with Col close behind. River followed, with two guards on either side and two behind. They came to the mouth of a rough-hewn tunnel that seemed to cut directly down into the earth. Suddenly, Dominik held up a hand. Everyone stopped. He pinned his sharp gaze on River, taking her in, from the top of her unbrushed head, to her dirty, bare feet. His gaze stopped on those, and her careful stance on the earth. He suddenly gestured to one of the guards, a woman on River's left.

"Take off your shoes."

It was a strange request, but she obeyed without hesitation, as if the order came from Grimald himself. When she was done, Dominik pointed at River.

"Put them on."

Her reaction was instant, and violent. She would not be trapped, blinded, like that. It was one thing to blindfold her eyes, but this was unthinkable. She threw herself backwards, trying to get free. Roots shot from the ground and tried to trip her guards. At the same time, moss and lichen crept over the floor of the tunnel. Suddenly, her world was spinning, and she was no longer touching the ground. Dominik was holding her in the air, one fist clenched around the collar of her shirt, and the other holding her up by the strap that bound her hands to her waist. She struggled to breathe.

"Put them on," he growled, "or I will knock you out and carry you the whole way. I will not have you compromising the safety of the whole group by leaving a trail for our enemies to follow."

River didn't have a choice. Even while he held her there, the two guards had grasped what was happening and were forcing the shoes onto her dangling feet. When she was set on the ground again, she walked into the tunnel without complaint. She was no fool, and she could see that it was no use fighting against this man until she knew more about him, and understood her situation better. He already had an alarming edge on her, by discovering that she had to touch dirt to use her power. Deeply disturbed by this, she ran along with the others down the tunnel, barely seeing where she was going. Barely caring.

16

The Hearer walked into the smashed-open warehouse, eager. He'd been carried on a covered chair all the way there, but now he was too impatient to wait. He wanted to see the fear in the rogue acolyte's eyes when he killed him. Then, he would need to figure out what to do with the girl. Given how many of his priests she had killed, he suspected it wouldn't be an easy fight to force her into submission. He approached the line of kneeling prisoners quickly, eagerly. There were ten, not two. He paused, staring at them. No. This couldn't be.

Kneeling in the dirt in front of him was a line of random, completely ordinary townspeople. However, the ground in the warehouse was covered in moss, flowers, grass, and baby saplings. He was sure the miraculous event had something to do with the presence of the escaped Messenger.

"Idiots!" he snarled. "These aren't the fugitives! They got away! find them!"

As the priests ran to do his bidding, he turned to the prisoners.

"Oh, and torture any of these that look like they might know something. Then kill them all." He walked away to the sound of wailing and begging. He didn't get to be Hearer by having a soft heart, or a conscience at all. As the religious guide of the world, he *invented* right and wrong. Anything he did was the will of the Gods, and no one could ever stop him.

Col knew his mother would never forgive him. He was getting himself into so much danger, the very thing she always warned him not to do. She had never even approved of his friendship with Rig. Now he had joined the rebels. She would never understand. He barely understood himself. All he knew was that River's arrival signalled a momentous change in the world he knew. All the turmoil of the past few days seemed to converge around her, and he needed to see this journey through to its end. He had started it, somehow, by touching the rock where she was imprisoned. He had no idea what manner of tyrant or monster he might have unleashed on the world, but in moments of weakness he had glimpsed a scared, broken girl inside her, and he needed to protect that girl from the chaos around her. *Instead of your family, Nikki?* He heard his mother question in his mind. He had no answer except a rush of guilt.

They continued through the tunnel, as it grew darker and darker. Sounds of chaos grew faint behind them. Surely someone would discover the mouth of the tunnel. Col's heart beat hard inside his chest at the idea of pursuit in the darkness behind them. However, soon the tunnel began to branch. It wormed its way deeper and deeper into the darkness, always headed downward. Col began to wonder where this tunnel might possibly lead. It seemed that they were now far beneath any point where they might intersect with a cellar or sewer. Dominik, walking confidently ahead, was continually checking various scratchings on the walls, taking turns based on these glyphs which seemed to be in an entirely strange language. The more Col saw of these rebels, the more he admired their cunning. Only, now he was one of them. He still found it hard to wrap his head around that decision he had made just a few days earlier. First an acolyte of the Hand, now a rebel. How quickly he had changed sides. In his heart, however, he knew his loyalties had never changed. Always, they were for the sake of his people. Only the group that he considered his people had now somehow expanded to include River. This change presented all manner of conflicting feelings inside of him. He watched her as they walked down the passage, at a slower pace now that the sounds of pursuit had vanished. There was nothing left of the regal, imperious bearing which she usually carried herself with. Her shoulders were hunched, and she kept trying to stumble and brush against the walls of the passage, but the two guards on either side of her held her arms. No flowers or moss bloomed in her wake, as he had become accustomed to seeing. He made a mental note of the fact that her powers seemed to desert her when she wasn't touching the ground. He'd been traveling with her for almost a week now, and he still had no idea of the extent of her abilities. Somehow, the good manners his mother had drilled into him made him feel that it wouldn't be an entirely polite thing to ask a lady. And, despite her lack of jewels and title, there was no doubt in Col's mind that this girl was a high-born lady in whatever world or time she came from. As far as he knew, there were very few things that you could politely ask that sort of lady. From his mother's descriptions they seemed to be extraordinarily thin-skinned creatures.

As Col tagged along at the back of the group, absorbed in his thoughts and feeling rather irrelevant in the company of the trained rebels, they came to a door that blocked the passage. Here Dominik, although he seemed the strongest of the group, stepped back and gestured for two of the other rebels to open it. Col realized with a start that he was one of them. Stepping forward with another young man, he tugged on the handle. To his astonishment, it came off in his hand. The metal was rusted and the mechanism on the inside completely rotted away. A shower of dirt fell through the hole. The other lad gingerly poked his fingers through, trying to find a way to unlatch it.

From behind them, Dominik snorted.

"Break it down, fools."

Col immediately flushed, feeling stupid, but also started to dislike Dominik for his overbearing tone. He rammed his shoulder into the door, and felt a slight give. Nevertheless, it took a good while between himself and the other lad to break down the door, and he felt his shoulder might break first. Despite its dilapidated appearance, it was very solid. When it finally moved and swung slowly outwards, they perceived why. The door led out of the side of a cliff. Some time ago, someone had piled dirt, bracken, and an assortment of trash onto the outside of it to hide the entrance from anyone on the outside.

The group emerged tentatively. The sun had set, and the outside world was hardly lighter than the tunnel. They were in one of the many chasms that cut through the land. High above them, faintly visible against the stars, was the city of the Hand, commonly called Kingsfall, capital of the known world, sprawled atop the highest series of cliffs anywhere. The tunnel emerged some twenty feet up the side of the cliff, with a narrow trail leading down. The gulley below was narrow, and filled with the refuse which a thousand citizens above had pitched over the edge. Rain had washed away some of it, but it still smelled awful.

The group descended carefully, following the dauntless Dominik. Col could tell how much wearing the shoes was bothering River, because even at the prospect of climbing down into the filth and the smell, she said nothing. She climbed down in a strangely awkward way even after Dominik unbound her arms, stumbling on occasion. Every time she grabbed a lichen-covered stone for balance, the lichen crept slightly higher on the rock toward her hand. It was an unnerving reminder that while she might seem like a mere girl, they were traveling in the company of a strange, otherworldly being.

She stumbled again, and Col, without thinking, caught her hand. A strange tingle ran up his arm, and he felt his cheeks heat. She looked up at him with a withering glare, and the feeling fled. He dropped her hand like it was a hot coal. Even in her current state, with her hair and clothes bedraggled from her imprisonment, her body hunched with misery, she could still make him feel small and inferior with one glance. As he followed the group through the pungent chasm in the darkness, stepping on things which he couldn't recognize and didn't want to, Col took a deep breath and told himself that he only had to put up with all of this until he was sure that the girl was safe. Then, he would quietly disappear and return to live peacefully in his tiny village with his family. Surely the

Hand would not know to look for him there. Caught up in this daydream, he barely noticed his bruises and the stench around him.

They travelled as the moon rose, and then the sun. They trekked through dry chasms, tangled thorny hollows, and deep ravines with slow muddy water trickling along in their depths. Always, they stayed in deep cracks in the land where the sun's revealing light could not touch them. Col began to suspect that Dominik was deliberately leading them through the most difficult terrain just to showcase his superior skills. He led them through the darkest holes where the cliff sides met above them, and the mud and thorns grew up to their knees, but seemed barely to slow down while the others complained and struggled. He avoided all paths, which seemed to make their journey four times as long. However, Col could not genuinely bring himself to hate the man who trekked tirelessly at their head, and even carried River when her leg injury began to bother her. Throughout the day, he gradually began to make friends with the other Rebels. There were two girls, named Annora and Belaflor. Annora was a scrawny, underfed young lady with a glint in her eye and a twitch in her hands. She was rather upset to be trekking without shoes, and resentful of River. Belaflor was a buxom middle-aged woman with a kind face who would have seemed a harmless baker's wife until you noticed that her arms were thick with muscle and not fat. The two men were Clement and Drew. Both were rather nondescript, large muscular men chosen as guards for River. Clement was missing two fingers on his left hand, which he told Col had been bitten by a drunk at a tavern and had to be removed before the infection spread.

"Don't need 'em, tho!" he laughingly confided. "Couldn't hit the side of a cliff with a bow or stick you with the sharp end of a sword even before I lost 'em. I'm more of a brawler, I am. Can wield a staff, a chair, or your grandma's soup spoon better than any man in our ranks. I'm right deadly with a soup spoon." True to his tale, he carried no bow or sword but a large iron club in his belt.

When the sun was finally threatening to reveal them no matter how deep the gulley they travelled through, Dominik finally called a halt. The entire party was staggering and barely awake, while even their intrepid leader seemed slower than usual. He had removed his hood, and his cloak was splattered with mud, which made him seem less ethereal, although no less fearsome. His dark hair was braided in a short tail at the back of his neck, with shorter strands curling out around his face. Col took some small comfort from the fact that his braid was damp with sweat. Dominik caught him staring, and gave him a vaguely condescending smile.

"Find us some brush-wood young brother, make sure it's dry so there will be no smoke. We will make camp in the woods around the next bend."

The "woods" he spoke of was a half-dead wilderness that filled a wide valley. The plants were rather too thick to be vines, and rather too vine-like to be called trees, but they stood twice as tall as a man and curled around each other to provide a thick cover from anyone looking down from the cliffs above. Inside, the place was a tangled maze. They made camp a few meters into the wood, and Col set off to find brushwood. As he tramped through the trees, he reflected how irritating it was to be once again reduced to the lowest level errand boy, after months of hard training as a priest. How tragic for all that effort to be wasted. Before his last trial, he had really been excited about how far he had moved up in the Order. He had seen a bright hope of helping his village. Now, he would have to return home empty-handed and rely on his family to hide him anytime a Priest-guard made the long trek out to gather taxes. Instead of a saviour, would he only be a burden to those he loved? Frustrated, he kicked a tree. A snake fell out of it, and he didn't stay to check if it was poisonous, but sprinted away as fast as his tired legs could carry him. Of course, then he had to re-gather all the brushwood he had dropped; so when he finally made it back to camp, exhausted, Dominik was not impressed. The infuriating man told him in a bored tone to "halve your time in the future or you'll be given a less pleasant task." Col ducked his head contritely, neatly hiding his scowl.

17

The four other rebels were sprawled on the ground. No one had been given time to pack bedrolls during the escape, but somehow one of the women had brought a large sack of supplies, from which they had all been cheerfully eating without him. River sat on a makeshift floor made from the rebel's cloaks. Dominik was taking no chances, and had lashed her firmly to a tree so that she was unable to touch any section of bare ground. She was asleep, and Col found her less infuriating that way. Rarely in his life had he met a girl who provoked much feeling in him, and now here was one who made him feel both protective, belittled, confused, compassionate and wildly frustrated by turns. He took both of their dinner rations, and settled down beside her to wait until she woke. It wasn't long, as she slept fitfully, sweating and twitching like a cat too close to a sizzling fire. When she snapped awake, her eyes fixed on him with shock, then a disappointed expression. He felt rather strange, as he offered her the food. She took it, sniffing with distaste at the dried meat and even drier flat bread.

"Is this what you feed royalty here?" she asked with disdain. He looked at her, and sighed.

"We're running for our lives, Princess."

She nodded.

"I'm aware. And I continually question why I chose saving the life of a peasant boy over a life of luxury as a queen."

"A puppet queen," he pointed out, reflecting that the power she craved probably wasn't what she would find as the wife of the high king. If she truly wanted power, she would have to join the Order of the Hand like he'd been trying to. She shot him a glare.

"Don't remind me." Frustrated, she thumped her fist against the tree she was lashed to. It burst into bloom and curled loving tendrils around her fist. She glared at it, and the tendrils withered.

"Even the earth forgets its place in this abominable land," she growled. Tired of her grouchy mood, Col left her and curled up against a different tree, reflecting that she had no right to complain. Dominik's method of ensuring that she couldn't touch the earth meant that she got to sleep on a pile of cloaks, while the rest of them did not even have a cloak for a pillow. Nonetheless, raised on a bed that was not much softer, he was asleep in minutes.

He was awakened by a shake of his shoulder. Dominik crouched over him, his face unreadable in the dark. Around them, most of the rebel group was asleep, and River snored softly on her pile of cloaks. Several rebels, he couldn't see their faces, were also stirring.

"There's been some suspicious sounds to the north of us," Dominik said softly. "It might be wild animals, but it might also be a camp of pursuers. I'll be taking Annora to investigate. Drew's on watch. I'm entrusting you to make sure the girl doesn't escape, since she seems to trust you. Clear?"

Still fuzzy-headed with sleep and confused, Col nodded slowly. Almost before he had blinked the sleep blur from his eyes, Dominik was gone. He sat up slowly. River was still sleeping. He stared at her, and found himself thinking how beautiful she was, with her long dark hair curving around her cheek, her delicate eyebrows raised slightly as if her dream amused her, and the sharp angle of her chin contrasting pleasantly with the softness of her lips. *Come on, Col. Snap out of it!* He rebuked his thoughts. *She's only pretty right now because she's not glaring at you or pinching up her face in disdain.* He looked away from River, staring into the fire. It crackled softly.

Suddenly, Col became aware that there were other sounds in the forest, other than the soft snores and crackle of the fire. Tiny, insignificant crackles, spaced far apart. At first, he assumed it was an animal foraging. However, the sounds came from all different directions. And no animal would move so slowly, only crackling a few twigs per minute.

Suddenly, Col was wide awake.

Self-preservation was not an instinct he possessed in large quantities. When the guard, Drew, let out a strangled yell that cut off alarmingly quickly, he didn't creep backwards into the bushes. Instead, he lunged for River, in his head a half-formed idea to somehow protect her with his newly learned combat skills. The rest of the group were starting to their feet, but Col didn't need to watch to see how this would turn out. By the sudden noise throughout the forest around them, he could tell that they were vastly outnumbered. In his desperate rush to protect River he hadn't considered that, while he had trained with practice swords, he knew next to nothing about fighting with his bare hands. He reached River and began yanking desperately at her ropes, hissing at her to wake up. Clement jumped up from his bedroll, bleary-eyed, only to fall down again as an arrow took him in the throat. The sight of blood and his friends dying made Col sick. Belaflor was a little wiser, grabbing up a cudgel and ducking out of the light of the fire. Col felt the first rope go loose in his hand, but there were so many. Dominik had been too thorough. River was awake now, and her haughty complaint died on her lips as she took in the scene in a moment. She began struggling, trying her best to help him.

Suddenly, men were leaping into the clearing from all sides. Belaflor leapt from hiding and began bashing men left and right with her club, but she was soon overwhelmed. River suddenly looked at Col, and her face set with determination.

"Get out of here, you fool!" she hissed. "You're no good to anyone dead."

Col set his jaw and continued to fiddle with her ropes. He'd never been good with knots. River wriggled one hand free of her bonds and slapped him in the face with it.

"Col! Run!"

He stared at her. She'd used his name, not Peasant Boy, Fool, or

Idiot. Just then, a knife swished past his ear and stuck into the tree next to River. He looked at her, and her face fell as she realized what he was planning. By this time, Belaflor was overwhelmed. Col couldn't see her anywhere. Men were still coming into the clearing, all of them looking half-starved, scruffy, and dangerous. Those who had previously been fighting Belaflor were now turning to look at the boy and girl by the far end of the small clearing. Col took a deep breath, and pulled the knife out of the tree. River groaned.

As the first man reached him, Col did his best to remember his weapons training. He dodged a blow from a club, then got inside the man's range and slashed at him. At the last moment, he felt a sick feeling in his gut and flinched, turning what would have been a killing blow to the neck into a cut that barely left a scratch on the man's shoulder. This isn't a priest-guard. He thought desperately, as he ducked and dodged wildly. He's just a desperate peasant. I don't want to kill him. The man finally gave up on the club. He threw it to the side, growled, and grabbed Col by the neck, fingers crushing into his windpipe. He gasped, struggling and slashing wildly. Suddenly, the fingers went slack. The man staggered away, then fell, the knife embedded in his ribs. Col realized with a feeling of horror that the man was dead. He didn't have time to reflect, however, as the entire horde of bandits were about to descend on him. River was struggling wildly against her ropes behind him. Hope seemed lost, but suddenly a wild, desperate plan began to form in his head.

Turning his back on the bandits, he sprinted to the tree. River glared at him.

" Leave me while you still can, little peasant. I already owe you enough. Don't you dare try a heroic last stand."

Col gave her his most charming grin, although his heart was pounding with panic.

"Don't worry, I won't," he assured her. Then he crouched down and pretended to take something from her. It was nothing, really. A small sack at her waist that probably contained some snacks. However, he cradled it in his hands and screamed,

"No! Foul ruffians will never get their hands on it! I will protect the gold at all costs!"

Then he turned and sprinted as fast as he could away into the woods, in the opposite direction from River.

The bandits had the camp circled, and Col found a man blocking his path. He brandished a large machete, a snarl on his face. Col couldn't slow down, and he barely ducked the first swing of the big knife as it swung at his head. His momentum carried him straight into the man, his face connecting solidly with a fist. His nose, so recently healed, sent spikes of pain searing up behind his eyes and into his brain. He could barely see, and desperately grabbed at the man's machete hand, trying to wrestle it away from him. The man socked him in the stomach, then shoved him hard in the chest. He flew several feet before crashing into a tree. Staggering forward towards the man again, He heard the sound of other bandits coming closer behind him. However, standing between himself and freedom was the man with a very large knife. He lifted it, closing in on Col. Suddenly, time seemed to slow. A flash of light glimmered at the corners of Col's vision, and he seemed to feel in slow motion a breath of air touch the back of his neck. Skin prickling, he lunged to the left. The arrow, which had been about to impale itself into his back, swished past him and struck the man with the machete. Col didn't stop to think. Didn't stop to wonder how he had dodged an arrow aimed straight for him. Instead, he grabbed up the machete, jumped over the dead man, and dashed for freedom. He barely noticed the pain of cracked ribs and a bloody nose as he sprinted off through the woods, hoping against hope that the bandits would give up on River to follow him.

The yells and breaking branches told him they had. Suddenly, he was terrified for himself and not just for River. His feet seemed to fly over the rough terrain, his breath whooshing out of him like an overeager blacksmith's apprentice pumping the bellows. The trees careened on either side of him, their gnarled trunks forming endless pathways that seemed to have no destination.

The pounding footsteps behind him receded, and he took several quick turns in succession. His pursuers were no longer a united group, but had started to spread out through the woods, searching for him. He finally found a small clump of bushes that hung low over a dry gully, creating a place where someone could crawl underneath and be completely hidden. Shortly after, several figures charged into view. Col could just make out their moving shapes through the shifting leaves of the bushes. He held his breath and held perfectly still. They did not slow down, leaping over the small gulley and continuing on through the woods.

As soon as he stopped moving, scenes began to flash through his mind again. The howling horde of bandits bearing down on him. Drew lying dead, Belaflor disappearing under a rain of blows, never to rise. Clement with the arrow in his throat, his lifeblood gushing out in sickening bursts. However, the thing burned into his memory was the image of River, tugging frantically at her bonds as the bandits drew closer. He felt a tense, hard knot in his throat that refused to go away. Something told him that all he had accomplished with his brilliant plan was to save his own life, leaving River to be slaughtered where she lay, tied to the tree. He cursed himself for his foolishness. He should have stayed with her. It was the right, the noble thing to do. Instead, he had tried to be clever. And, if his plan hadn't worked, he'd be left living with the guilt of her death.

He crouched until the sounds of pursuers had disappeared into the wood, giving them enough time to lose his trail but not enough time to grow discouraged and return to the clearing. Then he crept cautiously out and started walking softly back the way he had come.

18

When Col finally stepped into the clearing, he froze. The pale light of morning revealed the dark stains of blood everywhere, and he'd been gone long enough that flies and a few sinister ravens had gathered. Clement, Drew, and Belaflor were all dead, and he tried not to look at them. From his viewpoint, he couldn't see River. However, the ropes were still tight around the back of her tree, showing no sign of slackening, so he concluded she must still be tied there. Glancing carefully around, he dashed out into the area, rounding the tree. What he saw stopped him in his tracks.

The only thing left of River was the end of one finger, poking out past the cloaks she had been lying on and touching the ground. The rest of her body was completely buried in roots. The tree seemed to have tried to eat her, with the trunk swollen grotesquely and a huge pile of knotted roots thrust out over where she had been lying, bits of cloak shredded and wound around the roots. The ropes were no longer attached to River, only tight because the tree had swollen to several times its original thickness. Arrows sprouted from the bark like the bristles of a thorny desert scorpion, and the roots bore the marks of axe strokes. The dirt under the roots was stained dark with blood.

Col felt a wave of panic rushing hot through his chest. Clearly, not all of the bandits had chased after him, but several had stayed to finish River off. He hacked at the roots with the machete, but to no avail. They healed as fast as he cut them. Dropping the knife, he fell to his knees and grabbed them, straining to pull them out. It was rather like trying to move a rock that had long been mired in the bottom of a dried out riverbed. These roots did not act like they had been freshly thrust into the dirt. Rather, the tree seemed to be trying to pretend that it had grown that way for a hundred years. Col gave up, and started digging at the dirt around the roots with his fingers. He didn't stop until the sun had touched the tops of the cliffs above the wood, and his fingers were bleeding. Then he sat back with a gasp, viewing the one hand that he had only halfway freed from the tree. Even as he watched, the tree curled new roots over his work, hiding all traces of River completely. At the same time, a branch swept down and smacked him hard across the head. He fell to the ground in despair.

"River, I'm sorry," he whispered, choking through tears, "I couldn't save you."

There was no response, except that the tree suddenly began putting out new leaves and blooms; small, spike-edged red flowers the color of blood.

At the sight, Col suddenly grew furious. How could it look so beautiful when it had just swallowed his companion? He flew at it, grabbing up a discarded dagger from the ground and hacking at the bark.

"LET HER GO!" he roared.

A few Ravens fluttered away in fright, and the tree hit him with a branch again. Other than that, nothing happened. Col stood there for a long moment, a cold feeling of loneliness and defeat slowly spreading through him. He had nothing else he could do. He couldn't hurt the tree with the dagger, and his usual tactic, persuasion, wouldn't work on a tree. Finally, he fell to his knees and placed his hands over the place where he thought River lay.

"I'm sorry, River," he whispered. Then, feeling like a fool but with no idea what else to do, he glanced up at the sky. He could see little squares of light through the shifting branches of the tree.

"If anyone's listening," he began, his voice cracking, "tree, or god, or whoever or whatever might be in control of things here, I just want to say that I don't think this is fair. I've always tried to be kind, to protect everyone I can. And now everyone is dead, and I'm an exile. That's not fair. And this is especially not fair, because this girl is so special, she's like nothing I've ever seen. And she doesn't deserve to die here, like this, without any purpose or reason." He paused, knowing he was rambling and that it was dangerous to linger too long in the clearing. Nevertheless, he felt he couldn't leave without expressing his feelings to the tree, the ravens, the empty sky.

"Well, whoever you are, I'm sorry if I offended you somehow. But if I did, you can take it out on me. Just, please, I'm begging you..." his voice broke and he felt tears slide down his cheeks, the hot pain in his chest finally finding some relief in them.

"Give her back to me," he whispered.

The clearing was very still. All of the trees had stopped rustling in the breeze. Not even a leaf stirred. Then, slowly, the tree spread open its roots.

River was nestled in a soft hollow of moss and shredded cloaks, curled up with new flowers and leaves framing her body. Blood was leaking from her calf, where an arrow shaft was embedded, and she had a dark purple bruise at her temple. However, her chest rose and fell with steady, even breaths. When he took her hand, her skin was warm.

The tree had been protecting her, not eating her! He let out a soft gasp as hope flooded back into him. Her nose twitched slightly at the sound, but she didn't open her eyes. The little motion suddenly seemed to him the most adorable thing in the world, and a rush of affection filled him unexpectedly.

That was when he felt a knife point press into his back. "Well, this is interesting."

The voice sent chills down his spine. Despite its light-hearted tone, it was completely emotionless and hard. The knife poked him harder. He darted a glance to his machete, but it was several feet away.

"Turn around, lad. Let's see what kind of creature I've caught." Col turned slowly around, feeling defeated. The man behind him was middle-aged, very sun-browned, with a long, hawkish nose, thin, cracked lips, and dark eyes with as much expression in them as a dead lizard. His lips were quirked into a smile, but there was no kindness in it. He was worn, scarred, and savage-looking. The strangest thing, however, was how he was dressed. In stark contrast to his dirty, ragged appearance, his neck and arms were bedecked with a wild assortment of jewelry, from golden chains to finely embroidered beaded bracelets that would have looked at home on the arms of a rich noblewoman. His ears had at least five piercings, through which were threaded an assortment of ornate earrings. To Col's mind, he looked very similar to a Magpie, the bold, blue and black scavenger birds that had plagued the temple with their thieving habits, stealing anything shiny. The man looked him over as more bandits flooded quietly into the clearing.

"Well, well. What a handsome youth," he remarked dryly. "Too bad you've got no brains behind that face. Let me tell you something, lad. When hiding from bandits, it's not the best habit to scream and yell and wake the whole blasted forest."

The other bandits laughed harshly. Col gulped.

"Thanks, I'll remember that!" he forced his tone to be calm, despite his fear. The Magpie snorted.

"I'm sure you will."

He strolled casually around Col, and stood looking down at River.

"I really ought to thank you, however, for your stupidity. If it wasn't for you, my men would never have been able to get your girlfriend out of the tree. Now we can kill both of you so much easier! Convenient, isn't it? A shame you're such a pretty couple. But Lucan never spares people for their looks, not even the women. Give a woman to a group this big and it only makes my men fight each other."

He held out his hand to Col.

"Now, let's see that bag of gold, and we can get out of here, away from this demon tree that eats people."

Col's mind whirled as he slowly reached under his shirt and

pulled out the small pouch. The man snatched it, yanked it open, and eagerly poured the contents out onto his hand. A few tiny grains of something fell onto his palm.

There was a dead silence in the clearing as all the bandits leaned a little closer to see. Lucan's face pinched up into a look of dumbfounded fury.

"SEEDS?" he snarled. "Random weed seeds? Where's the gold?"

Col didn't let his panic show, but gazed levelly back at him.

"There isn't any."

The man's face set in stony anger.

"You're a dead man," he said softly. He drew his hand back with the knife. A desperate plan formed in Col's mind.

"We have something better," he continued, as if he didn't see the knife. As he had hoped, the man hesitated. Col looked at him, and tried to see past the stony facade to a man who might listen, who might care. He reminded himself that all of these men had probably once been starving peasants like his own family.

"We have the key to destroying the Priests of the Hand," he said, with all the confidence he could muster.

"And we intend to see them fall."

Several of the bandits muttered in shock, but Lucan sneered.

"Then you're a fool. The Hearer controls the world, and there's no force stronger than his warriors."

Col shook his head.

"I thought so too. But then I met this girl. Even the Hearer is afraid of her, afraid of how dangerous she is. His warriors are hunting for us right now, and the whole of Kingsfall has been thrown into chaos because of her."

He took a deep breath, looking around at the faces surrounding him, trying to see the honest peasants they might once have been.

"You hate the Hearer, I can tell," he said. "We all do. The warriors of the Hand took things from us. Land, family members, crops that we needed to get through the winter. Children to serve in their armies, friends to serve in their mines and make their weapons."

His voice took on a hard and angry tone, and he saw every face that looked at him start to reflect the same feeling, their anger diverted from him towards the order of the Hand.

"They took my father," he continued. "They condemned my village to starvation, driving them out of fertile land into a dry chasm where nothing grows. They've done something similar to all of you or you wouldn't be out here, hiding in the woods."

Men nodded. By this point, Lucan held his knife casually, as an old man might hold a pipe, and his face was no longer murderous. It was shrewdly thoughtful. Col warmed up for his final argument.

"They cliff-hanged me." He pulled his sleeves back, revealing the horrifying, freshly healed scars and scabs crawling around his wrists.

"The Hearer wants me dead, desperately, because I know things that can hurt him. He wants this girl dead, because she has the power to destroy him. If you kill us, you'll be doing him a favor. You'll be making him stronger, and making your own words true, that he'll be invincible. If you kill us, you kill the only chance you have to take down the Hand."

The crowd was silent, staring at his wrists in shock. Even more shocking than a tree growing huge and eating a girl, this was a sight that made even the roughest of them look scared. No one ever survived being cliff-hanged. Ever. Not in a thousand years of the Hand's rule. To see the marks on a living man was akin to seeing a man still walking around after losing his head. Col saw the belief and awe wash through the crowd, and his fear ebbed. These men were no longer his enemies. Dangerous? Undoubtedly. But they were his fellow villagers, oppressed, mistreated, and driven to desperate lengths to stay alive. Even Lucan looked taken aback, his eyebrows making a valiant attempt to climb into his hair. He looked from Col to River for a long time, considering. Then he nodded.

"Very well. We will not kill you. Not yet, anyway. But when this girl wakes up I expect her to prove her power. Should it prove a lie, you both will die. Nobody lies to Lucan."

Col dipped his head in acknowledgement.

"Thank you."

One of the bandits went over to try to wake River. He leaned down, and shook her arm with a grimy hand, long, dirt-caked nails pinching into her skin. Her eyes fluttered open, closed, then snapped open, fixing on the bandit's face with an expression of panic. She let out a yell of alarm, and several things happened at once. First, the tree she lay under began growing roots back over her. Several other trees around the clearing began lashing about as if in a strong wind, their branches bludgeoning bandits and their roots lashing around legs. Where Lucan had dropped River's pouch, several seeds had spilled out onto the ground. These instantly sprang up into strangling vines, coiling around everyone. Col himself was suddenly flung to the ground as a vine tried to tie him up. Lucan danced around, slashing at roots with his knife.

"Make her stop!" he cried in terror. "Call off your sorceress!"

Col struggled against the vines and glanced to where River was lying, her eyes wide and confused, fixed on the bandit looming over her, who was being slowly strangled by a root.

"River, stop!" Col yelled desperately. "We're safe! That man is not going to hurt you!"

She stared at him, eyes wide, then suddenly seemed to snap back into focus. She looked around quickly, then placed both hands on the ground, eyebrows knitted in concentration. Slowly, the thrashing subsided and the trees calmed, retracting their roots. Lucan's face was white with shock, his dead-eyed mask shattered in the face of events beyond his comprehension.

"What....... Was....... That?" he whispered.

Col took a deep breath, pulling a twig out of his hair.

"That is why the Hearer is afraid of her."

19

River cringed inwardly at the looks of terror directed at her. Oops. She hadn't meant to do that. Why was it that she always inspired fear in others, no matter where she was, or what she did? She tilted her chin up in pride, but secretly wished people would look at her the way they looked at Col, with admiration and fondness. She had no idea how he'd freed her from the tree, stopped the bloodshed, and somehow turned the bandits into allies, all in the time she'd been sleeping inside the tree. However, she was starting to suspect that she owed him her life yet again, and she hated it. He stood several feet away, quietly talking with a group of bandits. Even with sticks in his hair and dirt all over, he still looked perfectly charming. She glared at him. Col saw her grimace, and, of course, rushed over to help, assuming she was in pain. He knelt down close, pretending to check her head, and started whispering.

"Listen, these bandits aren't evil, they're just desperate men who've had their livelihoods stolen from them by the Order. I convinced them that we are planning to destroy the Hand, so they're letting us live. Just try to seem dangerous and determined, ok? I told them you have the power to destroy the Hearer."

River frowned, taking it all in. Clearly, Col considered this tale to be a wild fib, and wanted her to play along until they could escape the bandits. However, it struck her that he didn't seem to have a better plan of his own. To her, the idea to destroy the Hearer of the Hand seemed the best solution. Not immediately, of course. She would need resources, allies, and battle plans. But the Hearer stood between her and her birthright, the throne she was destined to sit in, ruling over all the world. Eventually, he would have to be killed. She opened her mouth to point this out to Col, but he pulled away as a bandit came towards them.

"We're moving," he said, nervously eyeing the two of them. "It isn't safe here. Bring the girl."

Col nodded, then looked at River out of the corner of his eye. She saw the expression on his face, and stiffened.

"Don't you dare pick me up, peasant boy. I'll walk."

Col just looked at her, then at the arrow shaft embedded in her leg. She reached down, gritting her teeth, and yanked it out. The tip was made of a smooth, sharpened stone, fortunately, and had no barbs. Nonetheless, it was incredibly painful, and blood began gushing out of the wound. She tried to hold it closed with one hand, grabbing a piece of the cloaks she had been lying on to bind the wound with. By the time she had stopped the bleeding, most of the bandits had already disappeared into the woods. Col was still standing there, and she noted with amusement that he was as pale as a drowned worm under his tan. She snickered, trying not to betray how much pain she felt.

"What's the matter, never seen blood before?"

He gulped, then blushed, looking at the ground.

"I prefer when it stays on the inside of people," he admitted. "Think you can walk now?"

River reached instinctively to pull off her shoes. Dominik had never allowed her to take them off. However, now, a different hand stopped her. Col gave her a pleading look.

"I know you hate them, but I don't think we're safe enough to do that yet," he said hesitantly. River felt a surge of outrage, but she couldn't deny his logic. She complied, for now, but resentment brewed within her.

She tried to stand up, but immediately regretted it, her leg screaming in protest. He reached out his hand, but she refused it. She would not be constantly relying on the help of this pathetic and infuriating peasant boy. Reaching out, she picked up a twig from the ground and held it in her hand, willing it to change. It was difficult. So much harder than it had ever been for her before coming to this accursed land. It felt as though she was screaming her requests at a half-deaf old man from several rooms away. The twig ignored her at first, then she felt it respond to her presence, but it took several more minutes for it to understand what she wanted. Gradually, the twig grew and shaped itself to her command, forming a crutch. It was the perfect height for her, with a smooth rounded portion to fit under her arm, a handle halfway down, and a tip that splayed out to help support her even on soft ground. When she stood up, she could take the weight off of her injured leg, and move quite quickly. She turned to Col and gave him a smug look.

"I don't need your help."

Several hours later, she was beginning to regret her arrogant words. The crutch was giving her blisters in her armpit, and the stick kept catching on brambles.

Col strode beside her, both of them trying to ignore the bandits around them. Col and River hadn't been chained or made to feel as though they were prisoners, but the largest, toughest bandits in the group kept close to them, their hands hovering near their weapons. After River's display in the clearing, all the bandits seemed on edge.

Col sidled up to her, a hesitant grin on his face.

"So... why were you collecting weed seeds in your pouch? Do you want these ones?" He proffered a handful of seed pods he'd plucked off a passing bush.

Thoroughly sore and grouchy, she glared at him and stomped stubbornly on without saying anything. A flash of hurt crossed his face. He blew out a frustrated breath, and moved away from her to strike up a conversation with a bandit. She momentarily regretted her harshness, but consoled herself by plucking some seeds for herself from a different bush. As if she needed his help to do such a simple task! Stupid peasant. She refused to be any more indebted to him than she already was.

That evening, footsore, lonely, and sullen, she wandered away from the group. The bandits made camp in a cave deep in the heart of the woods. It was a high and lofty cave, with dry walls and a sandy floor, carved into a cliff face with trees hiding the entrance. The bandits had a

stash of supplies here, and they were soon sharing a meal around a
crackling fire. Col, of course, was already being treated like one of the
group, but River created a bubble of wariness around her when she came
to the fire. So, she left. Outside the cave, in the darkness, she sat on a tree
stump and finally took off her horrible, blinding shoes. This deep in the
wilderness, she felt safe to do so.

The moment she touched the ground, she felt her irritable mood
fade away. Although it was dark, she felt as though a blindfold had been
lifted from her eyes. She became aware of the snap of every twig, the
drumming of a far-off waterfall, and the slow stretching of thousands of
roots into the earth. More than that, however, the earth became aware of
her. There was no obedience, no sense of friendship, but it reacted to her
presence as a pond reacts to a thrown stone. The trees were different,
when she touched them. Smaller, weaker, easier to command. She touched
a large, twisted one several yards from the cave entrance, and requested a
favor. Several moments later, she had created a bed for herself. It stretched
between two trees, made from interwoven branches and vines, with thick
moss lining the inside. Although it didn't seem to rain much in this
country, she created a rounded canopy and a curtain of thick leaves
hanging across the entrance. It was something she had done often, in her
past life, and the sight was so familiar it made her heart ache. When she
climbed inside, she could almost forget that she was in a different time at
all. She closed her eyes, and she was back in her father's garden. Any
moment now, Storm would come into the garden to find her, a torch in
hand and a smile on his face...

"River?"

Her fantasy shattered, as the leaves were pulled aside and a dark
head poked in, moonlight glancing off of unruly hair. It wasn't Storm. It
was Col. At the sight of him, her heart started to leap with joy, then
plunged back into misery. With a shock, she realized that she had always
harbored a deep, subconscious resentment towards him for not being

Storm. He wasn't the same, he wasn't good enough. His eyes were Storm's, but she resented the rest of him for not being someone else. When he saw her, he smiled.

"Hey, I noticed you didn't join us, so I brought you some food." He held out some shapes to her, and she couldn't quite make out what they were.

"They're not poisoned, I promise," he said, when she hesitated. "I think some of them are our own supplies, from the raid, and some were stashed here."

She continued to sit there, and he let out a sigh of frustration.

"Look, River, I know you hate me for some reason, but I can't understand why. You're the only person who's ever treated me like this, and I've spent every minute of these last cursed weeks trying to help you. You don't have to like me, but just try to cooperate, ok? I'm the only friend you have, and right now I think you need me."

I don't need you! I don't need anyone! her mind immediately screamed. But the practical part of her mind strangled this part before it could speak. She forced herself to take a deep breath and think.
She did need him, at least for now. And, as annoying as he was, she had come to miss his presence when he wasn't beside her. So, she reached out and took the food from him.

"Thank you." She took a bite, and found it to be a biscuit and piece of dried meat, too dry and too spicy, like everything in this country. Nevertheless, she was hungry.

"I don't like you," she said between bites, "and I hate how much I need your help, but... I do need your help. And you've been kind to me, which I must acknowledge. So, I will cooperate with you as long as our goals are aligned. However, we need a plan."

Col shifted, sitting down on the edge of her nest with his feet hanging out. He never seemed to respect her royal blood or personal space.

"Yes I've been thinking about that," he mused. "We need to find a way to escape from these bandits, and then we can go to my village. It's so small and insignificant, the priest guards hardly ever show up except for yearly taxes. My family can hide us."

She blew out her breath in frustration. It was as she had thought, he had no ambition whatsoever.

"Then what?"

The question deflated him, and he hung his head.

"I don't know. My village is dying slowly. Our livestock and crops get more pathetic every year, and the taxes take almost everything. I was supposed to save them, but I failed. Now I suppose I'll just have to stay and die along with them."

For a moment, River felt a sense of sympathy. It was a foreign emotion, but she reached out and put her hand on his shoulder without thinking.

"There will be a way to win," she said. "You can't give up so easily. You will still save them, and I will help you."

He looked up at her, surprised.

"How?"

"I don't know, but this village sounds like a good place to hide while we plan."

He looked at her for a long moment, and her heart fluttered strangely under his gaze.

"Thank you," his voice was sincere, "for your help."

She nodded and took her hand off his shoulder, feeling guilty. The only reason she'd promised to help save his family was because, if she had her way and ruled this land, all the villages would be free from the tyranny of the Order. It would be a natural side effect, not a favor specifically for Col. Suddenly uncomfortable with his open gaze, she shifted away from him, her cold demeanor returning. He seemed to read her posture, because he got up and left without bidding her a good night.

When he was gone, she lay down, trying to go back to her blissful imaginings. However, as hard as she tried, she couldn't recapture the feeling. What was worse, she realized that she couldn't clearly recall Storm's face. Instead, she kept seeing Col, his vibrant eyes shining out from his freckled face, nose crinkled up in a smile. So kind, so trusting. So perfectly handsome. Sleep was slow in coming.

20

When Col awoke, there was an excited atmosphere among the men. It appeared that Lucan's wasn't the only band of bandits in the area, and the bands even seemed to be on friendly terms with each other. A group of some twenty men had been seen by a lookout, headed in the direction of the cave. The moment Col was up, Lucan wanted to speak with him. He was leaning against the wall near the entrance, chewing on something.

"Those are Dirk's men approaching." He turned his cold, beady eyes on Col. "They're no threat, but after what your friend did outside, we're not going to be able to hide your presence." He looked at Col questioningly, and Col realised that he had won the respect of this man, transforming from prisoner to a sort of second-in-command. He was waiting for Col's opinion. However, Col had no idea what he was talking about. Disguising his confusion, he nodded thoughtfully, nonchalantly strolling to the entrance to try to see what Lucan meant without giving away his ignorance.

Although the doorway was crowded with bandits, over their heads Col could clearly see what River had "done" outside.

Over the bandits' heads, where there had once been the bare, dead branches of twisted trees clawing at the sky, Col saw lush green leaves, dotted with flowers the color of blood and whispering in the breeze. His breath caught, and he found himself pushing forward to see more. It wasn't just the trees around the cave. It was the whole valley. As far as the eye could see, all the ground at the base of the cliffs was now coated green. The dry dust bowls had transformed into soft meadows coated in thick moss, grass, and flowers. Every gnarled, dying tree in the valley had put out a thick crop of leaves, with new trees pushing up between them as if they had been growing there for centuries - strange, tall trees with thick, straight trunks and wide leaves. It was like nothing Col had ever seen before, like something out of the old legends or tales of faraway places. It felt like an alien world, or a different time.

River was nowhere to be seen. He glanced over to where she had been sleeping last night, and saw her strange tree nest still there, her shoes discarded on the ground nearby. Oh no.

Mind scrambling for a plan, he rushed up to River's bed. She was already awake, and as he approached, her head poked out of the curtain of leaves.

"Why must everyone make a ruckus so early?" she complained.

"Surely it was obvious I was still sleeping. It seems chivalry is dead among you people."

Col snorted, finding her objection hilarious.

"They're bandits," he pointed out dryly. "Were they known for chivalry in your time?" She seemed at a loss for an argument.

"But it's not very early, and you need to get up," he continued. He could see the sleepiness fading from her face as he explained the situation. Her eyes widened as she looked at the valley.

"I didn't make this happen," she whispered. "The earth no longer heeds me as it used to. It reacted to my presence against my bidding."

She looked at him, frustrated. "I can't undo this. It's too big."

He'd expected as much.

"We can't hide from this new group of bandits," he said, a half-baked plan growing in his head. "We'll just have to persuade them to join our cause, and then slip away later."

She stared at him, a look of incredulity on her face.

"You say that as if it's so easy. As if they'll just walk right up and want to be friends."

Her tone of scorn surprised him.

"Well, yes," he said, confused, "I've never had someone dislike me after I've talked to them. Except you, of course."

She was quiet for a long moment. Emotions chased each other

across her face, first surprise, then confusion, then jealousy.

"Such a gift... and yet you do not value it as you should."

She looked at him, her eyes critically assessing his every detail. He felt uncomfortable under the piercing gaze of this alien girl. In the sharp morning sunlight, her exotic features and aura of power made her seem distinctly inhuman.

"I see I misjudged you when we met," she said at last. "I thought you an ignorant fool. You are not ignorant, not in the ways of men, at least. You have great skill and tact in your words that inspires others. Perhaps you would earn a place as my general over this land, when I acquire my throne."

"Um...thanks?" He felt his face warm at her praise.

"But I was correct in judging you to be foolish," she went on, and his heart plummeted, changing quickly from a rush of pleasure to a feeling of affront.

"You are a fool to throw away such a gift." She pinned him with a resentful look. "If you can, as you say, win over these bandits to our side, why would you then want to throw away loyal followers? Why not use them?"

"I don't want followers." His irritation grew at the idea. "I don't want a revolution, or to give the Hearer bigger reasons to want me dead. I just want to slip away quietly and be with my family."

She looked at him, and he couldn't read her expression.

"We shall see if that is even possible," she said quietly. It was the most disturbing thing she'd said thus far, and he walked away feeling a deep dread growing. He pushed it out of his mind, refusing to consider that she might be right. The band of men were drawing nearer, picking their way slowly through a dry riverbed that ran through the valley, forming a rough, bramble-free swath that could be used as a road.

Col watched them come, mentally preparing himself with a regiment of persuasive explanations for River's influence on the valley, lined up like soldiers inside his head. Usually, words seemed to flow through him as he made things up on the spot. But right now he felt disturbed and distracted, so he felt it best to be prepared, just in case his wits failed him. There was a swish of motion behind him, and River stepped up beside the boulder he stood on, surveying the situation. Her hair was dishevelled, the tight braid losing strands, tangled with leaves and twigs. She was still wearing the same clothes he had found her wearing in the temple, which had by now become extremely unkempt and ragged. Her loose, hooded shirt was stained with sweat, and her face was covered with dust, nose burnt from the sun. Her grey pants, which had once been of the finest materials and latest fashion, were now thoroughly stained with dirt and old blood stains, with rips and slashes on her left leg, where she had sustained two injuries in their time together. Her thigh had healed, but her calf was still bandaged, although she had abandoned the crutch. Did she really heal so quickly? The wound to her thigh had seemed to take forever to heal, while she had been imprisoned by the Rebels. However, she barely limped now, walking barefoot with ease on the grass. He noticed a glow of health, almost like faint sunlight infusing her skin and the leaves of the plants around her feet. It was almost like they were feeding off of each other. Nevertheless, she did not strike an imposing figure. He gestured toward the cave entrance.

"I noticed our friends have a store of plunder in there. You could go try to find some new clothes in there, and try to make yourself look more intimidating." He made sure not to phrase it as an order, as she never responded well to those. Fortunately, she didn't balk too much at the suggestion, looking down at herself with a wrinkled nose of disdain.

"Very well. But if I catch any of these thugs peeking while I change, I will skewer them straight through with a tree." She noted that several of the nearby robbers were listening, and elaborated gruesomely for their benefit.

"A sharpened, wooden stake springing up from the ground

between your legs so quickly you have no time to dodge, and stabbing straight through your whole body, like a rabbit over a cook fire. Then, once you're dead, some leaves and flowers will grow out of your nose and mouth, and you'll become a lovely shrub."

Several of the men nearby, who had initially been leering when Col suggested River change her clothes, had now turned as pale as salt and were staring fixedly down the slope at the approaching visitors, several of them not-so-subtly shifting until they were standing on a solid rock like Col, not wanting to risk anything growing up under their feet. Col himself felt nausea at the description. Surely River could not have been well-liked, even in her own time. She was so grouchy and violent.

She stalked away, and he turned his attention to the approaching group. They were armed, but not brandishing their weapons. The same was true of the bandits in Col's group. In fact, as the men came close enough to make out faces, several of the bandits began muttering to each other, naming a few friends and relatives they recognized. Nevertheless, no one called out a greeting. The presence of Col and River had given the group a new mood of caution. Most of them had shown enthusiasm and support the night before at the idea of helping Col bring down the Order of the Hand, but with the approach of outsiders they were all aware of the danger of exposure.

As River approached the mouth of the cave, Lucan hurried out of it and approached Col.

"So, tell me, young hero." Coming out of Lucan's pinched mouth, the title could not be taken as anything other than sarcastic mockery. However, his tone was less harsh than the voice he usually used.

"Do you have a grand plan to keep this sorceress of yours a secret?"
Col gave him his most disarming grin.

"Trust me!"
He strode down the rock, putting himself in plain view of the

approaching men. They seemed cut from the same cloth as the men of Lucan's band, ragged and unkempt, a bunch of dangerous looking vagabonds. It was hard to see the farmers and villagers they had doubtless once been in their hard eyes. Col gave it his best effort. Lucan walked up beside him.

"Good morning, friends!" Lucan hailed them with a tense smile. A large man, clearly the leader with a forehead like a brick and an ugly lump for a nose looked him over, eyes narrowing as he approached to within a road's width.

"Lucan, What's happened here?"

"We-ell..."

Lucan hesitated, glancing to Col. The man followed his gaze, and Col sensed that if he didn't get answers soon he would get violent.

"Who are you?" His tone was aggressive. "Did you do this?" Col looked at Dirk keenly, trying to judge what kind of approach would best win over the giant.

"I am your friend."

The man snorted. "How can you be my friend? I don't even know you.

"Are you a friend of the Hearer?"

"No! Of course not!"

"Well, then I am your friend. Because I am the hole in the Hearer's armor, while you outlaws are the thorn in his sandal. We have so much in common." He said it loud enough for the whole band to hear, but quietly enough that they had to lean in, paying attention. Dirk still looked suspicious.

"Grand words, for a scrawny lad. I bet you've never even met the Hearer. What makes you think you're so special?"

Col drew himself to his full height, which was rather depressing, as he still didn't rise higher than Dirk's chin. It was hard to give a brave stare when he had to tip his head back to look into Dirk's eyes.

"I'm not special. I'm just a village boy. And that's what makes the

Hearer so afraid. Because I know a secret that can crush him. And anyone, any one of you, any villager, once they know this secret, can be just as dangerous to the Hearer as me." He turned and scanned the faces around him, most of them bearing an expression of confusion or disbelief. Realizing that he'd lost them, he hastily backpedalled.

"You hate the Hearer, the Order, the way they treat us," he stated, rewarded by some nods and a flurry of men spitting on the ground at the mention of the Order.

"You hate the way you've been driven from your livelihoods, your families, your homes." More nods, and mutters of assent grew louder. He sensed that, finally, he had their ears.

"Well, I'm here to bring you the glad news that a change is coming. The Order will fall, and it will be people like us, the nobodies the Hearer never cared about, who will bring it down."

There were several excited grins, but Dirk scoffed.

"That's not possible. The Order is far too strong to fight. They have thousands of warriors, not to mention that the Hand speaks only to the Hearer. Even the gods are on their side. I know Rebel propaganda when I hear it, and we aren't interested in those crazy Rebel plans."

"But it's not a Rebel plan," Col interjected, deciding not to mention that he was, technically, a Rebel now, and therefore any plan he made was a Rebel plan. "I was an acolyte in the Kingsfall temple. As far from a rebel as you could be. But on the day of my initiation, I was brought before the Hand, and I saw the sacred crystal break." He didn't give them time to voice their disbelief, but yanked up his sleeves, exposing his bare arms in the full light of day. The horrible scars caught every eye, their raw red color standing out against his skin, the jagged pattern unmistakable. The silence was instantaneous.

"The Hearer tried to have me killed for what I witnessed," Col let his voice rise with pain and outrage, remembering that night, "because he was terrified that others would learn what I know; that the people of the world find out that the Messenger never spoke to him, that the girl trapped in the crystal had never given him the laws he rules us with, that the whole Order is a lie."

No one was scoffing anymore. Every face showed belief, and rising excitement. Dirk stared at him.

"How did you escape?" he whispered.

Col played his final card to win them over. These were not cynical Rebels, these were simple village men who had been spoon-fed the Order's myths since childhood.

"The Messenger rescued me," he said. "I escaped Kingsfall with her, because the Hearer would rather kill her than let the people find out that she is not what the Order has told us she is." He spread his arms, gesturing at the thriving forest around them.

"She did this. And she can do it again," his words turned passionate, inspiring.

"Imagine a world where the Hearer doesn't tax us, where the land is lush and crops are full. Where little children never starve." He stopped, suddenly letting his own words wash over him. His words had whipped his audience into a near-fanatical frenzy of excitement, but he'd been so focused on inspiring the bandits that he hadn't truly stopped to think about the truth in his words. If River had done this, perhaps she really could turn the whole land into a paradise. Maybe the land could truly be free of the Order of the Hand, if enough people knew the truth. Maybe running and hiding in his dying village wasn't the only possible future. The vision took his breath away.

It was at that moment that River stepped out of the cave. Col was clued in by every eye suddenly veering away from him towards the entrance. He turned, and his jaw dropped.

He'd been expecting a slightly cleaner, more respectable-looking River. He'd expected to have to talk fast to assure the bandits that she was, in fact, a powerful being. But instead he just stared. She looked like an otherworldly enchantress. Her hair had been brushed out, long and silky and trailing to her waist. She was wearing a dress that hugged her figure, but flared out at the bottom. It had likely belonged to someone taller than her before, as it trailed on the ground. However, the result did not make her look ridiculous, but rather majestic. Having no way to bathe, she had gone the opposite way. Her face and arms were painted with swirling, mystic patterns of black, likely ash from the fire pit. The most astonishing thing about her was the vines. They swirled around her waist and trailed down her skirt with tiny dark green leaves. Roses bloomed at her waist, and around her throat like a bloody necklace, although all the thorns pointed outward so as not to prick her. Vines wrapped in a delicate pattern up her torso and flowed from her shoulders to the ground behind her in a living cape. They writhed and twisted in her shadow, thorned ends lifting up from the ground like snakes. As if that was not imposing enough, on her head she had actually formed for herself a crown. Sharp spines of dark, shiny wood rose in five wicked points at the front of her head, with smaller spines curving away at the sides and disappearing into her hair. Small white flowers twisted around and through the spikes, more beautiful than any gemstone. Two delicate strings of flowers hung down near her ears, framing her face and trailing into her hair. Her eyes were dark and impassive, her expression proud. She was breathtakingly beautiful. And also completely terrifying. A vision from a fairy tale, of some woodland queen surveying her magical domain. As one, the bandits fell to their knees. Even several of Lucan's band did, although they had seen River before in her bedraggled state. Some began weeping with joy, others clasping their hands, whispering, "Messenger!" Some covered their eyes. River drank it all in, standing taller, eyes glowing with pleasure at finally having the adoration she so clearly craved. For a moment, Col had a premonition that he was witnessing a monster in the making, a glimpse of a cold, prideful sorceress who could drink the world dry and still never be quenched of her thirst for power. River could become that, he realized. If she fully embraced this role as Messenger, she could wrench the religion out of the Hearer's hands and take it for herself, toppling the Order only to set herself up in its place, a new ruthless ruler. In that future, he saw the death of her humanity, of the serious, thoughtful woman and the sad, lost girl he glimpsed sometimes, desperate for love and affection. A man next to Col suddenly started chanting a prayer, one he recognized from his training in the temple, although he had never seen the sense in praying to a deity he didn't believe in. The wrongness of it wrenched him out of his glassy-eyed stare at River. This wasn't right. The religion of the Hand was a fake, and he had been travelling with her long enough to realize that River was not a god, she was just a very powerful, prideful human. He stared at the man, trying to shake his head, too confused to figure out how to voice his distress. He realized that, in calling her the Messenger to win the men over, he had caused this. His heart froze in horror at what his actions might bring about. River, too, looked sharply at the man. Her cold expression of pride faltered, her face suddenly showing misgiving. She looked at Col, no longer basking in the worship but suddenly looking lost, and a little guilty. He shook his head mutely, begging her with his eyes to stop this, not to let her pride control her and turn her into another false god. She wavered, but then he saw the pride fade and her expression turned serious. She turned to the man, pointing an imperious finger.

"Stop that," she snapped. "I'm a queen, not a god. You may bow, but anyone who prays to me, or the Hand, or any of the gods that the false Order told you about, can have no part in this. We are a revolution, not a cult. Understood?"

Hearing sharp, snappish words come from River's mouth broke her aura of mystic deity. She was still wickedly dangerous and mysterious. However she was also a full head shorter than most of the bandits, and obviously mortal. Even Col was taller than her. The men looked confused, but gradually came to their senses and stood up. Dirk looked around, suddenly feeling the need to re-establish himself as spokesperson for his men. He looked at Col, seeming vaguely betrayed.

"You lied to us? What is your name? And, if she is not the immortal Messenger, then what is her name?"

Col held up his hands to calm the man.

"I did not lie to you. She did come from the sacred crystal, she is the Hand, and has been trapped in the crystal for generations. She did create this forest, and she is powerful. But she is not an immortal messenger of the gods. The first Hearer made that up, pretending to be able to hear her when she could not speak inside the crystal. Her name is River, and I am Nikolo Wolf."

Dirk considered this, arms folded in an attempt at gruff disgruntlement. However, his eyes kept flitting to the forest, and back to River, and he couldn't keep the awe out of his expression for long. Finally he nodded.

"Very well. We will join you, Nikolo, and your terrifying friend. If there is indeed a chance to topple the Order, we want to be the ones to do it."

Col sighed in relief. Then he straightened up and shook the big man's hand, adopting a calm smile.

"A wise choice, friend. Together, we will do great things."

21

It turned out, "great things" involved a great deal of drudgery. In the aftermath of what had originally been temporary measures to secure his escape from the bandits, Col found himself suddenly with a small army of over fifty disreputable thugs looking to him for direction. He organized sleeping arrangements for the larger group, directed men to scout for food and danger, at the same time playing peacekeeper between Lucan and Dirk, both men who were accustomed to being the top dog in their own command structures. They had both pledged their loyalty to Col with little hesitation, after he had shared the full story of his escape from the Order with them and they had been fully convinced that a revolution was possible. However, their loyalty to each other was tenuous. To make matters worse, he was still confused as to what he intended to do about the future, whether he should escape with River or try to make use of these questionable allies. River wasn't speaking to him, which stung. Although the men respected her, they had all somehow assumed that Col was the leader, and looked to him for orders. River stayed aloof from the goings-on, but he could tell she was quietly fuming every time Lucan or Dirk approached him with an issue. He didn't understand why she blamed him. After all, it wasn't his fault that her interchanging brooding and imperious attitudes made her a miserable person to talk to. However, he wished she would help him, and mulled over ways to make amends. After several hours of struggling to coordinate everyone, he was at his wit's end. It was well into the afternoon, and still the bandits had made little headway in any direction. It was clear they were used to spending the majority of their time, when they weren't raiding, in a state of relaxed squalor. While they were still full of excitement and goodwill, they had little experience with organized activities. While they would initially approach a task with great enthusiasm, it was not long before they would get distracted or confused and come wandering back for new orders. Col slumped down on a rock, wondering how Lucan and Dirk got anything done. It was at that moment that River finally ceased her brooding and came over.

"It seems, despite these fool's devotion, you are not fit for the task of leading them," she noted with smug satisfaction. "You have little experience organizing troops. Nevertheless, if these men persist in refusing me as their leader, I will accept that you lead them. For now, at least."

Col let out a breath in frustration.

"Thanks, but I don't want to lead them. These men are awful at following orders."

River snorted.

"Or perhaps you are bad at giving them." She offered him a hand to stand up from the rock.

"However, since I hate to watch such incompetence, I will help you."

Col had grown used to ignoring the stinging barbs in her words, and saw through to the sentiment behind. She was getting over her resentful mood, and offering peace. He gave her a genuine, grateful smile.

"Thank you!"

She looked disgruntled, but together they walked to find Dirk and Lucan, her quiet voice all the while explaining the flaws in his tactics until he felt ready to shrivel with embarrassment. There was no impressing this girl.

"We need to move." Lucan's shrewd face was pinched up in worry. He and Dirk had joined them in the shadow of a large boulder, with several smaller rocks to sit on and the shadow of the cliff blocking them from view of the men.

"This region is far from any towns or main roads, but we've still got two, maybe three days before word reaches the nearest temple of what has happened to this valley, and they'll send Priest-guards to investigate."

River nodded seriously, brushing aside the fact that she had been the one responsible for the problem.

"Yes. If we are to escape these priests long enough to gather an army of our own, we must keep moving. I would advise all the men pack up immediately, and set out in multiple groups so as to leave several trails. Each group should have at least three scouts looking ahead, and several falling behind to cover any tracks. I expect both you and Dirk know of several discreet locations where we could rendezvous?"

Col winced. Her casual mention of an army unnerved him, and she was issuing orders to the two bandit leaders like they were her underlings, with the only nod to their station being the use of the word "advise". Both men looked to Col instead. He pretended to consider, although he had no experience in such matters.

"Hmm, yes that seems wise," he nodded sagely. "Dirk and Lucan, since you know this country so well, I'm relying on you to work together and find a route we can take to have safe places to camp while we visit remote villages, spreading word of the Hearer's lies. I'm thinking of Illbeth, Hammersound, Grayson's Shaft, and Bone Canyon as a start." He threw the name of his own village in with the others casually, making certain not to draw undue attention to the place. Let them think he simply wanted to rally the villagers there. The two bandit lords looked at each other, sharing a look that seemed to convey a mutual truce.

"We can do that." Dirk puffed out his huge barrel of a chest in pride.

"I know the land like the back of my hand, everywhere from Hammersound to here, where Lucan's territory takes over. I've got more men stashed in a cave near there too, along with my wife and boys. They'll be happy to join us."

Lucan nodded.

"The mountains between us and Illbeth are Hamon's domain, though. He could be useful, if we can persuade him to come out from hiding in those rocks. Just as likely he acts like a coward and decides to shoot us from a distance though. You never can tell."

Col put on the smile that he imagined an officer would have when awarding soldiers with medals for bravery.

"I knew you'd be the men for the job." Internally, though, his heart was still doubtful. Was he doing the right thing? Or was he setting fires too big for him to control? Regardless of her unpleasant demeanor, River was a brilliant commander. Within the hour she had the men sorted, and ready to move as soon as the sun left the valley floor. When it reached the tops of the cliffs, glaring brightly and causing the entire valley to fall into deep shadow by comparison, they marched out. Col found that his only role was to continue to motivate and inspire the men, as River's harsh words tended to slice a man's ego into pieces. Nevertheless, the orders, while harsh, were precise and clear so that the men never had to return to her for further clarification. Col watched closely, determined to memorize the way she worded things. After a while, however, he realized he wasn't paying much attention to her words. She had changed clothes again for the journey, and was wearing practical leggings, a loose shirt, and a coat that hung to her mid-thighs. As a reminder of her power, she had kept some swirling black runes across her chin and cheekbones, as well as a long vine wrapped around her waist. Her crown had changed to a sort of headband to hold her hair back from her face, with no decorations except for a few spikes and leaves jutting out behind her ears. She seemed to have put aside her dramatic sorceress act to focus on the task at hand, and Col found her even more mesmerizing. He shook himself out of it. He had a reputation to maintain as a leader, and staring gooey eyed at River wasn't going to help his image. He reminded himself how infuriating she was; he then turned to strike up a friendly conversation with the man beside him.

They had journeyed down from the cave and come to the bottom of the valley. At this point, the company split off into four groups, each heading in slightly different directions. Col and River remained with Lucan and three of his men, as well as four of Dirk's band. Dirk himself headed off with a different group to gather the rest of his men and his family.

They journeyed down a dried-up stream bed, as these scars across the landscape provided the best paths through the underbrush. Col marveled at the thriving plants that hung down over the edge. He had never seen plants so green and full of life, not to mention so many different varieties. In his experience, plants were primarily brown, with occasional tough green leaves. The air had a sticky, sweaty feeling to it that reminded him of when his mother boiled soup, and water steamed into the air as mist. Of course, she only did that indoors, and their chimney had a steam trap in it to turn the steam back into water. Here, it seemed the whole air outdoors had changed. Half an hour into the journey, Lucan's feet began to make a strange, squelching noise. He stopped, as did everyone following him. They stared at the path. The ground was growing darker in color, and in the dim light there were glimmering patches. Col reached down, and touched one. It was wet, as though it had just rained. But it hadn't. He was sure of that. River came up beside him and looked, to see what everyone was so excited about.

"It's just water," she noted, unimpressed. "Let's keep moving."

Lucan put out a hand to stop her.

"It's not just water, sorceress. Water comes from the rain, or from wells, or from the great river in the flat lands, several week's journey east of here. It has never run in this streambed, not for hundreds of years."

River shrugged.

"Well, now it is. There is just as much water in this dry land as there was in my time, the water is just deep, deep down. Only now..." she shifted her feet on the ground thoughtfully. "it's not so deep anymore. The trees' roots can reach it, and their leaves release it into the air. Why shouldn't it run on the ground?"

The men stared at her, then at each other, eyes wide. Water was not something to shrug off. Water was life. It meant the difference between a dead crop and a living one. Col had never thought about all the things that must work together for River to make her plants grow. Her power seemed even greater and more unnerving to him now that he understood it. She wasn't just changing the plants, she was awakening the very land itself, down to its ancient stone roots. Was it really true, the way she described it, as if the ground itself had a personality?

After a long moment of quiet exclamations, the group finally kept moving. As they walked, their feet began to sink into the mud. A little while further, and they had to leave the path and walk alongside it, as the mud was deep and sucking at their feet. Little trickles of water ran across the surface of the ground, forming pools in the hollows of rocks. The trickles soon joined together in a shallow sheet of water that ran across the ground, making a happy tinkling sound. Soon even that sheet was too deep to see the bottom clearly. By the time the sun left the cliffs and the moon rose, the water was so close to the edge of the bank that Col could reach down and run his hand through it. It was unnerving. Water wasn't supposed to look like this, all clear and cold and moving so fast. When Col had been very small, he had gone with his family to see the great river Thude, which was the only surface water near the cliff country. It had been a fat, brown slug of a thing, with thick sludge gradually sliding along and swarming with flies. This was completely different. Suddenly, River's name started to mean something much prettier to him.

As they walked, Col gradually began to hear a new sound other than the water and the scuttle of little nocturnal animals joyfully frolicking in the bounty of their new home. It was a distant thunder, but steady and unceasing. It grew louder as they continued, and Col could see that everyone was growing anxious. Everyone except River, that is. Without warning, the two scouts who had gone ahead burst out of the trees, waving frantically. Every man put a hand on his weapon before they heard what the scouts were saying.

"Come quickly! Come see!"

Col relaxed as he realized it was wonder, not fear, on their faces. They moved forward as a group until the underbrush fell away and they came into a clearing. The thunder was coming from a high cliff on the right, and what Col saw made him gape.

"What...?" He stared, entranced. River looked at him, and for a moment her expression softened in an affectionate smile.

"It's a waterfall, silly."

The name made it seem so mundane. But it was a silver sheet of thunderous momentum, endlessly cascading from the top of the cliff. A thousand droplets sprayed up from where it fell into a pool, shining in the moonlight. Col was awestruck. Even Lucan, who seemed to have the emotional range of a lizard most of the time, looked shocked. *Get it together,* Col told himself, and did. The men were turning around to see what he thought, and he wouldn't be caught gaping.

"Well, we should fill our bottles and wash our clothes," he said, pretending to be casual. Lucan let out a laugh of surprise, almost delight. It was strange coming from the impassive Magpie.

"A fine plan, my friend! Come to think of it, there isn't a man here that doesn't stink like a steaming pile of dung. Why don't we throw those temple dogs off our scent and take a bath?"

The mood was infectious, and all plans of further journeying were abandoned for the next hour. While River made a beeline for the woods, looking mortified, the tough bandits stripped naked and jumped into the pool, whooping like little boys and yelping at the cold. When he saw that the water was not too deep to stand in, Col joined them. He clung to the bushes and rocks on the bank as he eased himself into the water, wary of unseen holes in the bottom of the pool. In the Kingsfall temple there had been hot baths - an unimaginable luxury - but they had been shallow and he had never learned to swim. The moonlit pool was cold, and clean, and the most soothing thing he had ever experienced on his sweaty, aching body.

When the men had finally stopped splashing each other, pulled on trousers, and had settled down to the more serious task of washing clothes, River emerged. She had walked away into the woods by the water, and Col suddenly wondered if she had been looking the other way, or if she was the sort of girl to sneak a peek at the goings-on. An image flashed through his head of what he must have looked like, all awkward and naked clinging to a rock because he was afraid to swim, and he fervently hoped she hadn't looked.

She went to the pool and sat on the edge. The bandits continued their washing trying very hard not to look interested, but Col could tell that they were all wondering what she would do. He suddenly felt sorry for River, realizing that it must be embarrassing to be living in such close quarters to these rough bandit men, and being the only woman in the group. However, to Col's relief and several bandit's obvious disappointment, she found a solution. A circle of tall, reed-like plants sprang up around her, half on the bank and half in the water. They grew together so thickly that she had absolute privacy to wash, and when she caused the reeds to shrink back into the water she was fully clothed again.

They carried as much water as they could away from that place. The women of many villages had the skill of weaving together thin, waxy cords into bottles and jugs, so tightly woven that they could hold water. Each of these had a cork of soft wood, and the larger jugs had woven straps to carry them like a pack. They filled several of these, as well as a bottle for each person. The bandits were a well-supplied group. Col had picked up that they did not just get their loot from robbing rich city folk, but that their relatives in the surrounding villages also supported these men. Although few would resist the rule of the Hand, none liked it.

As they filed away into the dark trees, River fell into step beside him. She didn't say anything, but Col felt his heart grow lighter at her companionship. For the first time since he had escaped the temple, he was feeling hopeful about the future.

22

After about two hours of walking, they came to the place where River's explosion of power had ended. The jungle died out, and the land was divided along an invisible line. The green forest stretched behind them, and before them nothing but hard earth, sand, and rocks, bleached white in the moonlight. The same stunted, gnarled trees were thinner here than in the place where they had first been ambushed by the bandits, and they cast weird, spiky shadows on the ground. River fell behind here, and when she rejoined the group she was wearing shoes again. Col knew she was trying hard not to give away her weakness to the bandits, but she walked in a completely different way, transforming from a smooth, graceful gait to an awkward, shuffling stumble as if she'd completely lost her sense of balance.

As the sun was rising, the sky above the darkened cliffs turning a bright blue, Col suggested that they look for a place to rest. There was a sandy bowl ringed with trees, and Lucan directed the men to light a fire there, a safe distance from the dry brush. Col felt a twinge of satisfaction that it was no longer his job to be the one gathering brushwood.

There was a sudden whooshing sound, and a splattering of sand hit the side of Col's face. He turned, just as a scream rent the silent morning. Of the two men crouched in the bowl to light a fire, only one remained. He was half buried in sand, and screaming the wild, desperate scream of a man in horrible pain. The smoldering twigs of the fire had been scattered. Emerging from the sand, writhing and disappearing again around the man, were legs. Giant, segmented legs, with barbed elbows and long, furry sections, each leg ending in four claws. Col counted at least six of the monstrous limbs. Lucan leapt at the creature, chopping one of the legs off at the joint with a machete. A high pitched groan vibrated the sand, like the sound of a half-chopped tree as it breaks under its own weight. The head emerged from directly beneath the desperate bandit, and

Col saw with horror that the man's whole leg was caught inside the creature's mouth. With a flick of its head and a sickening crunch, the creature ate the rest of the man in one huge bite. It was the most horrible creature Col had ever seen. Coarse orange fur covered a wide snout in an oblong head with several small horns but no eyes at all. The only suggestion of eyes was two bald patches on the face, the hard hide beneath slightly transparent and bulging outward. Almost the entire length of the face was split in a wide mouth, curved upward in a permanent smile full of sharp black teeth. Long, almost transparent whiskers extended out from the eyebrow area. One of them was curled up and singed on the end, likely from the lighting of the fire. It turned in Lucan's direction, opening its mouth to emit an angry creaking sound.

Col stood frozen. His mind yelled at him that he must take action, but his limbs were locked up in indecision. Beside him, River was already crouched, her hands on the sand, eyebrows scrunched in concentration. However, there didn't seem to be many plant seedlings lying dormant in the sandy hollow, as only a few thin vines struggled up through the sand to cling to the creature's front legs. Lucan let out a yell of fear, backing away hurriedly from the monstrous head. It heaved itself up further from the sand to chase after him, revealing six legs and a thick body the size of a cottage. Col finally got control of his limbs and dropped his pack to the ground, grabbing a small hatchet out of it. He'd trained with battle axes briefly during his days as an acolyte, but the smaller weapon still felt awkward in his hand. Without giving himself time to second-guess his plan, he charged directly at the nightmare, yelling to distract it from Lucan.

It didn't seem to have ears, but its long eyebrow stalks twitched, and it turned to him. On its back, near the small pointed tail, two long arms unfolded, looking like nothing so much as a locust's hopping legs. However, they were attached backwards, waving in the air instead of braced on the ground. Col ignored them, sliding down the sandy slope directly towards the blind, grinning face. River screamed a warning, and out of the corner of his eye he glimpsed a flash of motion. The creature was whipping one of its long arms toward him. He stumbled to the side, as it stabbed past at where his shoulder had been a moment before. It had a bulb at the end, with a long, wicked spine emerging from it. The bright blue coloring at the base of the bulb, and the slightly transparent end to the spine indicated that it was, without a doubt, poisonous.

Too late, he turned to see that the second arm was coming at him from the other direction. His feet were sunk into the sand now, and all he had time to do was watch as his death flashed toward him. Lines glowed faintly at the corners of his vision, and suddenly the poison spike seemed to slow through the air. He threw his hand up to protect himself, and stared in wonder. His fingers seemed to be wrapped in glowing lines of light that trailed behind his hand as it moved before fading away. They looked exactly like the light he had touched in River's crystal prison, and as he moved his hand toward the approaching spine, it slowed down. He still didn't have time to dodge it, but he grabbed the base of it as it came at his torso and pushed it to the side. The strange light faded, and he was jerked up into the air, still clinging to the monster's arm. It tried to stab at him with the other one, but he was swinging wildly, and it missed. Praying that he didn't chop off his own hand, he hacked at the creature's arm with his hatchet. It snapped under the blade, and he fell to the sand, nearly stabbing himself with the poison spine still clutched in his hand.

River threw a handful of seeds onto the sand, and as Col scrambled to his feet he saw plants begin to spring up. The creature lunged at him but was held back by feet tangled in thick vines. Its monstrous mouth snapped closed just inches from Col's head, and he got a face full of the putrid smell of fresh blood mixed with rotting things. Without thinking, he chopped off the antennae it was waving in his face. It chopped off easily, and the creature snapped its mouth, shaking its head and creaking in distress. Emboldened, he smacked that horrible face with his hatchet. The hide broke under his blow, oozing dark goo, but the weapon stuck in its face like a new nose and wouldn't come free. The remaining spine stabbed down again, but missed him by about a foot. Still trying to tug his hatched free, Col lashed out with his other hand, plunging the creature's own spine through the transparent eye-like section and into its head. It screamed. The horrible breath washed over him again, and he scrambled backwards as it began to thrash and snap wildly. Lucan and one of his men had loaded crossbows, and they began shooting bolts into the thick body, as River's vines held it down. In a daze, Col watched River move in to finish the creature off. She had created an odd weapon, with a long, living wood handle. At either end, the wood engulfed the hilt of a dagger, resulting in a sort of spear that had long sharp blades at both ends. She danced lightly past the thrashing limbs of the beast, lopping off the remaining arm as it flailed, then stabbing her spear straight through its other eye spot until Col could see the end of the blade come through into the creature's gaping mouth. She twisted a couple times, just to be sure, and the creature stopped twitching.

Everyone stared at the gigantic creature, stunned at the sheer brutality they had just witnessed. Lucan finally shook off the shock and turned to Col.

"That was the bravest thing I've ever seen anyone do, Wolf. Not one of my men would have had the guts to charge at that thing head-on. Yet you showed no fear, and may well have saved my life."

Col was unused to being addressed by his surname, and even more unused to being praised for his performance in combat. He took a moment to recover from his surprise.

"Um, thanks."

"No, thank you." Lucan actually bowed. "I am your man, Wolf. I will follow you wherever you lead, and my men with me." His cold, expressionless eyes, for the first time, actually showed a soul behind them, burning with new loyalty. Col nodded his acceptance, knowing in his heart that things had changed. He could no longer go through with his plan of leaving these men. They were his people now, as surely as his village was, as Rig was, and as River, too, was. How could he possibly keep all these people safe? Nevertheless, he knew the option of hiding away in his village was no longer an option, not with all these people. This thing had grown too big, too important, for him to stop.

23

A half hour later, the scouts returned, as well as the two men bearing armfuls of brushwood. No one wanted to stay in the clearing, with the giant sand creature lying dead and twisted, so they moved on. The useful items from the dead men's packs were divided among the living, and Col found it strange how callous everyone else acted about the loss of lives. He had befriended all his companions during the day, and felt the weight of their deaths heavy on his heart. However, the bandits left the clearing without a backward glance. He jogged after, determined to prove himself the capable leader they all thought him to be.

As they settled down to sleep through the hottest part of the day, Col was pleasantly surprised to see River spread out her bedroll beside his. She made sure to touch the ground as little as possible as she curled up on it. He tried not to react to her presence, almost afraid he might spook her into going off on her own like usual. He lay back and pretended to sleep. However, she didn't seem interested in sleeping.

"That creature, are there many like it in this land?"

He gave up pretending and rolled to face her, eyes open.

"I've never seen one before. I've heard tales. They're called Scorpillon, I think. You see little ones that look similar, hunting bugs sometimes. This one was a Giant Scorpill-Tennebris, or a Canyon Scourge, as everyone calls it. I only know the proper name from reading books in the Temple. They're very rare. You can go a whole lifetime and never even see one of the smaller kinds. There are other kinds of creatures in the canyons, though. Lots. Few are bigger than a dog, though, and not very many will try to eat you. Some are even good to eat."

She sighed in relief, but still kept a suspicious eye on the night.

"This is a strange place. Strange creatures, and strange people. I think I know where we are, but in my day this land was a high country filled with falling water and rivers. The people who lived here would trade strange bird feather arrows and woven rope with my kingdom. I still see many birds, but it seems unbelievable that all the rivers could have disappeared in a heartbeat."

Col stared at her, astonished.

"You must have come from over a thousand years ago," he whispered, awed. "None of our oldest stories even tell of a time like that." She looked at him, and an emptiness showed in her eyes. She looked so lost, so distant.

"Everything I know is dead," she said, her voice dull, "not just the people, but the land, the memories, even the religion."

This got his attention, and his curiosity. She was finally talking about her past, and it was the opportune moment for him to ask the questions that had been gnawing at him.

"What religion did you have, in your time?" he asked. "What were your gods? Obviously you didn't worship the Messenger, since she's a fabrication centered around you. So if not her, then who?"

She shook her head.

"No gods. My people worshipped the Earth. They believed it created all the life on its surface, and that was why my bloodline was always revered. But I never believed it. I know the earth well, and it is far too dull an entity to have invented anything. It does as it is told, and follows the same patterns set out for it every year. I have always wondered who set out those patterns for it to follow. I never respected our holy men, though, as others did. I was so certain they were wrong."

Considering that he'd never seen her show respect to anyone, Col didn't find that surprising.

"I never believed either," Col admitted. "Despite being sworn into the Order of the Hand, I never believed what they told me. And I was right. You're no god, even if you are magical."

A frown wrinkled River's forehead.

"Yesterday, that man started to pray to me. It was disturbing. Do your people truly believe me to be a god? How could they believe that someone like me could have created the earth and life?"

"Well, no. Not just one person. Our people believe that there are lots of gods, and they all live on a mountain too high to see. We can't know them or see them, so the Messenger came to tell us what they wanted."

River snorted in derision.

"That's stupid. How could a group of people living up on a mountain have created everything? No group of powerful people can function without someone greater above them, telling them what to do. This is a law of nature and of all humans. I can only think that it would also be true of whatever created humans. If there were a large group of gods, all equally powerful but each independent, surely they would have torn each other and the world apart as they tried to decide how to run things."

Despite the fact that he didn't entirely believe in the things he had been taught, it still stung Col to hear her calling it stupid.

"Well, believing that a bunch of dirt and rock created everything is stupid, too," he shot back, but then felt silly. Why was he getting so defensive and arguing like a child?

She glared at him. Her mouth opened in a retort, but then she stopped, and looked confused.

"Yes, I suppose you are right." She flopped back onto her bedroll, and lay looking up at the bright sky.

"Neither belief seems likely to be true."

She was quiet for a long time, eyes half closed as she looked up at the bright sky through the bare branches of the trees above her. Assuming she was finished, Col was drifting off into sleep when she suddenly spoke again.

"I should like to know the truth, if there is one. It seems my only options are to embrace a faith that seems stupid, or reject everything and live filled with emptiness and questions."

Col was silent for a moment. He understood her feelings exactly, and remembered the moment in the clearing, trying to free River from the tree, when he had prayed to an unknown entity, frustrated that he did not know who or what, if anything, was listening. He couldn't deny the fact that the tree had let go of her not long after. That only gave him more questions, however.

"My mother believes in a different god," he offered. "She goes out to pray in the fields sometimes, and she says her god talks to her, and gives her strength."

River turned her head and fixed him with a quizzical look.

"Talks to her? Have you ever heard it?"

"No," Col admitted, "but I never followed her. Terren did, once, and claimed that he thought he saw a little boy around his own age holding our mother's hand. That doesn't seem like a very powerful god, does it? A little kid? I didn't think much of it. I was always too focused on joining the Order, and if I'd been caught claiming that a god speaks to me directly, the Hearer would probably execute me. They only tolerate the Silent Speaker guild because they are big enough to be too difficult to stamp out. But my mother hasn't been caught, and she seems happy. She's never broken, even when the Order took my father to die in the mines, or when food got scarce and she had to starve herself to feed her boys. Now she leads and feeds most of the village, somehow, and I think a lot of them believe that her god must be real."

A flash of pity crossed River's face, and he turned his face away, embarrassed. He didn't need her pity. Lots of people were poor. Most villagers had experienced starvation. But she didn't offer any trite little sympathetic remarks like many of his fellow acolytes would. Instead, she pushed herself up onto an elbow so she could still see his face.

"I should like to meet this woman, your mother." she said. "Perhaps she has some wisdom worth listening to."

Col swallowed back a surprised laugh. River, the magical, imperious princess from another time, wanted to meet his mother?

"She's a commoner," he reminded her. "Don't you, like, spit upon anyone who isn't royalty?"

She flushed bright red, and he felt a surge of satisfaction. Her haughty attitude made her delightful to mock.

"Of course not!" she shot back. "I'm simply not used to befriending them. However, considering the vagabonds we are currently employing as our troops, I doubt I could stoop any lower in my associations. Your mother, at least, is not a murderer."

Col grinned.

"How you have changed! Good job. I still remember how disgusted you were when we first met."

She gave him an exasperated look, not taking the bait.

"You were supposed to be a king, according to prophecy. Of course I was disappointed."

"Oh," Col felt his face flush. He smothered his feelings, refusing to reveal how much it hurt to be a disappointment to this woman. He turned away, vowing to himself that he would stop letting River's opinions affect him. He was so busy ignoring her, that he almost didn't hear her last words, muttered quietly as she curled up and closed her eyes.

"That was before I knew you."

She wrapped herself in the bedding and soon began to snore softly. Col was left suddenly very awake and desperately confused. What had she meant? And what should he do about it? His heart was pounding a rhythm quite contrary to his recent vow, and he lay there, wondering when he had grown so undeniably fond of the prickly, dangerous girl who lay sleeping a few feet away from him.

The Hearer was so astonished by the report that he actually cancelled all his plans, got into a carriage, and drove a team of horses at a full gallop all the way out to where the road ended. From there, it was several hours walk across the top of the plateaus until he could see the sight that the scout had reported.

It was incredible. Unbelievable. There, filling a massive valley and spreading across the landscape was a sea of vibrant green. It looked unnatural to his eyes. Poisonous. He was certain now. This strange outbreak of unnatural plant life was connected to the release of the Messenger from her prison. Having spent several hours every day in the presence of the crystal, he had no doubts about the magical properties of the prison and, therefore, was unsurprised that the girl within was more than merely human. However, the scale of this display of power boggled his mind. How did one fight a creature like that? He took a deep breath. He had to do this carefully, making certain not to aggravate her if he wished for her to be on his side. However, the boy had no strange powers. The moment the thought entered his head, the Hearer latched on to it. The boy. Nikolo. It was his fault. He was the one leading the Messenger astray. Take out the boy, and she'd be left lost in a strange world, uncertain where to turn. When that happened, the Order would be there. The Hearer smiled, slowly. His real enemy wasn't an otherworldly creature. It was a mere peasant boy. He turned to Eshbo, the Enforcer of God's Will.

"Put out a public warrant for the arrest of Nikolo Wolf. Make sure you specify I want him alive. I'd like to kill him personally."

The second day after the attack of the Canyon Scourge, River had recovered and was back to ignoring Col. He knew it was probably a good thing for her to recover from her trauma, but he selfishly missed the way she had been opening up to him. Traveling through the wilderness took a lot longer than traveling the King's straight roads on horseback, especially considering that they were trekking a convoluted course to avoid pursuit. As a result, they didn't reach the village of Grayson's Shaft until the end of the second day.

The canyons grew deeper as they travelled, with more and more forks, some so narrow that the cliffs closed back together overhead. The trees were gone, and they walked through a land of huge boulders and dry grasses. Signs of human habitation became evident in rope bridges crossing high overhead, and the occasional field of pale, sun-starved grain. It was early morning when they arrived. So early that the sun had not even risen in the land above, and they had to navigate by the light of the stars - as well as the small clusters of glow beetles that emerged from the dirt at night to scuttle across the canyon walls.

Most villagers would be awake by now. It was important to draw water during the morning, because by midday it would all have seeped away from the bottom of the wells. Nobody liked to drink mud.

Before they could make out the cluster of buildings in the gloom, they heard the dogs barking.

"Everyone except Lucan and River should stay back," Col ordered calmly. "The roads need to be watched for Priest-guards or visitors from one of the towns."

Lucan frowned.

"Shouldn't we bring more support? What if the villagers aren't friendly?"

Col grinned.

"I think River on her own is enough support."

He didn't say the real reason, the fact that this was where his family lived, and he wanted as few people to be privy to that information as possible. A fugitive's family was his greatest weakness. When applying for his role at the temple, Col had kept his family secret. They never assigned priests to gather taxes in their own village, and if he wasn't assigned to Grayson's Shaft he would not have been able to stop the extortion of his people. Lucan accepted his answer, however, without further questions. They emerged from the canyon onto a ledge. Grayson's Shaft opened up below them. It was a wide bowl far below, with sloping, hazardous trails descending into it. Some of the trails had collapsed due to rock slides, and the descent was perilous. The village itself was cuddled into the deepest corner of the bowl, with the more open area devoted to fields. Col knew it was silly, but he walked in front of River and took every opportunity to catch her hand when she lost her balance. Strangely enough, she didn't seem to mind. The trail was far more perilous than the main path that led to Kingsfall and other, larger villages.

When they reached the base of the cliff, five dogs were already there to meet them. Their growls turned to excited yips when Col greeted them. Lucan shot him a look of keen understanding, but said nothing about his suspicions. They passed through the fields with no one challenging them. However, several of the men out in the fields did not hail Col as usual, but instead eyed his companions with confusion. In the doorways of cottages, parents kept children from running forward. Lucan, with his weapons, garish jewelry, and grim face was a frightening sight, and River looked otherworldly with her aloof expression, vines flourishing impossibly around her waist.

The villagers might have held back, staring in fear, but Jehane, Col's mother, came running to meet them.

"Nikki!" She touched his face, almost fearfully, then tears welled up in her eyes as she pulled him close.

"Your cousin Naia came to tell us you were dead. She said she saw the squad march you to the cliff! We mourned you, and yet you are here!"

She pulled back from him to look him over, and her tone turned scolding.

"How could you put us through that? Where have you been? And who are these strangers you bring to our home?"

River looked at Jehane with new interest.

"This is your mother?"

Lucan just looked on impassively. Col looked around, noting villagers gathering at a wary distance, and considered where to start.

"Mother, how much did Naia tell you?"

Jehane shook her head in exasperation.

"Little enough. She said that she'd seen the Hand, and that you'd broken the sacred crystal, and that she'd been threatened on pain of death not to say anything about it to anyone. Surely that's not true?"

Col took a deep breath, considering the perfect words. But this was his mother. And she was looking into his eyes with those deep, perceptive wells of wisdom that had wrenched the truth out of him since he was a child.

His resolve broke, and the whole story came spilling out of him in bits and pieces like startled birds. She took it all in, emotions rushing across her face. Several times she looked about to interject, but she stopped herself every time and let him finish. When he was done, he noticed that nearly the entire village was gathered in a tight crowd around him, drawn in by the thrilling tale woven into reality by his earnest voice. Even Lucan, who knew a large portion of the events, was leaning in to listen. Col stopped, and was met with a moment of stunned silence and wide eyes. There was no doubt that they believed him. He was, after all, their boy hero. Then the questions started. Suddenly, everyone was talking. They wanted to know what he would do, what the Hearer would do, what kind of change they should prepare for. So many people started talking at once that Jehane had to flap her arms and yell to make them quiet.

"Calm down!" she snapped. "We will survive this, as we have everything else. In one hour, I would like the village elders to meet in my house, and we will discuss a plan with my son. Also, could someone please go fetch my boys from the field?"

Reluctantly, the crowd dispersed. Jehane turned to Col, and he anticipated a tongue lashing for getting into trouble and risking his family's safety. However, with Lucan and River close beside him, she seemed reluctant to vent her feelings. Instead, she was remarkably subdued.

"Would you like to come inside while we wait?"

The moment he stepped through the door, Col was met by the smell of home. A lingering scent of garlic hung in the air, as well as a dusty breeze through the open window, and the warm smell of a pumpkin and fig pie, which was currently cooking in the clay oven. He took a deep breath. River, stepping in behind him, looked around with curiosity. Jehane gestured for them to sit at the table, and soon served glasses of milk with hot slabs of the pie. Even in a time when food was scarce, she held to her belief of being a generous host. Tired of days spent eating dried travel rations, they all perked up.

"Thank you." Lucan gave Jehane a grateful, admiring smile, so different from his usual expression. Col suddenly realized that they were similar in age, and his mother still had a weathered beauty about her. He instantly caught the idea and sat on it, trying to smother it back out of existence. She smiled, but it was tight-lipped.

"So, you are the bandit who almost killed my son."

Lucan nearly choked on his milk.

"I assure you, once I understood that he was no friend of the Order, your son had nothing to fear from me," he hastily assured her. "In fact, I owe him my life, and he has my loyalty."

She gave him an unforgiving stare.

"If that is true, then I expect you to be willing to give your life to protect him, as he goes down this dangerous path of revolution." She said the word like it was a deadly disease. In that moment, Col understood all the things she wasn't saying to him, all the fears and worries he was causing her. Lucan nodded grimly.

"I am willing. If we succeed, we will be hailed as the saviors of all the people of this world. If we fail, at least we will have dealt damage to the foul Order that steals our loved ones and our food."

Col put his hand on the table, looking at his mother earnestly.

"We really can do this, Mother. I know the Order seems unbreakable, but if enough people know that it is a fraud, this world *can* change. This village could be free to live their lives without fear."

Jehane looked from Lucan to Col, her face full of trepidation. However, she nodded slowly.

"It seems the only path left to us. If we do nothing, the order will hunt you all your days."

She understood. Col felt a huge weight lift off of his chest. She didn't like it, but at least she didn't condemn his choices. He braced himself, preparing for a long, hard meeting of convincing his people to risk their lives for him, instead of the other way around. Of persuading them to secretly spread the truth about The Hand, and prepare themselves for some vague, unlikely day when the tables would turn against the Order, and they would be needed to join the revolution. It sounded foolhardy, even in his head. But he told himself that, if he were persuasive enough, they would listen.

25

They hadn't listened.

River wasn't surprised. Radical new ideas were never accepted by the men and women who had grown up around someone like Col. They likely still saw him as the little boy they remembered caring for, and not as a brilliant leader. They clearly adored him, but it was the adoration of fond adults cheering on a talented youngster, not the adoration of loyal troops ready to swear their lives to his service. The meeting had been a disaster.

Col was out in the field, now, walking with his youngest brother. The three other brothers and Lucan were still in the house, all four of them arguing passionately in favor of revolution. River trailed behind Col a few paces, walking in step with his mother, wondering how she could encourage Col. This place had begun to have a strange effect on her. Spending so much time with Col's charming, cozy family and thinking of him growing up here had made her feel strangely soft-hearted towards these struggling, starving villagers.

"How do you do it?" she asked suddenly. Col's mother turned and raised an eyebrow.

"How do you stand it, living in this place, while those Priest-guards slowly drain your life," River clarified. Jehane deflated at the apt description, but then lifted her chin in defiance.

"My god will protect me. He will keep my family alive because he loves us."

River held back the urge to snort in disbelief.

"How do you know that?" she demanded. Jehane smiled peacefully. Her eyes were too knowing, they made River nervous with the secrets they hid.

"Because he always has. We have been through hard times before. The Order took my husband away to work in their mines. He died there, as far as I know. And there was a summer when the Order took all of our bean crops to fill their coffers, and we had to survive on mere scraps. But through all of these times, I have gone out to the field to pray and my god has given me strength. I felt his love and comfort for the first time when I lost my husband and I was almost ready to break. He told me that things would get better. Every time, he provided a solution that would be just enough to keep us going. I trust that he will not fail this time either."

She smiled, eyes glowing with joy even after describing such horrible events. River was silent, staring at the woman in astonishment. She wondered whether the woman might be insane, believing that a god talked to her and *loved* her. Since when did gods care about humans? And yet, she seemed so wise and confident in her belief. River felt vaguely guilty for doubting her sanity.

"That's... hard to believe," she managed, "but I hope you are right."

Jehane gave her a calm nod.

"I am."

River felt unnerved, and hurriedly changed the conversation.

"These fields, what plants are they?"

"Beans.

Jehane bent down and picked a small, shriveled pod from the plant to show River. River accepted it, and stared at the sad little thing. The pod held a memory of what it was meant to look like, but there were whole fields of the things, and none of them was even half as tall as it was meant to be by this time of year. The morning light hadn't reached the fields, but it reflected off the white cliff above to shine a dull glare on the pathetic crop. River suddenly had an inspiration.

"I will help your village. Whether or not you support our cause, I will do this thing for you, out of kindness and because you are Col's people."

Jehane followed her, bewildered, as she turned and marched back toward the village, where a group of men and women were headed out toward the grain fields farther out in the canyon. She would want witnesses, for what she was about to do. If Col could not convince the people to support him, perhaps this would.

She kicked off her shoes discreetly at the edge of the bean field, then strode out onto the road to confront the group.

"Your boy, Col, is not only going to throw down the Order," she announced.

"We are going to remake the world. You can join us, or you can hang back and let a son of your clan march off to save you without raising a hand to help him. But either way, your world will change."

She turned, dramatically, to face the fields, head held high, posture regal. Then she stomped on the ground, mentally shaking the earth to get its attention. As soon as it became aware of her, she felt a leap of joy. This time, however, she determined that she would not let it get out of control. Again, a ripple of power rushed out from where she stood, gaining momentum in a joyous flood. However, this time, she tried to hold it back as it reached the edges of the canyon. She struggled and sweated, shoving it down into submission, railing at it to behave itself. It started to creep up the canyon walls, but finally relented.

The villagers stared, wide-eyed, as it happened. The wind turned warm, and wet. The ground softened, dry cracks smoothing out and fading to a moist, brown color. In the fields, things began to change in a rippling wave out from where she stood. Bean plants sprang up, growing as tall as her head, outgrowing the stakes set out for them and folding over to trail back down on the ground. Old, dry leaves broke off and fell away as new green ones unfurled in their place. Huge, juicy bean pods grew as thick as the leaves. Further out, the grain and corn grew a year's worth in one moment, shooting up, then turning from green to a rich, healthy golden color. Fig trees stretched tired boughs, the undersides of the branches thick with plump fruit. Squashes overflowed their patches, huge orange and yellow gourds growing so fast they popped out of the leaves like startled birds. Then it was done, and the rushing, rustling sound faded. The villagers were silent behind her. So silent that the only sound carried on the wind was the soft trickle of water as it seeped up out of the ground, making itself known in a place that had not heard the sound in hundreds of years.

"Imagine," she said softly, "how lives will change."

Of course, she didn't know if she could actually wake the earth for the whole kingdom, or whether it would go back to sleep again after she had left. She didn't know if she'd have to spend her whole life walking barefoot in giant circles through the whole kingdom to keep it awake. But let the peasants hope. Once she ruled them all, she could worry about those problems.

The silence broke as the peasants ran, laughing, out into the fields to begin the harvest. A few ran back into the town, shouting with excitement for others to come see. She wondered, belatedly, whether the astonishing spectacle hadn't driven her earlier words out of their minds.

Col came running, eyes fixed not on the beautiful valley but on her. He was grinning from ear to ear, and suddenly, before she knew what was happening, she found herself swept off her feet and spun around in an enthusiastic hug. It was dizzying, and lovely to be held in someone's arms again, after so long. She felt heat rushing to her cheeks. However, she came to her senses just as Col seemed to come to his. She locked away her emotions just as he dropped her, looking confused and embarrassed. She pinned him with a glare that would have melted stone. He backed away, and just like that things were back to normal between them. Jehane approached, with tears in her eyes.

"Thank you," she whispered, wrapping River in a motherly embrace that, somehow, River could not bring herself to pull away from. At some point that day, her impression of this woman had shifted, and she no longer thought of her as a common peasant woman.

"You have a great gift," Jehane told her. "You will help many people."

River didn't want to help many people. She wanted to rule many people. But she couldn't deny a deep feeling of satisfaction that unfurled inside of her, seeing the joyful celebrations all around.

A few minutes later, the council that had been conferring in Jehane's home came to witness the miracle. They regarded River with awestruck expressions. Col's brothers hissed questions at him in quiet voices, their eyes constantly darting to River, then away. Lucan was the only one who didn't seem pleased, when he came out of the village. He looked at River with distrust, and turned to Col.

"We should leave in the morning."

Col looked surprised, then shook his head with an air of authority.

"There's no rush. We have a harvest now, and there is plenty of food to go around. Fetch your men, and we will stay to help with the harvesting, filling up our supplies in the meantime."

It wasn't a very tactical move. River suspected Col was acting selfishly in order to spend more time with his family. However, he was so reasonable, so full of calm command and leadership, that no one questioned him.

They ended up staying for three days. By that time, the people had harvested their food and Col had won the village's promise of future aid. The waterfalls and springs in the valley had settled in to flow steadily with no signs of stopping. River had, initially, revelled in the awe she received, but now she grew tired of the constant attention. Of all the people she had encountered in this world, Col and his mother were the only ones who treated her like a normal human. Within the encircling canyon walls, there was nowhere she could go to avoid the admiring crowds, following her and waiting for something spectacular to happen again. She began to feel restless, and finally approached Col.

"We need to keep moving."

He sighed, but agreed.

"Alright, Lucan's been hounding me for days about that anyway. We'll leave with the sunlight."

26

Col watched River put on her shoes as they reached the path out of the canyon. It struck him as funny how bad she was at hiding her emotions. The fact that being separated from the ground made her powerless was a secret she tried to guard so well. And yet, her hunched shoulders and miserable face would have been plain to anyone watching. One would think the shoes were full of biting ants, the way she treated them.

They set off down a new path in the dusky evening. Col had no idea when he'd see his family again, and his heart wrenched at leaving them. But he couldn't ask them to join him in his hunted life.

As they walked, the plants began to glow with a dim red reflection. The sun was setting in a smoky red haze behind them. Then, Col started to smell the smoke. The two men who had been scouting ahead came pounding back down the trail, eyes wide. Col spun around, and had to hold back a shout of horror.

The sky behind them was lit, not by the sun, but by thick clouds of smoke, glowing from below with the orange light of fire. In that instant, all thoughts of tact, planning, and logic flew from Col's mind. He couldn't feel anything except a cold terror welling up inside of him. Without a thought for his own safety, he rushed back down the trail, desperate to find his family. When he reached the edge of the path, where it emerged from a crack in the canyon wall and descended down into Grayson's Shaft, he stopped. Clouds of acrid smoke were boiling up from the valley head. He had to get down on his stomach and crawl to the end of the ledge to avoid the worst of the smoke. Even so, when he put his head over the edge to look down onto his childhood home, the smoke stung his eyes. The fields were burning. The flames leapt up from every corner of the valley, greedily devouring the new crops where they stood. Fire licked at the low earth mound that surrounded the village, hungry to get through and devour the dry, straw-thatched homes inside. In many places, where storage barns had been built outside the makeshift wall, the fire had already begun its work, leaping high as it burned the precious food inside.

Several riders in the sleek black trappings of Priest-guards were riding horses up and down the wide roads between the fields, carrying torches. Other Priest-guards had dismounted and were dragging villagers out of their homes, inspecting their faces and then corralling them into the center of the village. From this distance, Col couldn't tell if any of them were his family members. River crawled up next to him to peek over the edge. He turned to her, frantic.

"We've got to save them!"

She looked at him, then shook her head sadly.

"I can't do anything from up here. And by the time we got down to the village we'd be spotted. If we kill the priests, more will come and kill the villagers as punishment."

"Then put out the fire!" Col insisted. "Can't you fill the air and the land with water?" His heart was pounding so hard he thought it might burst.

She gave him an incredulous look.

"Of course not! I can only awaken the earth, and it does the rest. When I do anything on so large a scale, I have very little control. The air and the water are just byproducts of the land's natural cycle as it speeds up. I can only directly manipulate plants and soil, and only those that are very close to me."

Col didn't understand a lot of the mechanics of what she had described, but he did understand that she was not going to be any help.

"But, my family!" he whispered, that horrible fear clutching at him. She sighed, looking sympathetic.

"The best thing you can do for them right now is to distance yourself. If the priests catch you trying to save them, they will only kill them and you. We have to get out of here before they realize we aren't in the village and come looking."

Everything inside of Col wanted to go charging recklessly down the cliffside, find his family, and throw himself bodily between them and any harm that might come to them. And yet, to his shame, the logic in River's words caught at him, holding him back. He wasn't a fighter, he knew that. River was the only one who had a chance at defeating the small band of priests destroying his home. If she refused to help him, he had no chance of liberating his village. Feeling like the most traitorous wretch in the world, he allowed himself to be led away from his burning home by River and the outlaw band.

He walked all of that night in a daze. He had failed his village, the people that he had devoted his whole life to protecting. He felt empty and lost. Without his village, who was he? Alongside these thoughts that horrible fear prowled, the fear that his family was dead. If they were, it would be his fault, he told himself. They continued through the wilderness for three days. Every time they stopped to rest, his dreams were full of fire and screams.

On the third day, they trudged down into a sandy, winding shaft that eventually opened up into a wide cavern with cracks in the roof high above that lit the space with thin sheets of sunlight. They were the first to arrive, and set up camp, waiting for Dirk and the rest of the men to arrive. The air was dry and cool, the soft curves of the sandy floor comfortable to rest against. Col hadn't realized his exhaustion before he sat down, and he drifted off almost immediately.

A familiar voice woke him up.

"Get up, you miserable log. We come all this way to find you, risking terrible danger, and you're just lying here snoring like a mud lump!"

Col's eyes snapped open. Just above his head, his older brother Tonis grinned down at him with astonishing cheer, considering the past events. He had a bit of soot smeared on his chin and one eyebrow was singed, but he was otherwise alive and well. Col was up like he'd been shot from a slingshot, and crushing the big dork in a gleeful embrace.

"You're alive!"

Tonis grunted, surprised at the uncommon show of affection.

"Of course, stupid. Everyone knows I'm stronger than you, so if you could survive a Cliff-hanging, obviously I'm going to survive when a couple snotty Temple Rats burn down our barn."

Col stepped back from him, and looked around. His younger brother Hankin was there, looking rather awkward in the midst of a large gathering of dangerous men, with a pack on his back that dwarfed him.

"The others? Are they here?" he asked eagerly. "How did you find us?"

Tonis gestured at Hankin.

"It's just us. Everyone else is in the village, but everyone survived. For now. With how much was burned, who knows how long it will be before someone keels over from starvation. A lot of people blame you for bringing trouble to us, but me and Hankin decided we wanted to join you and fight back against the Order. Mom said Terren is still too little, so he stayed. We followed the path you'd taken, and a day into the journey we stumbled into a bunch of bandits, but when they found out who we were they brought us here with them instead of killing us."

Col took the information in, feeling intense relief mixed with shame at the trouble he had brought to his village. Lucan spoke up, his back to the rock face, not looking up from the campfire he was poking at.

"Were you followed?"

Tonis shook his head.

"Not a chance. The Priest-guards had come from Henton. There's an outpost there, although there used to be only one guard. Word about the change in our valley spread faster than we thought, and they came out to investigate. We told them you'd gone to Bone Canyon, so they headed off down that way. We didn't follow you until we knew they were gone."

Col sighed. So much for his plans for rallying the Bone Canyon villagers. It was a bigger settlement than his village, and he'd expected to have an eager audience. However, the presence of his brothers filled him with joy.

"We'll make the Hearer hurt, for what he did to us," he promised, knowing it was what they needed to hear. He meant every word. Although he felt deep guilt for his village's sufferings, he also burned with rage against the brutality of the Order. They had burned his childhood home, and he would never forgive that, just as he would not forgive them for the death of his father. He straightened up to face the gathered men, steel in his gaze and his heart. The cavern fell silent, every eye turning to him. It was strange, how he seemed to always have that effect on people. It was something that had come naturally as he grew older, an ability to radiate a silent force that pulled eyes toward him. He never could understand what it was that people saw when they looked at him.

"We will make the Order pay in blood for every crime they've done to us," he said grimly. "After generations of ignoring us, they will finally hear the cries of the people they've stepped on, and it will be *their* turn to know suffering."

His words were answered by a cheer. Men who he'd barely had time to get to know, even some men who he didn't recognize, were looking at him with such admiration.

The day passed in a deluge of introductions, planning meetings, and preparation. Dirk had brought his family, as well as a large group of men from his base camp. They were all astonished as Lucan shared the tales from their trip. Several of the groups had met with success, rallying villages and hamlets to promise support. Some villagers had even left their homes to join Col's group. What had started with only a small band of outlaws had become over a hundred men by the end of the second day, well-stocked with provisions and bursting with energy. Col looked at the gathered crowd with a sense of astonishment. River approached him, and he felt his heart treacherously beating faster at her approach.

"Teach me to do what you do," she demanded. Although her tone was imperious, the words surprised him. Since when did River ever want to be taught anything?

"What do you mean?" he asked, confused. She gestured at the crowded cavern.

"This magic you do with words, tying men's loyalties to you like leashes. You are short, and bad at fighting, and yet you make people like you. Teach me."

His heart stuttered in his chest. Was that look in her eyes… *admiring*? Respectful, certainly. He wanted so badly to do as she asked.

"I can't," he admitted. Her eyes flashed with annoyance.

"Why not? Around others, you use these tactics, but when you speak with me you act like an irritating fool so that I cannot observe your techniques. I'm asking you to stop that, and teach me. Why not?"

Because you're beautiful, and completely out of my league. Because around you I get weak and lose all my strategies. He didn't voice the thoughts aloud. Instead he sighed, and lied.

"It's not something I do intentionally. It just sort of happens, and I don't know how I do it. Sorry."

Her eyes narrowed.

"I don't believe you. But fine, I don't need your skills, anyway. I don't need people to like me. They already fear me."

She turned and left, clearly stung. He watched her go helplessly, cursing himself for handling the conversation badly. The part of his brain that was always reading people noted that there had been underlying hurt in her words, not just at his lie but at the fact that people feared her. He subconsciously stored this information away for further study, but he couldn't bring himself to focus and puzzle it out. She always made him feel so small and useless. Girls had been chasing after him since he was young, much to the consternation of the bigger, stronger boys, and he had never before been so bothered by their attention as he was with River. She was, without a doubt, the most intimidating and yet intriguing person he had ever met.

27

The crowd gathered in front of the temple was restless, shifting uncomfortably. They didn't want to be there, huddling together and eyeing the guards blocking the gate out. After the most recent riot, the Hearer had simply had his guards drag everyone on the streets into the courtyard. There were several hundred who hadn't gotten off the street in time. The Hearer clasped his hands, standing on the dais at the great front doors of the Temple of the Hand. A string of priests stood around, prepared to catch his words and relay them to the furthest reaches of the crowd. It was beneath his station to shout.

"Your violence has grieved the gods," the Hearer said in a disappointed tone.

"You rise up against the Order, against me, against the very one who stands between this sinful nation and divine wrath. I am deeply grieved." He gestured to the priests, and they dragged out, at random, twenty people from among the crowd, uncaring if they separated family members. The Hearer had instructed them not to grab children, however. He wanted to inspire fear, not incite further rage against the Order. The Priest-guards forced the people to their knees in a long row. The Hearer raised his hands. It was a gesture of blessing, but the knife in his hand suggested otherwise.

"Twenty Priest-guards were killed this week," he cried. A ripple of anger moved through the lines of Priests listening, and a mirroring ripple of fear moved through the people.

"Twenty of your keepers," the Hearer repeated, "dead." He turned the dagger to point at the kneeling townspeople. They began to tremble and weep, beginning to guess at their fate.

"Violence for violence." the Hearer cried, voice rising. "You leave me no choice."

Deafening his ears to the cries of terror, the Hearer grabbed the nearest villager by the hair and killed him. Following his lead, nineteen other priests did the same. It was brutal, horrific, and so swift that the watching crowds had no time to react. The Hearer spoke into the stunned silence.

"Your hatred is misplaced. The real villains are the Rebels, those cowards who cause trouble but then slip away again, leaving honest people to take their punishment. From now on, a random person will be killed for every priest-guard that dies, unless the killer is brought forward."

The square exploded with sound. Screaming. Shouting. Blood spilling down the front steps of the temple of the Hand as if the gaping doors of the temple were drooling in hunger. The Hearer absorbed it all, feeling satisfied. Yes, oh yes. They would fear the Order now.

There was a sudden commotion at the far end of the cavern. Men were shouting in surprise, then outrage. Col ran in the direction of the noise, determined to break up whatever brawl was about to commence. These men were rough, and could be volatile. In their heightened state of excitement and bloodlust, it was hard to keep them from fighting. However, when he reached the edge of the cavern, he found a far more surprising sight.

Five men lay on the ground. Two were groaning, and Col prayed the other three were merely unconscious, not dead. Backed into a corner near the rear passageway out of the cavern, surrounded by men with swords and knives aimed at him, was none other than Dominik, the mysterious Rebel soldier.

"It's a spy, Sir!" one of the men exclaimed as Col stopped short, staring. The attack on the rebel camp seemed like a lifetime ago, and he'd almost forgotten that Dominik and Annora had been off scouting.

"He got past our lookouts somehow, and came sneaking all the way down the passageway without anyone seeing him! We caught him hiding in the shadows spying on us!" the man continued, his machete wavering as he pointed it at Dominik's face.

Col looked sharply at Dominik, and found his own surprise mirrored in the man's face.

"Sir?" he demanded. "So you're the leader of these brigands, not their prisoner? How could you betray your oaths, brother?"

Col raised his hands in a calming gesture.

"Dominik, It's good to see you are alive. I swear to you that I had nothing to do with the deaths of your comrades. However, these men aren't the enemy. The attack on our camp was a terrible accident."

Dominik snorted.

"You call three brutal murders an accident? Talk all you like, but you can't justify your alliances to me."

"They didn't know we were working against the Hearer," Col protested.

"These men have just as much cause to hate the Order as you Rebels do, Dominik. We have a common enemy. By all rights, we should be allies."

The crowd of men shifted restlessly. Col heard disgruntled murmurs.

"Foolhardy City Folk."

"Look what he did to Lilidan! He's barely alive!"

"Rebels just cause us more trouble than they solve."

Col did it again, that drawing of attention to himself. All he had to do was stand up straighter and shift a bit so they knew he was about to speak.

"I don't agree with the Rebel's plans. I believe we can take down the Order, but not in the careful, small way that the Rebels like to act. It isn't just about revolution, it's about creating a new, better world where water flows across the land and no one starves. We're fighting *for* this hope, not just against the Order. If you've been following us, Dominik, then you've seen what River can do to the land. She isn't a pawn to be sacrificed to topple the Order, she's a miracle."

Dominik's eyes were narrowed, skeptical.

"The Rebellion will never join you. You were supposed to be following our orders, not leading your own army. You're a traitor."

"I'm not asking for allegiance," Col said softly, "only alliance against a common enemy. Call me a traitor, but I have always been, and will always be, loyal to the people of this land, and an enemy of the Hand. You can hate me, but don't let that make you stupid and ignore wise tactics."

The tall man brushed his hand through his coal black hair, clearly conflicted. He sized Col up, and Col held his gaze unflinchingly. The atmosphere was tense, the silence thick with distrust.

"Alliance, then," Dominik agreed reluctantly, seeming to hold a new, grudging admiration for Col. "I underestimated you, boy. I should have known you wouldn't settle for a role doing Rebel grunt work. I'll pitch your case to the Rebels, but I doubt they'll agree. They're not going to forget your betrayal."

A thought struck Col.

"Is Annora still with you?"

Dominik nodded.

"I left her outside."

"Send her," Col decided. Dominik looked offended.

"But I'm much higher ranked! I am Grimald's secret weapon, his right han-"

"You're also a drag," Col cut him off, the words harsh, but his tone logical. "Annora is charming and persuasive. The support of your reputation is more convincing than your actual presence. You are many awe-inspiring things, Dominik, but you're not much of a wordsmith or politician."

The man bristled, his cool, dangerous composure fraying, giving Col a glimpse of a man who cared too much about how people saw him. However, he caught his outrage by the tail and dragged it back under control with visible effort.

"Very well," he said at last, stiffly. Then, as if to repair some of the damage to his image, he walked directly at the nearest weapon pointed at his face, forcing the man to step back and give him a path free of the bristling wall of blades.

"Let him go," Col ordered the disgruntled outlaws. "He may be fighting for a different cause, but the Rebels aren't going to give away our location to the Hearer. We can trust them that much."

He watched Dominik leave with the languid grace of a tiger. He hadn't shown it, but seeing the face of the man had dredged up so many bad memories. Of all the rebels he had come to know, Dominik was the only one he didn't like. The man was everything he wasn't: dangerous, imposing, and arrogant. He got under Col's skin with his dismissive ways, and while it irked Col to consider working with the man again, at the same time he mourned the loss of his other companions, slain by the bandits. It was an uncomfortable reminder that, while he inspired the loyal villagers at the heart of all his men, they were still thieves and killers, every one of them. He took a deep breath. Like him or not, he would have to work with Dominik for the sake of his cause. With the ruler of the known world determined to kill him, he could not afford to be picky about his allies. With a sigh, he determined to attempt to charm the taciturn rebel.

As the sky, glimpsed through cracks in the cavern roof, faded from pink to dark blue, the men settled down around campfires interspersed across the floor. There was singing, wrestling, and enthusiastic eating happening everywhere Col glanced.

"You've given us something to hope for," Lucan noted, poking a stick at the fire next to Col.

"I've never seen the men this happy."

Dominik said nothing, sitting reluctantly at Col's fire with ample distance between himself and the others. He eyed the raucous crowd with distaste. Col turned to consider the men. Over a hundred living, breathing humans, all flocking to the banner of an incompetent youth. He felt woefully inadequate.

"It won't last," he predicted grimly. "They'll feel invincible until the first group runs into some actual Priest-guards and gets slaughtered. Then they'll realize how outmatched we are, and turn back into the desperate men they were."

"But desperate men fight harder!" Dirk reminded him, his face jovial as he sat across from them, surrounded by his five sons with his arm around a tall, tired looking woman whom Col assumed was his wife.

"Cheer up Wolf! Tonight we celebrate a victory."

"What victory?" Col was confused.

"Why the victory of not dying yet!" Dirk rumbled. His laugh was so loud it echoed back at him from the far cavern wall. "The victory of growing numbers and food in our bellies."

Lucan raised a cup in toast to that, grim mouth quirking up in a wry grin. Col couldn't feel their cheer, however. He eventually ended up excusing himself, taking his food and wandering off in search of the one person who was conspicuously missing.

River sat in a little hollow of dry dirt just outside of the entrance to the cavern. When Col emerged from the narrow passageway, he could barely make her out among the tall rocks and tangled scrub growing on the slope. The canyon wall overlooked a wide swath of cracked dirt and sand, too dry to support a village or town. River sat in a huddled lump, her face glum.

He approached, pushing aside his own moodiness to better tackle the task of cheering her up.

"I brought you some food." The sentence had become a nightly tradition by now, his attempt at a peace offering to help him scale the walls of solitude she put up around herself.

"A nearby village gave us fresh vegetables. I thought you might cheer up if you got something other than all the dried spicy stuff we've been eating."

"Everything you eat is dry, even the vegetables." River eyed his offering disdainfully. "And how could you expect food to cheer me up? You don't know what it is to be lost, without anything in the whole world left to remind you of home."

It really did sound awful, the way she put it. He thought for a long moment, then made a daring move and sat down beside her without an invitation. The silence between them was tense. He wondered if she still resented him for lying to her. Certainly there was a new barrier in place between them, and words did not come as easily.

"Are the stars, at least, unchanged?" he asked at last. Both of them looked up, taking in the vast, brilliant display of sharp white lights above them. The moon was behind a cliff, and the stars shone all the more brightly for the lack of it, glittering in the dark blue dome. River let out a soft breath of awe, seeming momentarily shocked out of her defensive shell.

"They are familiar," she whispered, "but so clear and sharp tonight."

Col turned to find her staring at him, her expression unreadable in the shadow of her hair. She was breathtaking, as always, but breathtaking like a statue, not a living, breathing woman. She'd locked her humanity up so tightly inside of her that it hardly ever peeked through the bitter shell.

"I suppose I spoke wrongly," she said, her tone ironic. "Everything in this whole world is unfamiliar, *except* the stars... and your eyes."

What? Was she flirting with him? But her tone was far too

factual for that, and he couldn't imagine her flirting with anyone. He wanted to demand an explanation, but his sense of diplomacy told him to hold back the outburst. In this mood, it was the most likely thing to ruin the moment and make her clam up again. Instead, he held his tongue and looked back at the stars, waiting.

"I had a… good friend with eyes just like yours," she said, haltingly, as if the words were difficult. "Nothing else about you is the same, but your eyes are so alike, so unique. I am certain that somewhere in the distant past he was your ancestor." She stuttered to a stop, as if suddenly realizing what that meant. "He's really dead, and gone. Everyone is. It's not just that I left them, I outlived them."

Her eyes were wide and blank as she stared up at the sky, no longer seeing it.

"I hope he found happiness," she whispered.

Col was reeling from the revelation. Despite her calling the man a "good friend", the implications were obvious. She'd been in love with his distant ancestor. It was a horrible revelation. Was that why, despite her disdain for peasants, she had still rescued him? The reason behind all those looks, every bit of affection she'd ever shown him? All this time, he'd believed he was gradually breaking down her walls, charming her. Had she really just been thinking of a long-dead lover every time she looked at him? And, like a fool, he'd let himself be bewitched by her moments of vulnerability, her longing gazes, when all the while they had been meant for someone else! He felt so foolish.

He wanted to run far away, hide in a hole, or stand on a cliff and scream at the universe. Maybe all three at once. Instead, he forced himself to remain calm.

"I'm sure he did," he managed, his words a bit too stiff and unnatural, "but I'm also sure all the people of your land regretted losing you. I'm sure you were missed by many people."

She was silent for so long he thought she was angry with him again. But then he saw a glimmer of wetness on her cheeks.

"You don't know anything about them. Everyone hated me," she snarled. But the emotion was forced, and he could tell that the words had affected her deeply. He knew she wanted to be wrong. So, like he had always done since he was young, he pushed his own emotions aside for the sake of saying the right words to someone else.

"No one could hate you," he said, not bothering to wonder if it was true, "but fear and selfishness can push love down and smother it, making people treat others unkindly. Just because they didn't show you love doesn't mean it wasn't there."

Of course, Col had no idea if River's family had loved her, or if everyone had indeed hated her. But the poor girl had enough hurt in her life to make this burden one she didn't need to bear. She could never go back and find out what was true, but if she lived her life believing that she had been loved, surely that would help to heal the pain of losing her people. She started crying now, in earnest, and he knew from her body language that she didn't want him witnessing. His own emotions roiling like a sour stew inside of him, Col was only too happy to leave. He needed time alone to stitch his heart back together, and to erect some walls of his own between himself and this girl who, he was just realizing, he barely knew at all.

Getting up, Nikolo Wolf walked alone into the desert night.

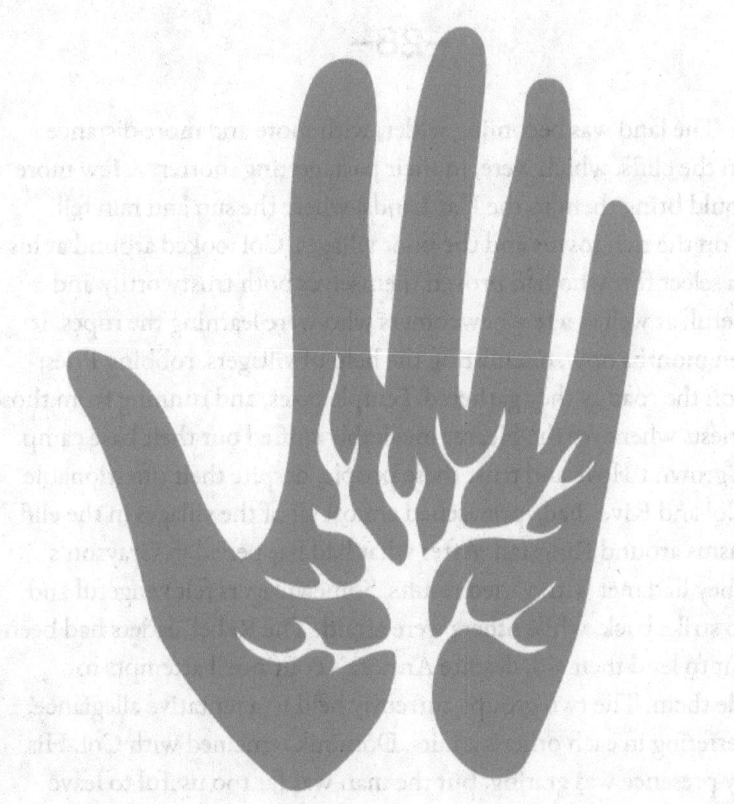

Part Two

The birth of a heretic

28

The land was becoming wider, with more and more distance between the cliffs, which were, in their part, getting shorter. A few more days would bring them to the Flat Lands, where the sun and rain fell equally on the rich towns and the poor villages. Col looked around at his band - a select few who had proved themselves both trustworthy and resourceful, as well as a few newcomers who were learning the ropes. It had been months now, of enlisting the help of villagers, robbing Priest-guards on the road as they gathered Temple taxes, and running from those same priests whenever the Hearer inevitably sniffed out their base camp. He had grown to love and trust these people, despite their questionable pasts. Col and River had approached almost all of the villages in the cliffs and chasms around Kingsfall. After what had happened in Grayson's Shaft, they had met with varied results. Some villagers felt vengeful and ready to strike back, while others were afraid. The Rebel leaders had been reluctant to lend their aid, despite Annora's continued attempts to persuade them. The two groups currently held to a tentative allegiance, not interfering in each other's affairs. Dominik remained with Col. His haughty presence was grating, but the man was far too useful to leave behind. Now, Col faltered as he looked out at the strange country stretching before him. He was leaving terrain that felt like home for strange, foreign places. But the rule of the Order extended far beyond the cliffs, and the time had come to take his plan one step further. One positive thing was that since the Hearer had no accurate drawings of Col and River, they could travel openly into these lands, far enough away that no one would recognize them. Hoisting his pack, he trekked resolutely onward.

In addition to the new habit of maintaining the awkward silence between them, River had taken to wearing sandals. It was a compromise between his constant fear of her powers giving away their location, and her fear of being separated from the earth. She left no trail of growing things in her wake, and the front lip of each sandal was cut short so that if she needed to she could stand on her tip-toes and create a connection to the ground. Col still worried, however. He needed her presence to convince villagers that they had a chance against the Order. However, her powers were growing more and more out of control. It was a difficult challenge, as they travelled and slept on the ground, to keep River from touching any dirt or living thing. The earth had begun reacting in a volatile way to her slightest touch. If even one of her hands slipped off the edge of her sleeping roll and touched the ground, they would wake to find themselves in a beautiful pocket of verdant woods. It was terrifying - the idea of leaving markers like pins on a map of places where they had been. How long would it take the priests to discover a pattern?

They were headed, at long last, to Illsbeth. Located on the slopes of a mountain thick with iron ore and at the mouth of the River Bleakley, it was an important source of weaponry for the Order, as well as a trade hub. Nonetheless, it was small enough that there would be no temple there, which was a relief. However, it reportedly had a garrison of King's men stationed there, and Col was nervous. Of course, he didn't show it. The village was still four day's travel away, and they had several small hamlets to visit along the way. There were many more immediate things to worry about, Col knew. Such as the fact that they were traveling into the domain of another bandit lord. They were traveling at a frightening pace, in fact. While there were main roads all throughout the region, cutting straight lines over the tops of cliffs with strong wooden bridges to make travel quick, those roads were constantly patrolled by Priests and King's men, with toll booths that would be sure to discover the group's identity. As a result, Col had become accustomed to traveling in slow, winding loops through canyons. Now, with the canyons falling away, he was unnerved by the straight line they cut through the wilderness.

As the hours passed, the land leveled out. Col could see his own thoughts reflected on the faces of his men, as they glanced around to find no cover in sight. The sky was so wide. Instead of a bright sliver directly above his head, it was everywhere, taking up an almost offensive amount of space in every direction on the dull brown plain, like a very large, very richly dressed lady in a roomful of orphan children, looking down with disdain at their drab clothes and grubby faces. The sun beat down like Col had never experienced it in the canyons, with dry, shrivelled scrub doing its best to drink up the light. Every now and then they passed a farm with wide fields around it. With all the new scenery, it took all of Col's willpower to maintain the calm composure of a leader, when his face kept threatening to betray him and gawk like a daft peasant. At any rate, he refused to look less composed than Dominik. Nothing seemed to faze the taciturn man. No matter what they encountered, he strode on with purpose and confidence. He had proved himself to be a reliable and powerful ally, but Col still disliked taking him on these trips. At that moment, Dominik was drilling the newcomers on how to attack a priest-guard. Most of the bandits relied on overwhelming numbers when attacking a guarded caravan, as they lacked the training and sophisticated weapons that every Priest-guard had. Dominik, however, was uncannily skilled with weapons. As far as Col could figure out, he'd never spent time training with the Order or as a King's man. It made no sense that he had the skills that even Lucan, with years of experience fighting Priest-guards, could never hope to match. River joined in, giving pointers to the men on using the terrain to their advantage, and suggesting techniques that Dominik didn't know. Together, they were the two most dangerous fighters Col had ever seen, even within the walls of the Temple of the Hand. He felt quite incompetent by comparison, and annoyed at the way Dominik and River regarded each other with such admiration. He still didn't feel comfortable about the fact that she had loved his ancestor, but he felt even less comfortable with the idea of her falling in love with Dominik.

"Too slow," Dominik barked. "If that bush had been a priest-guard, they would have dodged your first strike and had time to see the second one coming. In fact, they would have had time to skewer you in between. You're dead."

Doogal, a young bandit and a newcomer to Col's band, stopped whacking at bushes and threw his two hatchets at the ground.

"By the Messenger's glowing arse!" he cursed foully, "it isn't like I'd ever engage a priest-guard on my own, anyway! I'd have at least five men."

River's face paled at the foul language. She was, technically, the Messenger by which the man cursed. Col stopped walking and fixed the man with a hard stare.

"Doogal." he reprimanded sharply, "I know you're new to the group, so I'm giving you this one warning. We do not curse by the Messenger, or the gods, or any of the other lies that the Order has concocted. If you want to speak to the real Messenger, you may call her River, and you will be polite. Additionally, you may not have a choice to bring five men with you to attack a priest-guard. These tactics might just save your life if you ever find yourself alone with one, and you should respect the training."

River shot him a thankful look, and Col felt a surge of satisfaction. Doogal hung his head, mortified that Nikolo Wolf, king of the bandits, had reprimanded him. Col was still getting used to the power he held over men like Doogal. He hated being responsible for so many lives, but he couldn't deny that the instant obedience was a bit intoxicating.

"Forgive me, sir. I will do my best to learn."

Col nodded, accepting the response.

Not long after, they approached a small village. Col didn't know the name, but it was a scattered group of houses and barns with a few trees rising above the roofs, surrounded by a ramshackle fence. There was no hand symbol blazoned above the gate to the village, so Col knew that there must not be any Priest-guards stationed there. They entered without fear.

As they approached the village well, Col prepared to give his persuasive speech, throwing back his cloak to reveal his scarred arms. However, they found a group of women waiting at the well.

"We know who you are." A woman with tawny, tangled hair and a red sash gave Col a small bow, blushing furiously.

"We've heard of The Wolf, the man who freed the Messenger from the Temple of the Hand and fights against the Order. We know that you intend to change the whole world like you changed Grayson's Shaft, and the village has decided what to do when you finally came here." She took a deep breath, still blushing but regaining a measure of confidence.

Astonished, Col stood there watching as she pulled out a scroll and began reading out the villager's terms.

"We will agree to lend our aid to the Wolf when he needs it. We will give one tenth of our grain harvest to feed your men, and ten of our strongest men will join you if you teach them to fight and allow them to return to their village during planting and harvest. In return, we want the Messenger to heal our fields and cause our blackberry thickets to grow again. Do you accept these terms?"

She was calm as she read, like she was conducting a transaction. It took Col a moment to recover from his shock. He had no idea that the news of his deeds had spread so far. Behind him Sibyl, his trusted scout, laughed.

"It seems your reputation is doing our work for us... *Wolf.*"

Col cringed at the nickname. It seemed so aggressive and dangerous. He didn't feel either. Nevertheless, he knew a good deal when he heard one. He turned to River and addressed her in a hushed voice.

"Can you revive the blackberry thickets without making it obvious you were here?"

She looked uncertain.

"I can try."

"Good enough."

He turned back to the group of women with his most winsome smile. It was his most powerful weapon, and never used lightly.

"The terms are acceptable. We thank you for your support in this fight. It is because of people like you that the Order will fall."

The women reacted to his smile as most women did, like butter reacts to sunshine: growing soft and melting. River scowled at their flustered, blushing faces and shining eyes. For some reason, the scowl made him feel better than the swooning did.

The tawny-haired lass led them to the blackberries. Col learned her name was Eithne, and she was the only one in the village who had travelled to a temple to learn to write, making her the village Harvest Keeper, an important role in farming areas, as she would keep track of the Temple taxes, food rationing, and planting calendar. Without a rehearsed speech to fall back on, she was thoroughly flustered and spent most of the walk in awkward silence, eyeing Col every time she thought he wasn't looking.

As they left the village, Col turned to River.

"What's bothering you?"

River, who was clearly stewing, didn't need any further prompting.

"It's ridiculous." She hissed. "I'm the one who is destined to rule, I'm the one who can heal their land. But all these villagers think you're the big handsome hero, come to dazzle them with your charm, kiss their babies, and fight off anyone who might harm them. They see me as nothing but a weapon."

"I don't see you that way," he assured her gently. "I see you as a source of hope. I couldn't have done any of this without you. You're the hero, not me. This kingdom needs you to save them. Does it really matter what random strangers think, as long as we know the truth?"

She still scowled, but he could tell it was more for show than anything else.

The blackberry bushes were planted in several wide circles around the village. Had they been healthy, they would have provided not only food but also a substantial defense against invaders or wild animals with their thick tangle of thorns. However, they were brown, shrivelled, and dead with large patches of the dead branches taken for firewood, leaving nothing but stumps. River tentatively placed one hand on the ground, her brow furrowed.

For a moment, nothing happened. Then nothing continued to happen. Seconds stretched into minutes, and River's forehead began to bead with sweat. The ground began to tremble, but no greenery emerged at all. River was sweating harder now. Col watched in amazement, recalling how she had transformed all of Grayson's Shaft with barely any effort in comparison.

It took three hours. Col stayed with River, while the villagers came and went, then eventually stopped coming as they grew bored. The rest of the band left to have dinner in the village, but still Col stayed, and still River concentrated. The vines grew with agonizing sluggishness. Keeping anything else from growing was costing River so much that she didn't even have the strength to get irritated at his jokes and comments. Col took advantage of that, and started telling her a ridiculous story about a queen who outlawed burping. It was a tale that he made up on the spot but he told it like the solemn truth. There was no end to the ways he could annoy her, and he found it funny how she knew nothing of the history of his civilization, and so she believed almost anything he told her. Unfortunately, this time she didn't seem to be paying much attention to him.

Finally, River stood up.

"That should do it," she whispered, then staggered into him. He supported her, rather clumsily, as they headed back to the village.

The village was surrounded by several rows of tall, healthy hedges now. They had some blackberries, but the fruit was a normal size for the climate. The grain crops in the fields were thicker and taller than they had been, but not yet ripe. Everything was perfectly ordinary, and Col found tears of relief welling up in his eyes. After what had happened to his home, he was terrified every time River touched the ground that she would bring the wrath of the Order crashing down on them. As he watched her walk, dazed, into a crowd of cheering villagers, he felt his heart lift. Maybe this could really work. Maybe they really could outrun the Hearer and turn his own country against him.

29

Illsbeth was at the foot of a mountain. Everyone knew that about the mining town, but Col had never truly comprehended what that meant until he stood looking down on it. Avoiding the road had meant following perilous goat trails to the village, and when they finally caught sight of the place they were far above it, with the only approach a steep scramble which would be hazardous in the dark. The village sprawled on the slope, vastly dwarfed by the gigantic mound of stone it hugged. The iron-rich mountain was dark rock, patched with groves of trees. Where the stone showed, it had mottled colors on it like none Col had ever seen. He was used to rocks being brown and sandy, not these smooth, polished surfaces that glinted in the light of the moon.

Everything about Illsbeth was fascinating. The twinkling spread of lights in the darkness indicated more houses than any village he had yet visited. The houses spread across the gentle slope at the base of the mountain, then continued up in scattered lights to cling to the increasingly steep rocks until the builders gave up and the lights petered out as the incline became undeniably cliff-like. The walls were of wood, instead of stone or dirt. The white rush of the River Bleakley shone bright under the moon, as it leapt from a gap in the mountain with a roar, rushed through the town energetically, then continued in a calmer fashion to make its long journey to join the Thude in the Flat Lands. The most astonishing thing, however, was the building at the center of the village. High walls surrounded a gigantic structure that straddled the river, water flowing under a gate at one end and emerging from the other. It was thick, squat, and ugly, with none of the triangular windows and spiky decorations Col had come to associate with temples of the Hand. However, there was a massive hand symbol emblazoned above the main gate, so it was undoubtedly an edifice belonging to the Order. Guards with torches patrolled the top of it, but if the peasant's information at the last village had been correct, this structure was guarded by King's men from the nearby barracks, not priests. Despite his weak grip on the country, the king was not going to let the Order have complete control over the village that supplied the primary flow of wood and iron to the rest of the country.

Col had taken to silently praying, not to the Messenger or anything else, but to the mysterious force that had caused the tree to relinquish River in that clearing so long ago. He hadn't realized how common the habit had become until he caught himself doing it as they scrambled down the slope, silently begging for a smooth, uneventful visit.

The village had no gate. It was too spread out for that. As they walked between the houses unannounced, Col felt his tension ebb away. Other than the scrapes and bruises they had all acquired during the descent, they were unharmed and had raised no alarms.

They passed a house where, through the open window, Col could see a happy-looking family eating dinner. Three old people, likely grandparents, talked and laughed, while a younger couple listened politely and five children vigorously attacked their meal. He knocked, hoping to find a sympathetic ear among such friendly folk. The voices inside died down, then a man opened the door. He was, presumably, the father of the children that crowded behind his legs, eager to catch sight of the visitor.

"What is it?" he asked, his voice pleasant, but eyes cautious.

Col gave him a friendly smile.

"So sorry to bother you, friend, but could you kindly direct me to the home of a village elder or senior craftsman? I come bearing news that will have an impact on the village."

The man took in the sight of Col, a sun-darkened and mysterious stranger with travel-worn clothes. He didn't seem to catch sight of the crowd of rough-looking outlaws Col had brought with him, as they hung back in the shadows. However, his eyes did pick out River. Never one to simply let Col lead, she hovered at his shoulder. The man looked her over keenly, taking in every detail of her exotic features that could be seen in the shadows of her hooded shirt. Then he looked back at Col.

"I've some suspicion of who you might be, friend," he said, lips curling in a hesitant smile. "I won't call a village elder, but if you wait here I will run and gather the Guild leaders. The Iron-working guild is more influential here than our elders."

Col thanked him with sincerity. The man nodded distractedly, then hurried into the house to have a quick word with his wife before he headed off into the night. Col turned, his gaze seeking out Dominik in the shadows. The man was nearly invisible but his gaze was trained on Col.

"Follow him, make sure he goes where he said he's going, not to the king's guards," Col requested quietly. Dominik nodded approvingly, then slipped off into the night without a word. The family seemed lovely, but Col wasn't stupid enough to trust the safety of his whole group to his first impression of a person.

The street was eerily quiet now. As if the people in the houses had begun to sense the presence of outlaws creeping through the dark of the streets. The group retreated to the shadow between two houses as the sky grew from dark blue to pure black, and people began to blow out the candles in their homes.

At long last, Dominik slunk into view, melting out of the shadows. He approached Col and River where they crouched.

"He gathered the guild leaders into a house and seems to be coming directly back here," he reported. River shot him an admiring glance, which Col pretended not to see.

"Good work," he smiled.

At that moment, the man himself hurried up the street, trying not to look suspicious and failing. As he approached, Col stepped into the light. The man jumped, then calmed himself.

"If you'll follow me lad, I'll take you to see them," he said, looking nervously at the darkness behind Col, where the rustle of bodies and moving shadows made it clear Col was not alone. At the sound of the man calling Col 'lad', several of his men stepped forward, bristling. However, Col motioned them to stay back. He thanked the man graciously, then turned to his men.

"I'll take River, obviously, Dominik, and Doogal. Sibyl, I want you to stay and watch the roads for any... unexpected arrivals." She nodded, knowing he meant priest-guards.

As they followed the kindly villager down the road, Col could see very little of the village. The houses went from loosely scattered dwellings to a tighter arrangement, with orderly roads and signposts. There were several white sheets of paper pinned to these, but in the darkness Col couldn't read them.

Dominik took up a post by the door, as the rest of them were ushered into a large house, wherein Col found a group of about twenty people gathered. They were all men, all with thick arms and strong hands, even those whose hair was white with age. Shaking hands, Col couldn't help noticing that he was by far the youngest and slightest man present. Taking a deep breath, he shoved down his intimidation, forcing it to cower in the back of his mind as he let a more confident version of himself take over.

"You may have heard of me," he began, and the men fell silent.

"My name is Nikolo Wolf, and I have come to bring you news that will change the world."

"We've heard of you." An old man with bushy eyebrows leaned forward, fixing Col with a skeptical stare.

"We've heard many things, some too ridiculous to believe. They say you can cure hunger in the land, that you travel with a sorceress who can pull rivers out of nowhere. They say all kinds of things. But what they all agree on is that you're trying to fight the Order, like those dratted Rebels that are always causing trouble and bringing the Priest guards swarming around our ears. We want none of that, thank you."

A different man placed his hand on the old one's arm, silencing him.

"Not so hasty, Olger. At least let him speak."

He turned shrewd eyes on Col, sizing him up.

"All of the things we've heard have been hearsay. Why don't you tell us this news you say you have, and we'll withhold any decision until after we've heard you out?"

The others nodded with varying degrees of hesitancy. One of the men stood up.

"This will need strong drinks all around," he stated, almost glumly, and headed out of the room, disappearing deeper into the house.

Col turned to address the men, telling his story from start to finish. He found he had to tailor it carefully, as these were not poor villagers who hated the Hearer for personal reasons. Instead, he had to appeal to their honor and sense of outrage, convincing them to throw down the Hearer because he was a fraud who had deceived them and had no right to rule.

As he spoke, however, the men began to look more and more uncomfortable. It was distressing. He knew he was saying the right things, and if he had judged these men correctly they should be responding more positively. However, their silence was almost stubborn. Several of them were even glassy-eyed, as if they weren't paying attention despite the gripping tale his voice was weaving in the air around them. Col faltered, losing his hold on the story as he neared the end, letting it fizzle out instead of closing it with a rousing invitation to join his cause, as he had planned. The silence in the room was awkward.

Finally, the man who had initially invited him to speak took a deep breath.

"Fantastical as it may seem, I actually find myself believing it. They weren't kidding when they told us you were a charming man."

Col frowned. "Who told you?"

At that moment, Dominik burst into the room, his expression urgent.

"Sir, look at this!" He thrust a paper into Col's hands. It was of a similar size and shape to the ones Col had seen tacked to various posts around the village. He had to squint to read it in the flickering light of the room's hearth.

NOTICE

Be aware that a man calling himself "the Wolf" is abroad in the land. All citizens beware! This man is a dark sorcerer and must be stopped at all costs. Through profane magics this man destroyed our most holy artifact, shattering the crystal and freeing the Messenger. Through unholy arts he trapped the Messenger in a mortal form, and seduced her with his charm. Our holy Messenger must be freed from the thrall of this man at all costs. He is a heretic, possessed of unnatural charm and determined to destroy our link to the will of the Gods. Any sightings of this man must be reported to the Hearer immediately.

Any information leading to the capture of the Heretic will be rewarded by the Order of the Hand with twenty pounds of silver.

Any citizen caught aiding the dark sorcerer in any way will be guilty of crimes against the gods and sentenced to death by Cliff-hanging.

The message bore the mark of the Hand below it. Col read it in shock, then looked up at the guildsmen gathered in the room. A suspicion began to surface as he read the looks on their faces by this new light.

"We're really very sorry." The old man's bushy eyebrows were drawn into a pained frown.

"Especially after hearing this story from your point of view, this doesn't sit right with me. But even if you aren't an evil madman, you're still an enemy of the Order and we don't want any trouble with them. After all, the Order is the reason behind the Guild's prosperity. Surely you don't think they make their own swords?"

Col stared at him, barely comprehending. Dominik had drawn his blade and was hauling him backwards toward the door, waving it menacingly to keep the crowd of guildsmen away. River went up on her tiptoes, realized the floor was made of unyielding stone, and made a dash for the door as well. She whipped out her double-ended dagger/spear, which she had hidden under her cloak, the handle growing and elongating in her hands to its full length.

The group of guildsmen had mostly risen to their feet. There were a few of the older men still sitting in their chairs, looking confused and horrified. However, the vast majority seemed to know what was happening, and their faces were set in grim determination. Oddly enough, they didn't try to interfere as Col, River, and Dominik hurried to the door. Doogal, who had been standing quietly near the wall, goggled in shock, then pulled out a dagger and lunged toward the nearest guildsman, furious.

"No time, Doogal!" River snapped, intercepting him with the shaft of her spear. He glared red-faced at the crowd of men, but allowed himself to be dragged after her.

Col took it all in in a daze. He'd never before experienced this feeling of betrayal that wrenched at his gut. These were not priest-guards, these were his people. Fellow villagers who lived and worked under the oppression of the Hand, just like he had. How could they turn on him? Why? He'd been so trusting, so confident in the inner goodness of these people, that he had led his entire group into a trap. The horror of it stabbed into his heart. His feet moved mechanically as he was towed out the door by Dominik, who stopped abruptly. The road outside the house was crowded with King's men. The guards stood arrayed in ranks around the doorway, at least forty stern-faced warriors in dark grey uniforms. As one, they drew their cutlasses and pointed them at Col and his band. Out of the corner of his eye, Col saw the guildsman who had left the room to "get drinks" standing among them, looking smug. A man with the gold sash that marked him as the captain started speaking.

"Wolf, you have been convicted of treason against both the Hearer for dark sorcery, and against King Drystan for stealing away his betrothed." He turned his head to address his squad.

"Seize him. Kill anyone who fights, except the girl. She is to be treated with utmost respect as your future queen."

The guards surged forward. Col shook himself out of his surprise and reached for his hatchet. This time it was River who froze, watching the proceedings with indecision. Doogal began to fight wildly, demonstrating considerable improvement as he kept several guards at bay. Dominik was a blur. He moved with the speed and fluidity of a snake, not only fighting with his own dagger but even snatching weapons from the men who attacked him and using their own weapons against them. Col backed away instinctively, heart pounding as men yelled and bodies fell to the ground all around him. Four bodies already lay on the ground. The guards were attacking more hesitantly now, as between them Dominik and Doogal were keeping a swath of open space around the little band. Nevertheless, they were completely surrounded. Col tried to open the door they had just exited, but it was locked now. Col clumsily ducked a cutlass swing of a guard. He chopped at the man with his small axe, hitting him hard. The man's metal shoulder guard clanged in response, and the reverberation nearly made Col drop the hatchet. The man punched him. Col reeled, but stood his ground. He raised his axe in challenge, only to see the man die before his eyes as Doogal turned and sank his blade into the man's neck. Col reeled from the brutality of it. He'd seen men die before, but it hadn't dulled the horror he felt every time. He averted his eyes, feeling sick at the violence, and sick at his own uselessness in this clash of trained warriors. Over the heads of the guards, Col could see a glowing red light approaching down another street. It was torchlight, and the orderly marching feet indicated more reinforcements arriving even as Dominik killed three more men. He seemed about to be overwhelmed by sheer numbers. The King's troops, while much less versatile and deadly than the Priest-guards, were very organized and determined, their short cutlasses far more maneuverable in close quarters than the traditional swords of the Order.

"River!" Col screamed. She was still just watching, almost dazed, her face confused. She'd been offered a chance to walk away from the life of an outlaw and into a life of luxury. Despite the fact that it would mean the death of her friends, Col could see that some part of her was unwilling to give up the opportunity. It was the dark, ambitious side of her that he hated, flaring to the surface. His heart wrenched in fear. Not for his own life, not even for what she might do, but the fear of what she would become if she made this choice.

"Snap out of it. We need you!" he begged. At the sound of his voice, her eyes locked onto his, and her confusion seemed to clear.

"I need you," he whispered. He couldn't tell if she could hear him in the din, but the ambitious side of her seemed to be shoved aside, until it was only the girl, River, looking at him with her warm brown eyes.

She took in the situation quickly, then crouched, placing both hands on the ground.

The time for being subtle was gone. The ground trembled as vines and grass spread out across the ground, lashing around the legs of soldiers as they tried to move. There was a horrible, ear-splitting groan, as trees began to spring up, forcing their way out of the hard-packed earth. Even the houses, which were made of wood, had suddenly started growing branches that clawed out of the walls like many-fingered hands. In the direction opposite the reinforcements, branches and vines began grabbing at guards, shoving them aside and temporarily creating a gap in their ranks.

The King's men were in chaos. Luckily, all the members of Col's band had experience with River's work. Without a moment's hesitation, Col grabbed River's hand, helping her up. Followed closely by Dominik and Doogal, they rushed as one through the gap.

They dashed down the road, sounds of pursuit growing fainter as the reinforcements tried to fight their way through the mess of vegetation in the roadway. Where the city had once been silent, now it was alive with the noise of frightened villagers and surprised guards. Col was shocked to realise just how many guards had been patrolling quietly or having a drink in the various inns and taverns, as shouts came from all directions. Illsbeth was a wasp's nest, and they had just kicked it.

Suddenly, Sibyl rounded the corner and nearly crashed into Col, who was in the lead. She let out a little yelp of surprise, then grinned in relief. Behind her the rest of Col's party were hurrying to catch up with the fleet-footed scout.

"What's happening?" she asked, cheeks flushed with adrenaline. Col shook his head, catching his breath.

"No time. We need to get out, or find a place to hide."

She nodded, then took the lead as they hurried down the road.

Unfortunately, they didn't have much choice in their flight. With the city lighting up with torches and noise, Sibyl was forced again and again to simply choose the only paths without guards rushing down them. Before long, they came to the river and were forced to hurry along the bank, desperate for a way to cross. Col was reminded again of the feeling he'd had while being hunted in Kingsfall. He felt like an animal.

They came abruptly to the wall of the massive building straddling the river. Sibyl yanked the door open.

"If there is a door on the other side, we can cross the river through this," she said softly, eyes shining with wild excitement.

Despite the hurry, when Col entered the building he stopped short in amazement. He had never seen a room so massive. The room was filled with an overwhelming cacophony of noise, light, and heat. Despite the late hour, men still worked in the room, swinging hammers, tipping over vats of molten metal, and generally doing all kinds of dangerous, confusing things that Col associated with a Smithy. Except, this place made any smithy he'd ever seem look like a child's playhouse. Through the center of the chaos, the river Bleakley flowed, cutting a cold black swath through the light and heat of the factory. As it moved across the room, it turned an army of wooden wheels. These in turn caused all manner of machines to move without anyone manning them. Bellows pumped, grinding wheels spun, and massive hammers slammed down of their own accord, crushing ore as it slid down a chute. It was the most amazing construction Col had ever seen. Judging from the stacks of iron bars waiting to be forged, and the unfinished swords left lying on benches, he could finally understand how the Order could equip their priests so thoroughly.

They moved cautiously into the room, ignored by the various swordsmiths still at work at the late hour. These men were sheathed in a layer of sweat, concentrating on their work. Seeing that they weren't about to be set upon, the group began to move faster through the room. Doogal hurried until he could take a protective position in front of Col, his hand clamped over a thin slash above his elbow which Col hadn't noticed before. The man was just a villager, not very skilled with the sword, but he took his vow to protect and serve Col very seriously.

They came around the corner, and Doogal actually bumped straight into a man coming out from behind a large spinning stone. A man with a long, black cloak. A man with two swords strapped to his back. A man with a gold hand emblazoned on the front of his tunic. The grinding of the stone had made his footsteps inaudible.

Col froze in horror. The man stumbled back, then narrowed his eyes at the group.

"Hey! You aren't smiths. What are you doing here?"

And before Col could open his mouth to bluff their way out of the situation, Doogal, poor, foolish Doogal, reached for his machete.

Before he could even realize his mistake, Col watched him die. The inexperienced villager didn't even have time to unhook the machete from his side holster before the Priest-guard's sword stabbed straight through him, the sword entering below his ribs and angling up to spear his heart, the tip so sharp it split the back of Doogal's roughspun jacket, a horrible wetness glimmering on the point. His body fell to the ground, sliding off the sword as the Priest-guard shoved him, switched his attention to the rest of the group.

Col dodged the priest-guard as the man advanced on him. His band of loyal followers jumped forward to engage the man, protecting Col for the moment. Running to one side, he grabbed a round wooden lid off of a barrel full of metal scraps. He knew his small hatchet was no match for the double swords of the priest, but perhaps using this lid as a shield would help even the odds. However, running over to the barrel had separated him from the group. Looking back at them, he could see past the edge of the large stone block which they were fighting behind, River and Dominik keeping the priest at bay.

Beyond the group, on the other side of the stone block, was a long table with rows of beautiful sheathed swords on it, laid out in pairs. Several men were careful wrapping each pair in cloth and stowing them in boxes. Beyond them, waiting impatiently by a line of wagons, was an entire division of priest-guards. Dominik had the priest-guard by the throat now, and he was struggling wildly as River finished him off. Despite the arm across his throat, the man let out a choked yowl as he died. Instantly, the bored group of priests by the wagons came alert, at least half of them abandoning their posts and moving to investigate the noise.

"Run! There's more of them!" Col cried. His band reacted

instantly but with confusion, either following his orders blindly and running away through the machinery, running toward him, or running to engage the enemy depending on their personalities. Sibyl, incredibly loyal, ran to him with a man named Doug following. Three of his men ran away, but River and Dominik led a small group toward the priest-guards. At Col's outburst, unfortunately, two of the priest-guards redirected their attention and ran toward him. Col gritted his teeth, trying to remember his Temple training as he backed deeper into the factory. Despite their loyalty, neither Doug nor Sibyl really knew how to fight. The bandits could never hope to match the training and superior weapons of the Order, so they always relied on surprise and overwhelming numbers when they attacked caravans. Three on two was not overwhelming odds. Sibyl pulled out two knives, eyes shining in defiance as she moved to defend him. However, she was a scout, not a warrior. He couldn't let her die for him. Pushing her to the side, he charged the first priest-guard. The man swung his sword, and Col barely dodged. He ran into a narrower space between two massive crucibles, the huge pots suspended over blazing hot fires. The man followed, slashing at Col with both swords now. However, his swings were awkward in the narrow space. Using the flat side of his hatchet, Col slapped burning coals out of the fire below a crucible, straight into the man's face. The man yelled, dropping one of his swords to bat away the coals flying toward his face. Col lunged, his hatchet missing the man's chest entirely as the man jumped backward, but striking his forearm. With a clang, the priest dropped his other sword and cried out, grabbing Col's arm and trying to wrestle the hatchet away from him. He was so much stronger, despite the wound to his arm that gushed blood as he struggled. Col felt his grip on the hatchet weakening as the man yanked at it, peeling away Col's fingers. His hands were blistering from reaching into the crucible, and he could feel the hairs on the back of his neck singing away from the heat of the second fire behind him. The priest's hands were slick with sweat as well, hot blood sliding down his arm and splattering all over both men as they struggled. Col smelled smoke as the priest's cloak caught fire from the coals scattered on the ground. He felt his arms weakening, the priest gradually winning as he tried to twist the weapon away.

Col was no fighter. Despite months of stubborn training, he didn't have the knack for it. However, he was clever. With the man's attention focused on the weapon, Col suddenly let his hands go weak. As the priest triumphantly wrested the weapon from his grasp, Col kicked the man viciously between the legs. As he staggered forward with a shocked gasp, Col crouched low, utilizing his shorter stature to slam his shoulder into the man's ribs, then heaved, using all the power in his legs and back to throw his opponent upward and backward. The priest let out a scream as he was thrown over the lip of the fire. He smacked his head on the underside of the crucible, falling stunned into the flames. The fire leapt up, greedily devouring the luxurious silk cape and within moments the man's head and torso had been engulfed in flames. Col turned and staggered away, unable to resist the urge to throw up. The contents of his stomach splattered against the hot side of the other crucible, adding to the horrendous smell in the air. He staggered out from between the burning pots. Through the sweat dripping into his eyes, he saw Sibyl engaging the other priest. Doug lay on the ground, possibly already dead. Sibyl wasn't trying to attack the priest-guard, only defending herself as she retreated, blood seeping from multiple cuts. Col didn't think, he just lunged. He grabbed his shield up from the floor, and used both hands to bash it across the back of the man' head. As it was only a barrel lid, it didn't kill him. However, the man fell to his knees. He shook his head, dazed. Col raised the lid again, but the priest rolled out of the way, coming to his feet with a bit of a stagger. Sibyl lunged from the side. She knew enough to stab at the space just behind the man's arm, where there would be a gap in his black leather tunic. The man was still dazed, so she managed to stab him. However, her knife failed to slide between his ribs and instead struck the bone, only piercing a few inches before stopping short. He let out a roar, flinging her away with a blow from the hilt of one of his swords. She fell to the ground and didn't get up. The priest-guard turned, sword raised to finish her off, but Col was there. He caught the sword blow on his shield. The impact jarred his arms, but the blade stuck fast in the soft wood and he was able to wrench the sword away from the priest.

The man was angry now. Col barely blocked the quick succession of blows that came at him. His shield splintered, bits of wood flying off. He backed desperately away, all his attention on the man attacking him. The air filled with the sound of water wheels turning, gears grinding, and some slow, rhythmic thumping sounds like giant hammers. He tried to take a step back, tripped on a small lever on the floor, and fell backwards against a massive metal block. Putting one hand back, he felt along the top of the block without taking his eyes off his assailant. His hand scrabbled across the surface, seeking a weapon as the man struck at him again. The blow split a whole chunk of the shield away, and Col was left holding a half-circle with the handle threatening to fall off. With shock, he saw that the hand holding the handle had started leaving trails of light in the air. At the same time, he felt something on the table behind him. It was a thin metal plate. I wasn't much, but he grabbed it. As he did so, he waved his other hand threateningly at the priest, making the man back up at the uncanny sight of the glowing lines.

Then, without any warning, a massive metal hammer slammed down onto his hand. The world exploded in unbelievable pain. He heard a horrible, sickening crunch, his mind blank with panic and pain. The priest approached, picking up his other sword almost leisurely. Col dropped the shield and tugged desperately at his arm to free himself. It was too much. At his first attempt, the movement caused an even greater wave of pain to wash over him. His vision went dark. The last thing he saw was the priest approaching, sword in hand.

30

It was getting harder and harder to save face in front of the people. Especially the new King, because he had met the girl called River, and knew the truth. However, the Hearer knew that he had to keep up appearances at all costs. The room which he entered was vast, the stone walls keeping out most of the sun's heat. From where he stood, he could barely see the other end. The place was packed full. Not with peasants, but with important people. Dukes, Nobles, Priests of high rank, the king himself, and even some delegates from that Silent Speaker's cult. The Hearer stood before them and, despite the cool air, felt sweat forming on his forehead and in his palms. He had to convince all these people that everything was fine.

"We are a fractured people," he said, his voice echoing off the curved walls and reaching to the very back of the room. "Our charge, as leaders of men, is to keep the world ordered, righteous, and prosperous. We have failed in this duty." He said the words sharply, and sent his gaze sweeping across the crowd. "In our fractured state, in the selfishness of each one seeking their own gain and refusing the will of the gods, we have allowed a heretic to rise up among us. You know of whom I speak! This *Wolf*, this ruler of bandits and rogues, has spread his poison throughout our land, breaking it apart. This boy may seem like only a harmless brat, but he stirs up rebellion everywhere he goes. He has no respect for the gods, claims that the great Messenger is nothing more than a human, and even encourages the peasants to disrespect all of our authority as he does. He must be crushed. Such a foul heretic cannot be overlooked or underestimated. Any one of the people here may already have fallen prey to his lies." He went on, railing about the dangers of the Wolf, but really just emphasizing the idea of the peasants revolting. He knew that, if he could firmly connect the idea of the Wolf with the idea of revolt against all people in positions of power, and not just with revolt against the Order, he would sway this crowd. They might be fine with the fall of the Order, but every one of them took threats to their own power very seriously. By the end of his speech, he saw real fear in their eyes. All except for the king himself. He paid attention, but his face was inscrutable. The Hearer started to think that perhaps something would have to be done about him...

River had never before fought beside someone who was her equal. Dominik was that, and more. Although her ability to move the earth always tipped things in her favor, the man was so skilled he had, on multiple occasions, bested her despite her abilities when they sparred, dodging between her vines and strikes like a cat. Now, as they fought side by side, her admiration for his fighting skill almost outweighed her fear as the Priests of the Hand attacked. It was a bloody struggle, but their combined prowess made it almost a game to take down their opponents. River wielded her spear defensively with her hands, but her real focus was on the ground as she kicked off her sandals and controlled the earth with her feet. She wasn't just using her environment to her advantage, she was becoming the environment. Every footfall, every shift in weight as an opponent prepared to leap at her - she was aware of everything. There were no seeds to awaken in the dry, hard clay of the factory floor, but it was still earth, and she could use it. Even as she dodged and stabbed, her opponents tripped over rocks, and halted in their tracks as the hard ground enveloped their feet to the ankles. Dominik moved at her side, making use of every obstacle she introduced. Where she tripped men, he killed them while they were unbalanced. It was grisly work, but there was an art to it. The priest-guards were formidable adversaries, but they were no match for River on firm ground. She threw herself into the fight with frenzied intensity, pushing the priests further and further back. Her heart thrilled inside of her with adrenaline and excitement. The priests began to retreat, and she pushed forward with Dominik at her side, moving as one. She became aware of his every move in a way that had nothing to do with her connection to the earth.

Suddenly, she heard a shout. This was not out of the ordinary, as the fighting around her was causing both screams and yells of pain from all around. However, this was not a sound of pain. This yell was issued in a booming voice, and it had words in it.

"Stop the fighting!" a man yelled. "We have your leader!"

The words broke River's concentration, but she still had difficulty comprehending them through the heat of the moment. Dominik, however, stopped dead in his tracks. He was a cold-blooded fighter, not a passionate one. As he stopped, River followed his lead. No one was attacking them anymore, rather the Priest-guards were retreating to a safe distance. Slowly, she turned.

Behind them, a man stood with a sword drawn. In his other hand, he was dragging Col's limp body forward. All the heat suddenly leached from River's body. She froze, completely transfixed by the sight. He couldn't be dead. She refused to believe that he was dead. She couldn't lose him. He twitched, and it was as if a massive weight lifted from her. She could move again, breathe again. The first thing she did was to advance aggressively.

The priest shook Col. His head lolled, but then he gradually opened his eyes and looked around dazedly, taking in the scene. Two more Priest-guards dragged a defiant Sibyl forward. She was bleeding from the side of her head.

"Let him go," River seethed, her tone menacing, "or I'll kill every one of you." Dominik looked at her, then at Col, his eyes uncertain.

"Wolf?"

Col blinked bleary eyes, then came fully awake. His eyes were fixed on Sibyl, a blade held to her throat. Then he looked at the Priest-guards surrounding them, holding several other men captive. He saw the bodies on the ground. River could see his eyes fill with horror.

"Stand down," he whispered, his tone defeated. "No one else will die today."

"They'll kill you!" Sibyl protested, tone fiery despite being vaguely cross-eyed and disoriented.

"I will never stop fighting for you!"

River's heart echoed the same sentiment, refusing to simply accept defeat. However, the guard pulled Col further forward, and at the jostling motion Col slipped back into oblivion. He fell limp again. His body left a horrible trail of wetness on the ground, and River caught a glimpse of his other hand that dragged on the ground. Her stomach churned with nausea. Dominik, however, was looking at the sword in the hand of the man holding Col.

"We should surrender," Dominik said softly, looking to her. "The Wolf is right. Many more of our own will die if we fight. The Wolf will die. As long as he lives, there is still hope. And should he be executed, at least he will not be alone in that fate." He held out his weapon, prepared to drop it to the ground, but looked to her for agreement.

River stood conflicted, horrified that the decision rested on her shoulders. The heat of the fighting had turned to cold dismay inside of her, She wanted to keep fighting. She wanted to argue that they could still win, herself and Dominik. They could battle their way out and run off into the night, free. But Dominik had a steely determination in his eyes that told her he would not leave his brother in arms, that his loyalty to Col overpowered any affection he might have for her. She looked at Col again, at his limp form, and felt sick at herself for the selfish thoughts. If she fought, he would die. If they surrendered, they would probably all die, of course. But somehow that inevitable future death seemed far better than the idea of having him slain before her eyes, right now. Numbly, she dropped her spear.

"We surrender."

The priests didn't kill them. Not yet. There was a long and heated argument about whether to torture them for information right there, or take them to Kingsfall. The end decision was that they couldn't be sure what the Hearer wanted with the prisoners, and the risk of displeasing him was too great. They tied the prisoner's hands and River found herself thrown into the back of a covered wagon along with Col and Sibyl. Dominik and the six other men who hadn't managed to escape were bundled into a second and third wagon. The wooden door swung shut, leaving River trapped in a windowless box.

River looked at Sibyl, and then both women moved without negotiation towards Col. They couldn't bind his wounds with their hands tied, but they did their best to prop him up and support him as the wagon began to move, jostling the occupants. River looked into Col's face, his eyebrows singed and cuts everywhere, and her heart filled with guilt. How had she let herself get so distracted in the fighting that she forgot to protect him? Col was no use at fighting, she knew that. And yet, she'd left him to the mercy of the Priest-guards. After all the times he had saved her life, this was how she repaid him. For the first time, she considered that he was greater, more noble, than she could ever hope to be, despite her royal blood.

31

Sibyl had her hands free before the sounds of the factory faded behind them. She helped River untie herself, then stole the fine silk wrapping from one of the sword pairs neatly stacked in the back of the wagon. She ripped it into strips, then set about bandaging Col's wounds. He had smaller cuts and bruises, as well as singed skin in multiple places. However, when Sibyl went to bandage his hand, she hesitated, unsure where to even start. This time, River forced herself not to look away. His hand was mangled beyond repair. The ends of his two smallest fingers were missing entirely, and the whole hand was crushed horribly. Sibyl started crying softly as she ineffectively tried to staunch the bleeding. It was a pathetic sound, coming from the confident, energy-filled girl. Up until that moment River had been feeling useless, jealous of the practical skills of the other girl. However, now she realized that Sibyl must feel just as helpless. Gently, she took the bandage from Sibyl's shaking hands and set about doing her best to help.

Even when he wasn't bleeding anymore, Col was still frighteningly pale. Every bump set his eyelids fluttering, but he never fully woke, drifting from fitful sleep into a confused daze that wasn't much different. He was sweating, his breathing rapid, but despite that his lips and the fingers of his undamaged hand were flushed blue as if from cold. River was nearly frantic with worry. Sibyl had started praying, rocking back and forth with her eyes fixed on Col, her lips moving in the rote chants of the Order, petitioning the Messenger to speak to the gods on her behalf. River felt frustrated. Then she felt furious, as the useless chanting dragged on for what seemed hours. There was no Messenger, the chants were stupid, dangerous, even, as they promoted the ideals of the very organization they were fighting against. But she didn't have any better option herself, forced to watch Col suffering with no way to help, the guilt crushing her. Finally, she couldn't take it any more.

"Stop it, you're not helping!" she snapped, her voice filled with far more bitterness than she'd intended.

"Your stupid god isn't real, and your chanting isn't doing anything!"

Sibyl looked at her, eyes wide with hurt and surprise. Then she burst into a flood of tears. River instantly felt awful. Why couldn't she keep her angry emotions inside, why did she always spread her bitterness around like poison to the people around her? She was stricken with yet more guilt at her outburst. What right had she to judge Sibyl's actions, when she didn't have any better ideas? Following Sibyl's example, she felt tears well up in her own eyes.

River, daughter of General Ironwood, princess of a long-forgotten nation and betrothed to the king over all the known world, didn't cry. She hadn't cried since she left Storm behind. Technically, that had been hundreds of years ago. For her it was months. When the tears came, they poured out in a torrent. It was as if she had finally tipped over a bucket of emotions that had been gathering inside her, growing more and more full as she packed them away every day without dealing with them. She cried until Sibyl stopped her own tears to stare at her with concern. She cried until the guards riding beside the wagon banged on the side, calling for her to shut up. She wept until her eyes were puffy, her throat raw, and her nose runny. When she finally stopped, she felt utterly drained. At the same time however, she felt much lighter. She barely cared that Sibyl was still staring at her, looking uncomfortable. Sleep claimed her, and for the first time in months she didn't need to worry about touching the ground.

It felt like only minutes later that she awoke, groggy, to sounds of struggle outside. She sat up abruptly, realizing the wagon had stopped moving. Col was still pale and listless, but Sibyl was awake and crouched in a corner with a sword out. She hadn't been trained to use one, but she was certainly planning to try.

River got up instantly, reaching for a sword. Her eyes still felt puffy, so she knew not much time had passed. Outside the wagon, men were shouting and yelling. Swords rang, and a body was thrown against the wooden wall of the wagon, rocking it. Through it all, River could hear a horrible screaming sound. It was the sound of the horses, she realized. The wagon wasn't moving because the horses harnessed to it were being killed. She felt a chill. Whatever was going on, it wasn't Col's troops that had come to rescue them. The Revolutionaries never wasted resources, never killed trained animals but instead stole them for their own use. This was someone or something else attacking. She waited, tensely.

Suddenly, there was a horrible, jarring sound. Something smashed repeatedly against the multiple locks holding the wagon door closed. Metal shrieked, and wood splintered. River and Sibyl crouched down defensively as wood chips and bits of metal flew through the air. Gradually, a hole started opening up. The edge of an axe bit all the way through the door, letting shafts of early morning sunlight in when it retreated. Then the door was yanked open.

A man stood in the doorway, silhouetted against the rising sun behind him, the cool mountain air rustling through his dark beard, a massive axe propped against his shoulder. At the sight of the prisoners, his eyebrows shot up, chasing a ripple of wrinkles across the weather-beaten skin of his forehead.

"By my grandpapi's rotten teeth, these aren't swords!" he exclaimed, his leering grin revealing that his own teeth were in no exemplary state. His eyes roved over the two girls and Col's limp form, clearly unthreatened by their teary-eyed, pathetic state, despite the swords they held. Seeing that they weren't immediately going to be killed, River put down her sword and held out her hands in surrender. Reluctantly, Sibyl followed suit. River wasn't a very good actress, but she knew that if she could seem unthreatening they would likely let her get out of the wagon and put her feet on solid ground. The man leaned his head back and hollered to the side.

"Ey, Bogdana! I found some poor bedraggled folks in here! Seems like we swiped the Order's prisoners."

"In here too!" another man called. A woman marched into view. She was tall, with muscular arms and a braided tail of hair that was so matted it seemed to be just a giant fuzzy worm attached to the back of her head.

"There better be a full shipment along with them," she growled. The man scanned the interior of the wagon appraisingly.

"Yep, seems to be all here. They musta just thrown these wretches in on top of the goods."

The woman fixed River with a calculating look. Her gaze softened as she took in the girl's tear-stained cheeks, then melted completely as her eyes fell on Col. He was, if possible, even more handsome in his weak state, a tragic picture of perfect charm marred by violence. River marvelled that without trying Col could melt the heart of even such a burly thug of a woman as Bogdana.

"Bring them with us," she decided. "Any prisoner of the Order might just be a friend of ours, and even if they aren't, Hamon will want to make that decision."

Sibyl let out a little gasp. Too quietly for anyone but River to hear, she whispered, "Hamon is the worst bandit lord of all! He kills any group who tries to approach his mountain. This might be the only chance any of us will ever have to meet him and persuade him to join us!"

Or just persuade him not to kill us, River thought skeptically. She didn't have Col's charm, she knew. And without his help she didn't have much hope for their survival, let alone their acceptance into this rough group of bandits. As she stepped out of the wagon, however, she knew that she would have no choice but to try the path of persuasion. They were stranded high on the side of a mountain, with nothing in sight in any direction except sheer rock faces, spindly trees, and bandits. The horses were dead, as were all the priest-guards. River knew that even if she defeated the bandits, they would still be a long trek away from anywhere hospitable. Col would undoubtedly die on the journey. As she watched, bandits dragged the bodies off the road and hurled them over the edge of a cliff. There were a lot of bandit corpses as well, which received the same cold-hearted treatment. From the flood of men crowding the road, River could see that they employed the same tactics as Col's troops - overwhelming force and surprise - to combat the superior skill of the Order's priests. However, to her surprise she saw that they were all well-armed, not just with stolen Order swords but with battle axes, sabres, and bows. That was unusual, as the Hearer didn't allow anyone other than the King to manufacture weapons. She felt a flood of relief as she saw Dominik hustled out of another wagon, unharmed, and ushered over to join her.

The man with the axe turned to look back into the wagon at Col.

"This one's weak, we should leave him," he noted. Bogdana looked regretful, but nodded at the logical argument.

"No!" River cried out, her voice choked with fear. "Please, no!"

Bogdana looked at her, suddenly irritated.

"You should be grateful we're not leaving you. He's too weak to walk, and we need all of our men to carry these swords. A wounded lad isn't as valuable as weapons, no matter how pretty he looks."

"You're wrong about that," River snarled, prepared to fight every one of these bandits rather than let them separate her from Col. A man grabbed her, and she struggled violently, trying to call through the smooth, chiseled stones of the roadway to the earth beneath. She couldn't lose Col. Not now, not after she realized how much she needed him. Dominik spoke up quietly.

"Let me carry him."

The man with the axe looked him over, skeptical.

"It's a long journey. If you fall behind you're left behind."

"I will carry him," Dominik repeated, jaw set. "He is my brother and my master. I would rather die than leave him in this place."

River glanced at him sharply, shocked by the declaration. He was always so silent and proud. Never once in all the months River and Dominik had faithfully traveled at Col's side had she heard him voice such sentiments. She wondered when his loyalties had changed from the Rebels to Col. The expression of determination on his face now made it clear that, at some point, they had undoubtedly changed.

There was a moment of silence, and then Bogdana gave Dominik her approval, looking pleased with the decision.

The bandits herded all the prisoners into a group and began prodding them forward as even the wagons were rolled off the cliff, each bandit first filling a pack with as many swords as they could carry. They even gave the stronger-looking men of River's group packs to carry, not worried that the prisoners might fight back. It was no surprise, River supposed. The bandits had vastly superior numbers, and with their leader injured Sibyl and the rest had a subdued, beaten look about them. Dominik strode along undaunted, Col draped over his shoulders like a sheep. He had woken briefly when they brought him out of the wagon, however he was too weak to help much as Dominik lifted him. When Dominik grabbed his injured arm, he screamed. Then River saw him clamp his teeth down over the scream, jaw set in determination as his whole face flushed white with pain. He was unconscious again by the time Dominik had taken his first few steps away from the wagon.

River walked behind Dominik, watching Col's injured arm flopping limply against the taller man's back. Every time she looked at Col she felt horribly guilty, and yet she couldn't look away.

They left the road, climbing up a gravel incline and through several notches in the cliff side that had no discernable path. Far sooner than River had expected, they turned into a little ravine, crossed a stream, and then disappeared one by one behind a small waterfall that slipped down the side of a cliff. The entrance to the tunnel behind had almost the look of a spiky portcullis, with long, drippy spines formed of some kind of mineral hanging down from the roof like a second waterfall of stone behind the one made of water. They journeyed deeper into the rock, the ground sloping upwards as the tunnel began to look undeniably man-made, the chisel marks showing on the smooth walls. River felt the thrum of the earth under her feet, and hoped no one noticed the moss creeping along the ground in the dark, sprouting from her footsteps. She'd been able to keep the earth from noticing her on the hard roadway, but here, in the depths of the mountain, it was all around her. Instead of sensing trees and plant life, she became aware of hollow caves, mineral deposits, and veins of hard iron ore spiraling all around her. It wasn't dark - not to her. In fact, the moment she had stepped out of the wagon - sandals left behind in the fight in the weapons factory - she had felt unblinded. The others, however, stumbled and cursed. The bandits lit a few torches, but the flickering light was broken up by so many people's moving shadows that it made obstacles hard to see. River was careful to mimic the other's stumbling pace so that no one would guess her abilities.

The tunnel emerged after what seemed hours into much cooler temperatures. Cold wind and tall trees told River just how high up they were. They were in a mountain valley, protected on all sides by rugged cliffs. A thick forest filled the bowl of the mountains with green, climbing as high as it could up the stone faces until the cold and steep rock defeated it.

The descent from the tunnel mouth proved a grueling hike. When they reached the end, River saw that even Dominik looked exhausted. It made her feel better about her own weakened state, sweating from exertion and shivering from the cold by turns.

Despite his fearsome reputation, Hamon's fortress was little more than an encampment of wood and stone slab houses, clustered together behind a ditch full of sharpened branches. Nevertheless, River could tell that everyone was feeling her nervousness at meeting the bandit lord.

They were shown into a long hall with a fire roaring at the end. Beside the fire, in a large chair made from a massive tree stump, lounged a short woman with curly brown hair, a slight frame, and a face that would have been pretty if it wasn't for the suspicious scowl permanently etched into her brow. River couldn't believe it. The horrible, ruthless bandit lord Hamon was … a woman?

Her guess proved correct as their escorts bowed to the girl. She looked at them with irritation.

"Who are these miserable louts? You aren't supposed to take prisoners. Don't you know our codes? Why aren't they dead? For that matter, why aren't they even bound?"

Bogdana bowed low, looking terrified.

"So sorry lord Hamon, but these aren't our prisoners. They were the Priest-guard's prisoners. We didn't know what to do with them so we thought we'd let you decide their fate."

She was very careful to use "we" instead of taking ownership for the decision, and River saw the other members of that "we" trying to retreat without drawing attention.

Hamon's brows pinched even further in toward each other.

"Idiots! You robbed a prison convoy instead of a weapon shipment?"

Her gaze was furious until a robber hastily corrected her, spilling his pack of swords out onto the floor for all to see. She relaxed, leaning back into the giant wooden seat. Her sharp eyes examined the prisoners closely. Col's arms swung loose as Dominik held him, his scars exposed. However, Hamon didn't seem to recognize their significance.

"Who are you?" she demanded. Her eyes went to Dominik, not River. It made sense, considering his tall, brooding presence. He, however, turned respectfully to River. Despite the marked distance that had existed between the Wolf and herself since that night in the canyon, River was still Col's undisputed right hand when it came to rank.

River stood up straighter, trying out an expression of humility, which felt awkward on her face.

"Lord Hamon, we are a scouting group for the Wolf, enemies of the Order. We ran afoul of the Priest-guards in Illsbeth and were captured."

Hamon's posture was still aggressive.

"I don't believe you. What if you are spies, pretending to be prisoners so you could infiltrate my camp? There's no way to know. That's why we have our codes."

"They were taking us to Kingsfall for execution!" River cut in, desperate. "If you kill us, you'll be doing the Hearer a favor."

It was one of the arguments she'd heard Col use often. It sounded less convincing, coming from her, but still Hamon hesitated.

"I don't trust you," she said suspiciously. "How can I know you aren't lying?"

River gestured at Col, and several other men sporting injuries of varying severity.

"Would the Priest-guards have attacked us if we were their own spies?" she demanded. Hamon followed her gesture, and at the sight of Col's situation her gaze grew more thoughtful. River was looking at Col too, now, and growing more desperate. She did something she had never before done voluntarily. She got down on her knees and begged.

"I don't care if you trust us or not, but I appeal to your sense of mercy, or even just your desire to thwart the Hearer. Please let us have a healer. Our leader is injured."

"I can see that," Hamon remarked dryly. Then she sighed.

"Very well, have a healer tend to the injured, but lock them up. If even a single one tries to escape, kill them all."

River sighed with relief. At least they had survived.

32

The Hearer climbed the steps of the wide path leading towards the Sky Keep, one of the most beautiful towers ever built by the Order. The majestic tower rose from the very top of a cliff, reaching a height that boggled the mind. Blocks of white marble were placed among the grey stones of its wall. If you looked at the tower from a distance, the blocks formed intricate images depicting scenes from the Order's history. Up close, the pictures were lost. However, the city sprawled at the base of the cliff could clearly see the scenes, forever faced with a reminder of the Order's rule.

The peasants of the city of Keep's Sake had been unruly of late. Thus the Hearer felt it was his duty to visit the place in person. Perhaps seeing his golden robes and imposing entourage would remind the people that rebellion was pointless. If it didn't, he was prepared to deal out death and torment until the filthy peasants submitted. He had no patience for them, his thoughts occupied with the much bigger problem of organized banditry wreaking havoc on the main roads throughout the Cliff Regions.

The sound of hoofbeats disrupted his thoughts. The ringing sound clattered against the stone, and he turned to see a horseman pounding up the road at a pace that would likely kill the poor beast he was riding. Spotting the golden hand stitched into the man's jacket, the Hearer waved for his small army of guards to let the man pass.

"Your Divinity." The man leapt from his sweaty horse and let his momentum carry him to his knees in front of the Hearer, forehead pressed against the ground. The Hearer was instantly alert. People were only this grovelingly respectful when they didn't think he was going to like what they had to say.

"Speak," he snapped. The man raised his head slightly.

"The insurrectionist known as the Wolf, and the girl Messenger he travels with were caught, and sent to Kingsfall to await trial," the man panted.

"I knew that already," the Hearer cut him off. "The news reached me yesterday. You're late." He let out a rare chuckle. The news had been some of the best he'd ever received, causing him no end of satisfaction coupled with desperate impatience for the boy to arrive. The messenger shook his head.

"That's the problem, sir! I was trying to reach you before the first messenger. He was bearing false news."

The Hearer froze.

"*What?*" His tone was as menacing as possible. The man on the ground looked pale, but proved quite full of courage, as his voice didn't stutter when he continued.

"The Wolf was captured, but less than a day afterwards the caravan containing him was attacked. Every Priest-guard of the Thirty-fourth Calling is dead. We found the caravan smashed at the base of a cliff, with bodies of bandits mixed among the fallen."

The Hearer had never before experienced such intense rage. Perhaps it was because of the feeling of anticipation he'd been experiencing moments before, but he burned with a rage so blinding that he could barely contain it.

Moments later, the messenger lay dead at his feet. For the first time ever, the Hearer could not even remember what he'd done.

They took Col away. It felt almost physically painful to watch them take him. River never realized how much comfort she had been receiving from his mere presence, the ability to watch his chest rise and fall, to know that he was still alive. When they dumped her in a stone cell along with the rest of the prisoners who looked uninjured, then took Col,

Sibyl, and several others away, she felt ready to throw a fit and fight every bandit between herself and him. However, she wasn't stupid. If she rebelled, they would kill Col as well as her companions. He would never get the help he needed.

She seethed, then demanded, then seethed, then threatened in turns. The guards at the door would not budge. Finally, Dominik had to pick her up by her arms because her distress was causing moss and lichen to creep up in her footsteps despite the fact that she had mentally built a wall between herself and her connection to the earth. She didn't want its attention, but it still kept trying to creep back like a beaten dog. Despite the darkness in the cave, it wouldn't go unnoticed forever. Dominik set her down on a hastily spread cloak. Of all Col's followers, he was the only one who could get away with such behavior without being strangled. She glared at him, but with no real venom.

It took an entire night of her pestering before the guards would finally take River to see the wounded. When she walked into the small wooden hut where Col lay, she found a red-eyed Sibyl on a wooden bed in the corner near the door, her head bandaged but otherwise looking well. Col lay on a bed in the middle of the room, deathly pale. Sweat beaded on his waxy skin, and he shivered as if freezing. His lips were blue, eyes closed. An elderly man with a wispy beard and a balding head came in, bearing fresh bandages. However, he bustled right past Col's mangled hand and went to the end of the room, where a boy, not one of River's group, sat on a chair. He held out an arm for the man to bandage, with a small gash near the elbow. The man, who she took for a surgeon, wrapped it up neatly and then headed for the door. River couldn't believe her eyes.

"Aren't you going to help him?" she demanded, gesturing at Col's shivering form.

"He'll die!"

The man turned to her, face sympathetic. One of his eyes was cloudy with blindness, the other light brown.

"Yes, he will," he said, softly, "and that is why I am not going to help him." He held up a hand as River sputtered, distressed and outraged.

"I cannot do anything to change his fate," he explained, mouth pinched in an uncomfortable line.

"His injury is infected, and in such cases men much larger than him have died. I have never been able to save men whose limbs are crushed in such a way, once the infection sets in."

River reeled, her mind refusing to accept his words. She had little experience with wounds or death, but she thought back to her training lessons as a child, and her instructor, the old soldier with only one leg.

"If you... cut off the limb," she suggested, feeling sick at the idea, "would that stop the infection?"

"Perhaps," the surgeon acknowledged, "but he is far too weak already. The shock of the amputation would undoubtedly kill him. He'd either lose too much blood or die from the trauma when we cauterized the wound. If we do nothing, he'll perhaps have a few more days before the infection kills him. You'd best say goodbye."

He was completely serious, and sounded experienced. River stared at him, horrified. She looked at Col, and felt a grief well up, deeper than any she had ever experienced. Somehow, the thought of losing this man, of watching him die, was worse than the pain of leaving her world behind. She had left that place willingly. This was different. This was a ripping sensation, a taking against her will, as if someone had viciously yanked out a piece of her and left nothing in its place except a hollow void filled with pain. She sat down on the edge of his bed, numb. What would she do without him? He had, unwittingly, become her anchor in this foreign world. Her constant companion, a steady, reliable presence that had never left her side. Without him, she felt lost. How could she lead a revolution without his inspiring confidence and charm?

She looked at his face, so pale under the freckles. With his eyes closed, there was nothing about him that reminded her of Storm. And yet, his face was still so dear to her. She hated to admit it, but she cared deeply for this peasant boy. She reached out, hesitantly, and touched his sweat-damp curls.

"Please don't leave," she whispered.

In the doorway, feet shifted on the dirt floor.

"I hear you bullied my guards all night until they let you in here."

River looked up. Hamon stood in the doorway, her lithe body propped against the frame, her expression cautious, but not hostile. She was looking at River's legs, which were encased in Dominik's boots, with confusion. They were comically large on River's feet, but they kept the over-affectionate earth at bay. River returned Hamon's gaze. She didn't bother to hide her feelings. The loss she felt was too deep to hide.

"I'm sorry," she blurted. "I had to see him. They wouldn't let me see him. He's... *dying*." The word felt sharp and painful on her tongue. She felt herself coming apart, unable to reign in her emotions or put on a mask of cold pride.

"Please, Hamon, you have to help him!"

Hamon hesitated, looking at the surgeon. He shook his head firmly. A flash of pity crossed the girl's face.

"There's nothing to be done. It is a pity." Her eyes lingered regretfully on Col's face, then she turned to go. Before she left, she turned back to look at River.

"You may stay here with him until he dies."

River felt like railing at the girl, at the world, for not being able to do anything to change Col's fate. Instead, she nodded gratefully.

"Thank you, Hamon."

A flicker of a smile crossed the other girl's face.

"My name isn't Hamon. It's Helena. Hamon isn't real, he's a fictional warlord invented to intimidate the Priest-guards. For some reason, people refuse to see a young girl as a threat, no matter how many she's killed."

You're not entirely right about that. River thought, reflecting on the abject terror she inspired in the faces of so many people. Still, right or wrong, she was glad that the girl had confided in her. It seemed that the initial hostility Helena had viewed them with was wearing off. Perhaps being peaceable and submissive captives might be the best way to win the paranoid woman's trust. Remembering her insults and threats of the night before, River wondered how long she could manage to play along.

As Helena left, the surgeon following, River couldn't contain the tears that burst out of her. Knowing Col would die, her guilt redoubled for failing to protect him. Her distraction hadn't just cost him his hand, it would cost him his life. She sat hunched on the edge of his bed, arms wrapped around herself, trying to keep herself from flying apart, keep her body from cracking and flaking away like bits of eggshell until nothing was left except the swirling void of pain that consumed her insides. All her ambitions, all her arrogance, seemed pale and stupid in comparison to the looming darkness that was the death of a close friend.

People and hours came and went. River didn't see them. She let herself be consumed by her feelings, sitting alone in the cold, dark numbness of misery.

For a while, Dominik was allowed to visit the room. He didn't say anything to River, and avoided her eyes. Gone was the admiration he used to show her as they sparred and fought together. Instead, he focused his eyes on Col, and the only thing in them was shame.

"I failed you," he whispered, speaking to the unconscious boy on the bed.

"I'm sorry." He bowed his head, hands gripping Col's good one with fervor.

"I will seek atonement in the care and protection of your cause. I will see your prophecy fulfilled through your brothers, and your memory made eternal, this I swear to you."

He left after this strange speech, and River was momentarily confused out of her grief. Was Dominik also some kind of religious zealot? His talk of prophecies confused her. She had only ever heard one prophecy, and that had proved hollow. She had rejected the life of a puppet queen that it promised her. So what then was left for her? Without Col, the revolution seemed impossible. Now, even Dominik had rejected her, his shame at failing Col far outweighing any feelings he may have had for her.

The news of Col's doom apparently spread, because the rest of his men came to visit one by one. They gave River a wide berth, as if her aura of cold misery might infect them.

When everyone else had gone, still River stayed. She couldn't think of anywhere else that she could want to be except near Col. It seemed to her, as darkness fell and lanterns in other houses were put out, that there was nothing else in the world beyond the small circle of light cast by the lantern on the wall. She was alone on a tiny island in an empty sea, watching the only person she truly cared for die. As she looked at him, feeling helpless, she began to understand why Sibyl prayed. What else was there to do, when all other options were exhausted?

Feeling awkward, foolish, but mostly just desperate, River spoke into the empty air. How did one even start a prayer?

"This is a message to god, specifically the god of Col's mother, Jehane, because she has been devoted to you all her life, and I think you're the most likely to care for her son," she began, as if she was dictating a letter.

"I need you to please heal this man, Nikolo Wolf, that I'm sitting next to. I don't really know why you'd care to listen to me since I've never done anything to honor you, but his mother does seem to have a good relationship with you, and I'm sure she wants him to live. Also, if you do heal him, I promise to... believe in you, and be your follower, and do whatever I'm supposed to do to honor you, but I can't promise that I'll know what the proper things to do are, since no one's told me. Do you like sacrifices, maybe? Anyway, whatever it is, I'll do it. I swear on my royal blood. Just heal him please?" She was rambling now, she knew it. And probably offending the deity by praying in a disrespectful, disbelieving manner. Blinking back tears of embarrassment and grief, she thought that the lantern seemed brighter. It might have only been the coming of midnight, but a hushed silence had fallen over the world, almost a listening silence. Not even the trees rustled outside. River let out a small, hiccuping sob, dropping all pretense of trying to do a proper, persuasive prayer to the unknown god.

"Please!" she begged, "I need him!"

Nothing happened, and she felt the tears well up again. As they spilled out of her, she felt the void inside of her gradually fill with warmth. Somewhere out in the night, a voice started singing. It was a young voice, perhaps belonging to a child.

She awoke curled up at the foot of the bed, with one of Col's knees digging awkwardly into her stomach. Her knee, too, seemed to have a permanent dent in it from the hard round bone of his heel, where it was wedged against her. It was a small bed.

She sat up slowly, cracking the stiffness from her neck, then looked around in a panic. Morning light was spilling in the open doorway. How long had she slept? How many of Col's final hours had she missed? What if he had died while she slept?

She jumped up, rushing to the head of Col's bed and examining him. He was breathing, although he was lying alarmingly still in comparison to the shivering of the night before. She let out a little gasp of relief. His face seemed warmer in the sun's light, a peaceful expression making him all the more handsome. River stared at him, captivated. No one was around, and, for a moment, she let herself drop the facade of pride and strength.

"I love you, Co,." she whispered, feeling the words out in her mouth. She was shocked by how deeply they rang true within her. "I know you're a stupid peasant boy who can't fight, but I can't help it. And if you die today, I think I'll regret not admitting it."

He didn't move. Heart sinking, she looked at his face, memorizing every line, every freckle, every little scar and detail.

"Goodbye," she whispered, choking up with grief at the finality of the words. Then she leaned down, and kissed him gently.

His lips were soft and warm. Then, suddenly, she felt his hand slide into her hair and he was kissing her back. Her mind froze. *What?* She pulled away in shock, and found herself looking into the joyful, glittering green depths of his eyes, a stupid, delighted grin on his face.

33

Col felt as though he had been swimming through endless waves of pain for days. Everything was dark, and as hard as he tried to run away from the pain, it chased him. Then, without warning, the pain faded, and he fell into the gentle release of a dreamless sleep.

He awoke to River's soft voice, saying words he'd never imagined to hear her say to anyone.

"I love you." *What?* He couldn't believe his ears. He remained perfectly still, sunlight on his closed eyelids turning his world reddish-orange. He felt as though he was eavesdropping on an impossible event, and he knew if he sat up she would stop talking.

"I know you're a stupid peasant boy who can't fight, but I can't help it. And if you die today, I think I'll regret not admitting it."

He fought to keep his face calm. Even "stupid peasant boy" was an endearing term when it came from her lips. He wondered briefly if he was still dreaming, as the contrast of this beautiful moment to his previous painful existence seemed too dramatic to be real.

"Goodbye," she whispered, sounding so unbelievably sad. It broke his heart, and suddenly pretending to be asleep seemed like a cruel joke. He decided to drop the act, but then, the most wonderful thing that he had ever experienced happened. She kissed him.

The first thing he could think to say was,

"Um." For the first time, his quick wit eluded him and he was speechless. River stared at him, looking confused, embarrassed, delighted, and then angry by turn.

"You're awake!" she snapped. It was an accusation, despite the smile that lit up her face. She seemed to be trying her best to turn it into a frown.

"But, the surgeon said you were dying!"

"What?" Col sat up, looked down at himself, confused.

"But I feel fine."

Then a corner of the blanket shifted, and he saw his left hand. He threw up.

River took a quick step back from the bile and chunks of unidentifiable food that he spewed onto the clean bed. Her eyes went to his hand, but she didn't seem nearly as horrified as he felt.

"It actually looks better," she said, surprised. "It had all this angry redness and swelling, your veins turned red with infection all the way up the arm."

Col couldn't believe the cool way she said it. He couldn't believe his own eyes, looking at the injury. The memory of the giant block coming down onto the anvil where he had so foolishly placed his hand was too painful, too fresh to think about. Now that he was awake, and aware of it, the pain was creeping back. His hand was too nauseating to look at. He looked away, focusing on River, waiting to see the disgust in her eyes. Instead, she looked guilty, and oddly grateful.

"You're alive," she reminded him softly. He'd never heard such a gentle tone in her voice.

Taking a deep breath, he forced himself to look at his hand. It was horribly mangled, just a gnarled claw wrapped in fresh scars and scabs. He didn't see how he could ever use it again. *Wait, scars?* He looked closely. The injured limb had all the marks of a wound a few weeks old.

"How long was I unconscious?" he asked, frightened.

"Just over a day," she said. "We were rescued from the Priest-guards by Hamon's men, but they don't trust us and have us locked up."

Col shook his head, amazed.

"But these scars look at least three weeks old. That's not possible."

River suddenly looked deeply uncomfortable, almost spooked. For some reason, she looked at the lantern above his bed, which had burned out. She opened her mouth, eyes vulnerable, but then that distance between them surfaced again like it always did ever since that night in the canyons, and she put up a wall between them, holding back whatever it was she had wanted to tell him. He didn't know if she did that to protect herself or him, but he hated it. He felt like reaching out, grabbing her hands, telling her that she could let herself be vulnerable with him, that he would never hurt her. Instead, he sat there. Grabbing her hands would probably just make her pull away further.

She turned away, heading for the door without an excuse or farewell. As if the conversation was over, as if nothing had happened and she'd never kissed him. It was unbearable. She was already out the door before he finally had the resolve to say something.

"I love you too."

She froze, but didn't turn around. Then she kept walking. A few meters away, two guards emerged from the woods and trailed her. He stared after her, conflicted. He did love her. Or at least, he was pretty sure he did. He'd never felt so deeply captivated by any girl before. But a small part of him still questioned whether she loved him, or merely loved the reminder of her past that his eyes evoked. Another part of his mind was just exploding with joy and excitement over the kiss. *Stop second-guessing everything.* This happy side berated his skeptical side. *She's a beautiful ancient magical being. She's way out of your league, so just take what you can get and be happy about it.* He sighed, letting that part of himself take over. He was alive, which seemed a miracle. The girl he loved had kissed him. They had escaped the Priest-guards, and somehow, River had managed to persuade the mighty warlord Hamon not to kill them. He could barely believe it, and couldn't help being impressed with River. Despite her act of being a cold, prideful royal snot, she kept revealing more sides of herself that he couldn't help but love.

Feeling very weak, but otherwise fine, he got up and started slowly out the door, determined to figure out what was going on, his good hand trailing on the wall. He put a brave face on as he left. No use admitting how weak he felt, or how much his hand hurt. His real strength had always been his wits, anyway. If he acted crippled, he would always be seen as a cripple and wouldn't be respected.

Col emerged into a fascinating world of cool air, tall trees, and soft, moss-covered turf underfoot. His first guess was that River had been working her magic, but then he saw that all the houses were made from old, roughly hewn logs of the same wood as the trees. In the distance, looming over the trees in every direction that he looked, jagged peaks of stone stabbed the sky. He tried very hard not to gape, but failed.

Coming toward him through the trees was an elderly man with a bucket of water. One of his eyes was cloudy white, but the other fixed sharply on Col. He froze.

"Good morning, friend!" Col greeted him warmly, forcing a relaxed posture and his most good-natured, harmless grin. The man stared at him, goggle-eyed, looking absolutely horrified.

"What are you?" he gasped. Then, before Col could answer, he dropped his bucket and hustled away into the trees, moving so fast that it was painfully obvious he was trying to run away, but also trying to be subtle about it.

Col watched him go, then leaned himself against a tree to wait, looking relaxed, but knowing that he didn't have the strength to do much more than stand there. As he waited, he looked down at his hands. One mangled, the other whole. One ordinary, the other... changed, somehow, by his encounter with River's crystal prison. Bringing his good hand up in front of him, he thought hard about his fight with the priest-guard, remembering the glowing lines. As the image came into his head, he saw them again. Very faint and thin, but definitely there, parting around his fingers like strands of hair and streaming away when he moved his hand through the air. A thin, spiky leaf fell from the tree just then, and into the blurred trail that his hand had left in the air. It slowed, falling at such a gradual speed that he was able to move his hand back and pluck it from the air with ease. He was still staring at the leaf, fascinated, when news of his recovery spread and the people gathered.

34

Every five years, the Hearer would travel the whole land, visiting each temple and re-consecrating the priests there, rotating out any priests who were becoming too ambitious or corrupt, sending them to Kingsfall where he could keep a closer eye on them. Each Calling of priests was meant to be a united group, trained to work together since their days as acolytes, but sometimes a whole Calling became too close-knit, more loyal to their brothers and sisters than to the Hearer, and he had to break those up, as well. However, this was not the regular five-year check. Instead, he found himself suddenly motivated to do a surprise round of inspections around his kingdom, reassuring himself of his rule. This boy everyone was calling the Wolf was gradually becoming the stuff of his nightmares, constantly striking and then disappearing, causing an epidemic of unrest in the nation. The Wolf was clearly on the move, so the Hearer found himself terrified to be sitting immobile at Kingsfall. It was time for him to take action. It was time for the Wolf to see the full might of the Hand mobilized.

He looked out at the courtyard of panicked priests and servants, desperately trying to prepare for the surprise trip. The Hearer was taking almost all of his inner circle of priests with him, leaving only Grimald to oversee Kingsfall in his absence. A girl approached him. She was one of the former acolytes who had been witness to the shattering of the Crystal. He had kept them all close to ensure they didn't spread any rumors. However, this girl in particular had worked her way out of the Fiftieth Calling and into his inner circle with surprising swiftness. She was pretty in a dark, dangerous way, but too young for him. Instead, he liked her for her aggressiveness and distinctly bloodthirsty streak. She never shied away from any job he gave her. He was considering promoting her to oversee his spy network. The current woman in charge of that was getting old.

"Hello Amira," he greeted her first, waiving the need for a formal bow before she could address him. She still bowed, briefly.

"Arbiter of Wisdom, the scouts have been sent out to warn the temples of your visit. We can ride at your will."

The Hearer nodded, starting down the steps. Amira and Eshbo fell into step behind him. He knew they were giving each other dirty looks, but that was fine. Let his underlings fight each other for power; he didn't care as long as it kept them from ever raising their ambitious eyes any higher.

"We ride right now," he decided, heading for the gates. The Wolf was always three steps ahead of him it seemed, but the Hearer was determined to catch up.

Hamon did not like things that she didn't understand. This was evident in the way that she immediately had every one of Col's group brought to her main hall, as soon as she heard her people marveling and whispering. Dominik and River quietly filled Col in as they walked to the building. He read their body language, and was surprised to find that there was a new, uncomfortable distance between them, more pronounced than the distance between himself and River. They walked on either side of him, narrating the astonishing events that had occurred while he lay dying. Col became distinctly aware of the way that all the eyes of his men tracked him, especially Dominik's, with reverence and awe. He didn't like it.

"Listen, I had nothing to do with my recovery, ok?" he reminded them, for what seemed the thousandth time. "I usually heal slowly like anyone."

They didn't seem to believe him. Already, he knew, a new rumor was germinating, that the Wolf had cheated Death, not once, but twice. That he was unkillable, unstoppable. It made him very uncomfortable.

Dominik, whose arm he leaned on, patted his shoulder reassuringly.

"It isn't that you healed yourself that amazes me. I know you cannot. But it is the continued fulfillment of the prophecy that fills me with wonder. The hand of my god is upon you, blessing you and keeping you from death until you fulfill what is written."

Col looked at him sharply, then at River, who widened her eyes in acknowledgement that she, too, had noticed Dominik's strange, fanatical side. Col had rarely heard Dominik string so many words together at once, let alone spout lines about prophecies and gods. He glanced sharply at the man, wondering how much he really knew him.

"What prophecy?"

Dominik only smiled.

"You will know when it is fulfilled. To tell you would defeat the validity of its fulfillment."

They arrived before Hamon, or Helena, as River had informed him. He straightened and walked into the room without Dominik's aid. The girl lounging in the chair eyed him suspiciously. The hall was full of people, some of them the dangerous, thug-like types that Col could now peg on-sight as bandits and killers. However, there were many others. Old men and women, children, and people who looked like regular, harmless villagers. Col had begun to suspect that this mountain valley held far more people than he could have possibly imagined. It wasn't just a bandit camp, it was a bandit city, a safe haven from the oppression of the Order. However, he had also seen the many wounded in the huts near his own. It was a war they were constantly fighting, to keep this place secret.

Approaching Helena, Col went down on a respectful knee.

"Mighty warlady, I thank you sincerely for the liberation of my men from our captivity, and for sparing our lives. We are, all of us, in your debt."

Most women would have teared up by this point. However, Helena's expression became instantly more suspicious.

"What's your game?" she demanded. "I don't trust your innocent story and your miraculous healing. I interrogated some of your men, and they called you the Wolf. That doesn't sound like the name of a harmless boy who the Order kidnapped. Who are you really?"

Col immediately realized that he had misjudged her. This wasn't the kind of person you could sweet-talk and charm. The only persona she would trust was one of brutal honesty. However, it was too late to start over.

"Not harmless," he admitted. "I lead a large number of dangerous men. However, neither me nor any of my men would ever betray you to the Hearer, just as you would never betray us to the Hearer. To betray each other would be to stab ourselves in the foot, as the Hearer would be delighted to kill both of us at once."

Helena looked unconvinced. Belatedly, Col realized that perhaps he wasn't the right person to be doing the talking. Strangely enough, she was likely to trust someone like River far more, with her blunt and aggressive attitude. He opened his mouth again, but then hesitated, considering. Helena glared.

"What do you take me for, a fool? Why would I trust the word of someone I don't know, with the safety of my entire city at stake?"

Ah, so there is a city. Col thought, but he refrained from answering. Instead, he waited for River's inevitable explosion of outrage. She was being surprisingly tactful, holding herself back and remaining unthreatening. However, he could see that it was hard for her, and could see the urge to speak simmering inside, evidenced by her clenched fists. He waited. Then it happened.

"Stop being so paranoid!" River glared right back at the girl, her chin up in defiance.

"You would be a fool, to think that Col *intentionally* almost died, got himself permanently mutilated, and then somehow anticipated that he would be rescued and recover from a deadly infection, all just to get into your stupid valley, escape from it again without knowing how he got in, then betray your little band of outlaws to the Order, the *same* Order that mutilated and almost killed him. What kind of a psychotic madman would go through all of that? And why on earth do you think you're important enough to deserve such desperate hatred in someone who doesn't even know you?"

She looked ridiculous, actually, in her giant boots, while Dominik loomed next to her in his socks. However, she exuded such an aura of pride and righteous anger that she seemed to suck all the air out of the room. Her caustic tone made even the people she wasn't addressing wither and shrink away. Helena looked completely flabbergasted. River continued.

"This is stupid. I'm done being a meek little prisoner. All this suspicion and posturing is weak and meaningless. You confine me, and yet I could have broken open that silly cell hours ago. If we were your enemies, I would have destroyed this whole puny city already."

She turned and stomped away down the long hall in her big boots. Several guards jumped out to stop her, and she planted her hands on her hips, staring them down.

"I. could. *bury.* you right now," she snarled menacingly. The guards quivered in uncertainty facing the bottomless pits of her angry eyes, glancing from her to Helena for direction. Helena had risen from her seat, but she looked perplexed, confused, incredulous. The only emotion Col didn't see anywhere on her face was suspicion.

"Wait." Helena finally broke the tense silence. "Come back."

River turned to look at her, but didn't make any move to walk back to the front of the room. Helena sighed, running her hand through her bouncy curls, thoughts racing behind her keen eyes.

"I'll make you a deal," she decided. "You'll tell your story to me. Explain *everything.* I want to hear it from you, not this golden-tongued Wolf leader of yours. Then, if there is indeed no reason for you to be my enemies, I will set you and your companions free, to stay or go."

Silently, Col thanked any gods that might be listening for River's fantastic temper and vicious sarcasm.

Calmed down slightly, River looked to him for confirmation. Col nodded, and she agreed to Helena's terms.

The ensuing story took almost an hour to tell, even told in River's snappy, factual tone. It was truly abysmal storytelling. However, it still made for astonishing news. Helena was silent, riveted. Sometimes disbelieving, sometimes outright scoffing, but she always listened closely. Finally, River approached the section of the story that Col had missed. Col's men nodded along to her tale of his injury, their capture, and the bandit attack. However, when she continued to tell of her time in the medical hut, even they listened carefully. River hesitated. Her confidence evaporated, and suddenly she looked very vulnerable standing there. Her eyes sought Col's, and seemed to find some strength or resolve.

"He was dying. The surgeon said there was no hope. And... then..."

She sucked in a deep breath, looking terrified.

"I... *prayed*," she sounded shocked at herself, "to Col's mother's god. And then I fell asleep, and when I woke he was like this." She gestured at Col. He gaped, grasping the implications. Every face in the room looked completely incredulous except, strangely, Dominik's. He looked proud of her.

Helena crossed her arms.

"This is one of the wildest stories I have ever encountered," she remarked. "I can't very well ask for this god to show up and prove himself. However, I'm going to need some proof that you're really this Messenger or Sorceress or whatever you call yourself. What proof do you have?"

A spiteful gleam appeared in River's eye.

"You want proof." She calmly stepped out of the giant boots, barely having to try, as they were loose and simply fell off her feet.

"Be careful what you ask for." River's smile was dangerous as she stood, feet braced. Then her body tensed, almost as if she was about to leap. Instead, she remained rock solid and it was the *ground* that leapt. The earth under the hall quaked, and with a horrible, grinding sound a massive crack split the room in two.

Instantly, everything devolved into chaos. People screamed, wood splintered, walls bent, and roof timbers came crashing down. A few people fell into the crack and clung desperately to the edge, trying to haul themselves back up. Col lost his balance on his shaky legs and fell into a loose crouch, tempted to just lie down all the way from exhaustion. Helena's massive wooden chair was tipped on its side. She tumbled out, then sprang to her feet in a panic. However, the chaos had stopped. People were still terrified, clinging to each other or rushing out the broken doorway. The entire hall had cracked open like an egg, walls and portions of either side of the roof leaning crazily away from each other, sunlight shining down through the crack onto the mirrored crack in the floor. The massive fireplace near Helena, completely undamaged, continued to crackle merrily, trying to push smoke through a bent chimney. In the midst of it all, rock-solid, the only one still standing with perfect balance, River reached to put her boots back on, wildflowers blooming merrily around her feet like she was some kind of sweet, magical maiden instead of a walking natural disaster with a temper.

Helena's face was white with shock.

"You've convinced me," she gasped, voice shaky. After a long moment of looking around and getting her emotions under control, she added, "I expect you and your companions to help in the reparations of all this damage. Don't destroy anything else in this valley, or you will no longer be welcome here."

They were, at long last, able to explore the valley. Many of the men were excited, never before having been in a place completely safe from the Order. Sibyl was positively jubilant, exploring every inch of the valley while everyone else threw in a hand with the repairs. Col sat, ate, walked until he was exhausted, then sat and ate again until he felt rested. It galled him, being confined to the few minutes of exercise he could manage every day, while the rest of his men worked so hard. River "helped", but never stooped so low as to actually haul rocks with the peasant folk. Instead, she would stop by the broken hall occasionally, place a hand on the ground and, in a matter of minutes, do what a crew could not have done in hours, creating a whole new frame for the hall out of tall, straight trees, their trunks bending to interlace with each other in a high, arched ceiling that was stunning, compared to the rudimentary architecture of the former hall. Of course, she would then stroll calmly away and leave the others to do the menial work of stripping leaves and branches from the new pillars. It made Col wonder what an elegant paradise she might make out of a place such as Kingsfall, if they could find a way to live freely without being hunted.

Helena watched their movements, warily. She would check on him several times a day, and Col knew she had several people tailing River at all times. Col was determined to do absolutely nothing to spook the suspicious woman. He was the most boring version of himself that he had ever been, spending hours sitting in the sun watching the world move around him. Nonetheless, she never relaxed her guard. She was there hovering near him, a few days later, when Sibyl made the discovery.

Col was sitting in the sun on his chair outside the skeleton of the new hall. Carrying the chair there from the small hut where he slept had been his exercise for the day. It was a big step up, but he hated how weak he was. Suddenly, Sibyl came dashing down the hill and through the trees toward him, running as fast as her long legs could manage. She skidded to a stop, face red and eyes shining.

"Sir, I found something amazing! You'll never believe what these people are doing up in the mountains! There's a massive mine, and this HUGE factory where I think they're making weapons! The guards caught me and threw me out before I could see, but I'm sure that's what it is!" she finished, panting, as Col processed the incredible news. He looked up, seeing Helena swiftly approach, flanked by guards of an alarming size. Sibyl grew wary as their hulking shadows fell over her. Col, however, looked closely at Helena. If she'd wanted to cover up the secret, she shouldn't have let her alarm show so plainly on her face. Col didn't need her to confirm Sibyl's tale. Her darting eyes already had. He looked at her quizzically.

"That explains the well-armed nature of your men. Why the secrecy?"

She looked trapped. After a few moments of flailing for an excuse, she finally sighed.

"I suppose I couldn't expect to keep it from you now that your companions are allowed to roam free in this valley. But our weapons are our most valuable resource in our fight to keep this place safe. The Order mines much of their iron in this area, and it was no simple task to steal an entire mine without them growing suspicious. The Order thinks that this entire mountain has been mined dry of iron. They mine in the lower hills now, with no idea of the wealth we stole from them." She looked pleased with herself. Then her face turned serious. "This is a closely guarded secret, and cannot fall into the hands of the Order. I must ask you not to share it with anyone."

Col promised solemnly, his mind whirling. He thought about all the men who died for his cause because of the superior weaponry of the Priest-guards, and he realized he couldn't simply be satisfied with Helena's decision not to kill them. He needed her aid.

"I know I can't convince you to fight for my cause," he began, "but perhaps you would consider providing weapons?"

Helena threw up her hands, starting to walk away.

"I knew you'd ask for this. I decided not to kill you and suddenly you think you can take advantage of me."

Col called after her.

"But think of how many villagers will die when we overthrow the Order! If they had proper weapons, we could win this fight with much less bloodshed."

Helena wasn't listening. She kept walking.

"You can't have my mines and my weapons for your doomed revolution. Don't get greedy, Wolf. Be glad I let you live at all."

He blew out a frustrated breath. He wouldn't give up. Not yet. Helena would learn that he could be just as stubborn as she was. He turned to Sibyl.

"Don't go near the mine again. It'll just make her more paranoid."

35

Eshbo was a useful man, but not the wisest. The Hearer could tell this from the way the man decided to barge into his tent late in the evening, right as the Hearer was changing from his riding robes into his night clothes. Only certain consecrated servants were allowed to see the Hearer without his veil and robes. Servants, and also any women who caught his fancy, although they too had to be consecrated, and killed immediately whenever the Hearer grew tired of them, without ever being touched by another man. Upon entering the chamber, Eshbo immediately let out a squawk of dismay and threw himself facedown on the floor, shielding his eyes.

"Forgive me, Your Divinity!" he blubbered, "I only wanted to be the first one to give you the news!" The Hearer sighed. He would have to forgive Eshbo. The man was far too useful to put down, although the Hearer was tempted. He sighed.

"You're forgiven. Your news had better be that they found Eithne." The Hearer had been pleased by the tawny curls, ample figure, and rosy cheeks of the young Harvest Keeper in the last village they had passed, and had ordered a few men to bring her to his tent. However, when the priests had returned to the village, they had found the girl missing, and every villager adamantly claimed that they knew of no such person. All the villages had been subtly subversive like this, and the Hearer couldn't afford to slaughter all of his people anymore for such small disobediences. However, it bothered him greatly. He couldn't help but suspect the Wolf. Eshbo cringed.

"No, not her. Different news. But I promise you'll like it."

After listening some more, the Hearer did like it. He threw on his outdoor clothes again and ran out of the tent, leaving Eshbo still cringing on the floor. The Hearer wanted to hear the details himself, from someone a lot more intelligent.

Bursting into the main pavilion where he had just finished dinner less than an hour earlier, the Hearer found a group of his best tacticians huddled over a table of maps, talking excitedly. At his entrance, the head cartographer and tactician, Brenno, approached him, bowing.

"Hearer," he cut out the honorary titles, speaking in haste, "we've analyzed all the areas where the villagers have displayed rebellious attitudes, instead of just the locations where strange plant growth was found. Our best tacticians have thought long and hard about the patterns, and we believe we've discovered the Wolf's strategy."

Brenno led the Hearer over to the table, everyone else bowing and moving away.

"See, here where we've marked black circles are all the areas that we guess the Wolf has been. He's moving from village to town, seeking out the poorer communities but especially ones that are located close to our major caravan routes. And judging from the occasional plant growth nearby some of these, we think he still has the Messenger with him. And they're slowly moving south. If we just get a few more villages revolting, I believe we can pinpoint where the Wolf will strike next, with a high percentage of accuracy."

The Hearer just stared at the map. He didn't see the pattern, but that was why he had tacticians and cartographers in the first place, to do this sort of work for him. He found himself smiling, slowly.

"Look out, Wolf. I'm catching up."

Weeks passed. As Col grew stronger, he began to grow more antsy. Had everything gone according to plan, Lucan and his followers would be expecting a message soon. Col was supposed to have reached at least ten different communities by now, spreading the truth about the

Order. He couldn't be gone too long, or things would start to fall apart. Lucan and Dirk had been given orders that would keep them busy for at least three months, but Col didn't know whether they were succeeding, and it was making him feel stressed. He took to walking all around the valley, hiking through the woods as his strength returned to him, painfully slowly.

He came upon a trail that led upwards. As he followed it, he found himself climbing above the trees. He walked carefully, wary of the sheer rock face on his left and his own uncertain balance. He rounded a bend, and suddenly found himself on a wide shelf of rock, with a waterfall tumbling down past it in icy sheets.

River sat on the ledge, her legs dangling over the tops of the trees, her long hair whipping in the wind. Spray from the waterfall splattered the air and stone around her, catching the sunlight in a glittering mist. Her eyes were closed, expression peaceful, and she looked more beautiful than he had ever seen her. Col stood for a moment, admiring her. He didn't move, not until he knew if he stood silent any longer it would become creepy.

"Enjoying the view?" he asked, then felt stupid because, of course, her eyes were closed. She started, opening her eyes. When she looked at him, however, her expression was still peaceful. That hostile, prideful mask was somehow missing.

"I found this place a week ago," she said, trailing her fingers through the falling water.

"It is very calming. I promised your mother's god that I would serve him if he saved your life, so that's what I'm trying to do. I come here and I pray. I don't really know how, so I've just been saying, 'Thank you,' and then staring at the water and the sunset on the mountains. Sometimes... sometimes I think I hear someone singing, but a song I've never heard before, with words I can never quite understand." Her eyes were vulnerable, searching his.

"Do you know what I'm supposed to do?"

Col felt a warm affection for River filling him. For his sake, she had put aside her pride and was doing the last thing he would ever have imagined her doing - serving someone other than herself. He knew it was probably the hardest thing she had ever done, this girl who was convinced it was her right to rule everyone and everything else she met.

"No, I don't," he admitted, "but I promise you we will find out together. This is something that affects me just as much. And I promise I'll help you figure it out."

She seemed to accept the response, and smiled at him hesitantly. For a moment, he glimpsed the girl she might once have been - before she lost her world, before her head had been filled with ideas of her own greatness and destiny. The smile was so small and fragile, like the first leaves of a plant. It filled his heart with a nervous, fluttering feeling. He sat down beside her, and smiled back with his own heart showing in his eyes. No confident, carefully curated version of himself, just Col; nervous, a little awkward, and completely in love.

She read the expression in his eyes and suddenly her own smile faltered, eyes going big like a startled animal. She didn't look away, however, just held his eyes for a breathless moment. Suddenly, the cool mist-filled air seemed charged with electricity. Heart pounding in his throat, Col moved a little closer to her. She didn't move away, just kept staring into his eyes, her own wide, vulnerable, but also full of anticipation. Col was terrified of doing something wrong, of spooking her or misreading the look in her eyes. However, another part of him urged him to trust his instincts, and he was just as frightened of doing nothing and letting the moment slip away. Gently, he reached out and caressed the side of her face, letting his fingers slip into her silky hair, thumb resting lightly against her jaw. Her skin was cool, and her hair damp as the strands whipped against his hand in the wind. She didn't move, but a shiver went through her at his touch, a spark of something electric kindling behind her eyes. She was so close he could see every droplet clinging to her thick eyelashes, every fleck of color in her eyes. He kissed her hesitantly, then again more seriously when she didn't pull away. She seemed to melt into his touch, all stiffness and hesitation slipping away. The wind picked up and lashed the air with droplets of freezing water, but the kiss was so warm and gentle that he didn't mind. When he pulled away he felt as though every fibre of his being was crackling with energy. She smiled at him, and this time it was a bold smile, eyes alight. He'd never seen that expression on her before, and his answering grin was so big he thought it would break his face.

They walked back down the trail together, and she let him hold her hand with his good one, which seemed to him a greater miracle than his recovery. He had so much energy that she didn't even have to slow down for him to keep pace with her.

As they approached the camp, however, River's smile faded and she withdrew her hand from his, a measure of cold aloofness falling over her face. Nevertheless, he rejoiced. The wall was there, yes, but it was definitely thinner than it had been before. That spark behind her eyes still shone when she looked at him, and he knew that light burned for him, Col, and not a memory of some distant ancestor.

They met Helena coming through the trees, and for the first time Col saw a pleased expression on her face.

"The hall! It's finished!" she exclaimed, the excitement in her eyes making her seem ten years younger than her usual frown did.

"I've never seen any structure so beautiful, not even among the temples of Kingsfall!"

River acknowledged the praise with a gracious nod and a small smile.

"I am not always destructive," she agreed, "but don't expect me to build for you again, or grow your crops. Not when you refuse to help or join us."

Helena's lips tightened, but she nodded. Nevertheless, her eyes had a new, calculating look.

"Can you really do that? Just grow crops as fast as you did those tree pillars in the hall?"

River snorted. "Faster. But don't try to bait me into a demonstration. Besides, if you want this valley to stay undetected by the Order, I shouldn't make such dramatic changes. The effect tends to... bleed into the lands around."

Helena nodded again, but she didn't look happy about it. Her eyes, now, had a bit of a greedy look to them. Looking at her, Col was suddenly struck with a brilliant idea.

"Where is Dominik?" he asked, nonchalantly. "We're past due for a little meeting to decide when we'll leave this valley. I'm feeling well enough to travel, and the men are restless."

Helena said she didn't know, looking rather disgruntled at the idea of them leaving. The conversation ended as she hurried off. Col turned to River, grinning.

"I think I know a way to convince her to help us."

Dominik wasn't a man who was easy to find. However, Col never needed to find him. He let word get out that he wanted to speak with the man, and at some point as he walked around Dominik would step from the shadow of a tree and join him. Col had, gradually, come to accept the man's superior skills, and made use of them instead of resenting them. Dominik seemed good at everything. Not only did he possess astonishing fighting and survival skills, but he was also incredibly well educated, and had valuable insight on almost any topic. Not to mention, beautiful handwriting. This last one Col soon found out as they sat down together with paper and pen, and he explained his plan.

They approached Helena in the morning the following day, just River, Dominik, and Col. The woman was having breakfast in her new hall, gnawing on a half-raw hunk of meat like a starved animal, eating more and out-belching the large, thuggish men and women who sat with her at the table. Col had to admit, she put on a good show of being a bandit lord, despite her gender and small stature. When they approached, Helena waved for them to sit.

"What is it you want this time?" she demanded. "Come to say goodbye, or just hoping for free food?"

Col looked at her keenly, hoping he had correctly interpreted her emotions. She was determined not to join their cause, and risk losing so much. At the same time, he was fairly certain that she regretted losing access to the miraculous powers River possessed, and didn't want to be left out of the great things that were happening in the land. He took a deep breath.

"We'll be leaving soon, and we're grateful for your generous hospitality in allowing us to stay here, but that's not what we're here about. I know you won't join my cause. However, would you consider a trade agreement?"

At the mention of joining the cause, Helena's brows drew together and her mouth was already open to refuse. However, now she hesitated. Her eyebrows rose as Col flourished a paper, written in Dominik's lovely, professional script.

"A trade agreement? You can't be serious. What could you possibly have to offer me? Your witch admitted she can't grow crops without risking exposing us."

Despite her objections, however, she did take the paper when Col handed it to her. She squinted, mouth moving as she slowly sounded out the letters. As she read, however, she only grew more puzzled.

"Population? What does that even mean? How can you trade that?"
Col grinned, rather proud of himself.

"I noticed in the hospital that you take high casualties at the hands of the Order, but you don't have a way of recruiting more men, since you keep to your mountains. I, on the other hand, have men spread out across most of the known world, recruiting. I have hundreds more men sworn to my cause than I can find jobs for. I would be willing to send men to help in your mines and forges, also men to help defend the valley, if, in return, you manufactured weapons for me. If you keep reading the contract, you'll notice I'm also willing to trade food for your wood, as you can't grow many crops here. I'm sure you're tired of berries, weeds, and wild animal meat. There are a number of farming villages which are sending food to support my men, and we have enough to spare."

The men and women around the table mumbled their support, and Helena looked at them, then Col. He could see her resolve wearing thin.

"It *seems* fair," she admitted, "but what's this other thing? An... ore map?"

River stood up taller, chin tilted up in self-importance. She'd been happier than he'd ever seen her lately, but this time she was actually beaming with self-satisfaction. He still couldn't believe how brilliant her idea had been.

"That's actually something River is offering you in return for fully outfitting our group with weapons and supplies as we leave from here. She is willing to help your miners create a map of the inside of the mountain. So that they can find the iron ore. She can sense it when she's underground."

At this, Helena's mouth fell open.

"I don't believe that. How can I know this is true?" Col looked at River, who was preparing to be offended again. He put a hand on her arm.

"If we can prove that it is true, will you accept the agreement?"

Helena stood there, indecisive. She bit her lip, frowning. Then she looked at the people sitting around her, their excited eyes fixed on her, waiting for her response. She sighed.

"Very well. If the girl proves able to do what she claims, I will agree to this map in exchange for outfitting your group. However, further trades will need further negotiation."

Col released a huge breath. It was progress. It was more than he had ever thought would be possible to negotiate with this woman. However, even her intense paranoia did not make her stupid. She wouldn't pass up such a valuable opportunity. He gave Dominik an approving nod. It had been Dominik who judged the relative value of the various goods and services they had to offer, and drew up an agreement that, while heavily skewed in Helena's favor, would still give Col's people the weapons they desperately needed. They had a chance now. The odds of their survival and success were growing. He felt his heart lift. He still felt hunted, but now he could glimpse a way out.

36

As they left the hidden valley, Col felt all his anxiety return. Signs of the Order's oppression were everywhere, in every town and village. Col could almost feel a tangible difference in the air, making him feel nervous as if a Priest-guard could be around any bend in the road. Their guides led them out of the mountains and into the foothills. The dry, barren land made Col feel more at home, but ever since the encounter in the factory that had cost him his hand, he was constantly afraid of stumbling into an ambush. It didn't help that they'd left Sibyl behind. Although they had worked out a code of colored flags for future embassies to signal Helena's people, preventing themselves from being attacked accidentally, Helena still wanted a representative. She had insisted that Col leave behind someone who would be able to recognize his people, and verify their identities, lest any priest-guard imposter try to sneak their way into her hidden valley. Sibyl was the obvious choice, as she had worked at Col's side long enough to recognize most of the men and women making up his command structure. However, he couldn't afford to part with either Dominik or River. So, they were down to only himself, Dominik, River, and six other men. Five, as he immediately sent one off to get word to Lucan and Dirk of what had happened. Only two of those left were trained as scouts, a brother and sister named Caldwell and Kimia. They were older than Sibyl but less experienced, and it didn't help Col's anxiety to know that they were keeping watch.

It took two days on foot to leave the mountains. On the second day, the guides Helena had sent said their goodbyes. Without them, Col felt even more vulnerable. As they watched the men leave, River turned to him.

"Where to now, bold leader?" It was a touch sarcastic, still carrying the bitterness he knew she felt at being second to him in command. However, there was also a wry humor that he hadn't seen in her before. He looked around, thinking hard. He hated being the one to make decisions. But... maybe he didn't have to.

"What do you think?" he asked, turning to her. She cheered up.

"Well, we still have several months of time when Lucan doesn't need us back, and according to the plan we should already have contacted several villages. Things have changed with our discovery of Helena, but perhaps the old plan will still work. Organizing trades and shipments of weapons is crucial, but it's also something that we're not needed for. Other people can do that job. We have plenty of intelligent and shrewd bargainers. However, there's no one else who can do what I can do, and no one else who can persuade and inspire the peasants like you can. For you and I, the most important work we can be doing right now is gathering support. The Order controls the whole world, and we've barely traveled a quarter of that. Those who follow the Order still vastly outnumber those who follow us. I think we should keep traveling further away from our base."

She was right. Col knew her words were wise. However, he hated leaving the fate of his brothers, friends, and followers to someone else. He knew he should keep going, but he wanted to run back to make sure everyone was doing alright without him. What if the Priest-guards had found their hide-out again? What if they had moved, and his messengers couldn't find their new base? What if people had been injured, or killed, in the latest raid?"
He took a deep breath.

"We go onward, then," he agreed, feeling a strong sense of unease.

"Anyone know the way?"

Dominik turned, shouting down from where he had climbed up the side of a small hill.

"I can see a thin shining ribbon in the distance. There is only one river big enough that it can be seen from so far away. It will be the Bleakley, and if we follow it long enough, it joins with the Thude. All the large towns and cities in the Flatlands are built within an hour's walk of the water. It's crucial for trade and irrigation. The villages in the dry portions are small and scattered, usually too poor to spare food or working men to join our cause."

It was a callous tactic. Col bristled at the thought of ignoring the smaller villages just because they were poor. It was the poorest villages that his heart went out to. However, again, he had to let his mind triumph over his heart. It would take far too long to visit every tiny village. Before they could accomplish such a task, the Order would doubtless stamp out their little revolution before it could gain momentum. *Besides, there will be lots of poor people near the water.* He told himself. The whole kingdom was downtrodden, groaning under the weight of the Order's taxes and strict rules, topped with additional taxes from the King.

"Very well! Off to the water we go," he agreed, with forced cheer. "I do think we all need a bath."

The comment met with chuckles from the group, and they continued onwards with raised spirits. The prospect of seeing the great river Thude, even for those who grew up not far from the flatlands, was an exciting one, although everyone knew it was more mud than water, making the idea of a bath truly ludicrous. They chuckled and laughed together as they walked, their steps light. One of the men had a mother who grew up in the flatlands, and he even tried to teach everyone a song about the river. Within a few minutes, he had everyone singing.

> *My old grandpa fell in the river,*
> *thought he saw an eel!*
> *Slipped on a rock and sank in the river,*
> *twas a right ordeal!*
> *Oh the river's fine oh the mud is fun,*
> *when the season's dry, but listen son!*
> *When the season's wet and the rivers run,*

It was, really, a terrible song, made more so by the lack of skill of those who sang it. But they seemed not to feel the oppressive awareness of being hunted that he felt, and so he decided to let them have their moment of cheer. Putting on a cheery smile, he joined in.

They camped by the shore of the Bleakley that night, with proper sleeping rolls and rain-proof shelters from Helena. The shelters were made from the leftover molting shell of what the mountain people called a cave bleater. It was scraped incredibly thin, shaped like a dome big enough for three or more people, and made of a clear, flexible but stiff material unlike anything Col had ever seen. The amazing thing was that it could be folded, rolled or crushed down into any shape, then tied tightly, but would always snap back open into the same oblong dome shape the moment it was free. Col shuddered to think of the size of the creature that would have emerged from such a cocoon. At first, he had refused to accept the gift, until Helena explained that the creature was quite common in the mountains, and the fabric from the cocoon was used for many things in those parts, as well as shipped down the river. Nevertheless, he still felt conspicuous when they put up the domes, like a cluster of giant blisters on the landscape. The dark, cold flow of the water so close seemed to sober the group, and the next morning they were more cautious, glancing warily at the many other travelers heading up and down the road by the river. Col woke with a glimmer of joy in his worried heart. This was due to the fact that River would, occasionally, allow him to hold her hand as they slept, when it was dark enough that the others couldn't see them. He smiled at her as they ate breakfast, although she pretended not to see it. She was so very cautious with her affection.

By midday, the pathway down the side of the river was crowded with people. Some even poled their way on flat rafts up and down the current. People from all over traveled on the road. The traffic grew tight every time they reached a check-point, where guards were checking each person, making them roll up their sleeves and show their arms. This terrified Col. Either the Order had a general idea of the area he would be traveling, or they were searching for him the whole kingdom wide. He immediately ordered the group off the path the moment they saw the checkpoint in the distance, and they skirted the area, crouching low in the tall grass and creeping in a wide, roundabout trail until they were out of sight of the guards. Even when they had passed, Col's nerves remained taught as bowstrings the entire time they were on the road.

Sharing his identity in villages became perilous. Col lived with the knowledge that, in every meeting, he had to convince every person in the room to join his cause, or word would get out of his location, and the entire river road would become a death trap filled with Priest-guards. He plotted, he planned. He persuaded, argued and charmed every day until he was short of breath. Sometimes several times a day, as some villages and towns were clustered closer together. He worked harder than he had ever worked in his life, motivating his group, judging the characters of the villagers, and carefully selecting those that would be invited to join his meetings. Every choice was a reminder that he wasn't perfect, that even though he could read personalities and faces like open books, his judgement could still be flawed. He was haunted by the day in Illsbeth, when the weaponsmith guild had betrayed him. Every death that day had been his fault for trusting the wrong men. His mangled hand sent stabbing pains through him sometimes when he absent-mindedly tried to use it, and he almost enjoyed the pain, reminding him that at least he, too, had suffered for his mistake. He had always firmly believed that he would gladly give his life to protect those he loved. At first it had only been his family, but now his list had expanded to include River and every one of the men and women who served him. And yet, so many of them gave their lives for him daily, while he still lived. The thought was haunting. He was determined to prove himself worthy of their devotion.

37

Weeks later, there came a morning where the dawn broke brilliant red, silhouetting in sharp detail the walls and roofs of a city breaking up the flat line of the horizon. Col breathed a sigh of relief. They'd nearly exhausted their supplies, and he'd been forced to send all of his men except his two scouts off to report to his troops with instructions and updates. Soon, he'd have to turn back. However, they'd reached Wanderkeep, the heart of all travel in the far reaches of the world. To Col, it had always been a distant myth.

The Bleakley had joined with the river Thude, a wide, stinking expanse of slow-moving sludge that was too wide to see the other side. They had crossed the river on a barge, then continued downstream for days until the buzz of insects and the hot steamy stench of river slime became commonplace. Everyone except River came to accept the conditions. She remained disgusted, overheated, and generally cranky as she sweated, her pale cheeks blistering red from sunburn. Although she'd been astonishingly good-tempered for most of the journey, the stench of the Thude brought out the worse sides of her. At the sight of the city in the distance, she let out a huff of disbelief.

"Who would *choose* to live next to this stinking sludge? We don't have to go in there, do we?"

Unfortunately, they did. As they approached the city, Col grew excited by the wild variety of travelers he saw moving along the roads. There were people dressed in vests made from some kind of hard bark, men with their heads shaved in a strip down the middle, and even a group of people dressed all in yellow, leading Sliders to sell. The long, low beasts roamed in herds in many parts of the world, but Col had never seen people capture them. The creatures moved with an odd, rowing motion, digging thick, oar-shaped front claws into the soil and shooting themselves across the ground on their hard stomach shells. Each shell was made up of hundreds of large, spade-shaped sections which moved at the same time as the creature's paws, undulating to grip the ground and push the creature forward. Col had heard that they were physically incapable of backing up. It was very strange to see one for the first time, and frightening, despite the muzzles over their sharp teeth. As the group passed them, Col saw they left a trail of deep scores in the hard ground, and flattened grass.

Wanderkeep had no gates, nor were there any priest-guards checking travelers as they entered via the many roads and even docks on the river. Col marveled at the way the city was half built out onto the water on massive rafts, connected by swinging bridges. It was not too dissimilar from the way Kingsfall clung to the tops of cliffs, bridges spanning the many chasms. Except, it was flatter. And far more stinky. The stench of hundreds of sweating human bodies moving through the city, added to the smell of garbage that people dumped into the water made Col want to retch. To make matters worse, the city was surrounded by stables of a wide variety of animals, where greedy-eyed men were buying and selling steeds to cater to the many travelers. They, like everyone else, shoveled the refuse into the water.

Strangely enough, although Wanderkeep was further from Kingsfall and the rebel presence there than any place Col had ever heard of, Dominik approached the city with the confidence of familiarity.

"There is an inn on the water where the poorest of the poor gather," he told Col helpfully.

"Nobody there has any love for the Order."

Col nodded. "We'll stay there for a night, while we re-stock," he agreed, "but just one night. There are too many people here for my liking."

They entered the city and found the inn with little difficulty. The conditions were dubious, but after camping on the hard ground nobody complained about the quarters. Re-stocking was easy, as there were wares from all over the world practically being shoved in their faces by vendors at every turn. Col began to breathe easier as there continued to be no signs of recognition or suspicion in the people he passed.

As they headed through the crowded streets, he looked over at River, who trudged along in her borrowed boots looking overwhelmed. She tried to be so imposing, but in the overlarge boots and with her sunburned nose he thought she looked rather cute. Impulsively, he took her hand and pulled her behind him into the crowd, ditching the rest of the group in a moment of excitement. They were in a city he'd only heard of in tales, the woman he loved was with him, and his enemies were nowhere in sight. For the first time in weeks, Col let himself relax, grinning at River like a goon as she spluttered and protested.

"Relax, Princess!" he teased her. "We can't exactly visit the great Wanderkeep without getting a souvenir!"

Her eyebrows drew together in confusion.

"A... What?"

"It's like a gift to take home, to remember that you've been somewhere special," he explained. "My mother still keeps a rock we found on the bank of the Thude the one time we traveled all the way out to see it."

She nodded.

"I think I understand. My father used to bring home the weapons of conquered enemy generals, after he had killed them with their own blades."

Col coughed uncomfortably.

"Exactly! Just... less violent." He grabbed a necklace made of interwoven colorful cords from a stall and held it up to her neck, pinching one of the strings awkwardly between two crippled fingers of his bad hand.

"How about this? It looks good on you."

The greedy-eyed woman behind the stand agreed enthusiastically.

"Oh yes dearie! You look like a princess!"

River chewed her lip, looking unimpressed.

"I can make better ones from flowers."

Col deflated. It was silly, considering their situation, but in this little moment together in the Wanderkeep market he really did want to get a special present for his girl. He wanted to make her smile, to make her relax for a moment.

She didn't seem interested in shopping, and just trudged along behind him as they kept walking. He was starting to deflate, his excitement evaporating. Then, he heard her give a little,

"Oh."

He followed her gaze. There, in a little stall down a side street, a flurry of bright colors and fluttering leaves crowded the stalls. It was a collection of plant shops. River was completely fascinated. Col felt a surge of relief. As quick as possible, he steered both of them down the alley. He could tell she was trying hard not to look impressed, but she couldn't help the way in which she stared at the many different varieties of plants, seeds, and flowers on display. After a few minutes they came to a stall where River stood, transfixed, staring at a bush growing out of the ground near the stall with leaves that were bright blue, each covered in a soft film of silver fuzz. She touched a leaf, hesitantly, and Col was shocked to see her actually tear up.

"It's so beautiful," she whispered. "What is it called?"

The seller was a wizened woman with tough, sun-browned skin. She looked at River, then the plant, and laughed.

"Why, that's not a plant I'm selling! It's Dewbrush. You've never seen it before? It used to grow everywhere in the flatlands, although now it only grows in some spots near the river. It's rare now, but it's still just a weed. Needs lots of water, so it's leeching the run-off from the other plants I'm watering to grow here."

River just touched the soft leaves, speechless. Col didn't understand. To him, it was a scrawny little bush. He thought the flowers that River grew sometimes to twine in her hair were far more beautiful. However, River turned to him, amazed.

"This land is more beautiful than I thought," she told him softly. "I see now that it isn't dead, just wounded. Perhaps I can heal it."

Col didn't understand her enthusiasm, but he was glad she had something to get excited about in her future, instead of only pining for the land she had known in her past. He waited until River got distracted by a different seller calling to her, and then turned to the woman.

"Do you have dewbrush seeds?"

She started to laugh at him, but then saw his serious expression and her gaze turned crafty.

"Now, I told you it was rare, didn't I? I don't usually sell it, so you'd have to give me a while to dig some up from storage. Come back in an hour, and I'll see what I can do for you."

Knowing he was about to be charged a very steep price for what was essentially a weed, Col still agreed. It would make River happy, and that was worth any price to him.

Turning a corner, he came face-to-face with Dominik. The tall man was trying to blend in to the crowds of sightsee-ers, but that was like a sleek, dangerous panther trying to blend in to a crowd of happy puppies. The way he looked, even the way he moved was different. People parted around him warily.

At the sight of Col, Dominik caught him by the shoulders.

"Where have you been?" he demanded, eyes intense. "Where is the lady River? Kimia and Caldwell were following your lead, but when you disappeared they started acting like a bunch of gawking tourists, wandering off without any organization at all!"

Col felt guilt wash over him. He'd wanted to forget his stress, but as the leader of a group it was his job to stress. He couldn't wander off for a romantic walk with River without letting all of his men down.

"I'm sorry, I was distracted," he admitted. "But why don't we just let everyone have a bit of a holiday? Supplies are purchased, and people won't gather at the inn until evening. Besides, the more like gawking tourists we all act, the less conspicuous we will be."

Dominik considered that, but he still looked on-edge.

"I don't like this," he muttered to himself. "We shouldn't split up."

Col felt himself growing stressed again. Turning, he tried to spot River in the street full of plants.

She was blocked by a group of people moving down the street as well, several carrying large traveler's packs. Col didn't think much of it, until his eye caught on an object sticking out of one of the packs. It was a hilt. Not just any hilt. Criss-crossed with a tight wrap of black leather, flat silver end. Without getting any closer, Col immediately knew that it would have a tiny hand symbol stamped into the end, and that there would be a matching hilt protruding from the other side of the pack.

The man hadn't noticed Col, in his drab traveler's clothes. However, he was moving down the street in the direction River had gone. Craning his neck, he saw several shapes begin to rise from where they had been crouched behind stalls, the nervous, sweating merchants trying hard to pretend everything was fine. Several other people in the crowded street of plants were also moving in that direction, displaying a suspicious lack of interest in the wares displayed.

Panic clutched at Col's chest. He cursed himself for not disguising River better, at least covering the shining black waterfall of her hair. Dominik looked confused, trying to see what Col was staring at.

"Priest-guards," Col whispered, frozen between running away and charging into the plant market to find River.

"But they're dressed like travelers." It was brilliant, really. Col had never before heard of priest-guards going out into public without their official robes, so he hadn't thought to watch out for it. But the city had been too quiet, the street full of beautiful plants too perfect. He should have known it was a trap.

The moment he said it, Dominik was moving. He grabbed Col's arm before he could make a decision and started dragging him the other way. In addition to being almost a foot taller, Dominik proved to be incredibly strong. Col struggled, trying to break free of the iron grip and chase after River. Then he stopped struggling and started trying to move even faster than Dominik, because several men had caught sight of the struggle and were moving towards them with altogether too much aggression in their movements. Sure enough, Col caught the flash of bright silver steel and black leather in their hands. Side by side, Col and Dominik raced through the crowded streets. In the densely packed people, Col found himself pulling ahead, his small wiry frame better able to dodge and duck between bodies. He knew he should be planning, should be trying to find a way out of the trap, but he was too busy panicking.

Fortunately, the fact that the Priest-guards were in disguise proved a hindrance to them. People did not clear out of the way as they usually would, but pushed and shoved right back. The Priest's couldn't even brandish their weapons to clear space in the tight crush of people. Seeing this, Col signalled to Dominik. With the big man following, he turned onto busier and busier streets.

It worked! Although he found it hard to hear sounds of pursuit over the crowd and his own gasping breaths, Col soon realized that nobody was chasing him anymore. He flashed Dominik a quick grin of relief. Then, just as quickly, the good mood seeped away. *River.*

"We have to save her!" he said frantically. "Somehow, the Order knew we'd be here, and they set a trap for River in the plant market."

It made sense, really, now that he thought about it. Never having actually caught River for any length of time, the Hearer wouldn't know anything about River except the fact that she was causing magical flurries of plant growth in random places throughout the kingdom. With this knowledge, the best possible attraction to bait his trap with would be a market selling exotic plants. And it had worked. He turned in the crowded street, intending to go back, but Dominik stopped him with a firm grip on his shoulder.

"I can't let you do that," he said, his voice firm. He had been so obedient to Col over the past few weeks that Col was taken aback by the insubordination.

"You are too valuable to be risked for the sake of that woman, valuable weapon though she is." Dominik's face was set with determination. Col spluttered.

"What? That's crazy! Without River, I'm nothing! Just a scrawny village boy with a crippled hand."

"No." When Dominik looked at him, his expression was strange, almost reverent. "On the surface, yes. But you are far from ordinary. You are the fulfillment of prophecy, the future peace to this land. You are the Broken Man."

There was a weight to his words that sent a chill down Col's spine. The noise of the crowd seemed to dim, and he heard Dominik perfectly clearly, despite his soft tone. He took a step back.

"I don't understand. The prophecies of the Order are fake."

Dominik nodded.

"The Order is a fraud, yes. But not all prophecies are false. There are things far older than the Order itself."

Col's head was spinning. Dominik wasn't making any sense. Was he going mad? Or had he always been mad, just faking his usual calm persona?

"What do you mean?" he spluttered. "Who are you?"

At that moment, the ground shook. People started screaming, with the loudest screams echoing from the direction they had come. Dominik's face once again adopted his calm, dangerous mask.

"All will be known in time," he said, placing a hand on Col's shoulder and hustling him away. "Now, we need to run."

Col tried to shake Dominik off, but the man was strong. Additionally, there was a part of Col that had grown to see Dominik as a friend and valuable ally. His instinct was to simply go along with what his trusted commander wanted, instead of fighting him. Dominik had never before been this insubordinate since swearing allegiance to Col's cause.

38

River was staring, intrigued, at a plant which fluttered its leaves when she touched it, the whole bush shivering without any wind. The seller, who had been prattling on about which climates would support the delicate thing, suddenly trailed off. A breath of wind brushed the hair from River's neck. Too late, she realized that there couldn't be wind coming from that direction, as the street was tightly hemmed in with walls. A man grabbed her arm, and she spun, trying to kick her shoes off instinctively. They were new ones from Helena, and fit her feet better than Dominik's borrowed boots. However, it also meant they were harder to kick off, and clung to her feet. The man grabbed her face, inspecting her features with an intensity that scared her. Who was he? She tried to punch him, but someone behind her grabbed her arms. She struggled wildly. Unfortunately, despite all her weapons training, she was still a small woman. In these close quarters, with her arms pinned by someone with superior strength, a desperate feeling of helplessness threatened to strangle her.

"Is it her?" her captor demanded. The man holding her chin frowned, then let go to pull a piece of paper from his pocket, reading it over.

"I'm not sure. She's supposed to have very white skin, like paper. But this girl's skin is all red and blotchy."

The man behind her huffed out a laugh, his face so close that she felt his hot breath blow across the top of her head.

"It's called a sunburn, dummy. Other than that, does she match?"

River didn't give them time to decide. She thrashed, pulling her knees up to her chest so that the man holding her arms stumbled, suddenly forced to bear her full weight. Then she kicked his shins out from under him with both of her feet. Together, they pitched forward onto the ground. River's face slammed into the hard stones, and pain exploded through her. Her captor landed on top of her, knocking her wind out.

On the ground, dazed, with her arms pinned behind her, any other girl would have felt completely helpless. Not River. The man on top of her was cursing, getting up, pinning her down with one knee in the small of her back.

"It's her, it's gotta be! I'll hold her down, you give the signal."

There was the sound of a match scraping. Through the strands of hair tangled across her face, River saw a hand place a round green paper-wrapped package on the road a few feet away, then light it on fire. The little flame immediately started sending up a thick line of dark green smoke into the sky, consuming the package rapidly. People started shouting, and running.

River breathed out, slowly, blinking through the pounding pain in her head. She closed her eyes. Her lip felt swollen, and her nose was gushing blood on the ground. Her cheek was stinging, bits of grit and small rocks biting into her skin. But, through that pain, she could feel the cobblestone road. It was hard, unyielding. However, it was made up of rough, natural stones, with grooves of dirt between one stone and the next. She could still feel the earth underneath. It was distant, cowering like a kicked puppy. She'd been mentally beating it down over the past few months, distancing herself from it, afraid of giving herself away through a sudden outbreak of greenery. She felt a wave of guilt, suddenly, for the way she'd been treating her oldest friend. *I'm sorry.* She thought, whispering the words out loud into the stones, her breath sending puffs of dust out across the dry road. *I've been treating you like a slave. If you help me now, I promise not to push you away again.* She reached out, not to try to force the earth into submission, but with a tentative offer of friendship. It was strange, like straining a stiff muscle. She hadn't used her powers like this in years. For a long time, she had treated the earth like a weapon to intimidate those around her. However, somehow that approach didn't quite sit right with her anymore.

The ground trembled. People started screaming, but River didn't pay attention. At her offer of friendship, the long-dormant, wild creature that was the soul of this land drew closer, closer, power surging up from the depths of the earth to touch the surface where her body lay pressed against the ground. Then, it *remembered*. A flash of long-forgotten affection and familiarity reached out to brush against her mind. Once, long ago, she had also been its closest friend, a little girl with a deeper connection and awareness of the world around her than anyone else. As hints of that little girl showed through River's hardened personality, so too a hint of the earth she had once known peeked through the wild creature it had become. Joy flooded through her, and she almost forgot her pain.

The man kneeling on River's back suddenly let out a yell of surprise. Around River's body, grass and moss crept out over the stones like swiftly spreading water. As it radiated outwards, the stones began to grind and rip up out of the road, trees and bushes shoving their way up into the sunlight with increasingly violent speed. People screamed and ran, as walls began to topple, houses ripped apart as trees that should have taken hundreds of years to grow suddenly thrust their way straight through homes. Fortunately, most houses did not fall down onto people, but instead the sheer number of trees and branches broke the houses apart and hoisted chunks of walls, roofs, and balconies into the air. The whole city was in a panic before the trees had spread over two blocks, waves of people running for the countryside or the boats on the water. River could feel the thunder of their footsteps through the earth, drumming in an ever-expanding ring away from her as they fled the tide of trees.

Feeling strangely calm, River took control of a small portion of the earth near her, coaxing it to do her bidding. Two vines sprouted on either side of her, grabbing the man off of her back and hoisting him into the air. Several weapons fell off his belt as he dangled. River caught sight of the silver Hand of the Order on a knife. She reached out with her mind, and other vines grabbed people around her. They wore plain clothes, but she was sure that they were also Priest-guards, from the way that they had been running to attack her, instead of running away. In moments, eight men struggled and dangled around her. She clenched her fists, glaring at them as blood dripped down her chin. The temptation to crush the men to death with her vines was strong. She almost did it. But then she thought of Col's face. Somehow, she knew he would tell her not to do it. And it wasn't just Col. Her own heart told her he was right. She had killed many Priest-guards before. However, something about the fact that they were no longer fighting her, no longer a threat, made killing them wrong. She settled for squeezing them just a little, to make sure they knew she could kill them if she wanted to. Then she sat down and removed her shoes, tying two long straps together and looping them over one shoulder. She was *not* going to have to borrow Dominik's big, clumsy boots again.

Swiping blood from her upper lip where it gushed from her nose, River stood and set off into the crumbling remains of what had once been a market. She was small, alone, but she had the confidence of knowing that the earth itself was on her side. Picking up a stick, she took two daggers from under her cloak and formed the twig into a handle for them, making a spear with two ends. A spear was her favorite. She didn't like the close-quarters fighting that came with knives, and although she was an excellent shot with a bow, it wasn't practical for self-defense. Spears, though. A spear was elegant. The double headed spear was a weapon she had invented in her youth, fusing two spear handles together with her powers. Her weapons tutor, in particular, had admired it, and the way in which it could be used for much faster and more diverse strikes than a normal spear. Even her father had adopted the design and taken groups of men trained with the weapon into battle. She felt a pang of nostalgia as she gripped the shaft. With two feet planted firmly on the ground, and a spear in her hand, she felt more powerful than when all the hordes of Col's followers had been at her side. Thinking of Col, she quickened her steps, determined to make sure that he was all right.

39

A few blocks into the jungle, and River suddenly felt something. A shudder, almost painful, through the earth under her feet. She turned, slowly, as a sound came from behind her. It was the sound of chopping, marching, and a strange grinding sound. The pain came from that direction. River knew that a trap had been set for her, and yet, she couldn't just turn and run. That felt too much like defeat, like cowardice. Right now, she had the entire power of the earth under her feet. She felt invincible. She had to stop whatever was causing the earth pain. She *could* stop it. What if she could defeat the Order's armies right here, in the center of a city full of people? Surely then the people of this nation would see her as a true leader, with such a stunning victory. She didn't need Col or his men to be unstoppable. In fact, they were always holding her back, making her limit her powers in order to protect them. What if she could simply destroy this garrison of Priest-guards, and make Col safe from pursuit? She stepped forward, a fire burning in her heart. She wouldn't run. No. This time, River would stand and fight for herself and those she loved.

The drumming footsteps approached, and with them, pain. River felt her sense of strength weaken as the earth withdrew its awareness, shrinking away from the pain. Then, she saw them.

It wasn't so much a troop of Priest-guards, as it was an army. A garrison marched in front, hacking at the plant life with axes, machetes, and frightening wheeled monstrosities manned by ten men each. They rolled forward bristling with blades, grinding the underbrush into a pulp. Behind them marched a second row of men and women, but these each held a sack, throwing fistfuls of white dust onto the ground. It was *salt*. River knew instantly that this was the source of the earth's pain. As new plants and trees tried to push their way up from the soil, they withered and died even faster than they grew, shriveling into dried-out, brittle, bone white sprouts. A swath of white, dead ground extended behind the troop. Over the desolation marched still more priest-guards, as well as runners carrying more bags of salt to replenish the troops at the front. It was chilling.

Although she had come to respect them as mighty warriors, River had never guessed at the intelligent tactics, organization, and sheer overwhelming force of the Order. In her past, what approached her now would have been the full army of an entire nation. And yet, a part of her suspected that this was merely one battalion of the Order, one small fighting force mustered from a single temple. As the force spread out to form a wall of sharp metal pointed at her, her heart pounded in fear. She had only ever fought a few priest-guards at a time, and suddenly she realized that she might have miscalculated in her pride. Dominik at her side in that moment would have made her feel much better. However, River forced herself to stand firm. Stretching to her full height, she adjusted her grip on her spear, glaring at the priests in challenge.

"Turn back now," she shouted, "or I will show no mercy. Your blood will feed the ground, and the trees will consume your bodies, until there is no trace of you left for even the birds to pick over."

If she hadn't been surrounded by an awesome display of power, the priests would likely have laughed at the slight woman challenging their mighty ranks. However, she had just destroyed half a city, and the destruction was still spreading. Several men at the front of the line looked nervous, raising their weapons defensively. Then, an order barked from behind them. The voice was deep, cold, and harsh. To River's ears, it was vaguely familiar.

"She's the one. Take her alive."

Immediately, the men snapped to attention and charged forward. Clearly, they were more afraid of their commander than they were of her. Before the first line could even reach her, they were swept away by a fresh wave of tree growth, roots and vines grabbing legs, sharp wood shooting up from the ground and stabbing at the men. However, she could only halt the first wave. Once the trees reached the line of people throwing salt, they stopped growing. Sensing her weakness, these priests stepped forward, throwing salt over each step before they took it. It was infuriating and terrifying. River had no choice but to retreat before them, picking off anyone who stepped too close to unsalted ground, trying not to get surrounded.

At least they wanted her alive. As her opponents drew closer, River found them easier to defeat because they held themselves back using chains and clubs instead of their sharp swords, while she attacked with fury, uncaring how many she killed. Too late, she realized that her own fury was her downfall. In her deadly focus on her latest opponent, wrapping the woman in vines, she had allowed the salt-throwing priests to start surrounding her. Salt flew all around her, stinging her feet like hot coals when she stepped on it. The priest-guard who had been strangling in vines a moment before gasped for breath as the plant withered.

As the circle of priests closed in, River called tangling vines up from the earth to slow their approach. Pain instantly sliced through her like knives. The vines blackened and died even as they tried to grow, and she felt suddenly weak, as if the plants had sucked out her own blood instead of water from the ground as they grew. Her muscles shook, and her vision blurred with exhaustion. She barely dodged two priests who leapt at her. They were closing in from all directions now, and she couldn't keep track of them. Spinning in place, she stabbed and slashed with her weapon, clearing a circle around her the length of her spear shaft. How long could she keep this up? Even as she wondered, a man was shoved a little too close by the press of warriors crowding around. River impaled him before he could get any closer. At that moment, she was seized from behind by a crushing grip. She bent her knees, intending to throw her attacker off balance and break free. However, she was hoisted into the air like a thrashing puppy, her attacker seeming to have no trouble lifting her dead weight. The moment her feet left the ground, she felt completely blinded and helpless. Panic closed her throat. In her ear, the deep voice spoke.

"Not so powerful once you're in the air, are you?" the man hissed. River finally recognized that cold, hate-filled voice. It was the veiled man, the sinister golden robed priest who ran the Order.

In her moment of distraction, the rest of the priests had closed in, many hands grabbing at her spear shaft and wrenching it out of her grip. She thrashed, trying to hurt the Hearer. She punched him in the face, but her fist hit the hard metal of a helmet. Never one to shy from fighting dirty, River delivered a swift kick to where she thought his groin was. Once again, her attack only hurt her, as her heel slammed against the hard metal of a codpiece. The arms around her tightened in anger, crushing the air from her lungs.

"Give up, Messenger," the voice in her ear snarled. "You can serve me willingly, or I can break you first. Either way, you *will* be mine. No one can stand against me."

River's breath came in tiny gasps. She had never felt arms so strong, never encountered an enemy so full of power and violence. For the first time in her life, she understood how a mouse would feel, being crushed in the jaws of a snake. All the vengeful pride she had felt before was gone. In its place, only helpless desperation. The Hearer shifted his grip on her, capturing one of her thrashing arms and pinning it to her side.

"Now that I know your weakness, it shouldn't be hard to keep you contained." The Hearer laughed softly, as if holding her up in the air, struggling and kicking, was no trouble at all. As if he had already won.

"You'll never touch the earth again, never taste freedom, until you serve me," he hissed. "You'll say what I want you to, give demonstrations of power when I command, and the Wolf's little uprising will fall apart."

Never touch the earth again? At the Hearer's promise, sheer

terror and adrenaline flooded through River. When he shifted her weight again, gripping her in one arm while he reached with the other to capture her free arm, she thrashed.

Fingers scrabbling at his helmeted head behind her shoulder, she found the eye slits of the helmet and stabbed her fingers through. One finger felt something wet, and she poked him hard, directly in the open eyeball before he could shut his eyes. The Hearer let out a yell, staggering backward. The iron grip of his arm slackened slightly, and River used the opportunity to wrench herself free. Panting, she dropped to the ground.

The moment her body touched the salt-covered earth, she could feel the pain and death there. The ground was no longer living. However, in her desperation, River barely felt the pain. Knowing she had mere seconds before she was pounced upon, she blew hard upon the ground, brushing with her hands at salt that didn't blow away. Feeling horribly vulnerable with her back turned to so many enemies, she jammed her fingers down into the crack between two cobbles in the little patch she had cleared. Nails tore, jagged edges of the rocks tore bits of skin off of her fingers, and the residual salt on her hands only made the sting worse. However, River kept digging, wriggling her fingers down between the stones until she was sure they were going to be crushed. She could only feel the earth faintly, as it withdrew from the toxic ground upon which she crouched. *Please, God, help me! I can't be locked away from the earth, I'll die!* Her heart cried out in fear and anguish at the thought, tears of frustration dripping out of her eyes to mix with the blood, snot, and dirt on her face.

"What's she doing?"

"Stop her!"

"Get help for the Hearer!"

"No, first grab her, then help him!"

A cacophony of shouts and yells surrounded her, but River barely heard them. Instead, a calm swept through her. At that moment,

she felt her connection to the earth restored, through the tip of one
bloody, half-crushed finger wedged between the stones. She looked up at
the Hearer.

40

The Hearer was, if possible, more angry than he had ever been in his life. The cornerstone on which his entire religion rested was a diminutive young woman with unbelievable powers. This, in itself, would not have been an issue. He had figured out her weakness. Simply take her feet off the ground, and the awesome, earth-shattering forces protecting the girl disappeared. The problem was the girl's personality. He had to finally accept that he couldn't blame the Wolf for all of his problems. That brat of an acolyte may have stolen her away, but it was clear that the girl herself was also overflowing with defiance against the Order.

How was he to ever control someone who hated him with such passion? He was confident he could break her over time, but how much time did he have? He couldn't afford to have the core symbol of his religion missing for so long, or surely things would start to fall apart. And, there was the problem of his aging... Without the magic of the crystal influencing his body, he had noticed wrinkles appearing at a rapid pace. All of these things worried him as he seized his chance to grab the girl and take her away from her source of power. A moment of triumph. In that moment, he knew that he was the stronger one, that he could snap her like a young sapling. He savored her fear, and then - she *poked him in the eye.* Of all the degrading, humiliating ways to be beaten in combat, the Hearer had never anticipated that he would falter on the battlefield because an unarmed, feisty slip of a girl poked him in the eye.

It was astonishment and rage, more than pain, that stunned him. Within a few moments, he was striding forward again, shoving violently through the crowd of worried priests hovering around him. He would *break* her! How dare she! All manner of vile tortures and violent thoughts flooded through his brain as he leapt back toward where the girl had crawled off. His priests had not stopped her, sensing that the Hearer would want to finish this fight himself. It was a drawback of their warrior system. Only the strongest priest could remain Hearer, and so anytime that a Hearer fought someone it was seen as a duel of sorts. No one else could interfere.

The girl was kneeling on the ground, fingers wedged between some cobblestones. She looked up at him with a tear-stained face. Glaring at her through his one good eye, he felt a spike of triumph. She was crying, bleeding, on her knees. He knew she was defeated, and his heart was already racing, filled with anticipation at taking his revenge. Then, he saw a flash of something else in the girl's eyes. Determination. Before he could reach her, she used both hands to rip apart the stone roadway like it was a curtain, throwing herself into the chasm she had created. The ground shook, and a crash like thunder but a hundred times sharper split the air. When the Hearer and his men regained their feet, the chasm was gone. The girl was gone. She had been swallowed up by the earth as if she never existed. The stunned silence was broken by the Hearer's outraged yell. He had known nothing of this branch of her powers. How did she manipulate the earth in such a way? And why? Had it been suicide? Or escape? Either way, the Hearer didn't care. She was beyond his reach. The blinding rage that filled him had no outlet.

Never having lived in Wanderkeep, Col and Dominik found themselves turned around in the crowded streets. It didn't help that the streets that weren't overgrown with plants were now packed with so many people that the two men could barely move. Col's heart was heavier than it had ever been, feeling as though it was about to burst with worry. *I can't lose her.* He didn't care that she was a prideful, terrifying force of nature most of the time. He knew he loved River; he knew he would never stop loving her. If he lost her, his life would fall apart. The screaming was getting closer, but the crowd was packed too tightly to get away from it. Col turned, and then he saw it.

Moving through the crowd with a speed that only the threat of violence can achieve, was an actual army. A strange mix of Priest-guards in ordinary clothes, and a group of men in full, formal battle dress. Each priest packed more weapons than Col's entire group put together. Additionally, the group of men in the formal robes were surrounding a man on a horse, with the most brilliant golden battle gear Col had ever seen. Every inch of it was painted gold, with strips of thin cloth giving the impression of a robe, while doing nothing to hinder the man's movements, or hide the intricate armor. It could be none other than the Hearer himself. Even as Col realized it, the Hearer turned his armored head, staring in Col's direction as if he could pick him out in the crowd. Blood was smeared around one of the eye-holes in the helmet, making it look even more frightening. Col suddenly wished that Dominik, standing close by, was not so tall and conspicuous, with his dark skin and dignified bearing. Col started to back away, but the Hearer pointed straight at him.

"Wolf!" His voice was a snarl of rage, echoing out of the helmet and over the sound of the crowd.

"Do not think you can run from me! The Order will crush your little rebellion like it has crushed all others. I will hang your body from the highest cliff and watch the birds eat you!"

At his pointed finger, priests began to push their way toward Col. Dominik drew a sword, unable to back up any further in the crush of the crowd. Seeing he wasn't going to be able to talk his way out of this, Col drew his own. People were beginning to turn their heads and stare at the pair of fugitives.

"The Wolf? Did he say the Wolf?"

"He's right there!"

"The Wolf's men saved my uncle's village from starvation."

"Oh! He's even more handsome than I imagined!"

"Who's that with him? I thought the Messenger was a girl."

Something very strange was happening. Where once people had been scrambling away from the priest-guards, now they stood their ground. As a whole, the crowd began to draw close around Col, closing ranks to form a solid shield of bodies, hundreds of men strong. The harder the Priest-guards pushed, the more the people resisted. Col's eyes shone with tears of pride for his countrymen. However, at the same time his heart sank. They had no weapons. Behind him, people began opening a small path for Col and Dominik to retreat from the Hearer. They began to do so. Col ducked under arms and squeezed past shoulders, all the while touched by hundreds of admiring hands, surrounded by murmured blessings. Never had he imagined that so many people knew of him. His heart grew full of love for these strangers who cared so much for his cause that they would risk their own lives to save him. He tried to meet as many eyes as he could, memorizing faces.

Then, the Hearer's voice cut through the air again.

"Cut a pathway."

As one, the ranks of Priest-guards drew their weapons. Some even began to roll forward giant machines covered in blades to chop to bits any who stood in their way.

The murmured blessings turned into screams. Col felt, in his heart, the sudden weight of guilt. The crushing responsibility for hundreds of deaths came down upon him, and he could not leave. Even though all the people around him were trying to push him, standing in the way of the Priests while crying for him to run, Col couldn't move. He had run away and left River, and the guilt had been horrible. He would not leave a second time. Ignoring Dominik, who was looking back and waving ahead, Col instead turned and walked toward the lines of Priest-guards. He felt a dizzying sense of dread creep through him as he walked, like cold water in his veins. He had never felt particularly brave, and everything in him was desperate to get away from the bloodshed. But greater still than his fear was his love for the people of this land. Perhaps if he sacrificed himself fewer commoners would be killed.

41

River was a seed. Without breath, without sight or any other sense, she floated in blackness, wrapped all around by the warm, dark earth. She hovered in a state between waking and death, feeling her heart beat slowly, her need for lungs momentarily forgotten, feeling the earth sustain her as it did all the unseen life under its surface. She was warm, calm, and completely still. She no longer felt her scrapes and cuts, or her body at all. Instead, as the blackness cut off all senses except the warm dark, she began to sense another thing. The earth, which she usually sensed through the soles of her feet, was now all around her, touching every inch of her. She had never before felt so connected to it, like she couldn't tell where her body ended and the earth began. Gradually she reached out, like stretching a new muscle she hadn't known she possessed, and her awareness expanded to feel everything around her.

She sensed the entire city, then the entire country, then the entire world! She sensed living things all around, like the pulsing lights she sometimes saw on the insides of her eyelids when she rubbed her eyes. She felt the incomprehensible vastness of the earth, and her mind boggled that she had ever been so haughty as to command the thing like a pet dog. She felt a thousand thousand different kinds of trees, bugs, and creatures across its face, even more little creatures below the surface. And yet, as she watched she saw that every single thing was growing, moving, and working in tandem with every other thing. Together, everything played out its part, each tiny speck forming, when she sensed them all together, the most beautiful creation River had ever dreamed of. She would have wept, if her eyes had not been filled with dirt. To her, it seemed that even the smallest bug lived and worked in tandem with the Earth better than she ever had. She felt... inadequate. Ridiculous. As she sensed everything, she began to realize that there was a reason that each little creature and plant lived with a sense of purpose. All of them, even the great Earth itself, was following a rhythm established by a greater being. They were dancing to a song that sounded familiar. Only, this time as she listened she could hear it fully, and understand it. This time it was not the faint voice of a single young child singing in the night, but a sound so big it could not fit into any one body, so strong, so young, and so joyful that it shook the very fabric of the world, shaping everything. However, while it was more joyful than any voice she had ever heard before, it was also inexpressibly sad. As she began to understand the words, River felt she was seeing a faint echo of that greater being's heart. She sensed a loving hand carefully leading each little part of the world, caring for it, teaching it to work with all the other parts. Her heart filled with wonder. Then, she sensed humans.

Like a rash creeping over the land, humans tramped destructively across the earth, uncaring. They were broken, out of sync with everything else, wandering about killing each other, killing creatures, and killing the earth. As River sensed them, she began to feel deeply concerned. They were like a single voice screaming out in the midst of a beautiful song, disrupting everything. No wonder the singing sounded sad! No wonder the earth had dried up and gone wild! She saw now that it was shrinking back in fear from the hordes of destructive humans on its surface, allowing the ground to crack and crops to dry up. She wanted to make all the humans stop, make them sit still and listen to the music all around them until they could learn to sing along instead of wrecking everything. She tried, but her consciousness was spread so thin that her powers had no effect, she couldn't do anything except watch. The singing faded.

THEY HAVE FORGOTTEN ME.

A sad voice seemed to say the words, but River could not discover where it came from. It seemed to vibrate through the very fabric of the world, but it wasn't the Earth speaking. It was a very young voice, but at the same time more ancient than anything she had ever heard. River stopped her struggle to contact the humans, and instead grew still, listening.

River's consciousness snapped back into her body, with a feeling that if she had heard any more of that voice she would have shattered into a thousand pieces. It had been gentle, and grieved, like a parent softly speaking to a child, and yet it had been so powerful that it shook her very soul. The last two words kept reverberating through her like a heartbeat. *SHOW THEM, SHOW THEM, show them.* She huddled into herself, mind reeling. Had that been it? *The* singer? The one responsible for creating the pattern, the song, that all living creatures followed? Could it be the same one who had given Col back to her when he had been dying? Was there really only one being responsible for everything? If so, why did it choose to appear as a small child? How was a child powerful? How was she supposed to serve that being? Was *she* supposed to show the people? How? She had forgotten love and truth for so long, and was only recently learning to love thanks to Col. Surely she was the worst person to show those values to a world that only saw her as a weapon.

Suddenly, a commotion distracted her from her thoughts. The earth around her was cringing at a sudden flood of violence being committed close by. River reached out with her senses, pushing her awareness toward the location where the earth felt the most pain. It was a bit like intentionally giving herself a headache, but she pushed forward. She was curious. As she studied the surface, she felt the drumming of nail-studded sandals, the rumbling of wheels and clopping of hooves in an organized pattern. In addition, she tasted the horrible tang of spilled blood, the desperate slapping of feet running away, of bodies falling to the dirt. Then she sensed a set of feet walking *toward* the bloodshed, instead of away from it. Walking in a very familiar way... *Oh no.*

Suddenly, River was no longer content to be a seed. The soft, warm earth all around her felt much more like a tomb than a nice cozy bed. She shoved her way back through the earth, trying to feel her body. *There.* She forced herself to come fully awake inside of her own skin, fighting through layers of drowsiness to make her body wake up. While it was lovely to be so close to her old friend the Earth, River suddenly became very aware that she was also human. There was dirt in her eyes, in her mouth. Had the earth not been sustaining her with its power, she would have suffocated long ago. As it was, she knew that she could not stay there. It was no place for a living human, only for a dead one. Stay there, and she would gradually rot away, forgetting her body until nothing remained of it. Desperate, she reached out to the earth all around her, trying to explain why she had to leave.

I can't stay here. I have to stop the violence.

Col raced forward, fighting against people who were trying to back up. All the people too close to the Priest-guards, unable to retreat because of the crowd at their backs, had been cut down without mercy. Some had not even tried to retreat, but had fought back with unarmed fists. That was even more heartbreaking. Before any more could die, Col was determined to stop the fighting. At the sight of him, the Hearer also began pushing forward through his ranks, a bejeweled sword extended in challenge. Seeing the tall, terrifying warrior Col knew that this was a fight he could not win. He had never been much of a warrior, no matter how much training he was given. He simply didn't have the spirit.

Suddenly, Col was knocked from his feet. He scrambled up, only to find that the slaughter of innocents had turned into a mass of tangled bodies, people falling into each other and crashing to the ground as they tried to keep their footing. The ranks of Priest-guards were a mess. Even as Col tried to get up, he could feel the trembling in the ground worsen, until the houses and walls of the adjoining streets began to collapse. Even as the people tried to stand, the ground cracked, then the crack widened into a chasm separating the line of soldiers from the crowd of townspeople. Col scrambled back from the edge, kicking dust and pebbles down into the crack. They did not fall far, but only a few feet down he could see them caught up in a boiling, writhing mass of... *something* that was rising up out of the darkness. The lip of the chasm on Col's side began to rise, dirt and cobblestones bunching up into a sort of low wall, high enough that he could only see the Priest-guards heads over the top of it. Naturally, instead of trying to bridge the gap and attack the citizens, the priests were backing away in terror.

Only the Hearer pushed forward, eyes fixed on Col, bellowing in rage. He seemed to be trying to spur his horse to jump the chasm, but the creature took one look down into the crack and then shied back. With a sort of scream of terror, the horse bucked wildly, sending the Hearer flying before it took off running away at a furious pace, presumably headed out of the city. At that moment, a figure rose from the darkness. It was a human shape... maybe? The creature was completely dark, featureless, formed from dirt and mud rather than flesh. Around its torso and legs, a mass of dirt, mud, rocks, and vines lashed and swirled, spreading along the length of the chasm like a train. Everyone who saw it screamed in terror as it raised its arms, turning to face the Priest-guards. At the motion, there was a *WHOOSH*, and a geyser of mud exploded up out of the ground, shooting twenty feet into the air. Priest-guards screamed and yelled as the wave crashed down upon them, but on the other side of the wall, Col and the townspeople were only showered with a light splattering of mud. The dirt creature was obscured by the flood, as were the ranks of the Order. Gradually, the mud turned to clear water, and the geyser began to sink down, simply gushing instead of exploding.

Col stood with the crowd of people, staring with a mix of horror, awe, and fascination. On the other side of the low wall, a single woman stood, unbothered by the current. She was small, very wet, and dressed in tattered rags. All around her, gushing up from the ground and flowing violently away from the low wall, downhill towards the Thude, rushed a river of clear water. Here and there, the wheeled war machines stuck bent blades out of the water, broken and embedded in the riverbed. Further out, some Priest-guard heads bobbed above the water, fighting to stay upright as they were swept away by the fearsome current. Discarded weapons, armor, and cloaks tumbled through the water where the priests had thrown them off in the struggle to stay afloat. River turned, and waded toward Col. He stared at her in shock. He was glad, so glad, that she was alive. However, the joy was overshadowed by sheer amazement at what he had just witnessed. River had leveled an entire city.

Half of Wanderkeep was engulfed in vines, while the other half had just been washed into the great river Thude. Col was stunned that such unbelievable power could be contained within the slim, five-foot-nothing frame of River. Only her fierce eyes betrayed the power within. The very last portion of the city was rapidly being evacuated, as people fled to the countryside, eager to get onto stable ground. A small crowd remained on the edge of the new river, staring at Col and River. Some had begun caring for the dead and wounded. There were more people weeping than there were cheers. River stepped up to Col and hugged him.

"We need to go," she urged. "This was an inconvenience for the Order, but they will regroup. We need to be far away by then."

He nodded distractedly, feeling overwhelmed. His heart, unconvinced that he wasn't about to die, was still pounding. At the same time, River's nearness flooded through his senses. He'd thought he'd lost her and now, holding her in his arms, he couldn't decide if he was happy or afraid of her. Perhaps both. No matter what, he knew that he loved this wet, bedraggled, absolutely terrifying woman more than he had ever loved anyone. He held her tight, but she pulled away, frowning up into his face.

"Are you alright? You're shaking."

He nodded, trying to put back on the calm persona that was the Wolf. It was hard. He couldn't gain full control of his muscles, and they continued to tremble slightly. River's eyes took on a look of compassion, an expression he would never have associated with her.

"You're probably in shock," she sighed, glancing around at the dead bodies and demolished streets. "I don't understand how your soul hasn't developed a cold shell yet at this point, living amongst criminals and bandits. Your heart is always so raw and vulnerable, you should learn to protect it so things like this can't hurt you."

"I won't," Col vowed. "I can't. Caring about the people is what makes them follow me, and what makes me right and the Hearer wrong. If I stopped letting their deaths hurt me, I would be no better than *him*."

River looked at him strangely, head cocked as though the idea was hard to understand. But then she nodded her acceptance.

"Let's go."

Arm in arm, the two of them walked slowly out of the city, falling in with thousands of others that were leaving the destruction of their homes, some bearing bodies. Col's glassy eyes matched the look in many faces around them. However, he carried in his heart something none of the others did. Guilt. He had brought the fight to these people, he had been the one to poke the monster that was the Order and arouse it to violence. Col and River carried a secret that ensured the Order would never stop chasing them. However, in fighting back, they had involved hundreds of others. *No,* Col thought, *Thousands. By this point, it's thousands. But even with Hamon's weapons, most of them are untrained. How can we possibly fight against the Order?* What had seemed possible once, now seemed foolhardy. The Order had finally decided to retaliate, and at the glimpse it had given Col of the true might of the Order, he felt despair fill his heart. Was he a good leader, or was he merely a foolhardy radical leading his forces full-tilt towards annihilation?

42

They stopped outside the city, waiting to see who had survived. Col had set up several plans with his group before splitting up to gather supplies in the city. One plan had arranged a meet-up point outside the city in the event of an attack or separation. Col stopped by a large, flat rock sticking out into the water of the Thude, hoping he was at the right place. River, who had been very quiet the whole walk, lay down to take a nap. Col had far too much on his mind to sleep. The Thude was no longer the slow, muddy sludge it had once been. Now, rushing, clear waters of the new river swirled through the muddy waters of the Thude, making the whole river gradually change, becoming purer and faster downstream of Wanderkeep. The breeze blowing in off the river was cold and fresh, washing away the hot stench of rotten things. Going down to the riverside, Col threw rocks in the water, then stopped, noticing a lovely little plant with bright blue leaves on the bank. He gently touched the silver fuzz on the leaves, remembering River's enchanted look. His heart suddenly flooded with regret. How could he have been so foolish as to walk River right into a trap? And then to abandon her and run away... He bowed his head in shame, vowing that such a thing would not, *could* not happen ever again. He didn't ever want to leave her side.

It took a while for people to start arriving. Dominik was first. He looked at Col for a long moment, a question in his eyes. Col avoided looking at him. He didn't know what to do about his General disobeying him. He didn't think he could ever trust Dominik in quite the same way again. They could work together, but Col doubted they could ever be friends. He was starting to realize that, in his position as the Wolf, he couldn't afford to be friends with any of his men. Dominik's eyes became shadowed, and he put some distance between himself and Col, walking to stand guard over River's sleeping form. About half an hour later, Col was delighted to see Kimia come slinking out of a larger group of refugees toward them, her brother Caldwell not too far behind her. Both bore large sacks over their shoulders.

"Nobody dared to go into the jungle to start looting yet!" Kimia reported with a gleam in her eye. "Too many chunks of houses just hanging overhead, waiting to fall. But there's loads of stuff just laying everywhere, we've got enough supplies for weeks!" She had a rasp to her voice that was concerning, and blood trickled out of her brother's nose. Both were scraped up and covered in dust, but seemed otherwise fine. Col nodded his thanks.

With his whole team gathered, his instinct was to start moving. However, to his surprise, others started gathering. First ten, then twenty, and soon close to a hundred people came up to join him. Most were young men, stripped of their livelihoods in the city, awed by River's power, and ready to follow Col anywhere if it meant getting back at the Order. The bloodshed at the Priest-guards hands had been heavy, and there were few people who did not know one of the dead. They had died protecting Col. Many who gathered wanted to honor that, while others blamed Col for the deaths and demanded that he do something to help them.

Seeing their desperate faces, Col took a deep breath. It was that time again. The time for Col to do what he always did, put aside his own feelings and wear the face of the man that these people needed. Putting aside his own heavy heart, he listened to each person in turn, being the proud and strong Wolf for the young men wanting to follow him, then becoming Nikki, the compassionate boy of his village when crying families begged for his help. He gave the truly desperate ways to contact villages friendly to his cause who would provide for them. However, for most he simply assured them that the best way for him to help them was to leave, taking the Hearer's attention away from the city. He couldn't afford to care for all these people, not when he had to remain constantly on the run. He desperately hoped that the next time they encountered the Hearer, it would be in the deserted countryside where River could not cause so much destruction. Oddly, no one blamed her. Rather, they seemed to regard her as some sort of deity or natural disaster, and admired Col all the more for being able to keep her under control. River herself had been very standoffish, and hadn't spoken to anyone for a long time, even after awakening. The only time he had heard her speak, it was to correct some people attempting to worship her as the Messenger. Her voice was sharp, but not angry. Rather, it sounded fearful.

"I'm not a god. Don't call me that! The Order has told you lies. There's only one god. The Creator. Pray to *him*... if you can find him."

She sent the people away confused. When Col questioned her about this new conviction, she got all silent again and ignored him. He couldn't stop the fire of curiosity from growing inside of him.

By the evening, Col found himself with twenty men ready to serve him, even more setting off to join his army in other parts of the world, a stack of provisions, and no plan whatsoever. He knew he had to move soon, as scouts brought reports that the Hearer and his surviving men had been shipped off to the nearest garrison to receive medical attention, but that a replacement troop was already setting out for Wanderkeep. They were sure to arrive before nightfall. Col took a moment to sit down, feeling exhausted. He rubbed his head, wondering why choosing the next step was so difficult. He felt that whatever he did, the Hearer had already anticipated it. Having lived all of his life under the Order, Col had never yet felt the pressure of the Order's power as intensely as he did now.

Someone crouched down beside him. Col opened an eye, expecting River. However, Dominik squatted there, his expression uncertain, mouth pinched in a grim line as if he were about to say something he didn't want to.

"I know you don't trust me," he began, "and I do not blame you. I have kept my own council for so many years that even when I meet one whom I feel is worthy of my loyalty, I cannot bring myself to tell all my secrets."

Col looked at him sharply. "You can keep your secrets, as long as they don't involve me or my mission," he snapped. "If you've decided to make me your god, or prophet, or whatever you've done, I deserve to know. I can't have my men turning me into something I'm not. I'm your leader, nothing more, and nothing less. You will treat me as such."

Dominik bowed his head in acceptance, but Col could read in his face that it was only a gesture.

"As you wish, my lord." He was silent for a moment, and Col could tell he was wrestling internally. Then he seemed to come to a decision.

"There's something I've been keeping from you, but I feel it's time you know. I was never a Rebel."

"What?" Col demanded, shocked. "But you were the Grim's right hand man!"

"I worked for Grimald, yes," Dominik admitted, "but my loyalty was never to the Rebellion. Rather, I was sent by my people to seek a leader from the lands of the Order, one who might overthrow the Order and fulfill the prophecy. I thought perhaps that Grimald might be the one, but now I believe it is you."

Looking into the man's dark, unfathomable eyes, Col felt a shiver go through him. Yet again, he felt the movement of powers beyond his comprehension, and thought that he was caught up in something far bigger than himself.

"What do you mean, land of the Order?" he asked. "The Order rules the entire world."

Dominik looked around to make sure that nobody was watching. Then he leaned close, and his voice was low and dark.

"That's what the Order likes to pretend."

Col's mind reeled. He couldn't believe it.

"How do you know?"

"Because, I grew up in a land outside the Order's borders." Dominik's tone was guarded, but Col still heard the longing and homesickness in that voice, and he knew Dominik spoke the truth.

"My people live on a group of islands," Dominik continued. "We are not very many, but we are mighty warriors. The Order could not crush us, and so they finally decided to make us disappear. They cut off all trade, re-directed their shipping routes to other waters, and left us alone. We were not the only ones treated in such a manner, but one by one all the other small nations gave up, surrendering for the sake of renewed trade and prosperity. Not my people. We never broke, and though it has been many years since I left, I am confident that they still remain strong."

Col could hardly believe his ears. "That's wonderful!" he gasped, trying to keep his voice down. "Your people must be mighty indeed, to have withstood the Order for so long." Dominik nodded. "Our culture is deeply rooted in the ways of war. Before the Order, we were the mightiest of nations, conquering all our neighbours."

A thought occurred to Col, and he stared at Dominik, hardly daring to ask.

"Dominik, do you mean that everyone in this nation fights as well as you do?"

For the first time ever, Col was astonished to see Dominik, the cool, aloof warrior, blush and look embarrassed.

"No," he admitted slowly, "most are better, actually. I was never the finest warrior. That was the reason why my country decided to send me away to put a use to my other skills. I am an excellent spy and tracker. I was tasked with finding the prophesied leader, if I could, and if not to stir up insurrection against the Order however I could manage."

Col sat for a moment, thinking fast. Several of his men were watching him from a distance, so he tried not to let his excitement show on his face.

"Thank you for telling me." He smiled at Dominik, all grievances forgiven. "You have given me hope, and I now see what our next step must be. A next step the Hearer would never have anticipated! We will go to your country."

Dominik looked neither surprised nor happy with this decision. Instead, he looked resigned.

"I suspected it might come to this," he sighed. "But I must warn you, my people are a hardened group, set in their ways. It will not be easy to persuade them to join us."

Col smiled. In that smile, he saw Dominik understand, and his face looked more hopeful.

"On the other hand, it would not be easy for any man alive to know you and not be won over to your cause," he amended. Col laughed, finally feeling the weight and stress of the past weeks grow a little lighter. He had hope, he had a clear mission and, most importantly, he had finally found a task that he knew he was well suited for.

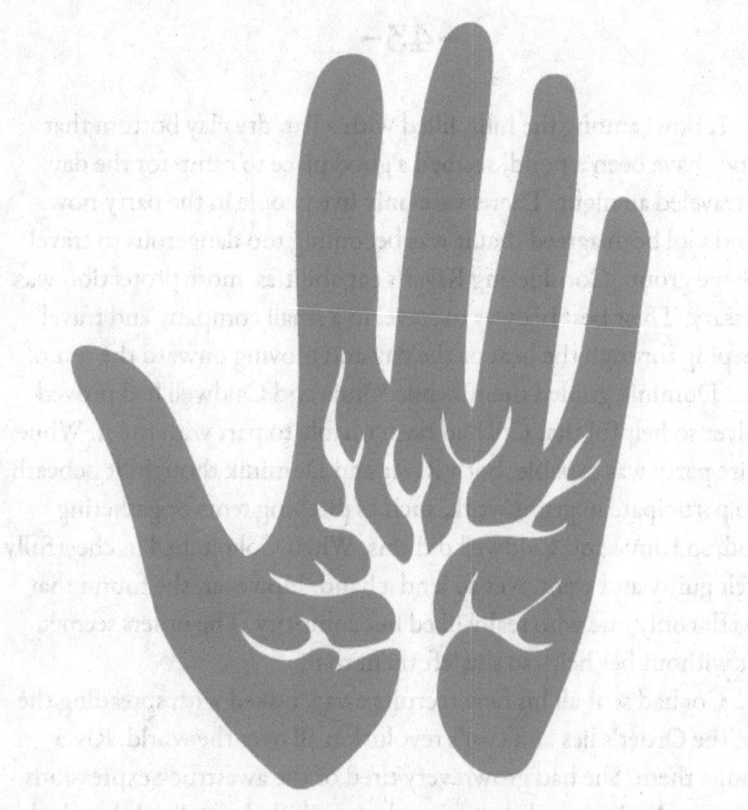

Part Three
The cries of a nation

-43-

A bowl among the hills, filled with a flat, dry clay bottom that must once have been a pond, seemed a good place to camp for the day, having traveled all night. There were only five people in the party now. River and Col both agreed that it was becoming too dangerous to travel with a large group. Considering River's capabilities, more protection was unnecessary. Their best bet was to travel in a small company and travel fast, sleeping through the heat of the day and moving onward the rest of the time. Dominik guided them, while Kimia and Caldwell had proved themselves so helpful that Col had been unable to part with them. While the entire party was capable, both River and Dominik thought it beneath them to participate in grunt work, such as pitching tents or gathering firewood, so Kimia and Caldwell did this. When Col pitched in cheerfully, River felt guilty and went over to lend a hand. However, she found that Col was the only one who really liked her company. The others seemed happier without her help, so she left them to it.

Col had sent all his new recruits away, tasked with spreading the word of the Order's lies and Col's revolution all over the world. River didn't miss them. She had grown very tired of the awestruck expressions, the whispers. As she paced along the edge of a hill, she realized that she had been going barefoot all night, and had left no trace of greenery to betray their trail. The Earth bore a new respect for her wishes that had never before existed. All she had done was ask nicely once, and ever since then the grass had stopped sprouting in her footsteps. A gnawing feeling of guilt tugged at her. She couldn't help feeling that it had been her fault that the Hearer had tracked them to Wanderkeep. What else could have given them away, except her uncontrolled bursts of power? She looked out at the dry landscape, a gentle wind rustling against her face. The country was beautiful, despite its sparse growth. The hills were gentle, sloping down into wide plains of old grass, white and yellow in the heat. There were a hundred different kinds of plants in this land, but River could feel most of them simply lying dormant in the dry soil. Looking at it, River could catch a glimpse of the way it would look in a kinder year, and her heart ached. In a way, the barren landscape reminded her of herself. She, too, was locked inside a hard outer shell. However, deep down a yearning had been growing within her, a yearning to be happy, to know her purpose, to thrive.

Col walked up beside her without saying anything. She loved that about him, that he could stand with her in silence, and the silence wasn't uncomfortable, but peaceful. Without thinking, she took his hand. It was the scarred and crooked one. She expected him to wince. Instead, he looked embarrassed. She knew that he felt crippled, useless; but she saw in his scarred fingers her own failure, and also a testimony to his strength. He shook off the momentary discomfort, and reached into his pocket with his good hand.

"I have something for you," he told her shyly, and held out a small, round, brown thing to her. She had never before seen him so shy and nervous. Usually, Col was the most confident and charming person in the world. The moment River took the gift in her hand, she felt life vibrating within it. It was a seed. And not just any seed. River felt within its slumbering heart dreams of soft blue leaves covered in a silver fuzz. She gasped, then felt her eyes filling with tears.

"Oh, Col! Wherever did you get it?"

Nervousness abating, a proud grin stole onto his face.

"I found the plant on the riverbank. It had only one seed pod, and the pod was half rotten so there was only one good seed. I thought, since you liked the plant so much, maybe you'd like a seed from it."

He reached out, brushing her hair back behind her ear with gentle fingers.

"Perhaps, when all of this is over, if we defeat the Hearer, and he stops chasing us, we can settle down somewhere peaceful and you can plant it."

River was deeply touched. Taking the seed, she plucked a few blades of grass from the ground and held them in her hands, pouring her intent into them. Swiftly, the grass grew longer and thinner. It twisted itself into thin strands, then twisted the strands into cords. The cords braided themselves together in a lovely little pattern, twisting strands around the round brown seed to encase it. She put it around her neck, and the cords fused themselves together, forming a delicate woven collar with the shiny brown circle of the seed at its center, like a bead. She smiled at him. However, a part of her thought his words were quite silly. He talked as if, once the Order was gone, he yearned to go back to a quiet life as a peasant. She couldn't imagine holding the kind of power he held over his people's hearts, and then simply setting it aside.

Heedless of her thoughts, Col kept talking.

"River, when I left you in the alley, surrounded by Priests, I thought I'd lost you forever." His expression was regretful, full of sorrow. "I can't lose you again, River. I love you too much. I don't ever want to leave your side. Which is why I need to ask. Will you marry me?"

The question shocked River. He was looking at her with deep, loving eyes. He looked so vulnerable, so desperate. She felt completely caught off guard. They had only confessed their love for each other a few weeks ago, and still hadn't completely figured out what to do about it! The proposal seemed so fast, so overwhelming, that River had no idea what to do. In her heart, she knew she loved him, and a large part of her wanted to say yes. However, then another voice rose up. *Could you be content with the life of a peasant? He has no ambition, no royal blood. Think with your head, not your heart. Would you give up your destiny because of your feelings for a commoner?* Even as she followed this train of thought, River could, for the first time, hear the falseness of the words. However, every fiber of her being had been groomed since childhood to believe them. She struggled within herself, knowing her pride was pushing her towards a choice that might destroy her happiness, but at the same time clinging to that pride. It was all she knew.

"I'm sorry," she gasped, rubbing tears from her eyes in frustration at herself, at him, at everything. "I can't marry you. It's too soon, it's too confusing, we're in the middle of a war, we don't know each other well enough..." However, she didn't voice the truest, deepest reason. The one that she refused to admit even to herself, as it carried with it a burden of too much shame and confusion. *I'm too proud to marry a peasant.*

As Col looked at her, she had the uncomfortable feeling that he saw through her words and her walls as if they were nothing. His cheeks flushed hot with embarrassment, eyes becoming veiled to hide the hurt. He sighed, tugging his crippled hand out of hers and looking at it bitterly.

"That's ok. I understand," he said hollowly. "I'm sorry for asking. You're right, of course."

He started to walk away, and she longed to run after him. Her pride held her still, heart aching. A few paces away, he turned back.

"It's probably best if we both try to forget that this happened... That way things won't change too much between us. I don't want to make you feel awkward." At that, he tucked his crippled hand away in his cloak, self-consciously tugged his sleeves down over his scarred arms, and walked off. River, looking after him, suddenly felt like a monster. Did he think she didn't want to marry him because he was scarred? Even covered in scars, and with a crippled hand, Col was still the most attractive man she had ever seen. His scars only made him more intriguing. Girls swooned over him if he simply smiled at them. Didn't he realize that? Filled with confusion, she watched him walk away. With Storm, things had never been this complicated. *But with Storm,* she realized, suddenly, *the bond was never this deep.* Perhaps the more you loved someone, the easier it was to mess things up.

44

River awoke to a dark sky. It wasn't night, but a mighty storm was brewing. The air crackled with energy, and the world looked gray. Caldwell had pinned a tarp over their provisions, but the edges of the tarp flapped frantically in the wind. She judged that it was still a long time until they were scheduled to set out, but something bothered her. Then she saw that Col's bedroll was empty, untouched. Why wasn't he sleeping? Curious, she got up and walked out into the grey landscape. She shivered, unused to the chill in the air. Over the sound of the wind, she suddenly thought she heard sharp pants of breath. Coming around the corner of several large standing rocks, River stopped. Col was practicing with a sword.

Ever since his injury, he had been forced to abandon the double-bladed fighting style that the Order had taught him, instead strapping a small shield to his forearm when he practiced. He was fighting in this way now, going through stabs and parries. However, he was fighting in the strangest way River had ever seen, always facing the same direction, moving side to side but never looking behind him. His back would have been wide open to any attack in a real fight! River was just about to go over and correct him, when she suddenly realized. The only reason that a man would ever have for using moves like that, would be if one man were trying to defend a group of unarmed individuals from multiple foes. He was trying to find a way to prevent the deaths of any more innocents.

Watching him, the desperate way in which he moved, the sweat dripping down his forehead, and the grim determination in his bloodshot eyes, she suddenly glimpsed a very different Col than the one he projected every day. In this moment, there was no confident leader, no charismatic hero, no calm peacemaker. Instead, she saw a tortured boy, a young man with the weight of a nation on his shoulders, the pain of all his people tearing at his heart, covered in scars inside as well as out. Suddenly, something began moving with him, trailing out from his sword hand. It left strands of light through the air, slowly fading. As he moved faster, the light began glowing more brightly, spreading, until his entire sword and arm left bright swaths of light through the air with each stroke. River caught her breath. He began working the light into his practice, slashing sheets of blue light-strands across his path like a shield to stall one imaginary attacker while he fended off another. The air in front of him began to look like a glowing mural of blue swirls and flashes. The light twisted down his arm and traced across his scarred forearm, making the scars look beautiful. Col looked like some ancient hero, even more ancient than River's people, fighting a monstrous evil single-handed. And yet, he was not enough. Watching him, River knew that, against the might of the Order, all he could ever accomplish in a fight like this would be to buy a few minutes of time for others to escape. She felt a deep sadness, and an odd sense of kinship.

"It's lonely, being powerful," she said at last. He jumped. When he turned to face her, she only caught a glimpse of the raw pain in his eyes before a veil hid it away. He looked at the fading light in the air, suddenly guarded.

"I'm not powerful," he said, "not like you. That's the problem. This light seems to slow down anything that passes through it, but I don't know what it is or how to use it. It won't do anything to stop the Order."

"That's not what I was referring to." River looked into his eyes, then found that she had to look away. His sheer presence was overwhelming in that moment, and she knew she had no right to melt into his gaze so soon after rejecting his offer of marriage.

"I was referring to the power you have over people." She studied his lips, his jaw, his neck, and then found that that was almost worse than looking into his eyes. She looked at her hands instead.

"To know you is to fall in love with you."

He laughed bitterly at that. She blushed. There was an awkward silence as they both knew what the other was thinking about, but neither wanted to address it. After a moment, he moved on as if ignoring it.

"And what good is that power in fighting the Order?" he asked softly. The pain may not have shown in his face, but it was creeping into his voice. "Shall I throw hordes of innocents at the Hearer? Just keep gathering followers and sending them into battle, until the Temples crumble under the weight of bodies, and the Hearer drowns in a river of blood? What will I have then? A free land, yes. But a land full of more pain than the Order ever caused by their rule." He stabbed his sword aggressively into the ground, blowing out a breath in frustration. "If that is a power, I don't want it."

"Your followers chose." River told him softly. She wanted to take his hands and hug him, but knew that she had given up that privilege.

"When they chose to follow you, they knew what it could cost them. They know that the cause is worth dying for."

He looked at her, running his hands through his hair. "Why?" he asked, helplessly. "Why do they follow me?"

River hesitated. A part of her was still very jealous of this fact, and she didn't have the answer, herself. Why *did* the people follow Col, when they could have had River as their leader? Why did they choose his charm over her power? What assurances did they have that Col would ever triumph over those who pursued him?

"I'm not sure," she said. "I stay with you because I like your company." At that, he smiled a wan smile. She smiled back, hugely relieved. Perhaps things wouldn't be so awkward between them anymore.

A crackling of dry brush sounded behind them. River turned, startled, just in time to see a dark shape disappear over the top of the hill. Perhaps an animal? If so, it had been a large one, and by the time they climbed the hill it was gone.

The following morning, or, rather, night, since they awoke in the evening to start their journey. River found Col waiting for her, a little away from the others. He looked very tired.

"Look, River, I'm sorry." He studied the ground in embarrassment. "I've been behaving badly since you said 'No' to me. I've been thinking about it all night and I really do think you're right. It was too soon, and there's a war to be thinking of. We have to focus on that. And I'm really sorry for the way I took your answer. I've been immature about it, and I'm going to do my best to keep my feelings of disappointment from spoiling our relationship."

He was really so sweet about it. River felt herself falling even more in love with him, for his humility and the way he was able to apologize for his mistakes. She forgave him, with equal sweetness. However, she couldn't shake the feeling that she was the one in the wrong. She hadn't really refused him for all the very logical reasons he brought up now. She had refused him out of pride. And she, too, had stayed awake long after others were sleeping, only she had been agonizing over her decision, wondering what would have happened if she had said 'Yes.' She didn't tell him this. She couldn't, because she knew that her answer had been the only answer she was able to give. Some things were too deeply ingrained for her to even consider changing.

45

There came a day when Dominik, who had been taking the lead more and more often as they progressed into lands no one else had ever heard of, decided it was safe to travel in the daylight. For weeks they had continued through rolling hills and vast, flat plains of grass, cracked clay-like dirt, and occasional trees, as well as a few rivers which they had forded with difficulty.

They were reaching areas that were on the scattered outskirts of the Order's dominion. While the Order still taxed the area, it rarely patrolled these people. For that matter, the presence of any people at all was becoming rare. There were no more cities, only farmland and scattered villages across the plains. Once, after a day of journeying through an especially uninhabited region, they came upon a series of hills, rough and crumbled at the peaks as if freshly forced out of the earth. A little further, and they actually saw new hills forming, with, not a sound so much as a faint trembling of the earth under their feet. In the distance, so far away that it was hazy and blue-tinged in the hot air, they saw the massive head of.... *Something* rather like a snake, but feathered with long spines. It reared majestically out of the ground, then dived ponderously back into the earth. Rocks and trees crumbled out of the way of its passing like so many small pebbles. Col's mind boggled at the sheer size of the thing, for its head was far in the distance, while its long body trembled the earth and formed little ridges not a stone's throw away from where he stood. All of the company stood transfixed in awe.

"I have heard of these in the Drowning Sands far far beyond the borders of all kingdoms," Dominik said in a breathless whisper. It was the first time Col had ever seen the man truly awed. "But for one to exist here, the summers must be becoming far hotter than they have ever been in the past. They cannot move without the warmth of sunlight. Supposedly, in the burning sun of the sands where they are born, they can move with a speed that defies imagining."

Col shuddered. No wonder no one had ever dared to explore beyond those sands. Shortly thereafter, they began to encounter something just as strange, but less alarming. The fewer people they encountered, the more often they saw Slider tracks.

"We are two weeks' journey away from the coast, the end of the world according to the Order," Dominik reported one day. Col felt his heart sink. They'd been walking for so long across the low hills, he'd expected them to almost be there.

"Is there no end to this grassy place?" River complained.

"Not that I can see," Kimia replied grimly, having returned from scouting. "I did, however, see some fresh Slider tracks. I wonder if they're good for eating?"

At the suggestion, Dominik's eyes lit up. He smiled, for the first time in days. Col had noticed that, the closer they came to his home, the more he had begun to be taciturn and moody.

"No one would dare eat them," he said dryly. "Have you seen their teeth, and claws? But they are good for something else! We should track down these ones."

The trail was easy to follow. They tracked the wide scores in the earth a little while, until they came up to the top of a little rise and looked down. Below them, sliders grazed and slid. The whole group lay down in the grass, cautious of alerting the beasts to their presence. Although the creatures ate grass, they were notoriously dangerous, and looked it. Their long snouts were hanging partially open, panting in the heat, and revealing large teeth. The most frightening thing, however, was the massive claws on their front legs, longer than swords, and the very front claw of the biggest ones as long as one of Dominik's own legs. These they used to dig into the ground and shoot themselves forward in a massive heave, sliding on their smooth, interlocked stomach scales.

"What are we doing?" Col demanded of Dominik. The man gave

him a sly smile.

"We are going to ride them! That is the fastest way to move across these lands, and no predator or bandit will interfere with a man riding a Slider."

There was a stunned silence. Everyone stared at him incredulously.

"*What?*" Kimia burst out. "Of course they wouldn't interfere! Look at those creatures! We shouldn't interfere with them either!" Dominik remained unswayed.

"It's quite simple," he said earnestly. "The brown-furred ones are female, the black-furred ones are male. The largest males are the only ones too aggressive to be ridden. In fact, don't let them catch sight of you at all. However, for any other one, you simply catch hold of the tail, and climb up onto their back, like climbing a tree. You hold on until they've tired themselves out, then steer them by kneeing the soft spot beside their front legs, or pulling on the long whiskers at the base of their neck for a sharper turn. They are nearly tireless beasts, and can carry a great deal."

There was a horrified silence. Then Col sighed.

"All right. I'll give it a try."

There was a chorus of hushed protests from everyone, including Dominik, who insisted it would be safer for him to catch and tame a mount first, lest the great Wolf be injured. Col ignored them. He wasn't a good fighter, and it seemed that everyone except him was allowed to risk their lives for his sake. He was tired of letting everyone else take the risks.

Swiftly, ignoring the lump that was growing in his throat, he crept down the hill towards the animals. A large brown female snuffled in the grass with her back turned to him. Making a careful approach so as to always keep several beasts between himself and the larger male's line of sight, he crept up to the creature. It gave a snort, raising its head to look around warily. Col gave up sneaking. With a short sprint and a flying leap, he grabbed hold of its tail. There was an awful snarling sound. Instantly, he was flying across the ground, moving at such a speed that he was very glad he had grabbed the thicker portion of the tail, closer to the creature's body. Had he grabbed the end, he would have had his arms and legs shredded from scraping along the ground. Still clinging to the thick, furry tail, Col began to inch his way up. It was very hard to do so without sliding back down. The wind buffeted his face, he felt it trying to lift his body away from the creature and fling him backwards. The tail thrashed back and forth. The smell of hot fur was all he could smell. He could even taste it, as dust and fur was getting in his mouth. He clung on with a grip that doubtless caused the animal some discomfort, for it started thrashing about even more wildly. Stubbornly, Col gritted his teeth and kept inching his way up.

"You're not getting rid of me that easily," he told the creature as he finally reached her back. The slider rolled her little eyes in fury at seeing the impudent face of a human grinning down at her from between her ears. She tried to slap at him with her long tail, but he was too far up on her back. From on top of the Slider, Col could now see that he was traveling through unfamiliar countryside. The massive muscles of the Slider's front legs thrashed as it dug its claws into the ground, moving forward in a swaying, sickening hurtle with no rhythm at all. Col felt nauseous. Every time they went down a hill, they moved with incredible speed, then the climb uphill was slower, but bumpy as the creature scrambled. Col began to worry that he wouldn't find his way back to the others. He kneed behind the Slider's front legs, but it paid no mind, seemingly as stubborn as he was. Suddenly, the Slider's motions changed. It stopped letting out angry snarls, and instead fell silent, pulling steadily at the ground and moving forward in long, smooth motions. Col dug his hands through the thick, smelly brown fur, then found what Dominik had told him to look for. There, protruding from the fur on either side behind the creature's ears, were several long, thick hairs. Col now encountered a problem. His mangled hand had difficulty gripping anything so small. Climbing up the tail had been mostly arm strength, but now he had to pinch the whisker awkwardly. Clinging on with just his knees, he used his good hand to wind the whisker around his bad one until he had a good grip. It was desperately precarious, but he managed it. Then he pulled. The creature let out a yowl of protest, but its head turned in the direction he pulled, with its body following. Col felt a grin spreading over his face.

"Giddyup, you overgrown mole!" he cheered, pulling harder to turn it all the way around. Sitting atop it, he felt far less afraid. Rather, riding a creature that was full of claws and teeth made him feel powerful. The gait was also far more comfortable than riding a horse, although the fur stank like hot swamp mud. Before they had gone far, following the trail that the slider had left in the earth, Col came across Dominik, astride a small black Slider. If he was relieved to see Col alive and well, he didn't show it. Instead, he simply gave Col a respectful nod.

"I see you have mastered the beast. Do not, now, dismount, or she will bite you. You must ride until she is completely worn out and falls asleep."

Col suddenly wondered what would happen if he felt the need to relieve himself before the creature had become exhausted. However, he didn't voice his fear. Riding back to the others, they found that Caldwell had also caught a Slider. The two girls were waiting by the packs, and had to approach the beasts very carefully as they danced in place, trying to move forward but held back by the yanking on their whiskers. By approaching from the top of a small bluff, the girls were able to very cautiously climb aboard. Kimia rode with Caldwell, and Dominik took the majority of the baggage aboard his animal, gesturing for River to ride with Col. Since her destruction of Wanderkeep, no one except Col felt comfortable around her. She climbed on behind him, and he felt a thrill as she clung to him tightly.

"This is worse than wearing shoes," she groaned. The thrill

evaporated. As the creature began to move again, picking up speed, her grip tightened, until Col thought his ribs might crack. It took half an hour of travelling in this way until she began to relax. Then, softly, she began to talk. Her breath tickled the back of his neck as she began to tell him of the things she had experienced while underground. As he listened, Col became more and more amazed. He began to understand why she had been so quiet, so much less contemptuous and bitter. She had been forced to acknowledge the existence of a power greater than herself, and the experience had changed her. Col had never before heard such awe in her voice. At her words, his own heart beat faster in excitement.

"This is incredible!" he exclaimed. "Do you suppose my mother sensed the same thing as you, when she spent all that time praying in the fields?"

She was silent for a while. Then she said,

"I think it is likely. The little child your brother saw holding her hand does strike me as similar to the personality of the Singer who spoke to me. That being doesn't seem inclined to grand displays of power, but uses a subtlety that I can't understand. Why would someone choose to hold themselves back, when they hold the power to crush every evil thing in the world? I'm not sure how to serve this god. I am so hot-headed, and the Singer is so gentle."

"So, she was right all along..." Col whispered. He felt a surge of shame for all the times he and his brothers had carelessly brushed off her beliefs, embarrassed that she was so vocal and warning her to keep it quiet, lest the Order execute her for a heretic. Now Col was a greater heretic than she had ever been. A part of him was terrified of the idea of a real god, because it meant he would have to change his plans, to find out what the god wanted from him before he made decisions. And yet, another part of him was thrilled. He finally knew the truth! There was an answer! And the truth seemed far better than the lies of the Order, or even the mystique of the Silent Speaker. He could read faces and voices better than anyone he knew, and so he knew from the way River talked that she was telling the truth. He knew, now, to whom he owed the thanks for his miraculous healing after the mangling of his hand. However, he still felt frustrated. What was the good of knowing that there was a god if you didn't have a priest or a book to tell you what that god was like, what the god required? He knew every detail about the Order, the Messenger, and their false gods, but knew almost nothing about the real one.

"You and I really are Heretics, aren't we?" he said with a laugh. "Not only are we trying to tear down the Order's lies, now we've got a new truth to replace it with."

She laughed, too. "It occurs to me that we are not so different, you and I, despite appearances. In my time, I was also a troublemaker and a threat to the ruling powers."

On the back of Sliders, their journey to the coast would take only a few days. While they were far more conspicuous this way, Col found that it was in fact safer. The rare people they encountered noticed them, but only shouted in astonishment from a distance, never daring to approach close enough to guess at the identities of the group of riders. They could have been anyone, from anywhere in the vast kingdom. The anonymity was refreshing.

–46–

The Hearer startled as a scout suddenly pushed his way into the war tent.

"I've seen the Heretic!" the man panted. The Hearer frowned. He wasn't about to get his hopes up so quickly, not after failing to catch that slippery demon so many times.

"How do you know it was him?" he demanded.

"A handsome boy with scarred arms was talking to a pale girl with long dark hair," the scout insisted. "And I know the boy was the sorcerer, because I saw him using dark magic!"

Wait, what? The Hearer inspected the man suspiciously.

"What do you mean?"

"Lines of light in the air." The scout traced twisting patterns in the air with his finger. "Like spider's webs in the light of the moon. I'd never seen anything like it."

I have. The Hearer thought. His mind was scrambling at the implications. This Wolf really was a sorcerer? How could that be? Could he use the same type of magic that had formed the Messenger's crystal? Suddenly, the Hearer was no longer stalling for time. He saw a way out of the mess the Wolf had created, a way to fix *everything*.

"Send out a message *immediately*." His voice was crazed with greed. "Double the reward. The Wolf must be captured alive. At all costs."

The sea. It was something Col could never have dreamed of. In his short life, rivers had been something to marvel at. This, however, was like seeing a thunderstorm after never knowing more than a single drop at a time. At first, it looked to him as though the sky was touching the earth. Then, as they got closer, he thought that the world was catching fire from the sun as it rose. The smell hit him before the sound did. It was hot, and wet, and smelled of salt. He had never before smelled brine, and didn't like it very much. But it was so different from the stagnant stench of the Thude, the clean, crisp smell of mountain waterfalls. It was a wilder, more alien smell. He couldn't help the thrill of excitement that ran through him. Then the sound. At first, it reminded him of the hiss of sand as a strong wind sweeps it over the rim of a canyon. However, it began to grow into a growling, thundering pulse that seemed to shake the air. It seemed amazing to Col that the whole earth did not give in to such a ceaseless onslaught, and simply slide away into the waves.

When they finally reached the beach, he was afraid to approach the ocean, afraid one of the surging waves would grab him and drown him. Growing up in a land where water was rare and precious, he had never learned to swim. Dominik was the only one who did not stand transfixed by the beauty and power of the ocean. He looked at the sea with a rather sour expression. At that moment, Col realized a very important problem.

"But if the kingdom we seek is on an island, how will we get across the ocean?" he asked, dismayed. Dominik's mouth quirked in a small, unhappy smile.

"Finding my people won't be the problem. The problem will be staying alive once *they* find *us*."

They camped on high bluffs overlooking the beach. Dominik had to warn the others not to camp on the beach, or they would undoubtedly have done so. No one else had ever heard of a tide, and the sand was so soft. However, as the evening fell and they saw the water rising until it touched the base of the bluffs, they were very grateful for the moody man's advice. Instead of keeping a low profile, they lit a large fire, and kept it burning throughout the night with dry driftwood. Col slept fitfully. In his dreams, the ocean gradually rose and washed higher and higher against the bank, until the waves pulled the entire chunk of land on which they camped into the dark water. He awoke with a horrible start, discovering a fear he had never before known he possessed. He was terrified of the deep. They spent a whole, boring day there on the beach. There was not another human living more than a week's walk from the water this far west. There were coastal towns further east, but here the entire countryside was barren, and it seemed to Col that they were people alone on the edge of the world. He began to be very bored, and even to wonder if Dominik had been lying about the mysterious island of warriors.

For two days, nothing happened. Then, Col woke up to River shaking his shoulder.

"Col! Look! Look at the ocean!" Her face was alight with wonder. Truly, River was a changed woman. Every day she was becoming less standoffish, more delighted by the things she encountered, seeing the beauty of every little thing. With a groan, Col got up, prepared to politely inspect yet another leaf or bloom that had caught River's fancy. Instead, he saw that the ocean had disappeared! Instead of huge, rolling waves, there was only a soft, thick whiteness.

"It's called 'fog'," River told him softly, leading him right to the edge of the water. "It appeared in the woods sometimes, at home, but only little wisps along the ground. This is like being in a cloud. Dominik says ships get lost in it."

Col looked back, and realized he could barely see the bluffs behind them. The fog blanketed everything, giving the illusion of privacy. In that strange place, he felt suddenly emboldened to reach out and take River's hand. She smiled at him, and it was for a moment as if nothing had come between them. Then, the first men leapt onto the shore.

Col had been so preoccupied with the beauty of River's smile that he hadn't seen the ships slide softly to the shore. They must have moved with alarming swiftness, although Col saw neither sail nor oars. The men who leapt onto the shore dressed in dark clothing. They had fierce eyes, but the rest of their faces were covered with scarves. They moved silently, with the same deadly grace as Dominik. They moved past River and Col without seeming to see them in the mist. The moment their feet touched the sand, River tensed, crushing Col's hand in a desperate grip.

"They're headed for the camp," she breathed. "We must get to the bluffs. I have no power here. The sand is too full of salt, and so shifty."

Even as she said it, men began to advance across the beach on the other side of them, as well. Col knew that the moment they moved, they would be seen. His white tunic blended in with the fog, but he still couldn't understand why no one had seen his sun-browned face watching them out of the mist. River crouched down with the dark waves lapping against her feet, blending in with her dark cloak so that she looked rather like a rock. He saw blades drawn, saw men climbing up the bluffs with deadly speed and silence. The others, he knew, were still asleep. His mind raced. The men were almost on his sleeping companions now, their dark shapes clinging just below the lip of the bluff. Hoping desperately that he was making the right decision, he suddenly cried out in a loud voice, a cheerful, welcoming voice.

"Dominik! Our friends have arrived!"

The men paused, looking around. A few whispered the name *"Dominik?"* as if with some recognition. Col's voice echoed strangely in the fog, both loud and muffled at the same time. Before they could pinpoint the source, he continued.

"Men of Artha, your arrival is expected! Your weapons are not needed, as we have nothing worth taking."

The men dropped down from their climb up the bluff, finally catching sight of him on the beach. Their weapons were still drawn, but lowered in surprise. It was as he had hoped. Most people, when intent on violence, were taken aback when greeted with delight. In that momentary pause, he hoped that Dominik and the others had awoken. The men approached him warily where he stood, a white figure wreathed in fog.

"Who are you? And how do you know our island?" one asked, his face indiscernible behind the scarf. Beside Col, River rose to her feet, a deadly determination on her face. Col saw her draw out her daggers, her hands gripping the short wooden handle, ready to lengthen the wood into a spear shaft. He put out a hand, stopping her.

"That will only spur them into violence," he whispered. Then, aloud, he addressed the men.

"I am the Wolf. You won't know of me, but-"

"Oh, we've heard of you," the man interrupted grimly. "Villagers cry that name like some kind of ward, sure that this Wolf will protect them. They never used to fight back when we raided their fields, but now they do, using your name as a battle cry. If you are truly the one behind this sudden uprising of fighting spirit amongst the pathetic coastal peasants, then you have caused us no end of bother."

"He's lying," another man spoke. "He's just a lad, there's no way he's the Wolf."

Col felt sick. He had no idea that his fame had spread so far. These were not noble warriors as Dominik had promised. They were pirates! Thieves who murdered the people of his country, and stole from them! They were no better than the Order, oppressing the people in the wild lands beyond the Order's aid. Had he traveled so far, only to discover another enemy, instead of an ally?

At that moment, Dominik slid down the bank onto the beach. He had his hood off, and his angular features looked haggard in the pale light.

"You would do well to respect the Wolf," he said sharply. "He has done more to hurt the Order than our entire nation ever has."

"It's not your nation, not anymore, Dominik. How dare you show your face here!" one of the pirates snapped. Col realized that not all of them were men. This voice belonged to a woman, although it was gravelly and low. She strode forward and made as if to slap Dominik across the face. Quick as lightning, he caught her hand mid-air. His face was astonished and bewildered. Reaching out, he tugged off the woman's scarf, revealing a strong-boned face with a sharp nose, narrowed eyes, and pinched lips.

"*Brea*?" he gasped. Then, to the utter surprise of everyone on the beach, he caught the woman around the back of her head and kissed her. It was brief, but passionate. Col felt he was about to fall over from shock. Suddenly, the woman twisted out of Dominik's grip and had a dagger point pressed to his gut. Her face was livid.

"How dare you? How *dare* you!" she cried. "No goodbye, no word, and now after ten years you think you can just show up and be welcomed?"

"I did not intend to hurt you," Dominik said, confused.

"Well, you did!" Brea snapped, her voice rising.

Everyone on the beach stood around the quarreling ex-lovers, looking more and more uncomfortable. River still looked ready to kill someone. Col, however, began to feel amused by the ridiculous situation. Of all the possible outcomes of their meeting with Dominik's people, he could never have imagined such a scene. At the very least, no one seemed ready to attack them anymore. Daggers and swords had been returned to sheaths except for the dagger now being brandished in Dominik's face by the irate Brea. He couldn't help the grin that began to spread over his face at the sight of the enigmatic Dominik so flustered. Finally, one of the pirates intervened.

"Brea, who is this man?"

"He's a traitor," the woman spat. "He left ten years ago against the express wishes of the Council, and he has been branded an exile. The Council ordered that he should never be welcomed back."

Col turned to Dominik, astonished and accusing.

"*What?* You failed to mention that."

Dominik looked surprised, and deeply hurt.

"I didn't know," he said. In his face, Col read another story. He *had* known, or had at least suspected, something of the sort. But he had been concealing it, putting Col's cause above his own safety.

"We should kill them," another man suggested. Col's heart fell. He had hoped to distract these men from that topic. However, Brea looked torn.

"No... We should take them prisoner... The Council may want to question them," she protested, feigning an uncaring attitude, despite the red rimming her eyes. No one was fooled. There was an awkward silence, as everyone looked at her. She looked back at them fiercely. Clearly, no one wanted to get involved.

"... Alright, then," a pirate voiced what everyone seemed to be thinking.

"But taking them home now will mean giving up on a hunt without anything to show for it."

"If this man is a traitor, maybe there will be a reward for catching him!" someone suggested. In the end, that decided the matter. Dominik was bound and tossed into the bottom of a long boat. Col and River were left untied, as they submitted peacefully. Upon inspecting the camp, however, the pirates discovered it empty. Kimia and Caldwell had escaped, along with two of the Sliders and all of the provisions.

47

The moment they cast off into the waves, Col felt a cold fear wash through him. They were setting out into deeper and deeper water, in nothing but small boats. Beside him, River clutched his hand in a white-knuckled grip. Her pale skin was almost green under her sunburnt cheeks. Col gave her a reassuring smile that he didn't feel. Then, to distract himself and her, he began questioning their captors.

"How do these boats move, without sails?" He asked the nearest pirate, as the boats slipped softly through the mist at a great speed. In answer, the man pointed. Col looked, and saw a young man in a boat near them, who looked almost asleep. He was hanging over the back of a boat, with both arms submerged in the waves up to the elbow. He had his eyes closed, eyebrows furrowed in concentration. Around his arms, the sea swelled and rippled in a strange way. These ripples spread out from him, catching each boat in the small fleet and propelling it forward in a surge.

"We Arthans have never needed sails," the man said proudly. "Sails are for weak landsmen who cannot speak to the sea."

"You mean... The sea can talk?" Col was shocked. The man hesitated, then scratched his head.

"Well, no. I'm not really sure. You'd have to ask one of our Tide Guides, like Dunca over there. But the sea responds when *he* talks, that's for certain. He knows the sea so well, I swear he breathes at the same beat as the waves against the shore. Swims like a fish, too."

Fish? To Col, fish had always been a legend.

"Fish are real?" he asked hesitantly. At that, the men in the boat began laughing. They laughed so hard and so long that Col could see the tears in some of the men's eyes.

"Real? Lad, you'll be wishing they weren't soon enough! Fish for breakfast, fish for lunch, and fish for dinner. That's what we eat on the islands."

"You're forgetting squid," one man remarked, smacking his lips. "Now that's a real treat."

Col forgot about his fear of the water below them. Instead, he was filled with wonder. Despite the disreputable nature of the island people, he couldn't help thinking that he was in the middle of an adventure more thrilling than anything he could have dreamed.

"Did you know the sea had a soul like the land?" he asked River softly. She shook her head, eyes wide.

"I've never heard of such a thing. I think it would be wild and violent, not an easy creature to befriend or master."

Col had to agree.

To Col and River's great relief, they caught sight of land on the horizon before the end of the day. The sun sank low over the glittering expanse of water, and in the far distance a low, bumpy patch of darkness did not reflect the light. The sight encouraged Col, even after the light grew dim and he couldn't see it. When they finally slowed, Col saw faint lanterns in front of them. A series of long white docks jutted out into the dark waves. At the end of one, an old man was sitting, his feet in the water. Suddenly, the waves around the boats began rising, forming a low wall in their way. A harsh current pushed them back out to sea.

"Ho! Who goes there?" the old man called suspiciously. He was met by a chorus of protests.

"Come now, you know us! Don't pretend your eyesight's gone, as well as your sense of respect!"

The wall of water disappeared. The boats nosed up to the pier, and Col heard the old man muttering.

"There ain't nothing to respect about a bunch of thugs making trouble where they've got no business. How about respecting the Tide Guides, and the old ways for once?"

Now that they were back on their own island, the pirates were surprisingly furtive. They quietly split up, sneaking off into the dark in silence. The captives were hustled up a steep stone pathway leading away from the ocean. Whenever they passed a torch or lantern set along the roadway, Col caught glimpses of dense jungle and majestic, pillared old buildings made from a yellowish, porous stone rather like marble, but rougher. Much later, he learned it was actually the dried-out husk of a type of sea tree called a coral. The entire way, Brea never spoke to Dominik, but Col saw her sneaking glances at him whenever she thought he wasn't looking.

After some time, they passed through a gate into an open courtyard, surrounded by high walls and dark doorways. It looked abandoned, with trees growing through the cracked pavement. It took some struggling for the pirates to open one of the doors. They pushed the prisoners in, then attempted to close and lock it. The bolt screamed in protest, and Col worried they might not be able to open it again.

Footsteps faded. Darkness closed in. Sitting on the cold, mossy floor, Col began to wonder if he had made the right decision.

"Well, Dominik," he said, forcefully cheerful, "I suppose you ought to tell us all about this Brea! You neglected to mention her."

Dominik just grunted noncommittally. From the noises that followed, Col guessed the man had turned away and pulled himself into a corner. He was surprisingly agile, even with hands bound.

Bored and worried, Col began to think. After a moment's deliberation, he knelt on the ground, hoping he was doing the right thing.

"God, the real god, I mean, the one who spoke to River, if you have power here, could you help me?"

He said the words under his breath into the dark. Beside him, someone shifted.

"I am, and I have been," said a voice. Shock rocked through Col. He turned, and there beside him sat a young man. At first he thought the man was around his own age, then he thought far younger, and then he became certain that the man was in fact much much older. Or, perhaps...

all three at once? He had a face that was so normal and nondescript that Col could never recall his exact features afterwards, not even his hair color. The youth turned his gaze on Col. Somehow, Col didn't wonder at how he was able to see the man perfectly clearly, although the rest of the cell was still dark.

"I help you every time you speak to crowds, making your words persuasive. Did you think your gift was an accident?" His voice carried mild reproach. He seemed so normal, and yet there was a depth to his eyes that made Col feel as though he couldn't look too deeply into them, or he might break. His form, sitting there beside Col, was so solid it made the rest of the cell seem insubstantial. Col opened his mouth, but was too stunned to know what to say. The man continued.

"I was there with River when she thought of you as you hung over the cliff, putting pity into her heart. I was there when you lay dying and she begged me to give you back to her. And I was there, thousands of years ago, when I first spoke to the people of this island, already thinking of you and plotting your destiny. Why do you still doubt me when you ask for my help?" Col felt a surge of wonder, followed by shame.

"I'm sorry. I didn't know. And, thank you," he whispered.

"You didn't know? Or you didn't want to believe?" asked the youth gravely. Col opened his mouth, at a loss for an answer. Before he could think of something, he opened his eyes, and he was lying on the floor of the dark cell. Only two other people breathed beside him. The hairs rose on his arms. Had that been real?

48

River found it very funny to be "locked up" in a cell which she could break apart with barely an effort. The ground beneath her feet was writhing with life and energy. She had never felt it so happy, so alive, even in the old country of her birth. Instinctively, she knew that she could not awaken or enrich *this* soil, any more than one could make water more wet. She awoke on the floor of the cell feeling more alive and refreshed than her time sleeping in the palace of King Drystan. She sat drinking in the sunlight that filtered through the barred windows for a while. Col was still asleep, and she couldn't help looking at him longingly. The sunlight turned his sandy hair into glimmering gold, and fell across the striking lines of his cheek and chin. He had a bit of moss stuck to his chin, which she couldn't help wanting to wipe away. She was tempted to do it, despite Dominik watching, when suddenly he awoke. His beautiful green eyes fixed on her, and she wondered if he knew she'd been watching him. She blushed, looking away.

"Do you want me to crack this cell open?" she asked. He shook his head.

"No. We're on an island, and the boats have no sails or oars. Even if we got out of this cell, we'd be trapped. The only thing for it is to talk our way out."

River couldn't help but groan. She hated the subtlety of such things.

"Fine," she muttered, "but they'll probably just let us rot in here and never come talk to us."

"Not Brea." Col said with a smirk. Dominik glared.

They needn't have worried. Before the sunbeam had moved halfway across the floor of their cell, someone came to fetch them.

He was a far different sort of person than the robed dark figures of the night before. Col couldn't know if he had been one of the pirates, but he seemed altogether cheery and civilized, with a clean green tunic that fell to his knees, brown trousers, high laced boots, and a floppy hat, the brim decorated with shells. His skin was of a similar shade to Dominik's, although his hair was shorter and curly, a few strands of it escaping from under his hat. An intricate line of some strange script was tattooed across one side of his jaw and down his neck. He sported a short moustache, the upturned edges almost giving the impression of a smile. He moved across the courtyard towards their cell with graceful steps. Unlocking the door took him several minutes, and when he did finally get it open he was winded. After a moment's breath-catching, he said,

"The traitor Dominik will stand trial before the Council this evening. Until then, he is to remain here. However, to you his companions, the Council wishes to apologize for the rough treatment you have received. You are free to go, and enjoy the hospitality of our island as you like."

Col looked at River, then at Dominik, his face conflicted.

"What will they do to you, at this trial?"

In answer to his question, Dominik simply knelt.

"Do not concern yourself with my fate, sir. I have brought you to the land of my people, as you wished. Do not now allow thoughts of my comfort to hinder you from achieving your goals."

River expected Col to protest, to refuse to leave Dominik. He seemed about to, but then he paused, considering.

"Very well, I'll go. But I will find a way to get you out of here. I swear it."

They left the cell. River couldn't help feeling a deep worry for Dominik. She looked back, trying to catch his eye, but he avoided her gaze, as always. Once, he had allowed her to distract him from his duty to protect Col, and Col bore the marks of that disaster forever. Dominik would never again allow himself to be distracted. Yet again, River felt a pang of jealousy towards Col. She loved him, but she couldn't help being resentful of the way that everyone else loved him, too. Far more than they loved her.

"What will they do to him at this trial?" she demanded of the dandified pirate. The man gave an elaborate shrug.

"There are many possible decisions the Council could make. Perhaps death, perhaps freedom, perhaps yet another banishment, or a beating. Who am I to predict their choices?"

"I'd better like their choice, or I'll predict *their* fates." River growled. Col put a hand on her arm.

"We're guests here," he reminded her. "Let's try to keep it that way."

He gave the man a pleading glance.

"Really, though. Can we see the council?"

"Anyone can see the council," the man replied calmly. "There are no restrictions. However there is usually a long line, so you may not get to see them before the trial. Just head up the island to the top of the highest hill."

With that, he left them. Col and River looked at each other.

"It seems these people have two faces," he remarked suspiciously. "One we saw last night, the other this morning. I'm not sure which disturbs me more."

River had to agree. They trekked up the hill. At first, there was only dense jungle on both sides of the path. Then, there began to be more houses. They passed terraces, arches, gates, and white towers sticking up through the tree canopy in the distance. Walls were decorated with flowing, beautiful designs. Thick swaths of flowering vines grew over everything. It was the most lovely place River had ever seen. She thought that they were probably in a vast city, but with all the trees it was hard to see anything except the very closest houses. People they passed gave them strange looks; and no wonder! Although Col's skin was a burnished brown, not too much lighter than the skin of some of the islanders, his sandy hair stuck out. And River knew her pale skin must seem almost ghostly in comparison with that of everyone else. Many of the islanders also had long tattoos of strange symbols on their wrists or necks. Col had shed his long sleeved shirt in the hot climb, and now he hiked up the hill with it tied around his waist. That was the most astonishing thing of all, and the reason everyone stared. Not that he was shirtless. This seemed to be rather common among the men and boys. No, what drew the attention of onlookers, and even caused River to stare occasionally, was his scars. She'd gotten used to the smaller ones on his face. She'd even gotten used to the sight of his mutilated fingers poking from the end of his sleeve. However, this was the first time she'd seen him walk about openly without hiding his arms. The scars were thick and horrible, having changed from angry red to a sharp white over the months. His arms were knotted with lean muscle, but where the thick white bands of his scars cut across the muscle, it dented in like cords cutting into the skin. When he saw her staring, he grinned.

"We're trying to get the council's attention, aren't we?" he laughed.

Suddenly, they came to a small hilltop, which was crested with a squat tower, its top merely an open courtyard rimmed with low walls. From the top of the tower, they could suddenly see the country all around them. The slopes stretched away downward, with a collage of forests and white stone architecture covering the land. Behind them, the slope ended in a small cliff overlooking the sea. The coast of the island stretched out into the sea like fingers or roots. Between each promontory, there was a calm bay. Some parts of the island were walled, while other parts were protected by sharp cliffs and high reefs in the water. However, the walls were ancient, crumbling from long neglect. Ahead of them, near what Col assumed was the center of the island, the ground rose in yet another hill, this one far larger. They made certain of their direction before descending from the tower. Once they were among the trees, it was impossible to see the large hill anymore. The trek was long, but it seemed easy for River, after her many months of walking all day. Something about the city felt strange to her, but she couldn't figure out what.

The top of the hill turned out to be a sort of dip or bowl. The rim was surrounded by old towers and walls, but there were no gates to keep people out, only archways. At the bottom of the bowl, there was a circular courtyard. Evenly spaced along one side were six thick trees, and as they drew closer River saw that beneath each tree sat a chair. Not a massive or elaborate throne, just a simple wooden bench. On each bench sat a very old person. They were not old and frail, neither were they old and fat. They were old and strong, with noble, weather-worn faces and straight spines. Looking at them, River thought of the type of tree that, when it grows old, does not rot on the inside or grow dry and dead, but instead the wood grows thicker and harder, until it is like polished stone on the inside. The type of tree from which her people would make handles for spear and sword. They were very like trees, these elders. They looked very stern.

There was a small crowd waiting in the courtyard, each taking turns approaching one or another of the elders and speaking with them. The soft murmur of voices in the courtyard mixed with the rustling of the tree leaves in the sea breeze.

River had been prepared to crack the stone, shake the island if she had to, anything to forcefully gain an audience with the council. However, now that she approached the place, her anger faded. She felt her heart fill with a quiet sense of respect. She could not imagine breaking up the solemn atmosphere with destructive power. She felt that to do so would be childish, the equivalent of throwing a tantrum to get her way. At the thought, she became aware of another thing. The earth did not *want* to quake, either. She doubted that she would be able to make it move at all. Here, and on the entire island, the earth felt completely at peace, like a cat in a sunbeam. She felt almost fearful as they approached. Col, too, seemed to sense the solemnity of the place.

They needn't have worried about an audience. As they drew closer, the crowd in the courtyard parted for them, eyes wide. With all of their faces uncovered, River could not tell if any of them had been in the boats the night before.

One of the elders rose and walked a few paces toward them, arms swept wide in a gesture that seemed welcoming. That was the moment that River realized what was strange. She couldn't feel his footsteps. She couldn't feel any of the footsteps of the people of this island, except for the pirates the previous night. It wasn't that they were completely silent. They moved with the dangerous grace of fighters, to be sure, but she could still *hear* their footsteps on the stone. The strange thing was that she couldn't feel their footsteps reverberating through the earth under her feet. They seemed to her like trees, or animals. The earth simply didn't feel their footsteps, didn't take note of them as it usually did with other humans. They moved across the ground in tune and in step with all other living things, making no ripple or disturbance in the song that beat through everything. River felt goosebumps rising on her arms. These humans were *not* normal.

Col bowed. River didn't. The elder sat back down in his chair.

"I assume you are the strange companions of our wayward kin, Dominik?"

The eyes of all six elders were fastened on them, on Col, especially, with interest. Col began his introductions, presenting their cause and his story with perfect elegance. He used the perfect words, paused at the right moments, and used his dazzling smile to devastating effect. The elders, the crowd, and even River herself stood spellbound. When Col wove a story into existence in the air, everything about him seemed beautiful, even his scars. It wasn't a facade, rather it was the genuine passion with which he spoke that was so captivating. When he described the things she had done, she blushed, for the way in which he painted her made her out to be far more noble, beautiful, and powerful than she felt.

When Col was done speaking, there was a hushed silence in the courtyard. He looked at each of the members of the Council, and his eyes held betrayal.

"I was told that this was an island of free people, of noble warriors who fought back against the Hand. And yet, I arrived here to find that you are instead pirates, oppressors of the innocent poor, just as the Order itself is."

One of the old women looked especially grieved at his words.

"We do not choose violence," she said, shaking her head. "Although some of the younger generations are rash and thirsty for revenge against the Order, we send raiding parties only out of necessity. Since the Order cut off all trade with us, we are forced to take what we cannot get any other way. We have given them firm instructions not to harm anyone who does not attack first."

Col and River exchanged a glance. The party who had apprehended them had clearly not been intending to follow such instructions.

"But why do you attack the poor villagers? Why not strike out at the Order itself?" Col asked. At his question, the faces of the Council grew dark.

"No. The Order is too big, and too far away. While the Order ignores us, we have peace. If we began to cause trouble for them, they would crush us."

"But you fought them once!" Col protested. The same old lady shook her head again.

"Once, we fought them, yes. But our people have dwindled in number, and our walls are crumbling."

"In those days we sinned," another elder chimed in. "Violence is not the will of El-Yos. Never again will our nation kill others except in defense of our homes and families."

River, again, thought of the way in which the pirates the night before had acted, and had trouble stomaching the irony of it. She thought that either these elders were lying, or they had grown out of touch with the ways of the younger generation.

Col spread his hands, pleading.

"But what of those without defenders? There are countless people suffering right now at the hands of the Order. They cannot fight. They do not know how. Can you, who preach peace, see all of that and do nothing?"

Several council members stood up, and went over to join others, talking quietly with their backs turned to Col. Then, finally, they addressed him.

"We will commence a private council to discuss this with you further. Such things are not meant for the ears of the public."

They took Col to a grand meeting hall, the pillars and roof rising higher than the jungle canopy. In front of the wide steps, there was a statue that Col found strangely incongruous, when paired with what he knew of the stern, warlike islanders. It was a statue of an assortment of different animals, gathered about a young boy with a joyful and yet solemn expression. He was feeding them, and did not seem afraid, even though there were Sliders and Scorpillon among the creatures. An eagle perched on his shoulder. The statue had holes in its palms, and water flowed out of them, pouring down into animal's mouths and then flowing in a little stream to the ground, where there were other stone animals lapping up the water. Col stood transfixed, staring, and suddenly his dream came back to him. Could the islanders' El-Yos, and the man who visited his dream have been the same person? If so, what did an island deity want with Col, a crippled peasant boy from the heart of the Order's country?

49

As they led Col away, River was at a loss. What should she do? What could she do to help? She knew that Col would probably tell her to keep quiet and do nothing. With her destructive temper, she was likely to cause more harm than good if she tried to get involved.

Bored and worried, she wandered the island. About an hour later, she found herself wandering onto a narrow path that led between tall rocks into a small, secluded cove. There she found something astonishing.

A woman was standing on the beach, long dark hair hanging almost to her knees, a tight shirt tucked into loose, baggy pants which were rolled up to mid-calf. The walls of the cove were dotted with nests, and grey gulls perched everywhere, even on the girl's head. She was feeding them, but with such aggression that some of them flapped away, crying their dismay at having been beaned in the head with a chunk of food. River recognized the sharp, angry motions, the harsh breathing. She was prone to such fits herself. The woman was seething with angry emotions. River felt a surprising pang of empathy, an emotion she had rarely experienced.

"Throwing it harder won't make them eat it faster," she said softly. The woman spun around, defensive. It was Brea.

"You don't know anything about gulls!" she snapped. Her voice cracked. River saw that she had been crying, as well as assaulting the poor birds with food. River took a deep breath and sat down on a rock.

"Maybe not, but I do know something about anger," she replied. At this, Brea looked offended.

"I am not-" she began, then deflated. "Alright, so perhaps I'm angry." She put the food away in her satchel, then continued.

"But I have every right to be! Dominik is a lout. A selfish, unfeeling lout!"

"He certainly does seem to have treated you poorly," River

agreed. "But some things, an ambition, a dream, or a prophecy, can cause people to do foolish things. They leave the people they love and all they have ever known to seek fulfillment. And yet, they still love the ones they left. They still miss their home every day. And sometimes they regret..." River trailed off, lost in the past. Brea looked at her with a new understanding dawning in her eyes. She seemed to calm down.

"You think he still cares?" she asked. River nodded.

"I've never seen him show so much emotion as he did when he saw you."

This seemed to placate Brea, for she sat down on the rock next to River, thoughtful.

"It was a prophecy and a dream that drove him away, like you said. So many of us wanted to take action against the Order, so we went on raids. But Dominik wanted to take it a step further. He wanted to see the Order brought down at last, and he was convinced we all had a part to play. The Council laughed at him. He was never the best of fighters. They warned him that he would only bring disaster to our kingdom. Then, one day, he just disappeared."

River felt awkward. She had never before been privy to emotional conversations with other girls. Other girls had always been afraid of her, or shunned her awkward bluntness. She hesitantly put a hand on Brea's shoulder.

"I'm sorry." She groped around for a change of subject, and her gaze landed on the small grey gulls gathering hopefully around.

"Why do you feed the birds, anyway?" she asked. "Isn't bread scarce on this island?"

Brea laughed.

"Not this bread! It's made from dried fish-meal. Nearly everything we eat is made from fish. Do you want to try?" She offered a chunk of the dry, crumbly stuff to River. It tasted awful. River immediately saw why it made better bird food than people food. Sitting next to Brea, she began to throw hers to the birds as well.

"Why do these birds need to be fed?" she asked after a moment. "Aren't they wild?"

"It's a sacrifice to El-Yos," the woman explained, a little ashamed. "It is His will that we care for all living things. Those of us who take our god seriously sometimes feel guilty about the violence we commit on raids. People say it's a necessity, but... well, sometimes it doesn't feel that way. I suppose doing service to El-Yos is a sort of penance."

"If this god doesn't approve of violence, wouldn't a better way of serving him be to stop committing it?" River asked with a frown. Brea looked at her sharply, as if she'd just been stung.

"That's the reality, isn't it?" Her voice was stricken. "But once something has begun, it's so hard to stop. All of the other young fighters do it, so how could I stop without looking weak? I'll admit it's not exactly a perfect situation," her tone became defensive, "but we're young, and full of energy. It has to be expended somehow. If we weren't fighting and killing, we'd be falling in love and having too many children and, well, the island can only support so many people." She shrugged. "The older Arthians are much better at staying out of trouble. I expect I'll be better too, when I'm old."

These just seem like excuses. River thought to herself. *Young people can be strong, too! Brea's energy and youth could be her strength, not her weakness.* She didn't voice her thoughts, however, reflecting on her own violent tendencies. She was no better. Instead, she tried to see something positive in Dominik's ex-lover.

"The others seem to respect and look up to you," she told Brea encouragingly. "Perhaps you could have more influence than you expect, if you started showing mercy to the innocent."

"Pah!" Brea spat. "Is anyone on the mainland truly innocent? They are all wicked men, worshipping the Order's wicked gods."

"Is your El-Yos not one of the Order's gods?" River had simply been curious, but at her question Brea looked horribly offended.

"No! Of course not! Our god does not need a Hearer to speak for him! Everyone is allowed to speak to him and know him, if they dare. It is a dangerous thing, serving El-Yos. He protects and loves those who are his, but he also can ask very hard things from us."

This intrigued River. She awkwardly apologized.

"I'm sorry, I meant no offense. I didn't know. Can I see his temple?" she asked. Again, for some reason, Brea seemed to think this a stupid question. She began to grow annoyed with River.

"There is no temple. Every beautiful thing we make is a tribute to him." There was a long silence, and she gave River a look of distaste, as River didn't seem likely to go away.

"I... can take you to see some of the famous old tributes, if you like," she offered reluctantly, after far too long a pause. River, for her part, was also beginning to dislike Brea's company. She hated being treated condescendingly. However, she refused to be driven away by the woman's unpleasant moods. Instead, she resolved to make Brea's day miserable by turning her into River's own personal tour guide.

"Oh, that would be delightful!" she said in a false, cheery voice. Immediately, she could see Brea regretting her offer.

The next two hours were spent trekking all over the island. The more sullen Brea became, the more cheerful River felt. A small part of her felt that it was wrong to be so vindictive, but a larger part of her didn't care. *Besides,* she thought, *I'm distracting her from her feelings about Dominik.*

Sullen or not, she was really starting to enjoy Brea's company by the end of the second hour. She didn't relish the thought of being left completely alone in an unfamiliar city. They were walking into a part of the city that felt really old, with stone worn smooth and polished by the sea winds. A winding path hugged the edge of a cliff that jutted out from the sea. On the thick wall protecting the path from the steep drop, there were occasional statues. Suddenly, River saw something that stopped her in her tracks.

It was a statue of a man without a face. The statue looked as though it had been smashed into pieces, and then put back together roughly, so that the cracks and jagged fissures ran through it. The arms were especially covered in broken lines, and the left hand was completely broken off.

"What is that?" she asked. Brea gave the statue a bored glance.

"Just some sculptor's rendition of a really old prophecy. One of those stories from the first island dwellers, after El-Yos raised this island from the ocean and wrote his words of blessing on the cliffs. I don't think it's true, just an explanation of why the strata lines and ore veins scribble across the cliffs in the weird way they do."

She moved to continue up the path, but River stood looking at the statue. Her heart was moved by it in a way she didn't understand. Thoughtfully, she sent a command through the earth at her feet. Immediately, the vines wrapping the base of the statue fell away, revealing the inscription. Over the months, Col had been teaching her to read the modern script people used. However, to her immense surprise, this inscription was written in two different scripts. First, there was an inscription in characters not unlike the ones her own people had used in the distant past. Then, underneath it, was a translation in the modern script. It was entitled, "The Broken Man"

He bears the pain of a nation.
Body and soul, his scars will never heal.
Alone, a desolate creation,
yet pain for thousands, he will feel.
His wounded soul will mend the land.
With broken hand, he will break the hand.

River felt a chill sweep through her. It was a horrible prophecy. She immediately felt pity for the subject, whoever it was, or would be. Uncomfortably, it made her think of Col, and her heart lurched with guilt and sorrow. In contrast, her own prophecy seemed blissfully bright. *It's not about Col.* She reminded herself forcefully. *It's probably not even a real prophecy... It can't be about Col. He deserves a happy ending. He will have a happy ending.* The more she told it to herself, the less she believed it. She turned away from the statue, thoroughly spooked. Already, she knew that every line had been etched into her memory.

Brea was staring at her, mouth open wide in astonishment.

"What did you just do?" she demanded. "How did you do that?"

"Hmm? Oh." River, distracted, glanced down at the vines around the statue's base. She shifted her foot, and they writhed up to cover the disturbing inscription again. Brea's eyes nearly popped out of her head.

"Your people can't speak to the earth?" River asked, bemused. "I thought, because of the Tide Guides..."

"No, I've never heard of such a thing!" Brea whispered with awe.

"We honor the earth, and take care of it, but it never does as we tell it to!"

Now that she was showing River a proper amount of respect, River felt herself liking the woman better.

"You do well," she said kindly. "Your people walk in step with nature, so that the earth flourishes under your care. I can sense that here, on this island, it feels at peace."

Brea beamed. Her face was really quite beautiful, when it wasn't all pinched up in negativity.

"We should go to the Elders!" she exclaimed. "They will want to hear about this!"

"They already did." River said, a bit testily. "They were far more interested in my companion than in me."

As if speaking of him had summoned him, they met Col a little ways down the path, as he came looking for River. Finally, Brea was released from her duties as River's companion. However, she no longer seemed to loathe River's company. She led them to a courtyard where a massive map of the island was engraved into the tiled floor, before taking her leave. When she was gone, Col turned to River, his face woeful.

"They won't lend us soldiers," he said, "not even a few to train my people to fight. They don't like the Order, but they don't trust me, you, or Dominik, and don't believe that their own interests would be looked after, if we should defeat the Order. It's just... so frustrating." For a moment, his face showed his weariness. River's heart ached for him. She stepped in close and slid her arms around his waist. He leaned against her, letting his cheek rest on her shoulder.

"I'm sorry," she whispered, feeling a weight settle in her own stomach at the implications of their failure.

"We won't give up, though. We'll find another way."

She didn't believe her own words. How could a crowd of untrained villagers and brigands, no matter how big, fight the overwhelming military might of the Order? They *needed* an edge. They needed real fighters.

50

"Lady River!" Both River and Col stopped on the crowded street, looking around for the source of the hysterical cry. They had been just on their way to find the new lodgings assigned to them by the Council, where they had been promised a good meal.

Through the crowd of faces, River caught sight of Brea. People were drawing away from her, as her frantic pace and wild eyes were unnerving. She dashed up to River, and caught her hand.

"They're holding Dominik's trial early! Please, come quickly!"

River immediately began following the woman, concerned. However, she was also confused.

"What do you want me to do?" she asked with a frown. "Shouldn't Col be the one to help?"

"You are powerful," Brea exclaimed. Clearly, she hadn't thought beyond that. "Just... protect him! Don't let them kill him!"

River couldn't help but notice the change in Brea's attitude now that the trial had begun. Despite her professed hatred for the man, Brea was revealing her true feelings. She still loved him. River hastened her steps. Behind her, she heard Col's stumbling pace. He was tired, very tired, and she knew he had been greatly looking forward to the meal. But, as always, he put the needs of his men before his own.

The late afternoon sunlight was slanting through the open doorways in the wall surrounding the bowl. The orange beams of light sliced through the air, leaving most of the gathered mob in shadow. River had to fight her way through the crowd until she could see what was happening. As if an invisible line had been drawn, the people held back from the circular courtyard in front of the six benches. In the center of this circle, Dominik knelt, his hands bound. It was all very formal, very solemn. One of the old men was just starting to speak.

"Dominik," he sounded weary, "we have considered your crimes.

You spoke treasonous words against the Council and our peaceful ways, stirring up trouble on our island. After being forbidden to leave the island, you disobeyed the Council's express wishes, going directly to the central city of the Order and stirring up trouble there, a foolhardy act that risked drawing the Order's attention to this nation. After being banished, you still dared to return to this land. Not only that, but you brought a wanted fugitive of the Order onto our shores, bringing even further risk. You are a traitor to our ways, our peace, and our safety."

As he spoke, River felt a dread sinking into her stomach. They were too late. This wasn't the beginning of the trial, but the end of it. Too late now for Col to change the Council's minds, as they seemed to have already decided Dominik's fate.

"We have decided," the old councilman went on, confirming River's fears, "that such actions deserve death."

There was a gasp in the crowd, and some cheers. Brea cried out in anguish. At her voice, Dominik's head snapped up. He craned his neck, trying to look over his shoulder and catch her eye. The old man held up his hand.

"However, we have taken into consideration that your banishment was issued *after* you had left our shores. Therefore, some mercy will be administered to account for your ignorance of the full repercussions of returning here. We sentence you to be beaten with a lash, and then imprisoned until such a time as we are convinced that you have fully forsaken your trouble-making ways."

Dominik bowed his head, squeezing his eyes shut. River saw pain on his face, but no surprise. She let out a breath. Well, at least he wasn't going to die. She felt sympathetic, but also confident that the revolution could proceed without him. Immediately, her mind turned to strategy, considering which of Col's men would be best suited to taking Dominik's place. Suddenly, someone shoved through the crowd, running out onto the courtyard. It was Col. He put himself between Dominik and the looming elder.

"Punish me instead."

River couldn't believe her ears. *What?* She had expected him to plead Dominik's case, but never this! It was tactically disastrous. What could they do against the Order without Col? How could the revolution survive without the Wolf to bring them together? The six elders, too, looked astonished. Dominik looked horrified.

"No!" he cried. "My lord, this is not your concern!"

"It is, though," Col said gravely. He turned to the Council.

"This man, Dominik, is not my companion, or my guide. He is my soldier, sworn to my service, and I am his captain. He did not wish to return to this island, but I commanded him to do so, against his will. It was my choice, not his. Should a man be punished for another man's decisions? The only fault in him is his loyalty to me. Would you discipline a man for his loyalty? It was my decision. I bear the blame. Lay the sentence on me."

River didn't know what to do. Dominik, it seemed, didn't either. Brea looked hopeful, and River instantly felt a stab of anger toward her. Only the Council seemed to be considering Col's offer seriously. They talked quietly among themselves, eyes wide, faces animated. Meanwhile, Dominik's two guards had seized Col's arms, uncertain now which of the men they were supposed to be guarding.

Finally, the same old man turned back to Col.

"Very well," he said, "take both of these men to the whipping posts. Tie them there. If, when morning comes, this "Wolf" still feels the same, Dominik will be freed, and he will receive Dominik's punishment."

River followed them. They wouldn't let her near Col, so she trailed along with the rest of the crowd, vacillating between being furious with Col, and falling deeper in love with him for his bravery. When he was tied to the post and the crowds finally departed, River rushed to him.

"Why?" she demanded. "How could you be so stupid?" By

Dominik's anguished face, she could see that he wondered the same thing.

"Please my lord, don't do this," he begged. Col looked tired, but he seemed resolute.

"I got you into this mess, Dominik," he said stubbornly, "I will get you out of it."

He never changed his mind. All through the night, they pleaded with him. He began to look more and more haggard, but never any less resolute. Towards morning, River finally fell asleep on the hard ground at his feet. Col, forced to stand upright with his hands tied above his head to the pole, did not sleep. When River awoke, he was still standing there, looking exhausted. The morning light was just touching the tops of the trees around them, and the clear space around the whipping posts was surrounded by silent islanders. River saw the six elders at the front of the crowd. Every one of them wore a solemn, almost reverent expression. She leaped to her feet, feeling desperate to fight someone, to stop this. But, what could she do that wouldn't make things worse?

"Will you still hold to your decision?" an old lady asked Col. He looked pale, almost green. But he set his teeth and nodded. Two soldiers untied Dominik and dragged him away, struggling and protesting. A man stepped forward, a whip swinging from his hands. He was massive, with veins and muscles bulging from his arms. The whip was long and thin, with sharp bits of shell braided into the cord. Col didn't even flinch. At the first strike, he did though. River saw his whole body tense, as blood ran down his back from a long, jagged stripe. He didn't make a sound. At the sight of his blood, River felt a hot rage sweep through her, such as she had never felt before. She was seized with an overwhelming desire to kill the huge man responsible.

The whip slashed across Col's bare skin again, then again. Col's eyes were squeezed shut. River was trembling with rage. Plants began thrashing around her feet, then the trees of the jungle around the clearing also shook as if in a strong wind. People cried out, as vines wrapped around their ankles. The man with the whip jerked his leg back, ripping a plant up by the roots as it clung to him. Then, in the midst of the chaos, she heard Col's voice, hissed through clenched teeth.

"Take her feet off the ground, before she kills someone."

Immediately, arms seized River. She let out a yelp of rage, horrified, betrayed that he should reveal her fatal weakness to these cruel islanders, that he should stop her when she was the only one here who seemed determined to help him. She struggled, but found that the arms holding her were too strong. The man was at least a foot taller than her, and so had no trouble lifting her off the ground. Trying to escape from him distracted her from the next two lashes on Col's back. He let out an *uhh* of pain, and she instantly stilled her thrashing, focusing her attention on him. His back was a mess of raw, torn skin and blood. His mouth, too, was bleeding, from where he had bitten his lip to keep from crying out. River had seen enough of battle now to be toughened to the sight of blood and injuries. However, seeing Col bleed had a far different effect on her. She winced at every lash. She saw Dominik where the guards held him near the edge of the crowd. He was weeping unashamedly, his expression wracked with guilt. He completely ignored Brea, who was trying to catch his attention. Nearby, standing among the adults, River saw a young boy also watching. He was looking at Col with a solemn expression and eyes that were... proud? River looked at Col, to see what could possibly have inspired that expression in a child. However, when she looked back, the little boy was gone.

In the crowd, the Council was becoming more and more agitated. Finally, one of them cried out,

"Enough!"

There was a silence as the beefy man withdrew, coiling up the blood-flecked length of his whip. Col slowly raised his head, blinking hazily. An old woman came forward, leaning down and cupping his face in her hands. River saw that she had tears in her eyes. Why? How could she be upset after sentencing Col herself?

"Such bravery," the old woman murmured, "such sacrifice." She raised her voice, addressing the crowd.

"We have tested him."

"And he has proved himself!" another old councilwoman cried.

"He treats our wayward brother as one of his own." The rest of the council was nodding their old grey heads in agreement.

"Here is a man we can trust. The hand of El-Yos is on him. We will give him our aid, and our allegiance."

River was finally released. She rushed to Col's side, helping to unbind him. He slumped to the ground. Tears ran down his cheeks. However, when he looked up at her, she saw with complete astonishment that they were tears of joy. His eyes were glowing with triumph.

51

Col was fed, bandaged, and then slept for a whole day. As soon as he was awake and able to converse clearly, he was summoned to attend a meeting. It seemed that, despite the finality of the Council's declaration, there were still a lot of negotiations to conduct. This time, River was permitted to attend the meeting, but only because Col needed to lean on her to make it up the big hill. They were both given new island clothes to wear. Col, mostly covered in bandages, did not cut a very striking figure, but River was delighted with her own outfit. The shirt was white and a little rough in texture, but the short, open sleeves left most of her arms bare, and kept the humid jungle heat from bothering her. Across her shoulders, a long tunic fell, folding together in front and cinched tight to her body with a belt where she could hang many useful weapons. Below the belt, the tunic hung in long strips, split down the sides along her thighs so that it did not restrict her motion at all. She also quite liked the trousers she wore beneath, which were comfortable and the color of rich earth.

"We won't have anyone on the front lines. No violence unless it is in self-defense." River heard this line so many times in the next few hours that she was sick of it. These cowards would let others bleed and die, while they sat back from the action! However, Col seemed to accept their terms calmly. He patiently hammered out conditions for using the Arthians as trainers, spies, and messengers, as they were one of the few people familiar with riding Sliders. He figured out procedures for keeping the Arthians from being discovered as they operated within his ranks, as their dark skin and hair would single them out as foreigners, especially closer to Kingsfall where the population was primarily light-haired. The Council was adamant that the Order could not discover any ties between themselves and the Wolf's forces. River began to be more and more impressed with Col's tactical skills. He had been learning much from watching River as she helped organize his troops, although she had often dismissed him as a figurehead. Unneeded, She began to zone out of the conversation, until the topic suddenly turned to a matter that neither herself nor Col had thought much on.

"Let us talk now of government, in the event that the Order is brought down," an old man said suddenly. "Who will rule the land, or will you divide it between your generals?"

Col gaped for a moment, his eyes bugging out in surprise as he floundered for an answer.

"Well, we've never really discussed our plans beyond the actual fighting of the Order..." he began awkwardly. "Perhaps we could organize some manner of council, where the poor people of the land have a say in how the kingdom is run..."

There was a chorus of laughter, old, wheezy laughter huffing out of all the members of the council.

"That is preposterous!" a man exclaimed. "A council can only work on a small island with few people, like our own. In such a great country, you could never have the peasants vote, no decision would ever be reached! No. You need a strong ruler, for strong decisions. The ruler can appoint advisors, but always it must be a mighty ruler making the big decisions! Even within this council, I am the leader, with the final say in decisions. Who will lead you, once the Order is gone?"

Col turned to River with a question in his eyes.

"River had once hoped to take the throne. She is of royal blood, the niece of a king, and formerly engaged to King Drystan. She is very strong. She has also spoken personally to the power that wove the world, I think the same one you call El-Yos, so she would lead the people wisely in ways that align with your own beliefs."

River suddenly felt very nervous, as all those old faces turned to inspect her. She looked back at them with cool pride, trying not to let their expressions bother her. They looked suspicious, unimpressed, even dismissive.

One old man began shaking his head, and gradually all the others followed suit.

"No. No. That won't do at all. We don't know her, we don't trust her." One old woman, especially, said something that cut River to the core. She looked keenly into the younger girl's eyes, and then pronounced,

"She wants it far too badly to be allowed to have it."

River felt her face flush hot with indignation. Before she could say anything, though, they were all looking at Col again.

"There is really only one solution we can accept," the head councilman said gravely. "You must rule."

Col looked as if he might faint. River felt the words hit her like a blow. Yes, she had seen it coming. But she had ignored the signs, clinging to the druid's prophecy and her own delusions. Internally, the old River raged. Col was a peasant! Col knew nothing of court life! He knew nothing of military strategy! He couldn't fight! She was stronger! And yet, she found inside herself a new River. This River was calm, happy for Col because she loved him. The new River knew that she was harsh, unloving, and prideful. She wanted to be different, but knew that she was still a hard person to love. She knew, although it was hard to admit, that Col was simply a better, kinder person than she was. Everyone loved him. He deserved the throne more, despite her royal blood. She didn't know which version of River to be in the moment, so she sat still, at war within herself.

Col looked crushed.

"I... I don't know," he finally said. "I need a few hours to think about it."

The hours were granted, and he walked out of the meeting hall leaning heavily on River's shoulder. She felt guilty for the jealousy that still raged inside of her. Col had always wanted a peaceful peasant's life. Not this. Why should she resent him for nobly accepting something he only saw as a burden?

Col sat down on a rock. His back was burning with every movement, but worse than that was the pressure of responsibility weighing down on him. Success was within reach. With just one promise, he could secure the help of a powerful warrior nation. And yet, that promise was the one thing he had been dreading ever since he first won the loyalty of Lucan and his bandits. Already, the responsibility of leading his men was a terrifying burden. He was so afraid of failing them, guilt-ridden when any of them were killed. But to rule the entire kingdom of the Order, really the entire world? How could he be sure of his own decisions? How could he be sure of anything?

From where he stood, he could see the slope of the island running away from him, the coast, with jagged cliffs and promontories, and then beyond that the glittering sea. He stared at the cliffs, and his heart cried out for answers.

"Is this really what I must do? How can I know I am leading the people right?" he asked. River didn't answer. Col looked at a cliff sticking out into the water. The stone was striped with squiggles and lines, chalky veins of marble or some such substance. Suddenly, Col realized that there were words written in the stone. Right before his eyes, as clear as if they were written on a scroll, but in a wild, spiky script, he read the words *I will guide you.* He stared. Then stared some more. As he stared, the words slowly faded, turning back into illegible lines. The hair rose on the back of his neck. Did he trust this mysterious deity to guide him? He'd already been through so much, and El-Yos hadn't stopped it. But then again, did he have a choice?

"Are you all right?" River was asking. She sounded alarmed, and he wondered how long he had been staring blankly at the coast.

"Um, yes... Sorry." He shook his head to clear it. "I just don't know how I can accept such a burden. What if I am a bad ruler? What if I make wrong decisions?"

River let out a huff of annoyance. She stomped over until she was directly in front of him, her arms folded over her chest.

"Listen to me, Col. You are a leader. People love you, and follow you. It's not something you have a choice about, it's just something that you are. You are, you have always been, and you will always be, a leader of men. You can't change that. The only thing you can do is decide what sort of a leader you will be. Try to reject the role you were destined for, and you will be a pathetic ruler. Keep second-guessing your decisions, and stressing over the consequences of every move you make, and you will be a weak leader. A failure. History will call you the man who failed because he was too afraid."

Her words were cutting. Col felt them dig deep into his heart, and worst of all, he knew that they were accurate. He was so afraid to risk men's lives that his indecision ended up costing more lives. However, River wasn't done. She put her hands on his shoulders, staring deep into his eyes. A fire smouldered in the dark brown depths of her own.

"But if you accept the challenge set before you," she whispered, "you *will* succeed. You will be the mightiest, most beloved leader this world has ever seen; " she hesitated, and there was shame in her voice when she admitted, "a better ruler than I could have been."

She turned away, walking to the edge of the hill. The sea breeze played with the soft strands of her hair and with the edges of her long tunic. The glittering of the sun on the waves beyond framed her body in a halo of shifting lights. Despite her small stature, she looked every bit the mighty warrior she was. And yet, there was a softness and kindness to her that had not been there when they first met. Her words now held a deep wisdom.

"So, Peasant-boy," she said, "which sort of a man will you choose to be?"

Col took a deep breath. Slowly, he stood up, walked forward, and took her hand. Together, they stared at the ocean. Col made his decision.

He walked away from River, even closer to the edge of the cliff, and knelt.

"El-Yos," he said, with trepidation, "I give in." As he said the words, his courage and confidence rose.

"Make of me what you will. I accept my destiny."

River sucked in a breath of astonishment, but when he looked back her eyes held admiration as well as fear for him. There, on that hill, he finally let Nikki the village boy die. The Wolf, Heretic, Insurrectionist, and Bane of the Order, walked down to meet the Council.

52

The Hearer fumed. Once again, right when he thought he had caught the Wolf, the boy slipped away. All the scouts, spies, and trackers in the Order had completely lost his trail. The Hearer had actually *seen* him, the last time, had been only a few yards away, when some strange mud monster had erupted from the ground to foil his plans. How many unnatural beings had the lad recruited? Thankfully, the unnatural occurrences in Wanderkeep had fully convinced all the other branches of the Order that the Wolf was, in fact, a heretic and dark sorcerer. He no longer worried about treachery among his own ranks.

"Your reports, Enlightened One." Grimald, the steward of the Kingsfall branch in his absence, came into the room. The Hearer took the papers, and began reading through them.

"Well done, as always," he gave a nod of approval. Grimald bowed, backing out of the room. The Hearer liked the big warrior. He was straightforward, and had kept everything running smoothly during the Hearer's absence. Even Rebel movement in the city had been at an all-time low.

Always badly timed, Eshbo burst in, right when the Hearer was settling down to read the reports in full. The Hearer gave him a glare. The little man was gradually wearing out his patience, and had already been demoted twice, much to the delight of Grimald and that dark beauty, Amira.

"You have some nerve, barging in unannounced," the Hearer's voice held a warning edge. Eshbo, however, didn't even bow and scrape as usual. His eyes were shining with a greedy light.

"I found them! I know where they are!"

River felt sad to set foot on the mainland again. After her time on the island, the land seemed even more dead and broken. Around her, the islanders splashed out of their boats. Two tide guides had accompanied them, and were now turning back, moving the entire fleet of boats back out to sea. A small army of islanders climbed the bluffs. Each of them wore dark clothes, with scarfs over their faces. In the moonless night, they were almost invisible. Even their movements were fluid, like shadows or cats creeping through the night. River scarcely knew how to command such deadly warriors, but Dominik did. His eyes were shining as he discussed with her the best ways to utilize these dangerous new troops. It was imperative that they travel only at night, and that they split the army into smaller groups, so as to keep their passage a secret. Of course, Dominik's shining eyes may have had another source. Brea had volunteered to join Col's forces. River felt less jealous of Brea than she would have expected. All of her affections had gradually been stolen away by a certain peasant boy, and she no longer felt such a strong need to win the love of anyone else.

The return journey made their first one seem tedious. Riding sliders most of the way made River feel as though the landscape was flying past. The faster they moved, the less time the Hearer would have to find out about their whereabouts. To her surprise, she didn't have to make nearly as many decisions anymore. Col had begun to throw himself into leadership with a passion that left her astonished. He could know a man's strengths after only a few minutes of conversation or observation. Within a week, he knew exactly the best way to utilize each man and where they would fit best within his ranks. River felt her admiration for him grow by the day. At the same time, her pride shrank. Nikolo Wolf, peasant-born though he was, was a more brilliant leader of men than she could ever have been. She found herself with only one ability that no one else possessed. She fed the troops. Instead of wasting time to hunt and gather food from the sparse landscape, River could turn a handful of corn kernels or pumpkin seeds into a bountiful crop. Even the plants could be fed to the sliders, which kept them docile and willing to remain with the company even after traveling far from their original grazing grounds.

It was here that River discovered a new and painful ability. After everyone had been fed, she was forced to leech the life back out of the plants she had grown. They couldn't leave any trace of her presence in the land. It made her feel sick and disgusted to command the lush growth to wither. It was like puking after eating a delicious meal; A gross perversion of her abilities that left her full of revulsion, drained, with a taste like ashes in her mouth. The men burned the dried-up plants, leaving no trace of their presence. She could still feel it, though. A patch of ground devoid of life, like a dark scar on the land. The rest of the land was dying. This ground was murdered. She had killed hundreds of Priest-guards without feeling. This act, however, left her feeling guilty.

"I can't wait to get back to one of our safe-houses," she said to Col mournfully one day as they dismounted from the slider they rode, named Dareth, or, as she liked to call him, "Death-Rat". She hated the monstrous thing.

"I'm sick of this."

He gave her a sympathetic hug, but then tilted her chin up to look into his eyes, an encouraging smile on his face.

"I know you are. But look! The ground is getting more and more dry! We're leaving the Flatlands!"

It was true. River could even see low cliffs on the far horizon, jagged in the early morning light. Soon, the Sliders would have to be left behind. She had never before been so happy to glimpse that hot, miserable country. It all came flooding back: Lucan, Helena, Dirk, all the bandit lords and their many secret hide-aways. The late-night councils, and the sudden strikes against the Order of the Hand. She found herself growing excited, and a rare smile touched her lips. Soon, she would become far more than just the woman who fed the troops. She would become a weapon. She would *fight*. And she would never again fail to protect Col.

Suddenly, a scout approached, bowing to the both of them.

"We have picked up the trail of two sliders," he reported. "They never travel in herds of less than ten on their own, so these must have riders. Shall we track them down?"

Col nodded. "Yes. But you only have an hour before we move again."

53

Dominik pushed the two prisoners to their knees in front of Col. However, he was suppressing a small smile. Col didn't even have to wait until he saw their faces to recognize them.

"Glad to see you're alright!" he exclaimed. "What news?"

Caldwell spoke up, his voice urgent.

"My Lord, we've been searching for you for days ever since the first of your scouts arrived at Hawknest base, reporting your triumphant return from Arthia. The Hearer has captured your mother and youngest brother."

The words cut through every layer of strength Col had built around his heart. He felt gutted, so stunned that he barely heard the rest of Caldwell's message.

"He demands that you and the Messenger give yourselves up at Kingfall in one month, or he will kill them. Your brothers are desperate to find out your response."

"How could I be so stupid?" he whispered. "How could I have left them unprotected?"

He had distanced himself from Grayson's Shaft and the people who dwelled there, careful to leave no traces for the Order to follow. The villagers had even been calling Jehane by a different name, so that no one could guess at who her son was. And yet, the Order had found them. Col felt so stupid. Of *course* they had! The villagers were loyal, but everyone had a breaking point. Either through money, threat, or pain, the Order had broken someone and wrung the truth from their lips.

The pain and horror threatened to bowl him over, but he forced himself to keep his composure. He took a deep breath.

"I will have an answer for you to take to my brothers by nightfall," he forced out numbly.

The more Kimia and Caldwell revealed details, the lower his heart sank. The Hearer was keeping his family imprisoned beneath the temple in Kingsfall. Col was only too familiar with the place, as well as with the small army of elite Priest-guards that not only filled the temple grounds, but marched constantly through the streets of the city as well. He knew the gates, the walls, and the buildings. He knew there was no way to rescue his mother. Not without alerting the Hearer to his intent. Such an act would only ensure the woman's swift death. River and Dominik began discussing possible rescue attempts. Col didn't join in. Instead, he turned and walked away. His mind was flooded with memories of little Terren, always following Col around and trying to imitate him, of his sweet and sensitive way of caring for his mother when all the other brothers failed to notice her needs. Then he thought of his mother, and he felt his heart was being shredded to bits as he thought of her wisdom, her strength, and her boundless love for her sons, even when they drove her to her wit's end. He knew that to leave her in the Hearer's clutches would break him forever. He also knew that he didn't have a choice. He couldn't trade River's life for hers. It was more than that, though. He was no longer Nikki the village boy. His family, while he loved them more than any others, were no longer his only responsibility. He had an equal responsibility to every one of his men, to the poor people of the land, to the entire kingdom. To choose his mother over them would be to doom the whole country for the sake of only two people. How could any man live with himself, after being forced to make such a choice?

    River followed Col. Her warning glare kept everyone else back, to give their leader his privacy. River firmly believed in protecting Col's private moments - except when it came to her. She liked to think that their closeness to each other had earned her the right to force her company on him even when he did not want it.

She found him kneeling in the grass.

"Col, you can't give yourself up!" she started arguing even before she had reached him, knowing how deep was his loyalty to his family.

"The country needs you! Besides, the Hearer wouldn't let them free, once he had you. He'd just kill all of you!"

She stopped talking, when she saw the tears running down his face, and heard his anguished sobs. She felt awful for scolding him. Instead, she rushed to his side, wrapping her arms around him, and rocking him as he wept. She knew she would soon be covered with snot and tears, but she didn't care.

"Hey," she comforted him softly, "why do you mourn as if they are already dead? There is still time!"

It was a long time before he could speak.

"Because, to me, they have to be," he choked out, the tears coming afresh. "For the sake of the world, I have to let them go."

River felt herself growing cold with horror. What a choice! What a sacrifice! She could not even imagine the pain he must be suffering. There, in that moment, as she held him, she knew. She knew without a shadow of a doubt that Col *was* The Broken Man. He was the man of that awful prophecy, whose "wounded soul will mend the land", and whose "scars will never heal." She felt a deep fear for him building in her heart, and she held him tighter. Gradually, another emotion began to stir. Anger. Anger with the Hearer, of course, but also anger at the mysterious El-Yos, this god who would comfort and bless them, who would bring Col back from the brink of death, only to allow something like this to happen. *Why?* She demanded silently. *Why would you do this to him? I thought you cared for him! What has he done wrong? What has his mother done wrong?* There was no answer.

She stared at Col, at his broken expression. *How can good possibly come from this?*

She wrestled with the question all through the heat of the day, while everyone else slept. Finally, she couldn't take it anymore. She went to find Brea. The two girls had grown more fond of each other over the past weeks, although River found it a bit sickening the way Dominik fawned over the woman. She shook Brea awake, a little more roughly than was necessary.

"Col has just started believing in your god, this El-Yos." she said, skipping all polite "sorry's" and "good morning's".

"And his mother, too, has been devoted to this god all her life. How could the loving Singer I sensed have allowed this to happen?"

"Hmm, what?" Brea looked very confused, staring at River with alarmed, bleary eyes. She took a moment to wake up, then needed River to repeat her question. It made her frown and think for a while, massaging her scalp.

"I am not one of the Elders, I don't know the answers to such things," she said at last, slightly annoyed. Then she saw River's frustrated expression, and her own expression softened.

"Who can know the ways of a god?" she asked gently. "El-Yos is far wiser than me. What I do know is this: I asked the same question of him when Dominik first left, and the Council said he could never return. For years, I thought El-Yos was punishing me by taking away the one I loved," she spread her hands helplessly.

"And yet, here we are now! Because Dominik left, he was able to meet your Col. Dominik was able to lead Col to our island, and inspire our people to take a stand against the Hand, Dominik's lifelong dream. Dominik and I are in love once more, and we are marching to aid the people of the world at this time of crisis, where our help may change the fate of the world! Did El-Yos plan all of this? I can't say."

Her eyes drifted over to Dominik's sleeping form, his head shaded under a small scraggly bush. She smiled fondly.

"I can say this," she admitted, "had I known this outcome, I would have gone through it all again, the same way, even though the years of separation were so painful. It's so wonderful to know the man he's become."

River mused on this, feeling vaguely comforted. However, she did not have long to muse. Brea's eyes were now filled with a giggly, girlish delight.

"Did I tell you? Dominik says that, when we have a quiet moment, he will get a *Shillin* for me!"

"Ummm a what?" River asked, hoping it wasn't something inappropriate.

"It's a tattoo," Brea tapped her jawline, "right here. And I will get the same one on my wrist. It signifies a lifelong oath of devotion to each other."

Oh, a marriage. River realized. *In the middle of a war. How sickeningly romantic. Well, I suppose they have waited a long time.* She felt unaccountably jealous of the happy couple, even though she had been the one to reject Col's offer. Brea was still talking.

"Every family has a symbol, and we will tattoo the symbol of my house, interlocked with his. Our children will inherit both, and so on, until the fourth generation. That is why you have some family tattoos that go all the way up a woman's arm, or down a man's neck. It is a very ancient tradition. Also, it helps to prevent inbreeding on such a small, secluded island community," she winked and laughed.

"In my country, we would just make the vows and the druids bless us," River remarked dryly. "It's less painful." She left without a polite goodbye.

River knew the topic was awkward, but after bouncing along for half the night on Death-Rat, holding on to Col's waist and mulling over Brea's words, she was too full of curiosity to keep it inside.

"What are the marriage customs of your country?" she asked. For a moment she thought he hadn't heard her, he was so quiet. She knew he had been grieving for the whole ride, although he wore a brave face in front of the men. Then, he shook himself out of his dark thoughts.

"Hmm? Oh. Well, there's the ceremony. You both kneel before the king and he approves the union, then the royal documenters make a note in their documents. Then the couple says their vows, and both families throw a big party for three days. During that time, everyone lays a stone into the wall of the couple's new house. They can just be rocks, or in the richer families the stones can actually be made of precious metals, or intricately carved marble. Everyone has a "wedding wall" in their house, and they can't ever tear it down, no matter how ugly it is. The couple each chips a piece of stone out of that wall and wears it on a necklace, to never forget their family or their promises even when they leave the house." His voice was sounding sad again by the time he finished talking, and she knew it had been a bad choice of topic to take his mind off of his family.

"That's a beautiful tradition," she said awkwardly. He nodded. His posture stiffened, and he was silent. River hugged him tighter, trying to comfort him. Gradually, he relaxed. As they rode along in the starlit night, River let her forehead rest between his shoulder blades. The air was growing chilly with the approach of winter and the speedy pace of their travel, but the warmth of his body gradually seeped through his clothes and spread into her. She let her mind wander and found herself daydreaming, a little guiltily, about what it would be like to be married to Col. She would never admit it to him, but the idea had become more appealing to her than any other future she could think of.

54

The woman, Jehane, lifted her eyes to meet the Hearer's. She sat in the same cell that had once held her son, the heretic. Her body was frail, her face lined, and yet she seemed to have an inner strength far surpassing that of any prisoner he had ever seen. Her son lay sleeping, with his head in her lap. The resemblance between the golden-headed child and the Wolf was remarkable. The Hearer immediately hated the boy.

"Will we die today?" she asked coolly. The Hearer smiled cruelly, trying to regain his sense of control.

"Not yet. Your blasphemous son has two weeks to offer himself up in exchange. If he does not come, then you die."

He scanned her face through the bars of her cell, and was rewarded by a brief expression of fear in her eyes. He felt some satisfaction at last. Like all good mothers, she cared more for the safety of her son than for herself. If he wanted to torture her, he had found his leverage. He began speaking of all the ways he could kill her son, hoping to terrify her. However, Jehane was a peasant of the land. She already knew everything the Order was capable of. She didn't give any response or further signs of terror, just leaned her head back against the wall and closed her eyes tight. After a while, he grew bored and strode away.

When he was gone, Jehane sighed. She looked up at the ceiling, a rueful smile on her lips.

"To think, Col. You were so worried about *me* being branded a heretic."

She gently stroked Terren's silky hair. He stirred.

"Mom?" he asked in a tremulous voice, "Col's going to come save us, won't he?"

Jehane looked down at him, and her eyes filled with tears.

"Don't hope for that, love. He *can't* come. We must pray that he does not."

The boy looked so confused. Col had always been his hero. "What?"

His mother lowered her voice.

"Col can't save us, because this is a trap set for him. If he comes here, they will kill him. This time, Terren, we must save Col. We must escape on our own."

The first thing Col noticed when he entered the cave was the overwhelming number of men packed into it. Where had they all come from? So many of the faces were unfamiliar to him, as they greeted him with almost reverential respect, and stared at his scars with wonder. The second thing he noticed was his brothers. The crowd made way for them as they approached. They had both changed over the months of living in the wild. They had both killed their share of men, and Tonis had even taken over as leader of the cavern Col was entering.

"I've sent word to Lucan and his group that you've returned," Tonis informed him promptly. His tone was flat.

"We're all very impressed by what you've achieved. We've begun training with these Arthians as soon as they arrived, and already our casualty rates have dropped significantly."

"I'm impressed with what you've done in my absence!" Col replied in an encouraging tone. It was a tricky situation, having his older brother as his subordinate, but Tonis had not yet shown any resentment. He looked around, noting that all of the men were well-armed.

"Hamon is living up to her end of the deal?"

Tonis opened his mouth to reply, but Hankin suddenly cut him off.

"What are we going to do about Mother and Terren?" he

demanded. "A week has already passed trying to find you! We've less than three weeks before their execution!"

His distress showed plainly on his face. Tonis had maintained better control over his emotions for the sake of his men, but Col now saw that the same question was burning within him. Col took a deep breath.

"I can't make the trade, nor do I have the ability to rescue her," he said heavily. "You should know that."

Before Hankin could voice the outrage that was on his face, Col held up a hand.

"It's not because I value my life over hers. If it was merely a question of that trade, I would give myself up without a second thought. However, to sacrifice both myself and River would be to sacrifice our cause, to give up all hope of victory and, worst of all, to doom all of the men who follow me to death or worse at the hands of the Order."

Tonis didn't look angry, only weary. He seemed to have already guessed at such an outcome. Hankin, however, still looked outraged.

"You're choosing a bunch of random men over your own family?" he demanded indignantly. "How could you? What happened to your loyalty?" His eyes narrowed. "It's *her* isn't it? You care more about the life of that strange girl than the life of your mother!"

Col's immediate instinct was to protest, to proclaim his devotion to his family. However, there was a new confidence inside of him, an inner grit that refused to second-guess his decisions or tolerate insubordination. He was a leader, so he had to act like it. He couldn't treat his brothers differently than any other soldiers. In his mind, River's words echoed. "*It's lonely, being powerful.*" He took a deep breath.

"I care more about my country than about any one woman," he said firmly. Hankin's eyes grew wide with betrayal. Col ignored him, instead turning back to Tonis.

"However, I will try what I can. Send a message to Grimald and our other allies within the city. We know they have peppered the Priest-guard ranks with their spies. Perhaps they can achieve what we cannot.”

His brothers looked at him with new respect, but there was also a new distance between them. Col had changed. He was no longer the boy they knew, and he knew their relationship would never be the same. He raised his voice, addressing the leaders who had gathered around him.

“We can’t afford to wait any longer. We either strike now, with all our force, or wait for the Order to find us out, like they did with my family. Send out messengers. It’s time to bring the Order down.”

55

The guard stopped outside. Jehane knew he would. She had seen the way he looked at her, leering, every time he walked through. Being the mother of the Wolf, she was by far the most interesting prisoner in the Order's dungeons. Although every part of her yearned to give him a scowl, bare her teeth, try to frighten him away, her practical side knew that she couldn't get out of the cell on her own. So she had acted pathetic, sad, and doe-eyed. Every day, his marching had grown slower when he passed her cell, his interest increasing as his caution decreased. Finally, he stopped, leaning one arm on the bars of the cell as he leered at her. Jehane pretended not to notice.

"They say the Wolf has a face like one of the gods, that anyone who looks at him loves him," the guard mused. "You're past your prime, but I can still see where he gets his looks."

Jehane looked up at him, her eyes big and scared. His grin turned more predatory and his eyes roved over her body.

"I wonder if the rest of your body looks as good as your face?"

Jehane made herself look as fearful as she could. It was difficult, as she was not afraid at all. She trusted her god to protect her and, if he did not, she trusted him to give her strength to endure whatever happened. However, she had seen this sort of man before, and she knew that her fear would intoxicate him, making him desire her even more.

"Please!" she begged, "Leave me alone!"

She saw the resolve harden in the man's eyes. He unlocked the door to her cell and closed it behind him, an evil light in his eyes. As he came toward her, Terren grabbed him from behind. He was a small boy, and had been making himself look even smaller as he pretended to sleep in the dark corner by the door. However, his skinny arms were made of wiry muscle, and he clung to the man's back, squeezing his neck with furious strength. As the guard struggled against her son, Jehane grabbed the sword from his belt and stabbed him through the stomach. She had only planned to knock him out, but seeing him struggling with her youngest son, his big muscles and violent movements had caused her to panic, desperate to protect her baby. His eyes grew wide as the sword went in, and Terren, as he had been instructed, clapped his hands over the man's mouth to stifle the cry. The man fell forward onto his knees, gasping. Jehane didn't let herself hesitate. She swiftly cut his throat. It was merciful, she knew, to give him a swift death, where the gut wound would have been slow and painful. However, tears ran down her face as she did it. *My god, forgive me. I have taken a life. He was an evil man, but to kill him is a still greater evil.* She stood over the body, blood covering her hands and the blade of the sword. Terren was shaking, his face white. Jehane pulled herself together. She took his chin, forcing him to look into her eyes instead of at the body. She gave him a fierce expression.

"Come, my darling. Be brave. We must run now. We must save Col."

They moved through the dungeon, slipping into the shadows of empty cells every time someone walked past. Tragically, there were not many cells that were empty in these days of turmoil. Jehane had no idea when the dead guard's shift would end, or when someone would discover him, but she knew they had to be far away before that happened. She held Terren close with one arm and clutched the stolen sword with the other, sure that it would prove little use against the strength and training of a priest-guard, should they encounter one. *God, please hide us from unfriendly eyes. Keep us safe.*

Her prayers seemed answered. Although there were Priest-guards everywhere, no one caught sight of them as they slipped out of the dungeons and through temple passageways, searching for a way out. They ascended a flight of stairs and ducked around a corner as people walked past. Through a window, Jehane could see a starlit sky. As soon as the hall was empty, she pulled Terren through it and out the window. It was only a short drop from there into a courtyard. Instead of jumping, however, Jehane edged out along a narrow parapet to the side. Wooden spikes stabbed outward from the wall at even intervals, and they carefully avoided these. Suddenly, a commotion started. At first distant, and then growing louder, voices were shouting. The slap of Priest-guard sandals echoed on the stone floors of the hall behind them. They crouched on the parapet behind a row of spikes, trying not to be spotted. Terren looked up at her, his eyes big and scared.

"What if they catch us?" he whispered. Jehane squeezed his hand, trying not to show her own fear.

"Then we will pray that Col does not come, and we die with bravery. Either way, we escape the Order."

Terren let out a little whimper. Jehane clapped her hand over his mouth.

"Don't cry. Remember what I told you about dying?"

The lad sniffled, then nodded.

"It will hurt for a little while, but then we get to see Daddy."

"Yes. Don't you want to meet your father? He will love you so much. And when we go there, to where my god is keeping him safe for us, oh! How wonderful it will be!" She kissed his forehead gently. "We'll never hurt again."

He brightened. He had never met his father, but had heard enough stories from his older brothers to be very excited about the prospect. He nodded firmly.

"Okay. I'm not afraid anymore."

She squeezed his hand, proud tears in her eyes, even as her own heart beat with fear for him.

"Let's go."

What followed was a frantic flight. They hurried along the parapet, jumped down into a second, quieter courtyard, then rushed across it to a door at the end. The door was locked. Jehane tugged at it frantically. Suddenly, she heard running feet behind her. A whole troop of Priest-Guards! She threw herself in front of her boy, facing them with defiance. At the head of the group were two striking individuals. One was a massive mountain of a man with a gruff face and a sneering mouth. The other was a young woman with dark hair and violent eyes. The man grabbed Jehane, wrenching her away from her son. She screamed and fought as the beautiful young woman grabbed Terren up, holding a blade to his neck when he kicked.

"We've got these two," the big man barked. "They were pathetically easy to catch. The rest of you, go reinforce the wall guard. We're expecting the Wolf to attempt a rescue any time now."

The Priest-guards reluctantly marched off. Jehane was shocked when the man holding her suddenly let her go. She turned to stare up at him. He wasn't sneering. He was smiling. It only looked like a sneer because of the scar twisting his lip. He pulled out a key ring and unlocked the door.

"Quickly now, before they notice we're not going to the prison," he hissed. Jehane just stared at the two of them. The woman no longer held a knife to Terren's neck.

"How... What?" Jehane asked. The woman exchanged a look with the man.

"We know your son," she said simply. No one needed to clarify which son. Jehane nodded her understanding, and hustled through the doorway.

"Stop!" The shout came only after they had passed through the last gate and were in the city. Immediately, they started running. The young woman quickly outdistanced Jehane and the big man, her long legs flying over the ground as she practically dragged little Terren. It was a straight street, with no side alleys to duck out of the way. Terror leant Jehane new strength as she heard running feet growing nearer and nearer behind her. She dropped the stolen sword, as it was only weighing her down. Around her, there began to be a sharp clattering sound, echoing off the walls of buildings. At first, Jehane didn't understand what was happening. Then pain lanced through her calf and she stumbled. At the same time, the big man let out a grunt, then a yell. He stumbled into a wall, grabbing at the stones to hold himself up. Jehane tried to take a few more steps, but her calf muscle clenched up, screaming with pain. A long arrow shaft protruded from her leg, its weight pulling at her awkwardly. Warm blood leaked into her shoe. Soldiers surrounded them, but hung back uncertainly when they saw the big man's face. Some even ran forward to help him up. There was a terrifying moment of silence, as more and more Priest-guards rushed to the scene. Jehane looked around, but saw no sign of Terren. The young woman had not stopped or slowed down when her companion fell, but had dragged Jehane's boy away into the night.

"Well, what an unpleasant surprise!" a deep, strong voice echoed through the street. Jehane managed to limp around until she could see the speaker. What she saw confirmed her fear. The Hearer stood in the street, shining brighter than everything else in his golden robes.

"Grimald, how could you?" the man said, his voice laced with real hurt. Jehane couldn't believe her ears. She had thought the man an unfeeling monster.

"What did the Wolf promise you that I haven't already given you?"

Grimald's head hung in a weary pose, darkness hiding his face. He had an arrow sticking from his back. Another had struck his shoulder, but fallen out again leaving a dark, seeping wound. However, a soft chuckle began to vibrate in his massive chest. It wasn't a happy chuckle at all, but a menacing one. Slowly, he looked up, and his eyes were filled with unveiled loathing when he looked at the Hearer.

"You have never possessed anything I wanted, fool," he sneered.

"Your power is corrupt, your religion hollow, and your empire crumbling. The only thing of value you could give me is the satisfaction of watching you die!"

With these words, he suddenly sprang at the Hearer, drawing his swords with a flash. The Priest-guards stood back, either from shock or conflicting loyalties, Jehane couldn't tell. What followed was a duel so ferocious that Jehane, looking on, could barely keep track of which of the four swords were being wielded by each man. Grimald was roaring, a terrifying sound as his face flushed red with fury. The Hearer was big, but Grimald was bigger. He threw all of his superior weight and rage into the fight, attacking with little regard for his own safety. The Hearer began to retreat, raw betrayal on his face. Jehane's hopes rose. Would the Hearer, at last, be defeated? What man could defend against such violent hatred?

However, Grimald's fury was short-lived. The more he swung his blade, the more the arrow in his shoulder shifted, digging deeper into him as blood poured from the wound. The sword strokes of his left arm began to be weaker, with an awkward hitch to them. It ended as suddenly as it had begun. One moment, the two men were locked in furious combat. Then, Grimald failed to deflect one sword stroke that the Hearer aimed towards his weak side. The sword sank deep into Grimald's neck, and the big man fell lifeless, his head almost completely severed by the Hearer's vicious blow. The sudden end was even more shocking than the violence of the fight itself. After a moment, some of the Priest-guards gave a half-hearted cheer, while others looked horrified.

The Hearer stood in the street, panting, his golden robes marred by a dark splash of blood. He kicked the twitching body, and let out a roar of rage.

"NO! Why?" he shouted. "I wanted to make you hurt! I wanted SATISFACTION! Must you take even the pleasure of your torture from me?"

The man was unhinged. Priest-guards drew away from him in

fear as he paced about. Jehane felt a chill as his face turned toward her.

" *Your* death will be slow," he snarled, "as will your son's." He strode forward and grabbed her roughly by the arm, dragging her back toward the temple. Jehane hadn't seen the blow, but the Hearer bled from a gash in his side.

Jehane closed her eyes.

"Thank you for saving Terren," she whispered. Somewhere in the dark night of the city, a little child started singing. The melody was serene, and a touch bittersweet. All Jehane's fear seeped away. The one thing that had terrified her was the thought of seeing her beloved little boy hurt. Now, he was safe. What more could the Hearer do to her? He could hurt her body, but her soul was at peace, knowing that those she loved were beyond his reach. She hoped desperately that Col would be smart enough to stay away.

56

Col winced as he pulled on a short-sleeved tunic. The scars across his back were healed, but still tender. Terren came into the room, carrying the small, triangular shield for Col to buckle onto his arm. The edge of the shield extended past his crippled hand and sharpened to a point, enabling him to use it to punch an enemy during close combat, suddenly rendering his useless arm useful again. It was Helena's invention. The woman was a genius when it came to weaponry. Col slid his twisted hand into the loop and pulled the straps tight. Terren helped Col with the difficult parts of dressing, such as the buttons on his leather vest. His eyes were big and dull. Col missed the way they had once glowed with excitement. Everyone said it was shock, and that it would wear off. Still, Col worried. He had been delighted to see Terren when a group of Rebels brought him into the camp late one night. However, seeing the boy's woeful eyes as he wandered about only made Col grieve for his mother all over again. He was sending Terren away that very night. It broke his heart, but a war camp was no place for one as young as Terren. In Helena's mountain fortress, he would be safe until it was all over.

"Thank you for all your help, kiddo!" Col hugged him. "I hope you're excited to go visit the mountains! Helena has promised to teach you how to fight!"

Terren's eyes brightened momentarily.

"Do I get my own sword?"

"When you're big enough to swing one," Col promised.

"I'm big enough!" the boy protested. Col smiled fondly.

"We'll let Helena decide."

As his littlest brother ran off to tell someone about his future sword, Col sighed. Thousands were gathering in the canyon outside, prepared to fight for him. Hundreds of thousands swore their lives to his service all over the country, readying in secret for war. Yet, Col had never felt more alone. He walked out into the bright winter sunlight. The air was cool. He stood on a little ledge, overlooking a wide swath of land. Deep canyon walls hid the place from any onlookers. Below Col, a horde of men and women filled the canyon from wall to wall, and as far in either direction as he could see. They were all armed, hastily trained, and wild with excitement. Freedom from the Order was within reach. They could almost taste it, and the hunger for it was driving them crazy. As Col emerged, they let out a cheer. It was not loud. They could not risk a yell or a shout. Instead, it was a low, *Huh, Huh, Huh,* of exhaled breath, accompanied by stomping on the hard earth. Multiplied by thousands of throats, the sound was vast and terrible, like the earth itself was rumbling.

Looking out at them, Col felt his heart filled only with grief. So many lives would be lost before they could achieve victory. Even if the Order was brought down, at least half of these eager soldiers would never enjoy days of peace. He felt the might of the Order overshadowing even this great army, and his heart was chilled. Nevertheless, he dug deep within himself and found the inner strength that had sustained him through all his years. Nikolo Wolf would never stop fighting for his people. Not while he still breathed and there were people to fight for.

Col spread out his arms, showing plainly the scars on the bare skin. A hush fell, so quiet Col could hear his own breathing.

"For thousands of years we have been enslaved by lies," Col sent his voice ringing, clear and cold, over the heads of the multitude. It echoed through the canyon.

"A succession of wicked men have oppressed this nation, each claiming to be the voice of the gods. They LIED." His voice filled with outrage. "For all our lives, we cowered under the thumb of nothing but a man, a pretender, a liar who hides behind his veil. They took our crops, our strength, and our freedom. They treated us as slaves. They took our *families.*" Here his voice cracked with pain. Wails and shouts of anger rose from the crowd.

"The Hearer hears nothing more than the rest of us. He never did. The sacred crystal is shattered, and we have seen for ourselves that the person trapped inside was no Messenger, no divine being too holy to look at. She's right here. Look at her." He gestured, and River stepped up beside him. She smiled at him, her dark eyes fierce and proud. She looked stunning in her battle gear, and for a moment he almost lost track of his speech, so tempted was he to stare at her like everyone else was doing. He shook himself out of his daze and turned back to the crowd.

"What right have they to rule us now? What power do they have, except the power we gave them by believing their lies?"

He drew his sword and raised it into the air. All of his soldiers mirrored the gesture.

"TODAY WE TAKE THAT POWER BACK!"

This time, they could not contain their noise. A fierce shout rose up, so loud that it sent the birds flapping out of their holes in the canyon walls. Col winced, praying that no spy of the Order lurked nearby in the wilderness. However, he also knew that the army needed to let off a little steam. It would be many hours still before they got to see any real combat.

As they walked back through the door leading onto the small ledge, River suddenly caught Col by the back of the neck and kissed him enthusiastically. The action left him flushed and staring at her, startled. They hadn't kissed since River rejected his proposal. She blushed, but didn't look repentant as she exclaimed,

"You were amazing!"

"Thank you," he blushed even harder, wondering why he could never keep up his calm guise when he was with her.

"Great speeches won't win this fight, though."

"No," River agreed, growing more serious, "but don't underestimate the power of morale. These soldiers will fight harder because of what you said."

But to what end? Col thought. He kept his gloomy thoughts to himself. This was a day for action, for valor, and for a last stand against the oppressive regime of the Order. It was too late now for doubts and second-guessing. Col had started the movement, but the tide of battle was rolling on now with or without him.

Several hours later, Col and a select group of fighters crouched in the piles of refuse beneath the very shadow of Kingsfall itself. High above, rope bridges swayed, but the canyon was too deep and dark for anyone looking down to perceive them. That was the hope, at least. An odd-looking boulder shifted, and Col was delighted to see, peering from the darkness of a passageway behind it, the face of a very old friend.

"You're a bit late," Rig observed, pretending to look stern. But then his face split into a huge grin. With a cheerful greeting, Col leapt at the taller young man and wrapped an arm around his neck. When he went to dig his knuckles into the crown of Rig's head, however, Rig grew more serious.

"That's not exactly an appropriate way to treat the new leader of the Rebels," he warned. Col let him go and stared at him, incredulous. There was a new look about Rig that Col had never seen before, a grim, calculating keenness about his face. Col wasn't sure he liked what he read in that new expression. Rig looked at the rest of Col's group, especially at River, with wariness.

"Really? What about The Grim?"

Rig's expression was guarded.

"You didn't hear? He was caught trying to flee with your mother. He fought the Hearer, and lost."

"Oh," Col wondered why Rig didn't seem more distressed, "I'm so sorry."

"His death won't be in vain," Rig vowed grimly. "Every man, woman, and child in the Rebellion is raring to get revenge. We'll prove your fiercest allies today."

"I'm counting on it," Col approved. As they entered the tunnel,

Col caught Rig looking at him with a strange expression.

"What is it?"

"Oh.. nothing. You've just changed a lot. And I'm not just talking about the fact that you look like you survived being chewed up by a Canyon Scourge. You've only been gone about a year, but you seem decades older."

"You've changed a lot yourself," Col remarked. Internally, though, he wondered. Had he really changed as much as Rig had? *Yes. He* thought. *The last remnant of the boy I was died when I condemned my own mother to her fate.* He was the Wolf now.

The whole group went silently through the dark tunnel in the stone, climbing ever upwards toward Kingsfall. The Hearer was expecting Col to attack at night, to attempt a rescue of his mother. The deadline was only three days away. However, Col would be attacking in broad daylight. Even now, the bulk of his forces would be marching on Kingsfall. The Rebels would start a riot in the streets, distracting the Order's troops for long enough to get across the bridges into the center of the city. The main danger lay in the risk that the Order would cut the bridges before the army could get in.

"Divisions of priests from the Sky Keep and even the Temple of Avowal have been brought into the city as reinforcements," Rig informed him. "My rebels will not last long if your troops don't come to the rescue."

Col assured him that they would. Even as they hurried up the winding tunnel, side passageways started opening up. Some swift-footed youths ran up to Rig with reports from different parts of the city. The news was grim, and they hurried their footsteps. Col raised an eyebrow at Rig.

"These tunnels are new?"

"We've been busy," Rig explained with a prideful smirk. "While the Order oppressed and punished our people for *your* acts of rebellion, we started building tunnels all throughout Kingsfall. We have secret escape routes from almost every area of the city."

"Impressive." Col's tone was admiring.

"It's structurally unsound," River remarked absently, from where she trotted along barefoot. She strode confidently unlike the others, who were all walking carefully, peering at the uneven floor of the tunnel in the flickering torchlight.

"Several tunnels are collapsed, and others were dug carelessly without accounting for the weight of the heavy buildings sitting above," she continued. Rig gave her a sharp look.

"Why did you bring *her*?" he asked in irritation. "If your freaky witch can't keep her nose out of Rebel business, she's not welcome in our tunnels."

"Well, I feel safer with her around," Col countered. "For one thing, she won't let any tunnels collapse on us."

Rig walked on in silence. A few turns later, they met a girl running down to meet them.

"The Wolf's forces have entered Kingsfall," she reported breathlessly. "There is fierce battle on every street of the lower levels."

Everyone in the group let out a relieved breath. Some even cheered. The bridges had been crossed. While there were still some sections of Kingsfall that could be cut off by destroying the bridges, the roads to the Temple and the King's palace were wide, crossing chasms with massive stone arches that would be nearly impossible to destroy in such a short time. However, their relief was short-lived. Another messenger arrived on the heels of the first.

"We can't advance," he panted. "The King has mustered his entire army, and they stand between our forces and the temple."

Col felt the blood draining from his face. He had been so certain that the king would not attack, but would hole up behind the walls of his mighty fortress. River had assured him that Drystan had no love for the

Hearer. Why, then, would he come to the Order's defense? What had changed? And how could they possibly fight two different armies at once?

River turned to Col.

"Send me," she begged, "I'll take care of the king."

"You're so eager to fight your former fiance?" Col asked incredulously.

"I'll stop him," River insisted. Col sighed, then nodded. As she hurried off into a side passage, following Rig's messenger, Col felt a cold fear seize his heart. What if she should die? What if he did? What if that was the last time they would ever see each other? *I am a leader of men*. He reminded himself. *Loneliness is my lot. I fight for a happy ending for others, not myself.* Grim, he pressed on.

"How close do your tunnels get to the Temple?" he asked Rig. His old friend grinned.

"Is *inside* close enough for you?"

57

Jehane was jerked roughly out into the bright sun of a courtyard. The massive golden doors of the Temple of the Hand loomed in front of her, the staggeringly large central tower casting a dark shadow over the entire courtyard. The main gates leading out into the city taunted her with the closeness of freedom. But the place was packed, end to end, with Priest-guards. On the dais, a little to the right of the temple doors, a wooden platform stood, with a contraption rather like an empty doorway built on top of it. *It's time.* She realized with surprise. *They are finally going to kill me.* Although she had been hoping and praying that Col would not come, she still felt a surge of fear and dismay. It was sooner than she had expected to die. Was she brave enough to endure whatever slow death the Hearer had planned for her?

She was dragged through the crowd, up the steps to the dais, then up a crude little ladder to the platform, and forced to stand in the empty frame. They lashed her arms tightly to each side of the door, then tied her legs down to the base of the frame. She had never in her life felt so helpless as she stood immobile, watching the executioner climb the steps toward her, a vicious axe swinging at his side. He unfurled a parchment.

"Hear the words of the Hearer, you accursed mother of a demon." Jehane was surprised the Hearer himself hadn't come to see her die. The man began reading, and in his voice Jehane heard all of the Hearer's hatred.

"Your son has forced my hand," the terrible man said. "You will die today. However, the manner of your death depends entirely on the next few choices he makes. The Wolf could save you, or he could watch you die. I wonder, will he still be so cold-hearted when I start to dismember you?"

Jehane felt cold horror fill her.

River hurried through crowded streets, ducking around hysterical citizens and armed rebels. These streets had already been conquered, but it chilled her to see how many regular villagers lay dead for every fallen Priest-guard. She stepped over bodies, broken doors and window glass, but no discarded weapons. Every weapon had been looted from dead bodies, as the residents of Kingsfall armed themselves and joined the fight.

The tunnel had let her out not far from the main road, and she quickly caught up with the bulk of Col's forces. They were standing in the middle of the road. No sounds of fighting could be heard. Confused, River pushed her way to the front of the crowd. There was a chasm in front of them. A wide stone bridge crossed it. However, on the other side of the bridge, an army stood. Rank upon rank of silent soldiers in dark grey. The sunlight lit up their shining helmets, their cutlasses, spears, and polearms. In the middle of the bridge, looking, for the first time, as if he actually had a spine, stood King Drystan. He was dressed majestically, in armor that was far less flashy and gilded than the Hearer's, and yet more noble. His helmet was under his arm, revealing rather mussed up hair. He looked as handsome as ever, but even more tired and stressed than the last time she had seen him. Although he maintained a stiff and confident posture, his eyes flicked nervously to and fro. River took a deep breath, wishing she had Col's ability to feign emotions convincingly.

"Drystan!" she cried out in a tremulous, breathy voice, running out onto the bridge. His face froze in surprise at the sight of her. As she had hoped, he was too stunned to react. Before either of the opposing armies knew what to do, she had flung herself into his arms. He closed his arms around her instinctively as she pressed herself up against him.

"Oh, Drystan, I've come back to you!" River cried dramatically. It was too forced. She knew the instant the words left her mouth that they sounded false. Drystan started to pull away from her, looking confused. However, before he could do so, she thrust a hand into his curly, sweat-dampened hair, pulled his head down, and kissed him passionately. She had to go up onto her tiptoes to do it, as he was so much taller than Col. The action felt all wrong and strange to her, but she didn't let herself think about it just yet. She pulled away, and gazed into his eyes. He was quite overwhelmed, eyes bright as his lips curled unbidden into a smile. He pulled her closer. She kept one hand curled against his chest, and slipped the other one up under his cloak, against his back.

"Call off your men, please, my dearest fiance!" she begged him in a breathless, feminine voice. He frowned.

"But the Wolf is invading *my* city!" he began to protest. Then, slowly, she saw his expression change as he became aware of the very sharp edge of a dagger pricking into his back, right in the open spot under his armpit where his armor plates connected. She slowly dug the point a little deeper, and saw the fear creep into his eyes.

"Call off your men," she repeated. "Have them turn and join in the attack against the Temple, and I promise you won't be harmed in any way."

He grew very pale. However, his voice was strong when he turned, somewhat awkwardly, to face his men. He kept his arm around her, and River seemed only to be reciprocating. With his thick cape, no one could guess at the weapon she was stabbing into his back.

"Stand down," he commanded his men. "I will not fight against the will of my own people. We will join forces, and together destroy the Order."

His voice sounded a bit forced and mechanical, his eyes shifting nervously. However, he was always nervous, so the change was not too noticeable. His men complied, captains barking orders as troops split away, marching instead toward the Temple. River gave the sweating, terrified king a kiss on the cheek.

"Good boy," she smiled at him wickedly. He returned her gaze with horror.

"What *are* you? What have you done to my country?"

"It's not your country anymore," she told him smugly, "not that it ever really was."

So, without a fight, or even a struggle, the puppet king of the world watched his reign fall apart. His face was pale, his eyes wide as he watched the hordes of angry villagers swarm past him. He sweated, and muttered under his breath. River found it uncomfortable to be so close to him. They remained standing there until Col's forces had swarmed around them, and she had found some big, strong men to hold the king captive for her. Then she ran off, hastily wiping her lips with distaste. If she had ever had any doubts, that one kiss had filled her with certainty. The only man she loved, the only man she could ever dream of marrying, was the same peasant boy she had rejected. She ran faster. She had to reach Col, to fight or fall by his side. Nothing else mattered anymore.

Col and his band hurried along the tunnel. Soon they would be going under the walls themselves, emerging into the cellars of the kitchens, which would connect them to the courtyard where the main gates were. Col already thought he smelled onions and spices. Suddenly, the man in front of Col stopped. The tunnel ended abruptly in a wall of dirt, with no way forward.

"I don't understand..." the man muttered. He was one of Rig's rebels, brought along as a guide.

"This used to be open-" He stepped closer to the wall. Too late, Col saw something glimmering along the ground near the wall. It was long and thin. Before Col could say anything, the man had stepped past, snapping it against his boot. Suddenly, the ceiling fell in. Rig's guide disappeared in a shower of rocks before Col could get to him. He jumped back, a wave of panic sweeping through him. Suddenly, time seemed to slow. Col threw out his hand in a useless gesture against the massive rocks falling down toward him. As his hand moved, a hurricane of light strands blasted outwards away from him, wrapping around the rocks like a shining web. They slowed. Not by much, but just enough that he was able to scramble out of the way with the rest of his band.

"Get back!" he shouted. As soon as the rocks had settled, Col saw something else descending. It was a group of Priest-guards. They had been ready for this. They landed in the rubble, swords drawn. However, they didn't seem able to see well in the gloom, blinking as they looked around to see if anyone had survived the rock fall. Col didn't wait for their eyes to adjust. Snatching a handful of dirt off the floor, he threw it in the face of the nearest priest, then charged in and attacked. The man was dead before he had blinked the dirt out of his eyes. Seizing on their leader's tactics, the rest of Col's men charged in, using dirt to blind the priests. Some even threw rocks. There was a horrible scuffle. The dark passage filled with dust, shouts, and the clash of steel. Within a few moments, all the priest guards lay dead. Even with the element of surprise, though, Col's band had lost five men. He looked around at the others, feeling his heart sink. He had no guide, no way into the temple, and too few men. How would he ever accomplish his task? Around him, he saw faces echoing his despair. He pulled himself together.

"Everyone is counting on us," he reminded them grimly. "Let's move."

Col popped up from a secret trap door in the cellar of someone's house. After so long in the wilderness, hiding in caves, it was eerie to walk through the decadent furnishings of a house that doubtless belonged to some high-ranking official. No one was home. Col wondered if the home owners knew of the tunnels beneath their house. They left through a back

door into a lovely garden. It was strangely peaceful. The noise of battle
was still far away, and the rioting in the streets had moved to other areas.
Pathways wound among elaborately stacked rocks, with large cacti and
desert plants blooming cheerfully on all sides. There was even a little
pond. The waste of such precious water was staggering.

They climbed over a high wall and found themselves within sight
of one of the temple gates. Everything seemed quiet, but there was a
telltale flurry of furtive motion on the walls. Every now and then, the
bright sunlight caught and glinted off the sharp metal edge of a spear.

"They're holed up in there, waiting for us to attack," one of the
men muttered grimly. "I don't like this situation at all."

Col was silent for a moment, thinking.

"We'll have to wait," he decided. "Get out of sight. Once the rest
of the troops attack, we'll look for an opportunity to sneak in while
they're distracted."
He didn't have to voice the urgency that they find an opportunity to get
inside the temple. The Order was a militaristic religion, and their temple
was a fortress. If they didn't find an opportunity to open the gates from
the inside, they could waste days in a siege. By that time, reinforcements
from other temples would arrive. In comparison to the massive might of
the Order, the rebellion was pitiful. They either had to win quickly or not
at all. Ideally, they would find the Hearer himself and kill him, thus
beheading the entire religion. Col knew that The Grim, a very mighty
warrior, had died fighting the Hearer. He knew that he had very little hope
of succeeding. However, he couldn't quench the fire that raged within
him as he neared the Temple, a deep yearning for revenge on the Hearer.
He hadn't been able to save his mother, but he was determined to avenge
her.

The sound of battle drew closer. Before long, Col saw Priest-
guards rushing about, most of them running to reinforce the north side of
the Temple, as Col's forces approached. Clad in Priest-guard cloaks that

they had borrowed from the dead, Col and his little band hurried out toward the wall. Suddenly, a sharp noise rang out, echoing through the whole temple. Col instinctively ducked to the side behind a tall statue that stood in the center of the wide paved road. It was a massive depiction of the first Hearer, with a long, flowing cape, mounted on a horse. Luckily, that very cape obscured the entire group from any watching eyes on the temple walls. The sound blared out again. This time, Col recognized it. It was the trumpet call that always preceded the Hearer's speeches. Col's eyes raised to look at the high balcony jutting from the Temple's largest tower. He knew that all the other residents of Kingsfall would instinctively be doing likewise. There stood the Hearer, resplendent in his brilliant golden robes. The sun set his robes on fire with reflected light, making him look like a god coming down to earth. He spoke, and the carefully positioned metal cones fixed to the railing around him caught his voice and sent it booming out over the city.

"I have a message for the Wolf," he cried, "this self-styled leader, this heretic who defies the will of the gods!" He leaned out against the railing, and Col felt an irrational fear that the Hearer could see him, even through the statue.

"For every foot your soldiers advance into my temple, Wolf, I will carve something off of your mother." The Hearer's voice was so full of hate and fury that he sounded deranged. "Let's see how brave and heroic you feel, when you hear your mothers screams as I cut off each of her fingers."

Col stood frozen. He couldn't think, couldn't move. Men ran up, giving reports, demanding to know what to do. With their leader indecisive, the rebel forces were stalled at the Temple gates, defending themselves from arrows but making no moves to push forward into the temple. Col knew something had to be done. However, he couldn't do anything except stand there. It was too much to bear. Too much weight on his shoulders. What man could ever make such a choice, to condemn his own mother to one of the most painful and gruesome deaths imaginable? He knew, without a doubt, that his mother was currently being held somewhere high up on a platform, so that he would be forced to watch every moment of her painful death. He couldn't do it. Dimly, he was aware of voices clamoring. River's hand fell on his shoulder, and she seemed to be demanding something urgently. Col paid no attention. His forces had the upper hand, but Nikolo Wolf was defeated.

River crouched at Col's side, feeling a panic course through her. The invasion was falling apart. What were they going to do? With Col catatonic, the soldiers were losing all enthusiasm for the fight.

There was the sound of more running feet behind her. River spun, to see Rig hurry up with a troop of soldiers. By now, the secrecy of Col's plan had doubtless been spoiled. River supposed that it didn't matter anymore, considering Col's state.

"What are we supposed to do now?" Rig cried in frustration. He seemed to have temporarily forgotten his dislike of River, as he looked at her helplessly. River realized with shock that the two main leaders of this revolution were little more than boys. She herself wasn't much older, but a lifetime of power and pride had hardened her beyond her years. She took a deep breath.

"Leave it to me," she said softly. Her voice was hard and cold. "Be ready to march into the temple as soon as the way is cleared.

Even Rig's cynical face betrayed a twinge of horror as he comprehended what she intended to do. However, he didn't protest. He just gave her a grim nod.

58

River looked up at the big wooden gates of the Temple, and her heart quailed within her. Not because of the soldiers crowding the top of the wall. Not even because of the arrows arcing down at the invading horde with deadly swiftness. No. She was afraid because of what she was about to do. *It's for Col.* She reminded herself. *I must do what he cannot. I must spare him this pain, by suffering it myself. I'm already a monster. My heart is already a cold stone. How much worse could I get?*

She gave the signal. Immediately, a small platoon of men rushed forward. They had shields held over their heads to protect from arrows, and they hustled River up to the gates in their midst. She winced at the sounds of pain some of them made as they ran. Two fell behind, struck by arrows. The rest of the group reached the shelter of the portico and relaxed their guard. Unless the enemy opened the gate now, they could not attack them here.

"...now what?" one of River's guards muttered. She didn't listen. Pressing both of her hands to the wood of the gate, she poured into it all her frustration, all her anger, all of her rage at the Hearer and the Order. *LIVE!* She commanded the thick planks, with all the force of her will. Instantly, she felt them spring to life beneath her hands.

"Get back," she ordered. The guards sprang back. The gates were vibrating now with pent-up power. River planted her feet, and gave them a single command. There was a ripping, screaming sound, as hinges tore free and metal bars twisted. The two gates warped and bent, breaking completely free of their frame. They sprang open, suddenly sprouting leaves and branches. New roots sank deep into the ground, anchoring the gates in their new position.

River was facing an army. Inside of the temple wall, the courtyard was packed from one end to the other with Priest-guards. They were momentarily taken aback, but they were all well-armed and ready for battle, with swords, spears, and axes. Some even had bows slung across their backs. At the far end of the courtyard was a raised wooden platform, on which a woman stood with her back to River, tied hand and foot. River didn't wait for the rest of the army to charge into the open gates. Instead, she charged forward alone.

The moment she stepped onto the oddly white stones of the courtyard, a horrible pain seared through the soles of her feet. She felt her connection with the earth retreating. *Salt. They were expecting me.* The ground was covered with it. She didn't have time to panic or retreat, however. She was already inside, separated from her allies, with several Priest-guards advancing warily. They formed a protective wall of bodies between herself and the platform. The executioner was approaching Jehane. River knew she only had a few moments to reach the woman before he started his gruesome work. Her hand closed on the handle of the double-sided dagger, drawing it out from her belt. She felt the living wood in her hand, and willed it to lengthen. It shot out quickly, five feet of glistening new wood. Even before it finished growing, she was ramming it through the stomach of a Priest. Her feet hurt, but the adrenaline pumping through her helped her to ignore it for the moment. Never before had she been so hard-pressed in a fight. Not only was she outnumbered and surrounded, but these fighters were extremely skilled. She wasn't attacking anymore. She was just trying to stay alive.

Suddenly, a cold feeling swept through her. There was a *clang*, and a sword that she knew would have impaled her from behind suddenly flew over her shoulder, clattering against the ground. She turned. Who had rescued her? She was still surrounded by Priest-guards. However, some of the priest-guards had begun fighting each other! She had two mysterious allies, no, three! Four! Heart racing, she spun and pressed forward through the throng of enemies, no longer forced to watch her back.

She was too late. Over the heads of the priests, she could see the executioner raise the axe. There were still at least twenty men between River and the dais. Her heart sank. *Oh Col, I'm so sorry.* A desperate, wild thought occurred to her. Turning, she snatched a bow from one of the rebel Priest-guards. His eyes lit up with understanding and he whipped out an arrow from the sheaf at his side, throwing it to her. Her hand closed on the familiar shape. Her fingers remembered, the bowstring sliding against old callouses. The axe was rising as she pulled back the bow, with only a moment to aim. She squinted along the shaft of the arrow, trying not to think too hard about what she was attempting. *Oh god, please let this work!* She let it fly.

Jehane didn't scream when the man with the axe approached her. She'd been praying almost constantly to her god since the failed escape attempt, with no answer. As the man approached, she felt fear finally consume her. She'd tried so hard not to be afraid. She was tough, and fearless. She was not afraid of death. However, seeing that sickeningly sharp axe, she couldn't quell the primal terror that surged through her. She felt so alone, so helpless.

"I have always been faithful, why is this happening to me? Why don't you answer?" she cried out, and realized that she had said it aloud, when the executioner looked around, confused as to who she might be talking to. Jehane felt a rush of shame. Would she spend her last moments falling apart and becoming insane, instead of remaining strong? Then, the air around her seemed suddenly silent. Inexplicably, she thought she heard a child's voice, singing. Her skin tingled. In the midst of that stillness, she heard a voice, hushed, as though breathed into her ear from a few inches away.

"I am here."

She gasped, relief flooding through her. However, the executioner was still approaching. Nothing about her situation had changed, and the fear came creeping back.

"Please, I'm afraid. Will it hurt?" she whispered. When the voice responded, the whisper seemed to curl around her, wrapping her in an intangible embrace.

"I will take your pain."

The executioner's axe was descending towards her wrist. Jehane felt no fear, even as the sharp edge bit into her flesh. Instead, she felt a peaceful smile light up her face. At that same moment, something hit the back of her head. She stumbled forward, and someone caught her. The person was wearing a soft shirt, with a leather vest that felt warm against her cheek from leftover sunshine soaked into the leather. The arms around her were strong, and strangely familiar. She didn't feel the axe. She didn't feel the blisters on her hands and feet from the manacles. She didn't even feel the sore spots in her neck and shoulders that had been bothering her for years. At that realization, she felt confused. What had happened? Hadn't she been tied up? With a battle raging only a little ways away? So, why was everything suddenly so peaceful? The only thing she could hear now was the sound of running water, and wind in the branches of a tree. The air hummed with a beautiful melody. It was no longer sad, but jubilant. The arms around her tightened. A hand rubbed her back gently, in a way that was achingly familiar. No one had touched her like that since... She pulled away suddenly, staring up into a face she never thought she'd see again. Wind-tousled brown hair, full lips, a strong nose, and chiseled jaw. Little crinkles appeared at the corners of his beautiful, laughing green eyes as he smiled at her.

"I've missed you, my love," her husband said tenderly. "What took you so long?"

River saw the body of Col's mother slump, saw the executioner stop his work and slam his axe into the platform in frustration. It was a superb shot, almost impossible. A direct blow right where her spine connected to her head would have caused an instant and almost painless death, robbing the Hearer of his leverage over Col. However, she doubted Col would ever forgive her. She had failed to save his mother. In fact, she had killed his mother with her own hand. Who could forgive that?

In her moment of distraction, someone slammed into her. Something hard hit the side of her head. The pain crashed through her senses, overwhelming her. Darkness closed in.

59

"Your mother is dead. She died painlessly. I've ordered the troops into the city on your behalf." Dominik's voice pulled Col out of the cloud of numbness in which he floated. The news brought a flood of relief from the agony threatening to crush him. He looked around as if just waking up. He had been propped up in a sheltered doorway. Hundreds of King's soldiers, bandits, villagers, and townspeople ran past in the direction of the temple gates. Dominik stood in front of Col, to shield his troops from the sight of their leader in such a pathetic state. The sounds of fierce battle raged just out of sight.

Col felt an overwhelming sense of shame. How many lives had his hesitation cost? In the final moment, when his people and his land needed him most, he had failed utterly.

"Who killed her?" he asked, trying to rally his strength enough to get up. Dominik opened his mouth, then closed it. He gave Col a strange look.

"A rebel Priest-guard," he said, finally. He was lying. Col could tell. However, he didn't have time to dwell on it, as the next words out of Dominik's mouth shocked all other thoughts out of his head.

"The lady River destroyed the gates, but was captured. Several priests carried her away into the temple."

No! Col had thought himself numb, after his mother's death. He now discovered that this was not the case. Horror and fear exploded through him. He had already lost everyone else, he couldn't lose River! He loved her more desperately and whole-heartedly than he had ever loved anyone, and the fear of losing her filled him with a surge of adrenaline. He leapt up.

"I'm going after her!"

Ignoring Dominik's protests, he charged towards the temple. The gates hung open, twisted, warped, and sprouting branches. There were still some priests shooting from the walls, but most of them had retreated. Col tried not to notice the bodies on the ground. It was even worse inside the temple courtyard. Priest-guards and villagers alike lay dead or wounded everywhere. The ground was no longer white with salt, but was also splashed red in many places. Col pushed through the chaos, making straight for the Temple gates without waiting for Dominik to catch up.

There were far more enemies than allies in the fight on the dais. Col found that his shield arm and short sword proved excellent for blocking sword swipes. He felt determination burning through him as he fought, his muscles remembering the motions that he had spent so many months trying to teach them. His short sword dodged through his enemies' guard as though each priest-guard was moving in slow motion. Then they really *were* moving in slow motion. His entire right arm began to blaze with blue fire, his sword slashing sheets of light through the air. He wove a tunnel of light through the melee, deflecting blows and slowing down attackers just long enough to slip past them. Several priest-guards froze up and died on the edge of his sword, not because of the magic, but from sheer surprise and disorientation as the light blinded their eyes. Col had never before felt such focus, such fierce clarity as he fought.

Col slowed in surprise when he found himself on the very doorstep of the temple. The great doors were open, as the Priest-guards had not yet abandoned the outer courtyard. He had killed at least four Priest-guards on his way in, each of whom would normally have been far more skilled than him in a fight. It was a new record, and if he hadn't been so worried about River he would have felt pride at the accomplishment. Instead, he ran through the open archway into the oppressive darkness of the Temple without another thought. It took a moment for his eyes to adjust in the gloom. The bright sunlight pouring in the archway behind him only made the far recesses of the vast temple even darker by comparison.

A massive hall faced him, leading to a gigantic prayer hall, he knew, where the Hearer would have his golden chair. To his left, a small door led to one of the many little side passageways within the thick walls of the temple, which would have stairs going up to the rest of the tower, and stairs descending down into the dungeons. To his right, a small black door held unpleasant memories of the last time he had entered this temple. He hesitated, uncertain. He had to decide quickly. Out on the dais battle raged, and deeper within the gloom of the temple he could hear Priest-guards rallying. Soon, someone would notice him where he stood by the entrance, caught between bright sunlight and musty shadow. He looked back and forth, torn. A movement caught his eye. On the right side, suspended in sharp shafts of sunlight from the doorway, the dust motes swirled a little faster than those on the left. It wasn't much to go on, but he made his decision, yanking open the door and charging down the dark hall beyond.

He didn't wonder that the door wasn't locked. He didn't notice that there weren't any guards. He just ran.

River opened her eyes. For a moment, she didn't realize where she was. The place looked so different without the crowd of priests and the bowls of blood and incense. However, the shape of the room and the melted candles leaving rivers of wax down the walls jogged her memory. Only a few of these were lit, making the funnel-shaped chamber much darker than when she had seen it last. She was hanging suspended from a hook in the roof like a dead animal near the spot where she had once been imprisoned. Another hook was on the roof near the other side of the dais, but this held a hanging brasier of incense. The air was thick with incense, which didn't help the confused fog in her mind. The thick rope dug into her wrists, but it was made from some sort of leather, not plant matter that she might be able to awaken. She looked around for a way out, cursing the pounding headache that muddled her thoughts. The motion of her head sent her body rocking gently, which made her nauseous. What had happened? How did she get here? She couldn't remember.

As she struggled to think, a single, piercing memory surfaced. Her fingers on a bowstring, the muscles in her back straining with the draw... the distinct thrum of the bow vibrating through her... the hiss of the arrow... and the sight of a woman's head jerking, her body slumping forward. *Col's mother!* She remembered. She had to get out of here, had to tell Col, had to explain... A motion startled her out of her thoughts. A man was sitting on the wide steps below her. From his golden robes, River immediately recognized him. However, his veil and headdress lay discarded on the step beside him. River saw dark hair, flecked with grey. At the sight of him, River felt her heart seize up with terror. His words to her the last time they had met came flooding back into her mind. *You will never touch the earth again.* Hanging there bound, with no way to escape, her fear was suffocating. Any moment, the Hearer would turn, and she had no way to protect herself from the horrible, violent man. She had never felt so vulnerable. He was running his hands through his hair and making occasional nervous, twitching movements. As time passed, he seemed to grow more and more agitated. He started muttering to himself, his deep voice echoing in the room like the growl of some wild animal.

"He'll come, he'll come. He *must*," he grumbled. Suddenly, a side door opened. A man with a weaselly, cruel face stuck his head in.

"Your Divine Eminence, the rebel forces are overwhelming us. We need to retreat and rally at another temple," he said, his voice sounding terrified.

"GET OUT!" the Hearer roared. "You know nothing! My plan is almost complete!" His voice turned scornful. "We aren't *losing*. I am about to WIN! Can't you see I have the Messenger captured?"

The weaselly man spared a quick glance for River, then turned back to the Hearer, looking desperate.

"I see that, but we could take her with us. It isn't safe to be this close to her without more protection. Can't I at least send in guards to protect you while you wait?"

"NO! No guards! They can't be trusted! I can handle the Messenger on my own." The Hearer's voice sounded deranged. Then he turned to fix suspicious eyes on the man.

"In fact, I'm not even sure that *you* can be trusted! How do I know you're bringing true reports? This might be another ploy to get me out of the way!"

The other man blanched.

"But-" he protested, but didn't finish his thought. He ducked back through the doorway, slamming it closed behind him right as one of the Hearer's knives buried itself in the wood. River held still, hoping the Hearer wouldn't turn that reckless bloodthirst toward her. Fortunately, he didn't seem to have noticed that she was awake. Instead, he hunkered down and kept muttering. Footsteps startled both of them. Someone was running, no, *flying* down the corridor towards the room at a reckless pace. A light began to grow in the dark tunnel. Not firelight, or even sunlight. No, this was a brilliant, pure blue-white light. The Hearer began to grow excited. Suddenly, the runner turned a corner and burst into the room. The dancing shadows cast by the candle flames were blasted away by the sheer brilliance of him. It wasn't just his hand that was glowing. Thick strands of blinding light radiated out from his hand and curled all around him, flickering with furious speed all across his body. The air seemed to warp around him. He took in River, the Hearer, and the chamber all in one glance, then whipped out his sword.

"Let her go," he snarled. His voice was chilling. Never had River heard anyone pack three words full of so much anger. The Hearer, however, chuckled. He rose to his feet, his massive shoulders almost blocking River's view of Col. He drew his own two swords, each easily as long as Col's own sword, with curving, wickedly sharp blades.

"You'll have to fight me to get her," he taunted.

River's head was still foggy, but her long years of training in battle tactics sent warnings flashing through her mind. The Hearer was very fast for such a big man. Col was clumsy, inexperienced. The Hearer had greater height, strength, a longer reach, and two swords to Col's one. Even with Col's ability to slow down the air, there was no way he could win. She felt terror seep through her, and struggled wildly to escape. She had to help him! She couldn't watch him die!

The Hearer seemed to have realized the same thing, as did Col. He began moving cautiously into the chamber, watching the Hearer warily.

"You can't hope to win," the Hearer noted. "Give up, and I'll even let you live."

The statement was so strange that Col stopped short.

"You would? How could you possibly benefit from letting me go?"

"All I need is *that light*," the Hearer's voice dropped to a hungry purr. "You will give it to me, or I will take it from you by force. Then I'll put the Messenger back into her prison, and everything will be set right. You have a choice, see. Either give up willingly, or die. Either way, I get what I want."

"You can't do that!" Col protested.

"Ah, but I can!" the Hearer cried wildly, leaping to the side to put himself more firmly between River and Col.

"I have studied all the ancient runes and cursed books that the Order ever found! I have travelled to the Founding Lands, and walked the depths of the very caves where the Messenger was first discovered! I have the Messenger here in this room, and the magic that first trapped her! If anyone in the world can re-create the spell, it is me!"

"Not if I stop you!" Col cried. River saw him grit his teeth, raise his sword. She felt a stab of fear.

"No! You can't fight him!" she shouted, just as he lunged. The Hearer was prepared for him, and countered with a violent swipe that Col narrowly avoided. He danced backwards out of the Hearer's long reach, his eyes wide. River saw him size up the Hearer again, and realize the same thing she knew. Nikolo Wolf was many amazing things, but he wasn't a fighter. He looked up and met her eyes. River held her breath. Then, he moved. He slashed a wave of light through the air, blinding the Hearer. While the Hearer was distracted, Col was already ducking quickly past him. He wasn't trying to fight at all. Instead, his sword slashed through a rope tied to the wall. It whizzed through the loop in the ceiling, sending River dropping to the ground. She was still a little disoriented, so she didn't land gracefully. Col was already jerking her to her feet before she had a chance to fall flat, sawing through her bonds with his sword. Wildly slashing light in the Hearer's direction, he pulled her towards the door. Touching the ground helped cure her dizziness. She joined him as they dashed away, her heart pounding. They couldn't fight the Hearer, not here. However, they could certainly outrun him, dressed as he was in full armor. River respected Col even more for the way he was able to put his pride aside, using wise tactics even in the heat of the moment.

60

"I love you!" River gasped, as the Hearer's raging cries echoed close behind them in the tunnel.

"*uh*-ve you too!" he replied, stumbling over an uneven bit in the hard stone floor of the tunnel.

"Coward! Fight me!" the Hearer shouted from close behind them. Col and River did not slow until they were dashing out of the temple doors. Bright sunlight blinded them for a moment. There were no sounds of fighting anymore. River blinked, and took in a horrible sight. The courtyard was mostly empty. Here and there, groups of men were carefully carrying the wounded out of the temple gate. The stench of blood and sweat hung over everything, and the ground was slick with blood and gore. The carnage of the battle in the confined space of the courtyard far exceeded anything River had ever seen. She had seen men die in skirmishes in the wilds, but had never guessed how much blood would be spilled. Without dirt to soak into, the blood pooled on the hard paving stones and under the hot sun the stench was unbelievable. River fought the urge to puke, and saw Col turn green. Even those who survived were splashed with blood and grime, so that for a moment she had difficulty knowing which side had won. Then, in the shadow of the wall, she saw a line of about thirty kneeling men. They were tied hand and foot, with guards watching them closely. The guards were dressed in rough, peasant garb, and the men kneeling each had empty double scabbards on their backs. Everyone in the courtyard had stopped their work to stare up at them when they burst out of the Temple doors. Several people cheered. River let out a breath of relief.

"We've won, Col!" she whispered in awe. Col, however, did not look delighted. He was staring at the dead and wounded with a hollow expression.

"And yet I failed so many of them." he whispered. Just then, the

Hearer burst out onto the dais with a roar. River jumped back. Col spun and ducked, narrowly avoiding the Hearer's sword as it swung at his head.

The Hearer wore no veil. Col felt a horrible shock as he beheld the man's face in the full, bright sunlight. He was old, but not old in a normal way. His muscles and build were still that of a much younger man, but they had shrunk greatly since Col had last seen him in Wanderkeep. An old man's skin was stretched across the shrunken muscles. His face was beyond old, it was ancient. Wrinkled, spotted skin stretched unnaturally across a young man's jaw. His eyes were sunken, staring at Col like two black pits of hate and hunger.

"Give me the light!" he snarled. "It's mine! I need it! I'll KILL YOU for taking it from me!"

Col danced back from the crazed man.

"Get back!" he called over his shoulder to River, as he began weaving light around the Hearer to slow him down. She had jumped back a few paces, but stood hesitant on the edge of the dais. Her bare feet were red and blistered where they touched the salted ground. She looked pale, but her eyes were fiery with determination. Her weapons had been taken from her, and the pile of weapons taken from the captive Priest-guards was too far away in the courtyard for her to reach. She was looking around frantically. Finally, she reached up and ripped at the necklace around her neck, yanking off the pendant.

The Hearer's roars turned more bestial as he was continually foiled. Every time he tried to strike at Col, a sheet of blue light slowed him down just long enough for Col to dodge. The more light he pushed through, however, the more the wrinkles seemed to recede from his skin. He seemed to grow stronger, more full of energy, even as Col watched.

His attacks began to be faster. Col struggled to keep any of the deadly blows from landing. As he jumped around the man again, putting himself between the madman and River, he heard River's voice.

"Col, get back."

"Stop dodging, you little coward!" the Hearer cried, as he swiped at Col again. "You can never defeat me! I will always be the strongest!"

Col retreated even further.

"I don't have to defeat you." he said, with a wry smile. "I've already won."

Light was growing on the dais where River stood. She seemed even more pale and haggard, with sweat running down her face. Sunlight seemed to bend and warp around her. She looked sickly, drained of life, and the very air around her seemed sucked dry of moisture. However, in her hand she held the most beautiful thing Col had ever seen. It was like a small, bright star, glowing green and almost exploding with vibrant life. The sunlight was bending into River's hand, coalescing on the thing she held.

The Hearer hesitated at Col's words, glancing around as if only just realizing that the battle was over, that the men tied up in the courtyard were his own priests. River threw the seed at him. It arched through the air, a tiny, brilliant orb of light. Confused, he instinctively swiped at it. He missed. The tiny thing struck against his armor, then fell at his feet. The moment it touched the ground, all the light sucked into it, leaving it a tiny brown seed. The Hearer laughed.

"What was that supposed to-" he began to taunt. Then, the seed exploded.

Roots thrust out, pushing through the layer of salt, through the rock, and into the very temple foundations. Branches whipped out, growing so fast Col could barely take it in. Tiny shoots grew to the size of Col's arm, then his waist, in seconds. The Hearer cried out and tried to jump away, but his feet were already anchored to the floor by thick, writhing snake-like roots. Wood encased his legs, bark grew over his golden chestplate. He tried to hack at the tree with his swords, but they both stuck into the wood, twigs growing out and encasing them, turning them into long branches. The Hearer's arms were encased in thick branches. He began to scream and shout, but then the tree grew over his face. In just a few moments, the Hearer was no more. On the dais, still growing and towering over the massive Temple doors, with a trunk as thick as a tower, grew the most beautiful tree Col had ever seen. Soft blue leaves unfurled, coated with a silver fuzz. The trunk was white, with little streaks of gold glimmering through cracks in the bark, the last remnant of the man it had swallowed. In comparison with the fresh, vibrant life of the tree, even the golden hand on the temple doors seemed dull. Col and River retreated, as roots spread out over the dais, breaking apart marble steps.

"You," Col said, turning to River, "are the most incredible woman in the world."

She smiled faintly. Only then did he notice how weak she looked. Her skin was as white as paper, and dark circles framed her sunken eyes. Even her eyes seemed dull and lifeless, her black hair completely lacking its usual shine. She took a step towards him, swayed, then fell. Col caught her before she hit the ground, but found that she was already unconscious. Her breathing was shallow, and growing fainter even as he listened. *Oh god, no! I can't have won, only to lose her!* Scooping her up in his arms, he found new strength to start running with her towards the open temple gates. Several people were already running up alongside him, offering to help. He ignored them, holding her close. Bursting out into the city, he heard a shout behind him. Dominik was racing to catch up. He had been in the temple with a group of soldiers, defeating the remaining Priest-guards and trying to find Col.

"Thank El-yos, you're safe!" he exclaimed. "If you died, there would have been no end to the war. We need you to take charge! Here, give her to me. I'll see that she's taken care of." He reached to take River out of Col's arms. His voice was reassuring, but an expression of doubt flickered across his face when he looked closer at the girl in Col's arms. Col didn't relinquish his burden. He knew, just as Dominik did, that River was dying. She'd poured her whole life force into that seed, to stop the Hearer. He didn't know what to do, but he knew he didn't want to be parted from her. Then, suddenly, a desperate thought entered his head.

"Come!" he snapped, and started walking again. Dominik looked confused, but instinctively jumped to obey, gesturing for several nearby King's men to accompany him.

The garden was just as peaceful as he had remembered. Strange, when all the rest of the city seemed filled with the cries of the wounded. Col laid River down gently in the dirt, then stepped back.

"Bury her!" he commanded. A few men stepped forward, but most hung back.

"But Sir, she's still alive!" one protested, after bending close to River.

"I said, bury her!" Col snapped, feeling a bit frantic. "Hurry!"

Dominik stared at Col in disbelief.

"Why?" he demanded, "Is this because she killed your mother? She did what had to be done! And it was a merciful shot, practically painless!"

"*WHAT?*" Col shouted. Dominik blanched, realizing he had said too much. Internally, Col reeled. He couldn't even begin to process the news. The woman he loved had killed the other woman he loved, and now she herself was dying. He didn't know whether to feel angry, betrayed, or frantic with worry. He settled on action. Snatching out his sword, he began to hack at the dirt, scooping up handfuls once it was loosened. Seeing his desperation, Dominik finally decided to stop questioning. He sent men running off to find shovels, and the rest got to work with their swords.

When Col finally laid River in the hole, he feared he was making a horrible mistake. Burying her was so horrible he almost couldn't do it. When Dominik patted dirt down, covering her beautiful face, he turned away, unable to bear the pain in his heart. Instead he knelt, placing his palms on the ground like he'd seen her do so often... Of course, he felt nothing.

"You swallowed her up and gave her back to me once, when I begged you," he said softly. "Now I'm trusting you to do that again. I can't help her anymore. Maybe you can. I know you care for her."

Nothing happened for what felt like forever. Col sighed, feeling such turmoil inside of him. However, he became sure of one thing. He couldn't be angry with River for what she had done. He loved her too much, and understood too well the pain of choosing the best of bad options.

"I understand why you did it, River. If you live, I'll tell you I forgive you first thing," he promised.

The ground trembled. People in the city screamed. Even the soldiers around Col looked nervous. Then, slowly, grass began to push out of the soft earth above River's body. Then little flowers blossomed. The greenery began to spread in a gentle wave across the ground, transforming the dry rock garden into a lush, flowery meadow. A beautiful scent wafted on a sudden breeze, carrying with it the rare smell of rain. Even the stone wall and the hard-packed streets outside the garden began to flush green with moss.

Suddenly, the ground cracked. There, sitting up slowly and pushing off the flowery turf like a blanket after a nap, was the most beautiful woman Col had ever seen. It was River, but she was simply glowing with life. Her eyes shone, her hair shone, and her smile when she looked at him was breathtakingly happy. Gone were the chapped lips, sunburn, and tired eyes. Most of her clothes were also gone, a realization that made Col blush furiously. Her clothes had decomposed at an impossible rate, broken apart by the moss and grass roots. She wore little more than rags, and Col was grateful when the flowers and grass began twining lovingly around her body, covering a bit more of her skin. He forced himself to turn away, desperately hoping that the other soldiers hadn't seen him blush. He needn't have worried. All eyes were fixed on River, except Dominik, who studied the ground respectfully.

River took in her surroundings sleepily, then she became far more awake as she realized how scantily she was clad, and became aware of the fascinated gazes of the King's men. In a moment, the old River was back.

"Look away, you drooling idiots," her sharp voice rang out, "before I poke out your eyes!"

The ground suddenly became the most interesting thing that anyone had ever seen. In a few moments, River marched indignantly past them, dressed in a practical green dress made, seemingly, from grass. Even with clumps of dirt in her tangled hair, Col thought she had never looked more beautiful.

61

Resolving the chaos after the battle turned out to be easier than Col had anticipated. When the King saw the way the tide had turned, he proved himself completely spineless, as usual, and swore allegiance to the victors with very little ceremony. With the Hearer dead, and both the King, the common people, and the Rebels on his side, Col was a force to be reckoned with. One by one, the other Temples of the Hand submitted to his authority. Now that the truth about River was out, they no longer had religious grounds on which to base their rule. Despite the victory, Col knew it would be many years of adjusting laws and policies before true peace could be established. He set himself to that task with fervor.

River slipped her arms about Col's neck. He hadn't seen her come into the study where he sat reading through reports. He'd barely seen her at all, actually. The past few weeks had been a never-ending stream of meetings and important decisions. River had often been there, but they'd never had a moment alone without five or ten people clamoring for their attention. Now, he wasn't even sure what their relationship was. The first words out of River's mouth were the last he would ever have expected to hear from her.

"Nikolo Wolf, I've decided to marry you."

He was glad to be sitting down, or he might have fallen over from shock.

"*What?*"

"You heard me. I want to marry you," her voice wavered, a little less confident and cocky. He got up and spun around to face her. Her eyes were big, and so beautiful, so hopeful. The request had caught him off guard, but everything in him wanted to say yes, to spin her around and kiss her breathless, to carry her away and marry her right that very moment. However, he didn't. Instead, he stood frozen, staring at her, trying to read her face and her intentions. She'd rejected him once, why was she proposing now?

Col was an excellent reader of people. However, in River's face he read too many things. Her stone cold mask was off, but what he saw beneath didn't tell him anything he wanted to know. He saw excitement, nervousness, pride, guilt, love, possibly even a touch of pity.

He thought, and he thought. Then, he opened his mouth and said the hardest words he had ever forced out.

"No."

Her face was blank, uncomprehending.

"What?"

Col took a deep breath.

"I love you too much to marry you," he said. "You didn't want me before, when I was an outcast. Now you do, when I'm about to be crowned king. I love you too much to marry you, knowing that what you want is my throne."

She looked shocked. Her eyes got even bigger, and they were filled with hurt. Then, the tears came. Only now, they were tears of rage. Her face crumpled, flushing red. A huge vase full of freshly cut flowers sitting on the windowsill suddenly curled up and died. The ground trembled.

"How dare you!" she spluttered, "after everything we've been through, how *dare* you say that!" She raised her hand as if to slap him, then stopped herself, curling it into a fist at her side instead. Without another word, she stormed out of the room. Col held his ground, back straight, jaw set, until she was out of sight. Then, he shed tears of his own. Tears of frustration, of pain, of woe. Why did he have to push away everyone that he loved? *This is why I never wanted the burden of Kingship.* He told himself. *The only thing I am destined for is loneliness and self-*

sacrifice. I need to just accept that.

River stormed for days. She didn't know if she was angrier at Col for his unfair accusations, or at herself because, just a few months ago, his judgement would have been true. She didn't want to have to face him with all the shame and anger inside, so she threw herself into the rebuilding of Kingsfall. Never before had fresh fruit and vegetables been so plentiful in the markets. She called a river out of the earth, and sent it cascading over the edge of Kingsfall's cliffs in a waterfall so long that it faded to mostly mist before it hit the bottom. She formed beautiful towers, half stone and half living tree, for those whose homes had been damaged by some of Col's more unruly troops. She tried not to be present at any of the meetings where she might see Col. However, some were too important to miss.

"The Rebellion doesn't recognize your leadership." The words weren't too surprising to Col, but their speaker was. Rig stood with hands on hips, the cold distance in his eyes making him seem an entirely different person than the boy Col remembered from acolyte training.

"What did you ever do for us, anyway, except get a bunch of us killed?"

Around Rig, several other Rebel representatives nodded their agreement. Col opened his mouth to protest, but Rig wasn't done.

"When you hijacked Order shipments, who did the Hearer

punish for it? Our people. When the battle began, who were the first to die? Our people. We hid you from the Hearer, we smuggled the Messenger out of the city, we supported you as allies. However, we got no thanks for it. I don't see why you simply get to lead us now, when all the hard work is done."

Col took a deep breath. He pushed down the hurt that Rig's words caused, and instead approached the subject diplomatically.

"It was never about, 'who gets to'." He made his voice reasonable, caring. "It's a question of who *has* to. I never asked for this responsibility, but our subjects in Arthia, the ones who *train our armies* won't trust anyone else. The people of the land chose me. The bandits would be pillaging and burning right now if it weren't for me. The Order of the Hand won't accept anyone's authority except the man who destroyed the previous Hearer. River did that..."

He turned to look at River, a question in his eyes. She wouldn't meet his eyes, but her voice rang out.

"But Col was the one who actually fought him. And, besides, I won't take the throne. My loyalty is to the Wolf." Her voice was flat and dead, but the words were all Col needed to make his point.

"So, you see," he said, turning back to the rebels, "I am the only one who *can* bring about peace for the entire nation after the Order's fall. Isn't that what you've been fighting for all along?"

Rig still looked belligerent. Col pushed on.

"I know I'm not your leader. However, I *am* a rebel. I took your oaths. I fought for the same reasons. I know your people, and I care for them." He met the eyes of each man and woman in the group, his own shining with sincerity.

"I know I am not the perfect choice. But I am the common ground, the acceptable compromise, the *only* path that leads to peace. Can you not see that?"

His words worked their magic on the Rebels. Every one of them, except Rig, voted to swear allegiance to Col. Rig, however, left Kingsfall and the Rebels that night in a rage. In one final moment, Col became the most powerful man in the world. In that same moment, he lost the last person he had ever counted as a friend.

Very few people could read the Wolf's thoughts. However, as he brushed past River on his way out the door of the meeting hall, she caught a glimpse of his heart through a crack in his mask. The Wolf was a victorious hero. However Col, the man she loved, was falling apart. Her instinct was to catch his arm. However, she was stopped, caught in the vice-like grip of her own pride. He had *rejected* her! He had maligned her!

A gentle tug on her sleeve snapped her out of her thoughts. A very small child was standing in the crowd, looking up at her.

"Go to him." The child urged. River stared into those deep, deep eyes, then looked away because she couldn't bear it anymore. At the simple little words, thoughts of Col began rushing into her mind, and suddenly the wall of pride seemed flimsy. She shut out all the thoughts about herself that whispered in the back of her mind, fixing her thoughts instead on Col, on how much he was hurting, and on how desperately she still loved him. With a massive effort of will, she took the first step after him. Then, before she knew it, she was running.

"Col!" Col froze. He didn't know what River wanted, but he wasn't ready to talk to her. It was too painful even to see her from a distance, knowing that he couldn't have her. He stopped walking, but didn't turn around. Her footsteps stopped a few feet behind him.

"I hate what you said to me," her voice sounded small, "but I don't blame you for saying it. It's hard to admit, but for the longest time you would have been right. I've been so prideful, and so blind."

She took a deep breath.

"But when I saw the way you acted in Arthia, I knew. I *knew* that you were destined to be king, and that I would make a horrible queen."

Her voice hiccuped, and Col suddenly realized she was crying. He couldn't help it, he turned around. River's eyes were red, and the expression on her face was more raw and vulnerable than anything he had seen before.

"I would have let you reject me, and left you to be king on your own. But now I know another thing, Col. You *can't* be king on your own. You can't push everyone away and rule the world with no love in your life. It's killing you, and it's killing me to watch."

Here she was really crying, her nose snotting and trickles of tears leaking down and dripping off her chin.

"I will *not* let you crush the man I love under all your stupid selflessness and sacrifice," she burst out, her eyes latching onto his with a fiery determination.

"I don't care if you are a king or a stupid peasant boy, and I don't care if I ever get a single smidge of power in this broken kingdom, I love you, Nikki! And I want to marry you!"

This time, Col couldn't read anything in her expression except pure, vulnerable love. It was hearing the pet name on her lips that finally broke him. Every wall he had built up to protect himself from his heart broke down, and tears leaked from his own eyes. He couldn't bear the pain he saw in her eyes, not when his own heart was overflowing with hope. There was still something that made him hesitate, however.

"I don't know if I can remember how to love again," he admitted.

"I care for you more deeply than I have ever felt for anyone, but my heart is so full of pain and covered in scars, I don't know if I can love you as you deserve."

"And I'm just learning how to love for the first time," River countered. "We're both broken, I know that. But don't you think we have a better chance at healing if we try together?"

Col had no resistance left. He didn't feel that he deserved to feel so happy, but River had cut through all his defenses, emotional and logical barriers alike. Finally, Col gave in. "I'll marry you!" he exclaimed, and the words felt wonderful. His whole body flooded with an intense feeling of relief. He caught her up in his arms, holding her close, then kissing her messy, snotty face until she gasped for breath. Her tears turned to hiccups, then a hesitant smile.

"Let's arrange it soon!" River beamed up at him. "I do need a new necklace."

The End

-About the Author-

Jessica Lietz is the author of Myth, this book, and hopefully many more! A middle child with seven siblings who are all creative, she seems to have a lot to prove, and continually strives to be the very best, or at least the most famous! She is married to Jesse Allen, a youth pastor in Lloydminster, Canada, and also the most fabulous husband who ever lived. In addition to writing, she practices a career in Graphic Design along with painting, sketching, crocheting, and many other hobbies in her free time. These include occasional cat wrangling, as she shares a house with an outrageous ball of fur and mischief, who goes by the name of Taco.

Jessica was raised on a diet of books, which pair very nicely with a good latte. She got her inspiration to write from voraciously devouring much quality literature, such as the works of J.R.R Tolkien, Megan Whalen Turner, Brandon Sanderson, and C.S. Lewis. Encouraged by many members of her family, especially her grandfather (another Tolkien nerd), her husband, and her little sister Haven (another voracious book devourer) Jessica has finally written this, her biggest book yet! She really hopes you liked it.

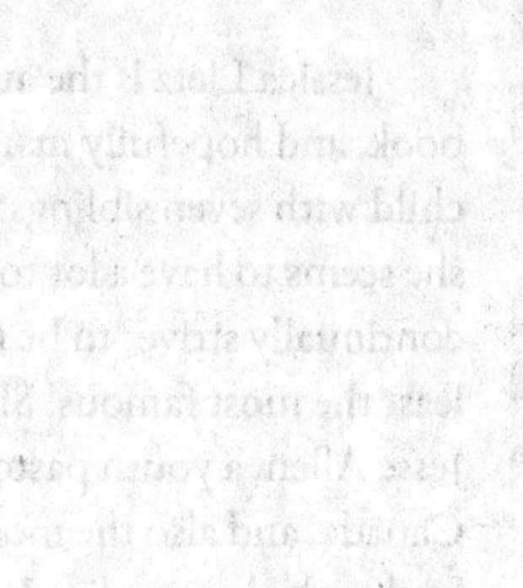